Midnight
Plague

ALSO BY GREGG KEIZER

The Longest Night

Midnight Plague

GREGG KEIZER

G. P. PUTNAM'S SONS

NEW YORK

G. P. PUTNAM'S SONS
Publishers Since 1838
Published by the Penguin Group
Penguin Group (USA) Inc., 375 Hudson Street, New York, New York 10014, USA •
Penguin Group (Canada), 90 Eglinton Avenue East, Suite 700, Toronto, Ontario M4P 2Y3,
Canada (a division of Pearson Penguin Canada Inc.) • Penguin Books Ltd, 80 Strand,
London WC2R 0RL, England • Penguin Ireland, 25 St Stephen's Green, Dublin 2, Ireland
(a division of Penguin Books Ltd) • Penguin Group (Australia), 250 Camberwell Road,
Camberwell, Victoria 3124, Australia (a division of Pearson Australia Group Pty Ltd) •
Penguin Books India Pvt Ltd, 11 Community Centre, Panchsheel Park, New Delhi–110 017,
India • Penguin Group (NZ), Cnr Airborne and Rosedale Roads, Albany, Auckland 1310,
New Zealand (a division of Pearson New Zealand Ltd) • Penguin Books (South Africa) (Pty)
Ltd, 24 Sturdee Avenue, Rosebank, Johannesburg 2196, South Africa

Penguin Books Ltd, Registered Offices:
80 Strand, London WC2R 0RL, England

Library of Congress Cataloging-in-Publication Data

Keizer, Gregg.
Midnight plague / Gregg Keizer.
p. cm.
ISBN 0-399-15319-5
1. World War, 1939–1945—Fiction. I. Title.
PS3611.E37M53   2005   2005047583
813'.54—dc22

Printed in the United States of America
1   3   5   7   9   10   8   6   4   2

BOOK DESIGN BY AMANDA DEWEY

To Keith

"And the plague lasted until . . ."

> —The last line of the last volume of *Nuova Cronica*, by Giovanni Villani,
> chronicler of Florence. Villani died of the plague in 1348

"Our landings in the Cherbourg-Havre area have failed to gain a satisfactory foothold and I have withdrawn the troops. My decision to attack at this time and place was based upon the best information available. The troops, the air and the Navy did all that Bravery and devotion to duty could do. If any blame or fault attaches to the attempt it is mine alone."

> —Note penned by Gen. Dwight Eisenhower, June 5, 1944,
> prior to the invasion, and to be used in case of its failure

Prologue

K irn leaned back to take in the steel cliff of the ship as the French workers wrestled lines of thick hemp around iron cleats big as sheep. The tub looked like it had sailed the seven seas. But the palm tree painted on the single red stack made him think those seas had been balmy waters, at least.

"I'm cold," Willi Kirn said. "Damn cold." Doktor Wollenstein winced. Kirn stamped his feet and jammed his one whole hand deeper into his overcoat pocket.

The two of them stood in the useless lee of an Opel too small to keep away the raw wind. "I swear, the only place colder is a hole in front of Moscow," Kirn said. "We packed newspaper in our clothes to stay warm, it was so cold. And then we ran out of newspaper." He brought up his two-fingered hand with the cigarette. But Wollenstein ignored him like he had these five days. Prick. Too important to talk to a detective from the Kriminalpolizei.

The doctor pulled his neck deeper into the collar of his expensive mohair overcoat. The black storm looked like it would soon sweep up the estuary of the Garonne; this tub had barely made it to Bordeaux before the weather closed in. Kirn pulled his coat tighter, but the buttons wouldn't reach their holes. He was big, not fat, solid in the chest and shoulders, with arms that filled the coat's sleeves. His hat, worn brown felt, was tight on his square head and at least kept that part of him warm.

Wollenstein had no hat, no uniform either under the tan mohair, just a smart wool suit like a rich doctor would wear. Not for the first time, Kirn wondered who Wollenstein was, what kind of pull he had to walk into the Kripo office in Caen and convince his chief to order him to mind the Herr Doktor. He'd tried to get it out of Wollenstein, but he'd had no luck. Not much of a detective, was he, if he couldn't dig out that.

"Where's this tub from? It's been to hell and back, looks like," Kirn said.

"Haiphong. Indochina," Wollenstein answered. "French Indochina."

"Really," Kirn said, mulling that over. Indochina was part of France's booty from long before the war, a place so far east it might as well be west. The Japanese fought the Americans on that side of the world. "Not the *Wulewubs's* anymore, is it? Belongs to *our* little yellow friends, doesn't it?" But that got nothing more than another grimace.

A stepped gangway pivoted from its spot and, on ropes held by four sailors, was let down to meet a hatch three meters above the dock. The hatch opened and a man leaned out. He wasn't proper Kriegsmarine, instead a brown nut of a pirate with a faded red sweater, denim trousers, and a crushed uniform cap once white but long gone to gray.

"Are you the ones for the box?" the pirate called down.

"Yes," Wollenstein shouted up. But he didn't step from the Opel nor take his hands from his pockets.

"Come get the damn thing," the pirate yelled.

"Go," Wollenstein told Kirn. "He'll show you. Go on, it's small enough to carry with one hand."

Kirn nodded, and banged up the metal gangway. He heard Wollenstein following, his feet slower on the steps.

"Where's Seishiro? The man who came with the box?" Wollenstein asked as they reached the top of the gangway, and Kirn slipped past him through the hatch.

"Sewed in canvas, at the bottom of the Bay of Bengal," said the pirate.

Wollenstein looked hard at the pirate, and for a moment Kirn had the feeling the doctor was going to bolt down the steps, but he stayed where he was. "Anyone else take sick?" Wollenstein asked. Kirn stepped back to the mouth of the hatch to better hear.

"How did you know he died of sickness?" the pirate asked. Wollenstein said nothing. "No, the only one was the *Japser*," the pirate added, using the name for the Japanese.

"You're sure?" Wollenstein asked and looked up. One of Wollenstein's eyes was gray, the other blue. It made Kirn uneasy. "You're sure?" Wollenstein asked again.

"I'd know, wouldn't I, being first officer," the sailor said, giving the doctor the eye. "What's in the box, Herr . . ." he asked, fishing for a name.

"Wollenstein," he said. "Sturmbannführer. SS."

SS, Kirn thought. It all made sense then, why his chief had bent over backwards to please this doctor. Damn SS.

"What's in the box, Major?" asked the sailor, who didn't seem impressed at the Sturmbannführer's rank. "The *Japser* comes aboard and even before he drops dead, he scares the shit out of the crew with that damned box he had us bolt to the deck of his cabin."

"What about his things?" Wollenstein asked, shivering. "He was supposed to bring papers and documents, too. Journals."

The sailor laughed. "I could barely get my boys to bag him and toss him over the rail, the way he looked. He turned all black like a negro. You think someone set foot in his cabin you're mad. Any papers are right where he left them."

"I must examine everyone," Wollenstein told the pirate.

"Examine—"

"I'm a doctor."

"Examine for what?"

It started to rain, first just a few fat drops, but in a moment, steady. Kirn watched Wollenstein rub his hands together and as they wet, they lathered just a little.

Prologue

"Take me to the captain, I'll explain to him," said Wollenstein. The first officer nodded finally, turned, and ducked through the hatch.

Wollenstein came after and brushed by Kirn, his eyes nervous. Kirn followed, wondering what was so wicked that it scared the SS.

Fucking SS, they were never scared of anything.

———

Thursday

War is the greatest plague that can afflict humanity,
it destroys religion, it destroys states, it destroys
families. Any scourge is preferable to it.

—MARTIN LUTHER

One

The little colored girl Brink meant to save shook under her thin blanket as if a gale blew through the packed dirt floor. She moaned, whispered, and finally turned her head to vomit. In seconds, the flies that had been stalking her mouth left it and made for the new pool.

Brink tried to breathe through his mouth to keep the stink from making him gag, but the thick Dakar air was oven hot in the tin-roofed shack. The mask itched and the rubber gloves baked his hands. He brushed away lank hair that had fallen across his forehead. The circle of yellow from the flashlight on the floor was only wide enough to show the syringe. Sweat dripped off his temples as he stared at the girl's arm, listening to her too fast, too shallow breaths.

He ripped the paper wrapping from a field dressing and used its dry white rectangle to wipe the sweat from her face, his hand feeling the heat rising off her even through his glove. As he daubed the hollow of her neck, she struggled against the weight of the blanket. And she coughed, her shoulders shaking, to rack out a long series, each harsher and wetter than the last.

He saw the splatter of thin liquid hit the blanket, froth at the edges of the stain.

That was all he needed to see. Here was proof that *Pasteurella pestis* lived in her.

Brink picked up the syringe, unstopped the glass tube, dipped in the needle, and pulled. He felt for a shallow vein, touched the needle to her skin. He said a prayer, his lips unmoving against the cloth. He'd found some religion in Dakar.

Brink pushed the needle. The girl moaned, her breathing slowed, and she coughed for more long seconds before sighing back into her blanket. He dropped the syringe and burrowed into the haversack for his notebook, black and held together with string. He glanced at his wristwatch—01:15—and wrote that, then the date. "3cc actinomycin-17," he penciled. "Colored, female, 45–50 lbs., approx. 4'2", age 8–10, adv. pneumonic, infected—??, first symptoms—??"

Brink glanced from his notebook to the girl. It was like time and place had been pinched between two glass slides, made thin enough to see from then to now. He was, for a moment, a thousand miles away from this African shack, back in the English room where Kate had poisoned herself.

"Hold on," he said to the little girl through his mask as he gripped her small black hand. He squeezed, but she only stared at him. "You'll be fine, I promise." She couldn't understand his English, but he was saying it for himself, not her.

Brink released her hand and used the field dressing to mop the new sweat from her, and as he did, he looked at his hands holding the gauze and felt a small amazement at how he tended her. Although there was paper that said he'd graduated from the University of Minnesota's medical college, he'd never had much bedside manner. He'd gotten better in the time on the wards, but even at the end the instructors had pulled him aside and said maybe he should think about being a surgeon since his patients would be unconscious. So when he went home to open his practice, he wasn't surprised that he'd lasted just two and a half months peering down the throats of fevered children and setting the bones of farmers. He left

8

doctoring for Kansas City and went back to the baseball he'd played sum-
mers to put himself through school.

He reminded people, some people, of Joe DiMaggio because he was tall
like DiMaggio, six feet two; had filled out like DiMaggio—he weighed
185—and his nose was long and sharp at its edges, a wedge of a nose. But
his hair was blond, not brown, and he knew he was nowhere near the ball-
player. DiMaggio had batted .346 and hit 46 home runs for the Yankees in
'37, the season Brink had caught for the Cardinals, batted .233, and plated
just three. So he was always happy when someone said he looked like
DiMaggio.

He heard the plank door squeak open and turned to look out into the
street. Squinting, he could make out the short, stocky Paré, the French
doctor from the l'Institut Pasteur who had promised to wait outside for ten
minutes in return for the three hundred francs Brink had pressed into his
damp hand.

"What are you doing?" asked someone not Paré. It was Morton, holding a flashlight so the beam hit Brink's eyes. Christ.

"I'm doing my job, that's what I'm doing," he said.

Morton came into the shack, swung the light to take in the girl. Morton
wore no mask, so he stopped five feet away. His flashlight caught the glint of
the syringe and needle, the glass tube of A17 next to them. "Is that penicillin?"

"No," Brink said, and dropped the syringe, needle, and tube into the
haversack. How the hell had Morton found him here?

"Then what—" Morton started, but his voice was shouted down by another round of coughing. Brink pulled the blanket closer to the girl's chin.
"She has the plague," said Morton.

"Yes."

"She's going to die."

Brink didn't answer at first. "No," he said finally, "she's not."

"What are you putting into her if it's not penicillin?"

"None of your business."

"I've been patient, Frank. I did what London asked, let you have the run
of the place to take your samples. But those orders didn't say anything
about you stealing my penicillin."

"It's not penicillin," said Brink. "I told you that."

The little girl coughed, shuddered in a series of jerks. Her back arched until her heels and the crown of her head were all that touched the blanket. After long seconds, she folded into her bed and was still. For a bit the shack was silent.

"Jesus, what did you shoot into her?"

Brink didn't answer. He didn't dare take his eyes off the girl as he looked for clues she was alive. Don't be dead, don't be dead, don't be dead. He prayed again that the antibiotic would work.

"She's gone. What did you give her?" Morton asked. "Morphine? You stole my morphine? You can't go around deciding when it's their time, not even for niggers," Morton said.

"She's not dead! She's sick, I'm helping her," Brink said.

Morton shook his head. "You gave her morphine to put her out of her misery."

"She's not dead!"

But Morton was gone. Brink slipped the notebook into the haversack and took a step to follow Morton, but stumbled just outside the door. He fell with his hands in the dirt, his shins across the white-wrapped log. Brink crawled off her, stood on shaking legs. *Goddamn.*

The little girl's mother lay spun tight in white cloth. She'd been dead by the time Diagne had called, but when he'd arrived she hadn't been draped, so Brink tugged aside her long, tight dress and used his flashlight to spot the buboes, a pair of raised lumps high on the left thigh, black against her black skin. Bubonic, the dead mother had. But her daughter had been clean. Not a single bubo. She was exactly what Brink had been looking for these eleven weeks in Senegal.

Plague, but not bubonic. Pneumonic instead. Deadlier still, quicker yet. Bubonic plague led, sometimes, to secondary pneumonic, where the *Pasteurella pestis* flooded the lungs and escaped in the violent coughs and sneezes as the body tried to expel the corruption. Anyone nearby could be infected, falling sick with primary pneumonic plague. The bacilli crept into the recesses of the pulmonary system where they waited some hours, or a day or two or three or even six before showing symptoms. And then they killed quickly, that very day or the next or at most the one after that. Every time, without fail, they killed. Even bubonic didn't do that. The thought made Brink shiver a moment in the heat.

There were no lights in the Médina, but the shack was just fifty yards from the docks and so the narrow dirt street was bright as a full moon. A crane chuffed close by, its donkey engine straining, and in the light from the lamps set atop the tall poles along the wharf, Brink watched a pallet heavy with bulging sacks swing high. Peanuts, that's what they shipped from Dakar. He tore off the mask and gloves.

Just then, two coloreds in bloodstained white passed him and went into the shack. In a few minutes they came out with the little girl slung in her blanket between them. The one at the rear nodded as he went by. Thick-chested Paré stepped out of the darkness under the tin roof's overhang, a good hiding spot for someone short. *"Ce n'est pas la peste, je vous assure,"* he said as he came close.

No, Paré, the plague *is* here. The dead mother with the buboes wasn't the first—she made a baker's dozen in his Dakar weeks—and the girl with the pneumonic made fourteen. Yet because the plague burned so low, so few dead in the three months, the l'Institut Pasteur de Dakar said *la peste,* officially, hadn't taken the city.

Paré turned on his heel and followed the coloreds, all headed north to quarantine on the rue Escarfait. Like the others, the girl would be put in a room alone.

Brink trotted to catch up with the girl in the blanket, his haversack bouncing on his hip, the glass inside clinking.

Brink tried to block out the stink of the rue Escarfait that lingered all hours, the smell of dried dung, the salt tang from the harbor, chicken ruined by charcoal, and the overpowering smell of peanuts. Roasted peanuts everywhere. It was like living inside a baseball park with an army of peanut vendors.

"Salam aleikum, Monsieur Brink. What do you have for me?" asked Diagne. His French had the lilt of every colored in Dakar. The thin man struck a match and lit a cigarette. Brink savored the odor, and wished he still smoked.

More than anything, Brink wanted to ask his own question—*How is the girl?*—because Diagne had just come out of the house with the high windows and the small letters QUARANTAINE hand-painted above its door.

She was inside this house. But there was a rhythm to conversation here, a politeness he'd had to learn, and so he answered rather than asked.

"*Aleikum salam*, Monsieur Diagne. Penicillin, like before. And something new," Brink said in French. He pulled the haversack's strap from his shoulder, and drew back its flap.

Diagne moved closer. "What is it?" he asked.

From the bottom of the haversack, Brink pulled a glass bottle no bigger than his thumb. "A vaccine against the pestilence, *dé*."

Diagne leaned against the wall. "The pestilence will not come," he said.

"It's here. You know it's here. In a few days, you'll be begging for this," said Brink. He pulled off his garrison cap, wiped his forehead with its edge, and put it back on.

"The doctors say no. Not like 1914. And if they are wrong . . . We have lived through the pestilence before, we will live through it again. Paré says the Institute will make a treatment, and they will not charge a franc. I cannot sell this to people if they can have the same for free."

Brink had heard the talk, too, that the Pasteur was preparing a vaccine against the bubonic plague—as they'd done during the Great War—but even if the French pulled it off, it would be weeks before it was ready.

"By the time the Pasteur cooks something, you'll be sick," Brink said. "You tell your customers that they have to take the vaccine three weeks before the plague. Three weeks. I'd start today. You tell them that."

Brink counted back on the calendar in his head. He'd been given a half cc of the army's killed vaccine twelve weeks before when he stepped onto the troopship in Portsmouth. Not that the vaccine would keep away the pneumonic plague; it only worked on bubonic, the plague brought by the bites of fleas.

Diagne moved his face closer to the bottle in Brink's hand, as if to see better in the dark.

"You should have this," Brink said quietly. He touched a hand on the cool stucco. Inside was the girl.

"What else will you give me for my news?"

"Penicillin, same as always," Brink said. He'd been carefully doling out the collection of tiny vials of penicillin powder he'd brought from England, knowing that in a place like this, the drug would be better than dollars for buying the information he needed.

Diagne struck another match and held the small flame in the mouth of the burlap sack, trying to see its crowd of brown and green and clear bottles. There were forty doses of the vaccine there, one bottle of sulfadiazine, a hundred tablets to the bottle, and ten vials of the penicillin. On the black market, the sulfa cost twenty francs for just two tablets, the penicillin ten times that for a single shot. The vaccine, well, he didn't know what Diagne could get, and tell the truth, he didn't care.

"More of the miracle water for the gonorrhea, *dé*?" The man's eyes, dark as Dakar's night in the fluttery light of the match, locked with Brink's.

"Ten vials, as we agreed," said Brink. Diagne's match guttered out. Each of the 5cc vials mixed enough for five 20,000-unit injections. One shot would clear up the clap and put two hundred francs into Diagne's pocket, the number sounding rich, which it wasn't and was: four bucks American and a fortune in Dakar.

"You want me to keep telephoning when I hear of people with the pestilence, that is what you want?"

"I have to know earlier," Brink said, sucking in the last cloud of the colored's cigarette. "You're calling when they're too sick. Especially the ones with the breathing pestilence." The antibiotic, his and Kate's A17, might only work if administered earlier in the course of the disease—that's why he feared the girl would not live, despite the injection. Maybe he'd gotten to her too late.

"I will try," said Diagne. "That is all I can do, yes?" He dropped the butt of the cigarette to the packed dirt and stepped on it with a bare foot. Brink handed over the burlap sack. The glass inside clinked one last time.

"You do this, *borom*, for what reason?" Diagne asked, lighting another cigarette from a new match. He breathed the smoke Brink's way. "I know you know the price of these things. You don't mean to trick this poor *bicot*, do you? No one gives these things for just the name of a sick person and the street where they live."

Brink couldn't tell the truth. Diagne wouldn't understand because it wasn't about money.

"I just want to help," he said, and Diagne dropped the cigarette, its end a small explosion of sparks as it hit the dirt.

The colored turned and ran.

The sound of heavy boots on beaten earth came up behind Brink, and something big trampled past. It was a man, in his hand a flashlight, and the dark shape merged with Diagne's and the two of them tumbled. The flashlight spun on the ground. When it stopped, it pointed at a black brassard wrapped around the man's upper arm, white block letters stenciled *M* and *P*. The uniform was army olive. The MP stood, dragged Diagne up off the dirt, and pushed him Brink's way, picking up his flashlight.

"Captain Brink," a voice said behind him softly. Brink turned. It was Morton, of course, with another MP. The MP held a big .45.

Diagne sprawled on the ground at Morton's feet as the larger MP shoved him. The policeman snagged the burlap bag, brought it up. Morton beckoned.

"What's in here?" asked Morton. He shook the sack and there was the thin sound of glass shards. "My morphine?" Morton aimed a flashlight at his face, and Brink put up a hand. "You're taking my morphine, and when you find niggers with the plague, you're using it to put them down. Your orders said nothing about that."

"You're wrong. I was trying to make her well," Brink said quietly.

"I didn't want it to come to this," said the colonel. "But after what I saw in that shack. You can't."

"I didn't kill her," he said, but not screaming like before. They'd made a mistake, he and Childess. They'd thought they'd be able to try the vaccine without Morton finding out or interfering.

"You're under arrest," Morton said. He turned to the MP who stood over Diagne. "Let him go." The big man pulled Diagne to his feet, the colored confused in the flashlight's beam.

"My police are taking me away, *dé*," Brink said to Diagne. "Tell them to give the girl sulfa. I'll come as soon as I can, with more medicine."

"The little one? From the docks? Allah, forgive and have mercy on her."

In the background, Brink heard Morton say something, and again he felt a hand around his arm.

"She died before we carried her into quarantine, *borom*."

The MP tightened his grip, but Brink barely felt the pressure.

Two

The surf, louder now, told Alix that she had brought Papa's boat near the English shore. The smell, bigger now from the open hatch near the bow, told her that the cargo had gone foul.

Alix Pilon tucked her short hair back behind each ear, one side at a time, felt the wood under her bare feet as she shifted her legs to brace against the crash sure to come, and gripped the wheel harder with solid, callused hands. Papa was part of that cargo dead and dying in the hold. Thirteen, all women and children, and Papa.

She had let the door of the wheelhouse hang open and it knocked quietly as it swung against the frame when the long swells rocked the boat. The sound of the surf grew, disappeared. She wondered if there were rocks ahead or a sandbar shielding a cove. Alix had never sailed so close to England, and although she could guide Papa's boat into home's harbor with her eyes closed, this was foreign.

Helping the Jews had been her mistake.

They'd come from the two *boche* trucks she and Papa and Tardif and Clavette had surprised on the N13 east of Formigny in Normandy before dawn the day before. Killed the drivers she and Tardif did, but when Papa and Clavette opened the back of the German trucks, expecting to free eleven captured *maquisards*—Resistance fighters—that they'd been told were being motored to Caen's Petit Lycée and the Gestapo who lived on its second floor, instead they'd found Jews. Most were sick with a fever, coughing and vomiting. Three were dead and their skin had strangely turned as black as dried blood.

She had been the one who said that the thirteen living Jews must be taken to England. Juniper had told her to keep watch for the strangely sick. Juniper had said to get word to England if she heard of a large number ill. But passing word the usual way was impossible, for the *boche* radio detection trucks had grown thick, rolling up roads at all hours, the Germans arrogant enough to park in front of Port-en-Bessin's church two days straight with its hooped antenna swiveling like an evil eye. She'd buried the radio in the garden after that.

She'd convinced Papa that they must take the Jews to England because there was no other way to get the news to Juniper, but the convincing had been selfish. It was an excuse to see Juniper again as much as to help these people.

Papa had nodded and taken up the chore of arguing with Tardif and Clavette until finally they agreed to take the Jews in one of the trucks to the harbor, hide them aboard Papa's boat, and then ship them to England. But by the time they'd left the quay, her and Papa running the single sail up the mast in the middle of the afternoon—Tardif and Clavette had not come, the cowards—and catching the breeze to chart a course north by northeast, those Jews in the hold were miserable. Five had died during the hours crammed under deck, gone to blue and purple and black, and the eight remaining were sicker than before. Coughing and spitting and vomiting every one of them.

Nine hours clear of the harbor, long after they had finished pretending to fish and with the sun already under the horizon, Papa had fallen down in a heap in the little wheelhouse, shouting the *boche* were everywhere although the Channel was empty of Germans. It was the same nightmare he had at home, from his time in the Great War. In the moon's light she could only watch Papa crawl for the hold and drop out of sight while she took the wheel with her fisherman's hands.

Alix returned to the present only when the surf pinched the stern and swung it to starboard and the wheel turned so quickly it flew out of her hands. For a moment, she thought the boat would broach. She had fished with Papa since she was twelve—fifteen years pulling cod and cuttlefish from the nets—but none of her skills could help her here.

The boat went aground with the sound of a hundred rocks rubbed against a wood wall. She lost her footing as the gunwale dipped and the deck fell from under her feet. Her head struck the frame of the narrow wheelhouse door and everything was quiet and then far away and finally dark.

When she woke, the boat was still. She raised her head, and the boat tilted, or so it seemed. She felt the small lump above the temple at the edge of her hair. She struggled until her back was to the wheelhouse, her feet against the gunwale. Water lapped against the port side behind her, the sound loud in the darkness, but too weak to shake the hull. She'd run Papa's boat aground. For a second, she panicked. What would Papa say?

Papa. The hold. Jews.

She crawled to the opening. Papa had pulled off its cover to give the Jews air, and she dropped into the dark. She breathed through her mouth against the stink and felt her way over bare wood. The Jews had been tumbled to the starboard side, heaped there out of her way. She kept on until she touched Papa's worn sweater. He had pulled himself up to put his back against the hold's bulkhead. He moaned loudly.

There in the blackness she blindly wiped the sweat from Papa's face and held his hands until it was nearly dawn, when she fled back to the deck and the cleaner air and tried to believe none of this was happening.

Then she climbed over the gunwale, stepped into the biting water that came up to her waist. The dress she wore, stupidly thinking she would want to show Juniper her legs when she got to England, was soaked. Alix waded from the stranded boat to the pebbled shore, found a large rock above the tide mark, sat there, and waited for dawn.

Kirn had put Wollenstein out of mind for a year and a half, but it took only an hour and a half to renew the acquaintance and make him hate the doctor again.

Kirn looked at Wollenstein, the man tall and thin, with that habit of always rubbing his hands together. The doctor's eyes darted here and there in the bright Normandy mid-morning light, first to the abandoned truck plugging this dirt road just off the N13, then to Kirn.

"You must find my Jews," said Wollenstein.

"I don't know any Jews," Kirn said quietly. He pulled a package of Ecksteins from his coat pocket with his left hand, the one with all its fingers, and carefully shook out a cigarette. He pinched it between the thumb and first finger of the right, all that remained after the shell fragment had sung through the air and stolen the rest. He lit the Eckstein with the lighter he'd made, the one fashioned from an Ivan's 7.62mm cartridge case. "Your men would do better finding Jews," said Kirn, nodding to Wollenstein, with his peaked hat with the SS bones and skull pinned on it, and the gray uniform with its silver lightning flashes at the collar tab.

"I don't have anyone who knows the countryside like you do," Wollenstein said. "It's why I asked for a man from your office. The Kripo knows Normandy, doesn't it?"

"Yes, Herr Doktor." Kirn had to be polite. Wollenstein was SS, but there was more to it than the collar flashes the way Kirn's commander, Isselmann, had jumped up when the doctor walked into the Kriminalpolizei offices this morning bright and early, and showed him a much-touched piece of paper. Wollenstein had pointed to Kirn, the doctor had remembered him from Bordeaux, it seemed, and said he wanted him to look for stolen Reich property. He hadn't mentioned the property was Jews.

"They escaped yesterday morning," Wollenstein said as Kirn drew again on his cigarette. "Thirteen Jews. Their trail will be fresh, you won't have trouble finding them."

"What were they doing in this?" Kirn asked. He glanced at the gray-green Daimler with a closed-up wooden box on its back rather than the usual loose canvas top. There was a door framed at the rear of the box, but no windows.

Wollenstein said nothing.

"I can't help if you don't tell me what's going on," Kirn said.

"They were being taken to Caen, to the rail station," the doctor said finally. "There were two trucks, another that looked like this one."

"To Caen from where?"

Again Wollenstein hesitated.

"This won't work—" growled Kirn.

"My farm. In the Cotentin, north of Carentan. About thirty-five kilometers from here." Kirn knew the Cotentin, he'd searched for smugglers there twice. It was even more cut up by the maddening hedgerows than the ground here.

"But they didn't get out of your trucks by themselves, did they?" Kirn could see the Daimler's rear door had a broken latch. He stepped toward the truck, but Wollenstein reached for his coat sleeve, making him drop the Eckstein.

"Don't," Wollenstein said.

Kirn looked in the doctor's eyes, the one blue, the other gray. But Kirn shrugged his arm from the Sturmbannführer's grip, slapped at the latch with his right hand, and tugged open the door with his left.

The blast of stink backed him up one step, two.

It took moments for his eyes to adjust to the dimness. Kirn moved closer and with his left hand over his mouth and nose, peered inside. Bodies. It was hard to count because they were snarled into a knot at the far wall. The smell made his head hurt. They'd been dead a day at least and they'd gone dark, like the dead do when the weather's warm.

"What's this all about?" he asked, not able to take his look from a child's face—a little boy, he thought—who stared back with clouded eyes from the jumble.

"The Jews were ill, sixteen of them," Wollenstein said behind him, the words rushing out. "That's why I sent them to Caen. For a train to the East." The mysterious East, where Jews went but never returned.

"Ill? With what?" Kirn faced Wollenstein now, finally able to break the stare from the boy, but the stink still boiled out of the truck.

"Typhus."

"Typhus . . ." Kirn said, and stopped. He'd seen typhus in Russia—it had laid low a fifth of his company that December in front of Moscow. The lice had been ferocious. "You were treating them for typhus?"

"You could say that, yes," Wollenstein answered.

"But . . ."

"But I was unable to help them. And then someone stole them."

Stealing Jews, that was new. Who would steal sick Jews?

"Someone ambushed these trucks," said Wollenstein, "and took them."

Kirn already knew that. Black boots and the hint of gray trousers showed in the grass beside the Daimler—the driver of the truck. The *maquis* had done it, of course. They were the only ones with guns, other than the German soldiers, the *Landsers*, who lined the Normandy coast in their Tobrucks and trenches waiting for the invasion.

For the first time Kirn looked closely at the two SS enlisted men standing beyond the Daimler, both with rifles slung over shoulders. Like Wollenstein, they kept distance between themselves and the truck, and they, too, wore rubber gloves.

"So the Jews have typhus. They've run and you want me to find them—"

"Before they infect others," Wollenstein said. "I'm worried that they'll infect our men. The Wehrmacht, I mean." Wollenstein rubbed his hands together.

Kirn nodded. There was something else here. Kirn had been in Russia, he had seen how the SS treated Jews. He doubted the SS had ever given a Jew so much as an aspirin.

"You'll find them for me," said Wollenstein. It wasn't quite a question, not all command. "They were sick, very sick, they couldn't have gotten far. But they may infect others."

"You said this is typhus," Kirn said, stealing another glance into the mouth of the truck's door. "How will I know what to look for?" He wished Wollenstein would stop rubbing his hands; the squeaking was already under his skin.

"It's a different typhus," said Wollenstein, the words coming off his tongue quickly. "A fever, chills, and chest pains, and when there's a cough, it looks watery first, but bloody later."

That didn't sound like typhus—the typhus in front of Moscow had been a rash and fever and a dry, hacking cough. "Medicine?" Kirn asked.

Wollenstein looked toward the Daimler, then back to him. "Anyone found with this typhus must be quarantined. Wear a cloth mask, or come no closer than a meter or two, and you'll be safe," he said.

Kirn found another Eckstein, lit it. "I'm no doctor. What you described could be anything. Influenza, it sounds like. You'll have to point it out." He waved the hand with the cigarette toward the truck.

Wollenstein's eyes got very large, like when the doctor had stepped across the threshold into that rusted tub from Indochina. Kirn wondered then if there was a connection between this typhus and the wooden box they'd found screwed to the deck of the *Japser*'s cabin. The Jews in the back of the Daimler were turned black, like Africans. The *Japser* on the ship tied to the Bordeaux dock had been made into a negro, said the Kriegsmarine pirate.

"No, I have work . . . much work, important work . . ." said Wollenstein.

"Then I won't be able to find these Jews."

Wollenstein pushed his hands into his coat pockets. "Yes, you're right. But only today. We find one or two, and you'll know what to look for."

Kirn nodded, satisfied. "Sixteen, you said. Counting these or not?" he asked. He waved the stub of the Eckstein at the opened Daimler.

"There are three in the truck. Thirteen escaped."

Kirn nodded, dropped the cigarette to the dirt and stepped on the butt. "My car," Kirn said as he gestured to his little boxy Renault twenty meters down the road.

"One moment," said Wollenstein. He skirted the Daimler as he approached the SS.

Kirn squeezed behind the wheel of the Renault and watched through the flat windscreen. Wollenstein talked to his SS a moment. They nodded and headed back to their Mercedes truck up the dirt road. As Wollenstein walked toward the Renault, Kirn watched the two men lift petrol cans from the back of the Benz. One splashed fuel across the hood of the Daimler, the other dragged the dead driver by the boots through the grass along the road. Together, the two SS lifted the dead man—one by the feet, the other by the arms—and swung him up into the Daimler.

"Typhus?" he asked as the doctor settled into the Renault. Kirn started the car and put it into reverse. "Wouldn't it be easier to just delouse the truck if it was typhus?"

"Yes, typhus," Wollenstein said beside him.

By the time he had turned the Renault around, Kirn could see the flames lick at the Daimler in the side mirror.

Brink sat in the right-side seat, the African sun baking the top of his skull, as the jeep braked to a stop and he had to put a hand out on the frame. They'd taken his garrison cap hours ago and for some reason hadn't given it back.

The only shade was thirty feet away under the long, thin wings of a four-engined airplane. Two men handled a machine gun through a large, square opening halfway between the wing and two-finned tail. Another passed out long belts of bullets.

An hour ago, Brink had been sitting in his closet-sized room in the government house on the avenue de la République, an MP standing outside the door left open. But when Morton stepped into the doorway, he told Brink to pack, then watched while Brink stuffed his duffel with clothes and books and shaving kit and his black notebook. Morton made him leave the A17 he'd brought from England, and the blood samples he'd drawn and the cultures he'd grown, those in the battered General Electric that Brink had scrounged and hauled to his room.

The ride here, with the MP driving and Morton squatting in the back holding his hand atop his cap, had been quick.

"Get out," said Morton. "Someone wants you in England." His voice was thick and angry, its patience seeped away. Morton nodded to the plane, and the MP pulled Brink's duffel from the back of the jeep and shouldered it to the front of the bomber, tossed it onto the metal planking. As Morton walked him to the plane, Brink wondered who was calling him home.

"I'm not under arrest anymore?" Brink asked, and enjoyed the pained look that crossed Morton's face.

"Yes, damn you, you're under arrest," snapped Morton. He pulled paper from his pocket, unfolded it. "'Return Captain F. C. Brink England by fastest transport available. Urgent he arrive soon as possible,'" Morton read. "They're going to stand you before a court-martial." His mouth made a thin line.

An airman got to his hands and knees and crawled under the airplane, dragging Brink's duffel. The man stuffed it through the nearly hidden hatch and disappeared after. Things were moving fast for a court-martial.

At two this morning his arm had been in the grip of this MP. By nine, he was being shipped home.

"Get in," Morton said, and pointed to the airplane.

"Whose name is on that?" Brink asked, nodding to the signal slip Morton held.

Morton looked at the yellow paper. "Childess, Paul."

Brink breathed. It was going to be okay.

Brink squinted to read the letters on the small pad of paper the sergeant held out. The plane's engines hammered and every rivet vibrated like it would worm loose. It was just the two of them in the clear glass nose of the bomber, the pilots' cockpit above and behind them; a crawl through narrow spaces connected the two.

The sergeant leaned closer and handed the pad and a pencil to Brink. 3 HRS. MORE, the pad said. Brink drew a line through the words and scribbled WHERE R WE?? before giving the pad back.

The airman—MY NAME'S NAWLS, he had written on the pad not long after the airplane left the hot metal planking of the Dakar airfield—grabbed his map again, held it in front of Brink, and pointed to a spot. The map was so small that the finger could have been pointing to Spain, the ocean between Spain and France, or France. Still a long ways from Portsmouth on the south coast of England, their destination Nawls had written hours before.

They'd talked like this because some idiot had torn out the headsets everywhere but up in the cockpit, thinking that a few pounds of stuff would save a thimbleful of gas. Brink had tried to sleep, but the constant shaking and the occasional thump made it impossible, so they talked with paper to pass the time.

The pad came back to him, now with HOW DID U KNOW HE WAS STEALING 2ND? Nawls had seen him play ball last October when the 505th Parachute squeaked by the 306th Bomb Group at Thurleigh. Once Nawls found out he'd played part of a season for the Cardinals and had known Dizzy Dean, baseball was all he'd wanted to talk about with the pad.

Brink remembered the game at Thurleigh. It had been bottom of the fifth inning, one out, the 306th ahead by two runs, and their leadoff man had walked, then edged out from first. He'd thought the guy was screwing with Watts, trying to keep the pitcher's mind off the batter. But when the count ran two and one, the runner had glanced over to the stands. He'd followed the glance and seen a pretty blonde sitting there watching, must have been his girlfriend. He was gonna steal to show off. Brink had stood up from his catcher's crouch and slung the ball for second base just as the man took off. The ball reached Mitchovsky at second base long before the runner started to slide. The easy tag had been the second out, and that had been the moment when the game turned. The 505th had come back to score three in the top of the eighth, Brink driving in one with a single, scoring a run, too.

All that was too long to write on the pad. Brink just scratched GOT LUCKY and showed it to Nawls. The sergeant grinned. Next, Brink scribbled TIRED, GONNA TRY SLEEP AGAIN. Nawls nodded.

Brink leaned his head against the flying jacket crammed as a pillow between him and the shuddering glass and closed his eyes.

After a bit, Kate came to him on the inside of his eyelids, like she almost always did. In the mirage, she was tucking her long dark hair behind an ear and had her head cocked to the side that way of hers. Then she turned her back and he gave her a long look, top to bottom, from the crown of her head to the sweep of her hips under her dress to the kink in the seam of her left stocking. He stepped up behind her, put his arms around her waist, and pulled her close, bent his head and, after brushing aside her hair, kissed her neck. She leaned into him.

One year, seven months . . . and six days since he'd met her. Four months, three days since he'd lost her. He'd walked into the lab to find her on the floor with the anthrax powder lightly dusted on her nostrils and the syringe near her hand.

Ironic, really, that she had died while he watched. He had thought he'd left death behind when he'd walked into Paul Childess's office months before and told him he didn't want to quit, didn't want to let anyone down, but the anthrax animal experiments and their bloody results gave him such nightmares he couldn't sleep.

Childess had shouted at him, but gave in and removed him as head of the team trying to puzzle out how to spray the anthrax from airplanes.

They'd come to an agreement, he and Childess. He would stay at Porton Down and work with microbiologist Kate Moody on her antibiotic.

The work had been good for him and his sleep, Kate even better for both. Six months together and they'd made love that night after drinking too much champagne to celebrate A9, their first antibiotic that stopped the growth of the *Bacillus anthracis* in the petri dishes. Righteous work, his father might have said if he'd known what Brink was up to. Brink thought of it that way. It was to keep the plagues at bay if the Germans managed to recruit sickness, God forbid.

But Brink wasn't stupid, and he and Kate had argued about the actino-mycin. Building any antidote made it easier for the British to give in to temptation and use anthrax as a weapon. Kate, however, had sworn it wouldn't happen. I've been promised by Dr. Childess, she said over and over, that we will not use our darlings first. She used that word *darlings* as substitute for the anthrax's real name, like all the English at Porton Down. Most of their arguments were after they'd made love, so she would slide closer until her so-warm back pressed against his stomach. What we make, she said, you and I, only saves. We are lucky, so very lucky that way, aren't we, she said. Our conscience is clear.

He'd learned only later that before him, she'd been having an affair with Paul Childess. And even later still that conscience is not always either clear or cloudy, but sometimes in-between.

Brink opened his eyes because the airplane's engines changed their pitch, and a moment later, the world slipped. Nawls slid across the space between them and they tangled together in a ball as the airplane tilted. *"What the fuck?"* the sergeant shouted. Brink could hear him now, since the man's mouth was only a few inches from his ear.

He had a hard time breathing because Nawls's weight was pressing on his chest, but he turned his head to the right to look out the clear nose. First he saw clouds below them like always, but then a gap in those clouds showed they were over land. Off course somehow, because Nawls's finger, when it had traced their path from Dakar to England, stayed off the coasts the whole way.

A blur caught his eye, but it was gone, past and under them, too fast for him to have seen what it was. The airplane rocked, pitched into a dive.

As the bomber pointed for the cloud cover below, Nawls tumbled into the very tip of the glass nose. *"Dammit!"* Nawls yelled. Above his shoulder, Brink made out a black bird with a yellow nose. It was coming from below them, and in just slices of seconds it grew in size. Another airplane, he made his mind think, and lights winked on its wings. Shooting—

And then there were holes in the glass, holes as wide as his fist. The air screeched into those holes and a small piece of glass brushed against his eyebrow. Nawls's leg exploded and the hurricane wind blew blood everywhere.

The airplane leveled out and the scene beyond the glass was only white. They'd made it to the clouds.

The engines still made as much noise as before, so when Nawls opened his mouth, like he did now, Brink couldn't hear any screaming. Nawls had to be screaming, his leg shattered like that. Brink reached out and grabbed Nawls's flying jacket and dragged him closer, laid him out as best he could in the cramped space. Blood ran out of Nawls's leg as if the leg was a leaky pail. Brink looked at what remained of the limb and wondered what he'd remember of doctoring, it being so long.

He had his answer in the quick lightning flashes that were the glances he gave Nawls. He remembered fine. Brink saw the white of a shattered femur, marrow exposed, the *rectus femoris* muscle shredded from a projectile that had likely penetrated the *gracilis* at the back of the thigh. The blood came from the *profunda femoris*, but the artery was hidden.

Brink put fingers into the wound—Nawls opened his mouth against what must be the pain—and felt. If he could find the artery and pinch it, the bleeding might stop. But all he touched was torn muscle and some sharp fragments, bone or metal. The artery had retracted when it was severed. He'd never find it without a forceps, never clamp it without a hemostat.

Nawls moved less now. Brink looked around, but there was nothing, no line no cord, to use as a tourniquet, and only after several more seconds did he remember he wore a belt. He scratched that away from his waist and used the olive green canvas webbing to cinch above the wound and just below the pelvis. He pulled and pulled on the belt until it was as tight as he could make it, then tied its end in an awkward half-assed knot to keep it there.

"You're gonna be okay!" Brink shouted into Nawls's ear. The boy looked up at him with distant eyes. He'd not heard, Brink thought. So he rummaged around the bloody nose of the airplane until he found the pad of paper and pencil, tore off sheet after sheet on the pad before finally getting to a clean one, and wiped the pencil on his thigh. He scrawled the words and showed Nawls.

The sergeant didn't look.

Brink dropped the pad and put a finger at the man's throat to feel for a pulse.

He stayed next to Nawls as long as he could, but the wind through the holes in the glass was so cold and so damp. Finally he crawled away from the dead man and went to find some other place to sit in the shaking, vibrating hell.

Three

Beneath the airplane's wing, Brink raised his hands over his head to stretch for the first time in ten hours. Muscles popped. He twisted his neck and that cracked, too.

Shadows ran long across the concrete and the sun was half hidden by the trees at the west edge of the airfield. He looked at his watch: past eight in the evening.

Brink touched the tape above his right eye where the glass had cut a short, shallow groove. It had stopped bleeding hours ago and he'd closed the wound with white cloth adhesive from the aid kit. But the memory of Nawls's death wouldn't end so fast, not the way the wind had whistled through the plane and blew what Brink swore was the smell of blood through the plane.

A tall man stepped toward him across the tarmac. Dr. Paul Childess held out his hand, the arm frozen in mid-gesture. "Frank, what happened?"

Automatically, Brink took Childess's hand. The handshake was dry and light, very British. "Are you hurt?" Childess asked.

Brink turned to look at the airplane. A pair of men had climbed up into its belly through the hatch after he'd wriggled out, and now they returned, wrestling a lumpy blanket between them.

"What happened?" Childess asked again.

Brink shook his head. He must look like hell, Nawls's blood painted on him by the wind. He scratched a finger across his check, and looked at the dry brown caught under the nail. "We were talking about baseball, and then he was dead." He was too tired to say more.

The balding Englishman touched Brink's elbow to guide him to a waiting Dodge, once American, now British. He could tell because although it was now dark blue, the painter had missed a patch of olive on the front fender.

"Wait," said Brink. He freed his arm from Childess's touch and went to the two men and the sagging blanket between them. He ordered them to put Nawls down, and they did what he said because he had captain's bars pinned to his filthy collar, and he opened the blanket to get his belt to hold up his pants, but when he touched it, he realized the idea had been ridiculous. His fingers came away sticky. He wiped them off on the blanket, nodded to the men and told them to take Nawls away.

The young co-pilot pulled himself out of the hatch, dragging Brink's duffel. He handed it to Brink and as their hands touched a moment, he gave Brink a forced grin. Brink nodded, turned, and walked past Childess for the Dodge and tossed the duffel into the open boot.

"Everyone loves base ball, don't they?" Childess asked as he joined Brink. Childess was an unusual Brit for his love of baseball. He'd spent a summer in Washington before the war, got hooked then on what he called "base ball," always saying it as two words, a pause between them, and he yapped about the Senators and Griffith Stadium, and how he'd always wondered why they didn't cut down that tree to straighten the right-center wall. Childess had told Brink all that the first time he'd asked for gasoline to get him to the try out for the 505th Parachute's regimental team. Baseball was how they'd become friends.

Brink ducked into the backseat of the Dodge and Childess followed. The woman behind the wheel, Childess's regular WAAF driver, smoothly put the car into gear and steered it across the concrete and out a gate manned by a pair of sentries. The road left the airfield behind, and as it took a curve, Brink saw they were on the west side of Portsmouth harbor, heading north on the ribbon that hugged the shore and followed it toward the city.

He'd never seen so many ships. Not dozens in the harbor like usual, but hundreds. Long freighters with forests of cargo booms, and things with strange square-cut bows, and needle-nosed warships, and boxy little boats that looked like they'd swamp as soon as they hit the Channel. Enough ships to walk dry from here to Whale Island, clear across the harbor. A thicket of cables held down fat barrage balloons that floated over the fleet, each cable connected to a ship, and made the sweep of the water look like a kind of garden, the balloons its flowers, the cables their stalks. Brink closed his mouth.

"Part of the invasion fleet, I believe," Childess said quietly as he leaned back.

The light was fading, and when Brink looked at Childess he couldn't see if the man was serious.

"Is it time?" Brink asked. "Already?"

"I'm not in the know on the date, Frank, it's just what my eyes tell me." Brink thought he was lying—Childess always knew more than he let on. "Dakar, how did it go?" Childess asked.

"Dakar has the plague, like you said." Brink looked out the window again at the harbor.

"And?"

"It's a natural plague."

"The blood samples and cultures?"

"I had to leave them." Brink glanced at Childess.

"Pity."

He'd gone to Dakar to track the plague, to see if the outbreak was just bad luck or something more. Childess shifted beside him. Here it comes.

"What in God's name were you thinking?" Childess asked. His voice stayed soft.

"The charges are crap, Paul."

"We had an agreement. You would be careful. You would not make trouble." Childess's voice got quieter yet.

"I needed to find the sick before they made it to quarantine, didn't I, and Morton wasn't any help, so I used my penicillin to get information. How was I to know he'd think I was stealing morphine and overdosing them. That's crazy."

Childess went back to staring out the window on his side of the Dodge. "I had to make some very embarrassing calls to get you home. Very embarrassing," Childess said finally. "It was fortunate that our secret didn't spill out, Frank."

What secret, Brink wondered. There were so many.

That Childess thought the Germans might be behind the plague in Dakar? That was one secret, as outrageous as it sounded. Or that Frank had carried a haversack to Dakar filled with A17, Kate's new antibiotic, and would try it on the plague victims?

"That was always the risk, wasn't it?" Brink asked. "That we'd be found out. We should have told them in Dakar."

Childess turned from his window to look into the car. Brink tried to see his friend's face in the twilight of Portsmouth's streets, for the Dodge had reached the city outskirts and its flat-roofed warehouses, some just standing shells from the bombing four years earlier. The two-story flats the car passed next looked like they should be let to rats rather than people.

"So it was natural," Childess said, almost to himself. "And the other . . . the antibiotic? Tell me everything."

Brink had regularly cabled Childess with the barest details—no one outside Porton Down was to know what they did in its brick buildings of Wiltshire, so he had to pick the words carefully. All he'd been able to tell was the number of sick he'd found and the number who still lived each week.

"Does it work?" Childess asked when Brink didn't speak.

Brink told the truth as he knew it. "I think so."

"You think—"

"It wasn't exactly a meticulous trial, was it?" Brink said, his voice larger in the car. "I was trying to save them." He caught himself, breathed a time or two. "Yes, I think it works," he said finally.

Their antibiotic, their actinomycin, the clear liquid he'd injected into the little colored girl, was to be part of the defense against German anthrax, if it came to that. Penicillin showed efficacy against *Bacillus anthracis* in vitro, but Kate had argued that her antibiotic would be even more effective. So when they'd heard that the bubonic plague had snuck into Dakar, Kate lobbied to take A17 there. Even though it had been conceived with anthrax in mind, it should work against gram-negative bacilli like *Pasteurella pestis*, too. Childress had finally agreed, but not until Kate was dead.

"I found fourteen with the plague, and only one of them with pneumonic. I gave each of them the actinomycin. Ten, no, eleven died." Eleven, that was the little colored girl. "I have all the details in my notes." In the black leather notebook with the string holding it together.

"The one with pneumonic, did she—" Childress started.

"No, she didn't make it." Brink rubbed his eyes. So damned tired.

"Only three pulled through? That's not any better than you'd expect without any treatment," Childress said.

"I got to them too near the end," Brink said. "I'm sure it would be more effective if I'd diagnosed and started treatment as soon as the symptoms showed."

Had they missed a turn? The car headed east rather than west toward Salisbury and Porton Down. Then it slowed and stopped to wait for a convoy of Chevy trucks to trundle by. Two GIs leaned out from under the canvas at the back of one as it rolled past.

"Cairo didn't work out," Childress said in the idling car.

"Cairo?" The lack of sleep muddled his head.

"The army's doctors in Cairo have been using penicillin against a plague there. It's not been effective against either bubonic or pneumonic. Not effective at all."

Brink pinched the bridge of his nose, hoping that would clear his thinking. The woman put the Dodge in gear and in a few minutes the darkening streets of Portsmouth turned into a highway and they left the city behind.

"Did the A17 *kill* anyone in Dakar?" Childress asked. Sooner or later, Brink knew, it had to come around to this.

Diagne had said the girl hadn't made it to the quarantine. "No."

"That's good," Childress said. "You have enough on your conscience."

"At least I have one," Brink said. They'd had this argument, but it never got old.

"I've put mine in the cupboard for a bit, true," said Childess. "But not all of us have the luxury. Some of us have to be as wicked as the other side, or we'll lose this war. But Kate, that's another story, Frank."

"It wasn't my fault," Brink said.

"She loved you. She would have done anything for you. And you knew it. That's why she took the powder, gave herself the damned thing the two of you cooked up."

"Kate was . . ." Brink started—he wanted to say she was crazy. He closed his eyes a moment. That was a lie. She wasn't crazy, but she'd done a crazy thing. She'd been so sure that they had finally gotten it right, and wanted to prove it to him, him who always doubted, and maybe even to her former lover, Paul Childess, who wouldn't give them an answer about taking it to Dakar and using it to crush the plague. We need a rabbit, she'd said to him the night before when they lay close, but he hadn't picked that word out of all the others to hear what she meant.

"God, what a mess," Childess said very quietly. It wasn't the first time they'd done this since January. It had been all so civil between them, that Kate had been sleeping with Childess, that their affair was on its last legs, or so she said, when Brink came to her lab to work with her. So adult, the way they didn't talk about it, the way they'd never come to blows over it, Childess's anger at losing Kate mostly hidden. Brink's own unease—he refused to call it guilt—at loving the woman his friend had loved, still loved, was buried no deeper.

Brink opened his eyes and he saw a sign that read HARVANT in the dim light of the Dodge's masked headlights. "Where are we going?"

"To a hospital in Chichester, a dozen miles on. A boat came ashore near there first thing this morning. I want you to look at the passengers. Most of them didn't finish the trip."

Brink was confused. He wanted a cigarette. But he'd quit, hadn't he, because Kate had asked him, saying she'd read research from John Hopkins that claimed it ate years from your life.

"I brought you home because you're the only one who can help," said Childess. "Some at this hospital believe the French have—"

But Brink didn't give Childess a chance to finish. He understood. His work, going to Dakar, the little colored girl, the bomber flying light and fast for England, the memory of Kate and the death of Nawls, all the steps as clear as the scoring of a double play, 4-6-3. "Christ, it's the plague, isn't it? They've sent it here."

The car swerved as the WAAF driver twitched at the wheel.

He's the only one left alive?" Brink asked.

The nurse shook her head. She was old, her face lined like a street map. "No, sir. A young woman down the corridor."

Brink stepped toward the metal bed in the stark hospital room. The light cast mean shadows on the man under its sheet. He was unconscious, his face washed with sweat like rain. His lips were the color of lilac.

"Don't get too close, sir," the old nurse said. "The two others they brought, they passed early this afternoon."

"The woman?"

"Another French. But she seems fine. This is her father. It's his fishing boat that ran ashore, she says." She pointed to the man under the sheet.

"You're the one who suspected plague?" he asked, still staring at the man. He wished he had his A17, but although Childess had telephoned Porton Down to have it driven here, the car hadn't appeared.

"Yes, sir. I spent enough years in India to know what I see when I see it." She looked at him carefully. "You're an American, sir?" she asked.

"Yes."

"But you're from the Ministry—" she started.

"Yes, from the Ministry," he lied. She gave him a look that wondered what an American was doing giving orders from the Ministry of Health.

"You're a doctor, sir? You have experience in this?" She glanced at his clothes. Nawls's blood on his shirt and the beltless pants loose on his hips didn't instill much confidence in his doctoring skills.

Brink wasn't sure what to say. Lots of secrets all around. "He could be sick from a dozen things," Brink said, looking at the Frenchman again, knowing that wasn't so.

"The others were the color of the *mariyamma*, sir. I spent time in India, I know how it happens."

"*Mariyamma?*"

"Their name for the black death, sir. I've seen this, sir. The kind without the buboes. It's in the lungs. The sputum, see?" Brink had already noticed the faint line, barely visible against the pale of the man's face, that etched from his blue lips to the white sheet, where pink wormed the line. There was a dusting of froth at the turn of his mouth.

"Has he been given anything?" Brink asked.

"Sulfa, sir, but I think it's long past that."

"No buboes, you say?"

"I checked him very carefully, sir. Armpits, neck, and groin, the whole lot."

"There's no mask on him. Why not?"

That lined face of hers twitched. "I wanted to put one on him, but Doctor Tadwell, he said a mask was unnecessary. But I spent time in India—I know I'm right."

"Find a mask for him, then leave us for a bit."

"Yes, sir. Of course." She brought him one, but drilled him with her bright eyes as he shut the door on her face.

He tied the mask on over his own mouth and nose, then bent over the Frenchman. *"Monsieur, réveillez, vous Monsieur,"* Brink asked through the cloth. The man refused to stir. *"Monsieur, vous prie, où donc avez vous trouvés les malade?"* But the Frenchman couldn't tell him where he'd found the sick ones, could tell him nothing other than what his symptoms said: that he was very sick. The man breathed quick, his face was flushed, his nostrils and lips blue. Brink rolled down the damp sheet, hesitant, cautious, careful not to touch the sputum that had dribbled onto the white cotton. The man's naked chest was like the nurse said: no buboes. *"Je vous prie Monsieur, serait-ce la faute des Allemands?"* Was it the Germans who did this?

No answer.

When he tucked the sheet back under the Frenchman's chin, the man's eyes snapped open and his hand snaked out to grab Brink by the throat. His fingers dug in. *"Nous devons aller de l'avant, ne devons prendre de l'avance!"* the Frenchman shouted hoarsely. Brink clawed at the hand, but the man was strong and he couldn't break the grip. The Frenchman yanked at his mask, the ties bit into his neck and snapped, the cloth was suddenly in the man's hand, and Brink's face was unguarded.

"En avant! Aller! Aller!" the Frenchman shouted—the words *forward, go! go!* hollow in Brink's ears—as fingers dragged him closer. He smelled the man's hot sour breath, and the Frenchman coughed deep and wet right in his face. Brink felt the droplets sprinkle his skin.

The Frenchman collapsed under his sheet and Brink lost his balance, knocked a metal waste tin with his foot, and fell to the floor.

"Sir!" outside the door. Someone tried the latch, but he'd locked it.

He lay there on the floor, his hip hurting where it had caught the bed, the voice in his head shouting "Oh Christ, oh Christ." This isn't happening. His breathing quickened, just like the sick Frenchman.

"Sir! Is everything all right?" she shouted through the door.

He didn't know if he'd pulled enough *Pasteurella pestis* into his lungs to kill him. He didn't know how long it would take for it to work its nonchalant evil.

"I'm okay," Brink yelled finally, blinking fast to make the panic go away. "Stay out!" The Frenchman thrashed in the bed above him.

Brink breathed shallow, wondering whether drawing deeper breaths would bring on the plague sooner. He shook his head: one breath of the *pestis* didn't have to end up as pneumonic. That thought calmed him for a moment, although a cousin—that a mouthful was more than enough—wormed right back into his head.

Brink used the edge of the bed to pull himself up, and staggered for the door. "I'm fine," he said to the woman outside. "Give me a minute." He went to the small cabinet tucked under the window beyond the bed, pawed through its drawers, found a half-filled bottle of medicinal alcohol and a clean cloth. He drenched the cloth and wiped his face, under his nose, across his lips, scrubbed as far up his nostrils as the cloth would go, that stinging like hell. It left his face cold, evaporating quickly like aftershave. He even took a swig and swished it around in his mouth, then spit it onto the cloth.

He tossed the cloth into the bin, pulled the mask from the Frenchman's fingers by one of the ties and dropped that in there, too. Then he opened the door.

"What happened, sir?" the old woman asked. She glanced over his shoulder, took in the room. Her stare stayed a moment on the Frenchman and the awkward way he'd fallen back onto his pillow.

"I'm okay," he said.

"Should I find one of the other doctors?" She had an idea what had happened.

"No, I said I'm fine."

"Sir, you need to go into—"

Brink moved closer. "Nothing happened, do you understand?"

"Sorry, sir, yes sir," she said. But she wasn't ready to back down. "He'll die, won't he, sir, like the others." Not much of a question, since she was telling him another way that she knew or at least suspected.

"Can you keep a secret?" Brink said, and waited again for ages. The old woman nodded. "Not everyone with the *mariyamma* has to die," he said.

Brink followed Childess down the wide staircase at the heels of the two old doctors who ran St. Richards, the one balding, the other with a badly cut shock of white hair. Everyone's shoes clicked on the tiled steps. The bald one was Tadwell, the one who'd told the nurse she was wrong, the other was Holden.

The staircase emptied into a cool basement smelling of mold and bleach. Holden shoved on a set of swinging doors to take them into a long, large room with too much light and a too-low ceiling. Two women were stretched across porcelain draining tables, shallow tubs with worn raised edges. Brink stepped to the first, noticing the gray powder spread a good yard around the table and sprinkled over her. Brink's shoes left footprints. DDT. Childess must have told the hospital to use delousing powder to kill any lingering fleas, in case this was bubonic.

The corpse wasn't black like Dakar's coloreds, but gray from the DDT against the porcelain's cream. Naked and thin, very thin. The other was even thinner. He asked for gloves and Holden handed him a pair; he pulled them on and gingerly raised first one stick of an arm, then the other. No buboes.

Brink stepped to the second tub. The same, except this one's fingernails were dark blue. But there could be a score of reasons for the cyanosis: severe pneumonia or a heart failure or even drowning.

He fingered her wrist, ran that finger up the arm, and used a rubbered thumb to scrub away the powder at the hollow of her elbow where he thought he saw a discoloration. He scrubbed again. There, at the median cubital vein. The beginnings of a bubo, he thought, and looked closer. No, only an inflammation, and in its center a bump of a pinprick. She'd been stuck with a needle.

Brink went back to the first, scrubbed away her powder, too, and found several marks in the crook of her left elbow.

"Something, Frank?" Childess asked behind him.

Brink looked at the punctures, almost invisible. "Just looking for buboes." He glanced up. Childess stared at him a moment, but nodded. "Where are the rest?" Brink asked. He needed to see more elbows.

"In the truck, I'm afraid. We didn't want to bring them . . ." Holden said, his voice tailing off. "We thought it best to leave them where they were." He sounded embarrassed.

Brink looked at his watch. Hours in the trucks, no telling how many hours dead before that. And the day had been hot.

"I need to see them," he said, and asked for a mask and flashlight. Holden nodded, and led them down a long hallway and up a short flight of stairs. They came out at a side entrance, the loading spot for hearses. Parked at the far side of the small graveled lot was a Bedford, its high hood easy to see as a silhouette in the moonlight.

Ten feet from the truck the smell wriggled through the mask, and as he touched the Bedford's canvas side the odor pushed deep into his mouth. When he exhaled, he tasted the stink on his tongue. Only Childess had come this far, and he suddenly bent and heaved, spraying shoes and gravel and even the cuffs of his pants. Brink gagged, swallowed, and swallowed again. He hoisted himself into the Bedford, and the canvas fell into place and the space closed. He swung the flashlight. Bodies, tangled.

Jesus Christ. He waved at the flies that slowly rose from the dead with the flashlight. I can't do this.

But Brink made himself look. At the left breast of every dress or shirt, a yellow star was stitched. He focused on the face of a girl—maybe ten— framed by dark tangled hair and stained with a goatee of red and pink. She stared at the underside of the canvas with china doll's eyes. In the flashlight, each face was dark. Light blue some, others sliding near purple, one or two almost black. But whether from plague—the color caused by the respiratory failure—or decomposition he couldn't tell.

Jesus jesus jesus.

Porton Down, the low brick buildings where rooms were crammed with glass pipettes and petri dishes, swam in his head. He'd seen *Pasteurella pestis* under his Watson microscope, the safety-pin shape impossible to miss. But he'd never taken the thing to its conclusion, from the safety pins under glass slides to a real person really dead. Even the girl in Dakar had still been alive when he last saw her.

What a fool I've been. Fools, all of us. Childess should see this, too.

Then, because he couldn't think of any other way, he touched the hem of the nearest dress, raised it, and looked at the thighs in the flashlight's glare. They were unblemished. Brink pointed the light at her neck. The skin there was dirty or just purple, but without a lump of something darker. Her elbow next. He held her arm, twisted it to show the inside curve, and put the light full on her skin. Nothing.

On hands and knees, he went from one woman to another, lifting skirts like a Peeping Tom. Clean, clean, and clean. Peered for pinpricks in elbows, and found five women marked. The children he left untouched. He couldn't bear to bother them.

On one of the last women he found it. Two inches below her ear was a swelling. He traced its contours with his gloved fingers, pushed on it, felt it give. In the yellow cone of the dying flashlight it was only a hint blacker than her skin. She had no needle marks.

Brink retraced his trail across the bodies and shoved aside the canvas. Outside, he pulled off his mask to breathe the air, now like sugar, and climbed down and walked to the doctors standing stiff near the door that led to the morgue.

The needle marks and the plague. Someone had given these people pneumonic plague and then nicked only some with needles. Someone had tested a cure on part of the group, and not on others, the control. Someone across the Channel was testing his work.

"What do you think, Frank?" asked Childess as Brink reached them.

He could tell them to have the two in the morgue cut open and their blood drawn and cultured, order them to put the tissue of that one bubo in the truck under a microscope, all that taking hours and days, and he wouldn't have anything more than what he had now. This was pneumonic plague. The pink, frothy sputum was one sign, the lack of buboes on the thighs, another. The third, that was the single cervical bubo, for pneumonic plague very occasionally produced those.

And the final, well, that was the mortality. Eleven in the truck, two in the morgue. Thirteen of thirteen. And the Frenchman would soon make it fourteen.

"The nurse is right," Brink said.

"No, that's impossible," said Tadwell. "It could be any number of—"

Brink understood the stubbornness. It had been centuries since the plague had come here.

"This must be a mistake," said Tadwell, pleading to Childess.

"Dr. Brink is the expert," said Childess.

"Quarantine," Holden said. Brink flinched, knowing the nurse who suspected he'd been exposed would think he should be separated, too. He hoped his denials to her had been convincing.

"We can't close this hospital and turn it into a quarantine, we have sick people here and a staff that needs rest," said Tadwell.

"Nonsense, we must notify the police first, but I imagine soldiers next," said Childess, speaking mostly to Tadwell. "We'll say it is an outbreak of influenza."

"This is absurd. You go on the word of one woman, a nurse at that, and a doctor I've never met, an American—"

Brink moved closer to Tadwell, who backed up. "I know this," he said.

Childess stepped between them. "You realize what we have here, don't you, if this gets out? Not only the plague, but the talk."

White-haired Holden was the one who answered. "Of course, Doctor, we understand. And we'll cooperate, I assure you."

"Damn that nurse," muttered Tadwell softly, but Brink heard him.

"If it wasn't for her, you'd be dead, too, in a few days," said Brink. "You should thank God for that woman."

"Dr. Brink, we should find you some soap," said Childess. "And some clothes." He nodded to Brink. "Go, Frank, go wash up. I have some calls to make, and we'll talk."

Brink left the three Englishmen, walked down the stairs. He had questions for the daughter of the fisherman. He wanted to find out how they came to be, the plague and the needle marks, and she was the only one left to ask.

Four

Brink turned the corner of the linoleumed hallway, saw the constable leaning against the wall next to the door, cigarette in his mouth. That would be the girl's room. He switched the small metal tray from his right hand to his left, the syringe and vial snicking together on that tray under the white cloth as he did.

The constable nodded. "Sir," he said as Brink came near. "The nurse, she's—" but then it didn't matter, since the door across the hallway banged open against the wall and the nurse herself flew out the door. A metal tray followed, bits of food trailing, and skipped on the floor before clanging into the constable's chair.

"*Père? Père? Mais où est donc mon père?*" a woman's voice screeched from inside the room.

A blur followed the shouts for her father, and the girl—all Brink caught was bare legs—was out the door and across the hallway and on the constable. Her surprise was complete, and the first slap was enough to send the constable's cigarette sparking. Before he could reach them, the woman had grabbed hold of the constable's tunic, next his throat. She kept her hand pinched under his chin, but turned to look at Brink.

"*Je souhaite parler à mon père,*" she said.

Her face was square—strong, his sister might have said if she'd met this woman—and her nose was wide for the face. Her lips were full and her neck slender, graceful, as it disappeared into the collar of her dress, a shapeless thing mended on the sleeve and tight under the arms. Her hair was dark and short, cut so it barely covered her ears.

"*Vous etes la fille du pêcheur?*" he asked. The fisherman is your father?

"Yes, we are fishermen," she said, Brink understanding her French. "I want to talk to my father," the girl repeated.

"He's sick," Brink answered. The constable squirmed a bit under her hand, but she squeezed on his throat and muttered something Brink didn't catch and the man stopped.

"And you . . . you are . . ." she asked.

"I'm a doctor of medicine. I've examined your father." He looked at the constable, then her. "Let him go, we'll talk."

She had green eyes, he noticed. She nodded, released the policeman, who rasped for breath and staggered to his chair. The girl held her hands in front of her, as if afraid that the constable would now retaliate. From his spot a yard away, Brink quickly examined her. She seemed fine. She had no sign of fever, her breathing sounded normal, and she hadn't coughed.

"Please," he said, gesturing to the open door of her room. She nodded, he followed, and after he'd put the tray on a small table, she sat on the bed. There was no chair.

She pulled a finger from her hair where she'd been twisting strands mindlessly, and rested her hands in the lap of her dress, fingers criss-crossed and folded like a small shield. She looked down at her lap, back to him, to his face once more. "My father?" She cocked her head to the side.

She looked strong enough to take the truth. For a moment, sitting there with her head tilted, she reminded him of Kate. There was nothing re-markable about her except her green eyes, but the way she looked at him made him think of Kate and how stubborn she'd been.

"He's sick," Brink said. "Very sick."

She kept staring.

"Tonight, tomorrow perhaps," Brink said. He matched her stare. She nodded finally.

"Et alors il va mourir bein," she said quietly, the words at first refusing to move into English.

"Oui," he said, yes, then he will be dead.

"I want to see him before he's gone," she said.

Brink shook his head. "Too dangerous. You might catch it."

"I already have it." As she said that, she looked at her hands in her lap. She was lying—she wasn't sick.

"No, no you don't."

"Please, let me talk to him, only a moment, please." She leaned forward from the bed where she sat and he couldn't help it—he looked at the swath of white skin at her throat where it disappeared into the scooped bodice of her old dress.

"Answer some questions for me?" he asked. She looked hard at him, her eyes as still as those in a bronze statue gone green with age. "Answer the questions, and I'll let you see him. For a minute or two. But you have to tell me the truth." She nodded slowly, and her fingers, clenched in her lap, finally relaxed.

She told him where she was from, how she and her father had found the Jews, how they'd gotten to the boat, how they'd sailed and her papa had collapsed in a fever shouting at imaginary enemies. It had all been *erreure monumentale*! she said. A big mistake. Her face had an expression that took him a moment to puzzle out. Sad, he thought at first. More than that. Heartache. But she couldn't say what had made the Jews sick. When he asked about a doctor or a doctor's bag or needles anywhere, she said no. It all sounded like the truth.

He could tell she wanted a turn asking questions. It almost moved her lips.

Her father would soon sweat out his last rough breaths, but she might be fine. If she had stayed away from the Jews. If she'd kept distance from her father. A whole bushel of ifs.

He went to the metal tray he'd left on the table. Brink pulled back the white cloth to reveal the syringe and A17. The car from Porton Down had finally shown up and he'd intended to give himself the needle first to show her it was safe, then prick her second. Maybe the actinomycin would work as a prophylactic, keep the *Pasteurella pestis* at bay. Sulfadiazine worked like that sometimes, and A17 was magnitudes stronger than sulfa. But when he picked up the syringe all he saw was the contorted face of the little colored girl who'd died after he'd injected her. What if Morton had been right? What if his cure had killed her?

"Monsieur?" the girl asked, and Brink realized he'd been staring at the syringe. There was plenty of time. He'd wait to see if symptoms appeared, *then* give them each shots. That would offer much more time than the coloreds in Dakar had had.

He laid the syringe back on its tray, it clinking against the steel.

Brink turned to the girl. He thought of Kate a moment, how he'd not been able to do a thing for her. He could do better for this woman.

"Yes?" she asked.

He went to her bed, extended his hands. She looked at them, her face uncertain, but there was glitter in the corners of her green green eyes. Her hands were dry, talcum almost, and warm when he took them in his. It had been a while since he'd touched a woman's hand like this.

"You don't have the pestilence," Brink said quietly, though he had no way to know. "You're fine."

She tightened her fingers around his hand. *"Merci,"* she said, the word sticking in the French.

Their hands touched for one, two beats, and then Brink pulled his fingers from the twining of hers. He went to the door, pushed the latch, and was halfway down the hallway before he realized he'd not even asked her name.

Wollenstein watched over Sillmann's shoulder as the pilot brought the Storch into the wind. The little aircraft flicked over a final tree, the nose dropped, and Wollenstein's stomach went with it. Sillmann pulled on the stick to pop the Storch level and settled the aircraft on the grass, the bump no rougher than stepping off a street curb. They rolled across long shadows, the Storch's engine falling softer as Sillmann worked the throttle.

He waited until the engine switched off before raising the door on its hinge. When he glanced at the grass a meter and more below him, he noticed a leafy branch pinned between axle and tire on the landing strut. Sillmann liked flying low.

"Pull it against those trees," he said into the cockpit after he'd jumped down. Wollenstein pointed to the green line that defined the landing field. There was a ruined, yellow-nosed Messerschmitt 109 near the edge of the strip, a relic of 1940 and the war against England. At the far end was a shiny Junkers 52, a three-motored transport just like the one under netting back at his farm.

"Don't worry, Sturmbannführer," said the young pilot he'd cadged from Brussels.

He always worried. He'd worried the two and a half hours from Chef du Pont as Sillmann brushed the Storch against trees all the way north along the coast to the Pas de Calais and Flers. Unlike Sillmann, he'd not worried about Allied fighters that might pounce, but rather about the missing Jews and the vulgar Kripo, Kirn. How together he and Kirn had not found a whisper of sickness, even though they'd been to half a dozen villages near the abandoned Daimler and talked to almost that many doctors during the long day.

Wollenstein tried to put those worries out of his head as he walked to the waiting car, a tiny cloth-topped Kübelwagen. The driver, a Luftwaffe enlisted man with a greasy face, ground the car into gear and bounced it across the grass. Ten minutes later, after too many turns to count, the driver braked. Two concrete paths, separated by a meter of grass, disappeared into darker trees a hundred meters away. Wollenstein pulled himself out and stared into the twilight.

"Down that way, Major," shouted the driver, not shutting off the Kübelwagen's toy engine. He pointed at the paths. "They're waiting for you." As soon as Wollenstein slammed shut the door, the driver and his car rolled away.

Wollenstein walked on the right-hand concrete line, smelling the early summer's green from the sun-warmed leaves on the trees to his left. Lindens, he thought. The gloom there made him nervous and he put a hand on his leather holster, the Walther inside it, to make himself feel brave. He'd not been to this part of France—the bulge of coast that swung out nearest to England—and although it had looked the same as his farm, more or less, from the air and the Storch's backseat, it certainly felt foreign. But Himmler had told him he must come to watch this Luftwaffe demonstration, and so he was here.

Near the trees that cut across these paths a man stepped out of the long shadows and asked for his papers. The sentry was young and smiled a pleasant smile. He switched on a torch to see the pages, then aimed the beam at Wollenstein's face to match it with the photograph in the small identity booklet. The boy waved him on with his rifle, telling him to keep to the paths and he'd be there in a bit. Once through the thick stand of trees, a small woods really, where the darkness was almost complete and the small sounds in the uncut underbrush made him flinch, Wollenstein stepped onto a long, narrow field. At its edge was another sentry who repeated the looking at papers. This one was older and all business.

Down the length of the clearing was what Wollenstein first took as a strange shed, a long, thin triangle with one end at ground level, the other ten meters in the air. Then he saw it for what it was. A ramp. The peak was forty or fifty meters away. A knot of men worked over something poised at its near, low end. Lights had been strung on poles, and in their glare Wollenstein saw a long tube, eight meters perhaps, with a sharp nose and stubs for wings and a pylon at its rear on which perched a drumlike cylinder. A Fiesler, the Luftwaffe's flying bomb. He had documents and photos back at his farm that Himmler had sent for his opinion on whether the machine could carry the *Pasteurella pestis* in its warhead.

The final sentry was an officer at the door to a squat building not far from the ramp. He, too, looked at Wollenstein's *Soldbuch* with a torch, then at a page in a small notebook he held, nodded, penciled a line through an entry, said, "Welcome, Major," and pointed to the thick door.

The unshaded electric lights inside made Wollenstein squint. This bunker was made smaller by the crowd. Three sat at a table covered with radio equipment and a small box no bigger than two thick books laid side by side. Eight others stared out the narrow open slit that was the room's only view, and looked, he assumed, onto the field. All but one wore Luftwaffe blue, most with braid twining on their tunics' shoulder boards and collar tabs. Colonels and majors, he thought, from their age. None turned to look when he closed the door behind him.

Only one of the men wore gray. He was slim, shorter than most, with blond hair that showed under his peaked hat. For a moment Wollenstein thought he would be sick. Of all the people. . . .

"How much longer?" Kammler asked the blue-clad men, the words clipped. Impatient. Kammler had not seen Wollenstein enter the bunker.

"We're ready now, General," said one of those in Luftwaffe blue. He hovered behind the men at the table with the radio and the small, odd box with the cloth-covered wires out its back.

A Luftwaffe officer at Wollenstein's right looked Kammler's way. The man's eyes went to the bones and skull pinned on the Obergruppenführer's hat, then his face went blank and his eyes emptied.

"Show us how the Luftwaffe will save us all from the English, Wachtel," said Kammler.

A Luftwaffe officer nodded to one of the men seated in front of the box. Wollenstein peered over shoulders to the viewing slit. Someone had switched off the lights outside. Even the ramp had gone into the gloom.

"Clear?" asked a voice to his right. Another voice answered. "Start, then."

Out in the dark a small circle of blue light first, then a quick sound—a *duv-duv-duv-duv* that was like an unmuffled motorcycle—and a three- or four-meter-long stream of flame, mostly blue but with touches of yellow, lit the field. In its light, Wollenstein saw that the flame jetted from the cylinder atop the Fiesler.

"Engine start, running strong," called a voice. A heartbeat or two of listening to the strange pulsing noise, then another yelled, "Launch!"

Wollenstein thought he heard a hissing over the *duv-duv-duv*, and the little aircraft lurched ahead, then flung itself the length of the ramp. It leapt off the end and into the night, the *duv-duv-duv* fading faster than the flame. But the dot of flame fell and a fireball replaced it, all yellows and reds. As the fireball rose, twice as high as the trees, the sound of an explosion echoed against the walls of dark woods.

No one in the room said a word until Kammler broke the silence. "That's not London."

"No," said Wachtel.

"What happened?"

"It's gone down." Someone choked back a laugh in the corner.

"I can see that," Kammler said. Had he not heard that half laugh? Perhaps not; Kammler still stared out the viewing slit.

Wachtel looked like he was about to shrug his shoulders, but only shook his head. "Another malfunction. I'm sorry, but we thought we had the launching problems solved."

"It seems not."

"I'm sorry, General, but the deadlines, they cause—"

"How often do they do that?" Kammler pointed at the tree line, now dark.

"One out of six, one out of five. But we'll fix the problems. Four days, five days, no more, and we'll be ready. We have enough stock to send off fifty the first day, eighty the next. London will be in flames, I promise."

Kammler shook his head. "Thank you for the demonstration." He turned for the door and saw Wollenstein for the first time. His small eyes didn't register surprise, and he only nodded.

"We can prepare another, it will only take an hour or so," said Wachtel.

"I've seen enough," said Kammler. "Herr Doktor, please?" he said and gestured to the door, but didn't wait. Because he was slow following, Wollenstein heard someone in the bunker snort and softly say *"Ofenmann"* to Kammler's disappearing back. Wollenstein smiled. "Oven man," yes.

Kammler waited in the dark. "Doktor," he said, as Wollenstein approached and smelled tobacco and garlic on the man.

"I didn't expect you here, Obergruppenführer," Wollenstein said.

"The Reichsführer asked me to come see this thing of Göring's," said Kammler. "To give my opinion of the Luftwaffe's magic weapon."

"Today?" Wollenstein slipped toward thoughts of the Jews he'd lost and the disease they'd stolen. If Kammler learned of it, he'd go right to Himmler and tell the Reichsführer of Wollenstein's blunder. Kammler was jealous of his work.

"He and I are inspecting the launching sites being built for my rockets," said Kammler. "Farther north, in Belgium. I flew in this afternoon. He told you, certainly, that I'd be here."

No, he hadn't. Wollenstein wondered what Himmler was up to.

"I'll take you to your aircraft. You landed on the same field as my *Tante Ju*, yes?" Kammler said, and before Wollenstein could answer, the short man started walking, his strides slow and deliberate across the field that now smelled like petrol exhaust.

"The Luftwaffe can't hit a plate with its fork," said Kammler, his voice raspy. "And if it does, it's more likely our plate, not England's." Kammler stopped, spun to face Wollenstein. "It's madness to put your warheads on this. The Luftwaffe would end up infecting us all. One crash like that and the sick would drop from here to Warsaw. And suddenly the war wouldn't be so important." He lit a cigarette, and his angular face with its large nose and sharp cheekbones showed its shadows as the lighter's flame moved in a gentle wind. The lighter clicked shut and Wollenstein smelled the heavy smoke.

"That's the problem with some inventions, isn't it?" Kammler asked through the stink. The ember end of the cigarette glowed. "This is insanity, thinking we can shoot your *Grabbringer* into the air on Göring's fool flying motorcycles. Idiotic. My rockets now, they're different. Safe. We've done a dozen test shots this past week without a single malfunction," Kammler said proudly. "That's a record."

Wollenstein remembered the trip last July to the Baltic coast, Peenemünde cold even that summer day. Kammler had been there, too, at the test firing of the A4, the arrow-nosed, black-and-white torpedo standing over a concrete pad. Tall as a four-storied house, the A4 had belched flame, raised smoke and dust, and on a long yellow flame, rose straight into the air. Even standing behind a concrete wall, he and Kammler and Himmler and a host of others—some in suits, others in uniform—the noise had been of three dozen trains rushing through one tunnel. And in an instant the rocket was climbing and in seconds gone from sight. A few days later, Himmler had given the A4 project to Kammler, even though Kammler was no engineer, only a builder. He'd built camps for the SS in the East, built the crematoria in that place in Silesia, Birkenau, so went the talk. *Oven man*, the Luftwaffe officer called him. *Ofenmann*.

Wollenstein found Kammler beside a dark thing he recognized as a boxy, high-wheeled Horch when the driver turned on a torch and opened the rear door. Kammler climbed in, Wollenstein after. A fat man spread across two-thirds of the front passenger seat. Folds of skin layered the back of his neck and flowed into his tunic's collar. He smoked a cigar, fat like him, and each time he flicked its end, ash floated in the car.

"The secret is safe, yes? Your *Grabbringer*, that's what I mean," Kammler asked.

Wollenstein's heart hammered a time or two in his chest, he swallowed, searched for spit, and swallowed again. "Yes, of course."

"Anyone been snooping around your farm?" Kammler asked.

"No." Wollenstein's head was crowded with the moment when he'd stepped up to his truck and found its door open and his Jews missing.

The driver switched off the torch, climbed behind the wheel, and as the Horch rolled down the concrete paths it didn't rattle or squeak like that toy Kübelwagen. "Remember what I told you. If the Wehrmacht hear of it, they'll want it," said Kammler.

"Yes, I remember," Wollenstein said. How many times had Kammler pestered him like this?

"You should think about my offer," Kammler said. "It would make things so much simpler." Kammler's cigarette smoke joined the fat man's cigar.

Wollenstein cranked down the window on his side to let in the night air, thicker now after the warm day. Move his project to the Reich? No, France was the right place because it *wasn't* the Reich. He was far from eyes over his shoulder, he could run the farm as he wanted, not worry about Himmler poking his nose into things. "Very generous, as always, Obergruppenführer, but no."

"You say that every time," Kammler said.

With each passing moment that Jews didn't become the subject of the conversation, Wollenstein felt better. "And I will each time," Wollenstein answered.

The Horch made one turn, another, and the headlamps showed the landing field where Sillmann waited with the Storch. And the Ju-52 at its far end, the *Tante Ju*, Kammler called it, that must be the Obergruppenführer's. The solid car braked to a stop and its lamps fixed the Storch against the trees. The bright tank on its belly caught the light.

"Still spraying potatoes, Herr Doktor?" asked Kammler. He'd seen the Storch.

Wollenstein opened the Horch's door and stepped out. "Your rockets won't be ready until September, yes? My potato spraying is the only hope if we're to crush their invasion."

Someone switched on a lamp inside the Horch and Wollenstein shaded his eyes against the sudden brightness. Through the slits in his eyes he saw

Kammler's narrow face go even thinner. "Not again," said Kammler, his voice sawing at the air. "We've talked this to death. The English will shoot down your aircraft long before they reach their target. This isn't 1940."

"But you're not the one who makes the decision, are you?" Wollenstein asked.

"You shouldn't talk to me like that, Herr Doktor. Even if you are Himmler's pet." Kammler reached for the door and slammed it shut in his face. In that instant, the fat man in the front seat turned, a counterfeit smile around the cigar clenched in his teeth.

June 2, 1944

Friday

Diseases desperate grown,
By desperate appliance are relieved
Or not at all.

—WILLIAM SHAKESPEARE, 1601

Five

The man's charcoal-gray suit didn't fool Brink. He stood too stiff to be anything but military, or maybe once and since retired. Brink stepped into the dim room, which was lit only by a cheap floor lamp.

The man was fifty, give or take, with a clipped mustache that looked even more army than the way he stood. He had the shifty eyes of a coyote. Childess stood behind him, his face half hidden in the gloom. "Gubbins, Collin Gubbins," the man said, and grabbed Brink's hand in a fierce grip. He sounded like a Scot, but the accent wasn't thick.

Brink looked around the room. It was nearly bare; only three chairs and the lamp. No carpets on the floor, no paintings on the wall, furniture that looked hand-me-down, and with an unused smell like a dusty back storeroom. No. 10 Downing should look more impressive, even at two in the morning. Gubbins caught his glance.

"Everything moved out years ago, when the Blitz made them say it was too dangerous for the prime minister," Gubbins said. "He lives in the Annex, next over, that and in his caves underneath."

Gubbins folded his large frame into one of the chairs. It creaked. Like everything British, it seemed ready to give up the ghost. He waved a hand at the two empty chairs, then reached inside his dark jacket and came out with a dented tin cigarette case. From it he pulled a half-smoked butt and fiddled with its burnt end. Brink wanted that cigarette. What harm in smoking, now that the Frenchman had breathed on him? But he'd promised Kate.

It hit Brink then why this room felt odd. Dark as it was in the corners, bare as it was on its floor, the light and chairs made it feel like a theater's stage, with Gubbins only an actor playing a part. A play was pretend, and this had the same fake feeling. There would be secrets here at least, and probably a lie or two, so the feeling fit. Brink looked at Childess, but he was studying the bare floor, then back to Gubbins, who struck a match on the outside of the case to light his cigarette. "Who are you?" Brink finally asked.

Childess jumped in. "Frank, there's—"

Gubbins waved his cigarette at Childess, its plume making a ragged circle. "I speak for the prime minister," he said. The way Gubbins put it, Brink knew he wasn't supposed to ask more questions. Gubbins took a puff of his short cigarette. "Did Jerry put sick Jews on this boat and send them our way as a weapon?" he asked, picking tobacco from between his teeth.

There was an awkward silence. Brink had assumed he'd been flown to London to report only on what he'd found in the Chichester hospital, and the question took him by surprise.

"No time like the moment, Doctor." Gubbins breathed out smoke. "Answer, please." Ordering now, not so polite.

"You're the expert, Frank. Tell him what you think," said Childess from the other chair. He crossed his legs carefully.

"No one meant for the Jews to come here," said Brink. "If they had, they would have sent ones who were not yet presenting."

Gubbins looked at the lit end of his cigarette. He put it to his lips, sucked deeply, then pinched off the ember and let it fall. "You're not speaking English."

Brink tried to keep the irritation from his voice. "Someone with symptoms of pneumonic plague can spread it to another with a cough or a sneeze. Like with influenza. The plague is carried on the tiny droplets expelled from the lungs when people cough. Or sneeze. Okay? Pneumonic plague is fatal, every time, and it works fast. If the Germans meant for it to spread they would have sent people only just infected. That would have given more time before the disease presented and perhaps was diagnosed, more time for the Jews to disperse so they could infect people in a greater area. But nearly all of them were dead by the time the boat reached shore." He caught his breath. "It was a mistake." *Erreur monumentale!* the girl with the green eyes had said, and Brink knew she'd told the truth. The Germans hadn't meant for the Jews to end up in England.

"How astounding. Like influenza you say," said Gubbins. In the distance, an air-raid siren warbled. It went on and on, and only after it faded did Gubbins talk again. "Extremely dangerous, then," Gubbins said.

"It's been contained," Brink said.

"No, I understand that. In France, that's what I mean. What if this disease is loose in France?" Gubbins leaned forward, the chair protesting and his eyes under the coyote eyebrows.

"I don't—" began Brink.

"We've always assumed Jerry worked on the same things we did," Gubbins said. "But not this. Correct?"

No one had figured out how to release *Pasteurella pestis* without resorting to fleas, and fleas, well, fleas were crude and dangerous. "Correct."

"Could they spread this as we intend the cattle disease?" Gubbins busied his hand with the cigarette case again, but kept his eyes on Brink. The room was quiet; the air-raid siren had gone silent. If it was another false alarm, the all clear would come soon. "Yes, I know about the anthrax. You were part of that, weren't you?" asked Gubbins. He lit another cigarette, breathed in, breathed out.

Brink held the stare with Gubbins. The clustered bombs that released a cloud of anthrax, enough to kill half of those within a mile. They'd left that Scottish hunk of rock, Gruinard Island, filled with dead sheep. Brink remembered the sheep, and the three days it had taken them to die. His job had been to watch those sheep through a brass scope set on a hill three hundred yards away from the wooden frames the animals had been tied to.

"Or other means. Dr. Childess says Porton Down worked on ways to release anthrax in a cloud, like the one that drifts from the spray I pump on my roses. What if Jerry's perfected that?"

Brink shook his head. "We've tried to aerosolize anthrax, but we've had no luck. It's a very difficult process, technically, to dry and grind it into a powder, and produce uniform-sized particles that properly release in a spray. I don't think the Germans—"

"But it's possible."

"It was a dead end," said Brink.

"However they ended up here, these Jews are proof Jerry has something . . . something wicked," Gubbins said. "So perhaps they're more capable than you think."

Brink held Gubbins's look. He had worked more than a year on aerosolizing anthrax and had given up. Even his experiments in freeze-drying plague vaccine to concentrate and purify it—the reason why the army had come to him four years before to ask him to volunteer, the reason why the same army had handed him to the Brits a year later—hadn't helped.

"They had rabbits," Childess said. "That's why they succeeded."

"Rabbits?" asked Gubbins.

"Subjects for experiments," said Childess. "Rabbits."

Gubbins cleared his throat. "You must go to France, Doctor, and search out this disease," he said, his voice deeper now, even less Scottish.

The words hit Brink like hammers. France? "I don't understand."

"The invasion, Doctor, to be blunt. Our armies under such a cloud, think of that," said Gubbins. "Panic, at the best, and thousands die. At worst, Jerry pushes us back into the sea. Another Dunkirk. I don't think we could take reversal like that. We might not be able to try again until next year. Perhaps never."

"No, I don't—"

"You're the right man," Gubbins said. "You've seen the disease firsthand, Childess says. You'll recognize it, and the kind of place needed to create it."

"I can't go to France . . ." Brink said. Gubbins looked at him through the haze of his cigarette smoke.

"And if Jerry acts, we will be forced to reply in kind," said Gubbins. "With the anthrax." Gubbins flicked ash off the cigarette. "Do you know Shakespeare, Doctor? The prime minister does. He pulled a line out of his head soon as Dr. Childess telephoned. 'A plague of all cowards, I say, and a vengeance too,' that's what he said."

Brink looked at Childess, Childess looked back.

"Jerry has other weapons, Doctor, almost ready," said Gubbins. "Rockets and aircraft without pilots that could sow this on our island in an instant with us able to do nothing more than wag a finger back."

Brink looked at Gubbins, or tried to, for the man's coyote's eyes wouldn't stay on his.

"We have been looking for this coward's thing three months. Looked very hard. But we've had no luck. And now time is running out," Gubbins said quietly, taking pause to light yet another cigarette. He breathed its smoke. "Days only now. And this place from where these Jews left France, that, too, is special."

Brink thought of the armada choking Portsmouth. It would sail soon for France, that's what Gubbins was telling him—and for the part of France where the girl and her father came from.

"What do you think, Frank?" asked Childess.

Brink couldn't stay in the chair a moment longer. He stood so quickly that the straight-backed chair rocked a bit before he put out a hand to steady it. He thought about bolting for the door, but instead went to the nearest window and brushed aside the blackout curtain. Brink didn't care if light spilled into the street. It was 10 Downing; who would complain?

Brink saw Kate on the tiled floor of his workshop, her feet tucked under a table, blood on her temple where she'd cut it falling and a streak of that blood on the table's edge.

"A hero's no braver than the next man, he's just braver five minutes longer," Gubbins said behind him. "All we're asking for is that five minutes, Doctor."

Brink looked out into the dark street but saw only the empty syringe in his head. Things came almost as clear as his reflection in the glass. The needle marks in the dead at St. Richards meant the Germans understood the rules of *Pasteurella pestis* just as the English understood *Bacillus anthracis*: bacilli didn't respect borders, couldn't honor uniforms. It would be madness to unleash the plague without an antidote. The Germans had an antibiotic, too. Maybe it wasn't any better than his actinomycin. But what if it was?

He let the curtain fall back into place and turned to squint at Gubbins through the man's smoke, wanting to taste it. "I look through microscopes, I don't know anything about—"

"My F Section, SOE, here in London. They have a man who knows France. You'll be . . . think of yourself as a guide to the disease. All you have to do is help him find it. He'll take care of the rest," Gubbins said.

"I'd like a cigarette," Brink said softly, breaking his promise to Kate. But he'd keep the important promise, the one he'd made after she'd died. Finish the work. Find the antibiotic. Destroy the diseases.

Gubbins took two cigarettes from his battered case, scratched another match on that case, and leaned forward. The flame fluttered briefly until Brink pulled hard on the first cigarette, drawing the cottony smoke into his lungs. His head felt light and his throat hot.

Even if the Frenchman hadn't coughed in his face and given him a selfish reason, he would have decided this.

"I'll go," Brink said. He took another puff of Gubbins's cigarette.

If he couldn't kill plagues with her antibiotic, he'd have to kill it with theirs.

Childess stepped from the doorway of No. 10 Downing to stand beside him. Brink didn't move from his spot at the curb, where he'd been told to wait for the car that would take him to F Section and the SOE, whatever that was.

Brink lit the second of Gubbins's cigarettes off the end of the first—it had been a long time since he'd chain-smoked—and listened to the dark city. Another air-raid siren wailed in the south. Across the Thames, Brixton maybe. Another false alarm more than likely; the Luftwaffe was nothing now, not like the old days.

He listened, just in case, for engines but heard nothing except the siren. If Gubbins was right and the Germans had aerosolized *Pasteurella pestis*, all it would take would be one plane droning overhead.

Brink smelled the air, found the cleanliness within the cigarette smoke. London always smelled better during warm weather when people put away winter's coal. He wondered what it would smell like if the plague came back. Not like this. It would smell like the back of that Bedford. He pulled his borrowed coat tighter against the early summer morning.

"You knew the Germans were close to this," Brink said, waving the last cigarette at Childess. "That's why you sent me to Africa."

Childess said nothing for a moment. "We always knew there was a chance they'd play with the same genies. That's why your work, yours and Kate's, is so important."

"You knew about the *pestis* and the Germans," Brink said.

"Of course I knew. Five months ago, Gubbins came to me saying his people had heard talk in France. Something Jerry calls 'grave bringers.' '*Grabbringer*' they say. But F Section hasn't been able to find a trace of it."

"We were so stupid. We thought we had to talk you into letting us go to Dakar."

"I would have sent you even if you hadn't asked," Childess said. "I needed to know if the antibiotic would work on the *Pasteurella pestis*. That's all. But then she . . . and you . . ." His voice drifted off.

"You should have made up your mind earlier and sent us both," Brink said. "She'd still be alive."

"Frank—"

Brink didn't care to go down that road again, and made a fork in the conversation. "Why didn't you tell me about the Germans, Paul?"

"There are some secrets even I'm not allowed to share, Frank."

The sound of a car came up the street. It got louder still, and the small car, black as the pavement, showed the narrow street in its shaded head-lights as it pulled to the curb. A driver got out. "Mr. Brink?" a girl's soft voice asked in the dark.

"Give us a moment," said Childess, and the driver backed away a step or two. Brink moved for the car, but Childess laid a hand on his arm. "It's good to see you believe in something again, Frank," said Childess.

"Get to the point, Paul," Brink said.

"This is one of those times I take my conscience out of the cupboard for a walk, Frank, so I want you to know exactly what's at stake. If you don't . . . find this . . . and they use it against us . . . I won't be able to stop the PM. We'll want to be as evil as them, I think, and he'll use the anthrax."

Brink pitched the second cigarette into the gutter and watched it spark, then ducked into the car and the driver shut the door behind him. Childess was trying to give him another reason to find the *pestis*, but he didn't need more than what he had. Childess rapped on the window. Brink cranked it down as the driver walked around the car and got behind the wheel.

"He's fond of Shakespeare, Frank, and he likes to sound grand, but this isn't talk. He'll use the anthrax."

Brink wished he had bummed a third cigarette from the Scotsman. He could use another. "You promised, Paul, not to use the cakes if we found an antibiotic."

"No I didn't."

"You promised Kate."

"Yes, I promised. But only that we wouldn't use the cakes without provocation, and that's—"

Brink wished there was more light so Childess's face was more than a narrow shadow. "You're a shitty liar, Paul. She loved you once, too, for Christ's sake."

"I'm not clever enough to lie."

"Don't use the cakes, Paul."

"You expect us to die from the *pestis*, Frank, and do nothing? That's easy for you Americans to say. It's not your home they'd destroy, is it?"

"It won't do the dead any good," Brink said.

"Find it, Frank, stop it."

"Sir, we have to go," the driver said.

Brink stared through the window at Childess, who leaned against the car. "Good-bye, Frank," Childess said. Brink cranked up the window, and the car bumped over the cracked pavement of Downing Street.

Six

Tracking the sick Jews had not been easy. Kirn had spent the day before with Wollenstein, and hours more this morning alone driving the Renault from one dreary hamlet to another. In each town he'd find the doctor if there was one, and demand to know of anyone with an odd illness.

Finally a wrinkled bird in a threadbare black suit from Étréham, less than three kilometers from the torched Daimler, admitted yes, the family Tardif had fallen sick, he'd treated them for pneumonia the afternoon before. Strange this time of year, the old doctor said. The wife was most ill, her fever 39.5, the daughter running a fever, too, but Monsieur Tardif, he looked fit.

Kirn drove, with the creaky doctor guiding, until the Renault ended up within sight of a farmhouse surrounded by its brick wall. Tardif, said the old man, pointing through the poplar trees. Satisfied he could find this place again on his own, Kirn returned the doctor to Étréham and used the telephone in the village post office to ring Wollenstein and give directions, then drove back to the Tardif farm and parked behind that same stand of poplars where he could watch the gates to both the house and, across the lane, what looked like a barn.

Wollenstein arrived in a canvas-covered Mercedes, the same faded-blue truck as before. He stepped down from the cab and a half squad of gray SS uniforms piled out its back. The roof of the house was visible above the wall beyond the poplars.

"Finally, my Jews. This took you long enough" was first out of the Sturmbannführer's mouth.

Prick.

Wollenstein pulled a cloth mask from his mohair overcoat and tied it around his neck, but didn't pull it over his mouth. A pair of rubber gloves followed, and the doctor snapped them on. He motioned to his men and they jogged through the trees. Some disappeared around the back corner of the wall, others through the open gate to the farmhouse. He and Wollenstein followed the last bunch. One of Wollenstein's men, a fat Unterscharführer, pounded on its door with the butt of his machine pistol. The door swung open.

Kirn put a hand on Wollenstein's sleeve. "I want a mask," he said.

Wollenstein dragged another from his coat pocket. "Let's find my Jews," he said, and pushed open the broken door with a rubber-covered finger.

The farmhouse was dark and smelled of bad meat. One of the SS yanked at the blackout curtain over a window and it came down in a small landslide of dust. Wollenstein told the three SS crammed into this kitchen to stay, and he walked toward the back of the house where the smell was a January cloud heavy with snow, thick and thicker. Kirn followed.

A sitting room of sorts, with a pair of chairs and a small table, and on the table an oil lamp and a radio. In one chair sat a girl, her head back and her legs splayed. Flies buzzed across her mouth and crawled in and out of her nostrils. The radio played static. And the stink . . . Kirn put his half hand up to pinch tight his nose.

Wollenstein stopped a meter from the dead girl and raised his cloth mask and tied it over his mouth. Her face was dark, the front of her dress darker, and for a moment Kirn thought she'd been cut across the throat, but he looked closer and saw it was whole. She'd been dead awhile.

"Typhus?" Kirn asked quietly. Wollenstein said nothing, only rubbed his rubber-clad hands together. Then he grabbed the hem of her dress and raised it, revealing black legs and white underclothes.

Kirn heard Wollenstein mumble something behind his mask. *Die Pest,* he thought it was. The plague?

"What are you doing?" Kirn asked, but the doctor only looked at the girl's naked thighs, then let the dress fall back. Wollenstein didn't answer, only turned and pushed past Kirn.

The girl's dress was in disarray, and Kirn felt he should straighten it to give her back some modesty, but he didn't touch her.

They found the stairs to the second floor and clumped up, their boots loud questions that no one answered. The first room on the small floor was empty, an unmade bed the only furniture. The second, though, was occupied by a bed, table, and washbasin propped on the table. A man and a woman lay side by side, both covered by the same green blanket. The woman was curled into a semicircle, her eyes open and unblinking, a dark dried line of black spittle running from the downside corner of her mouth across the blanket. The line continued to the floor and met a splattered chamber pot, its lip stained like the girl's face downstairs. Flies settled on the rim of the pot, rose, settled again. The woman's face was the color of watered ink.

For all Kirn's time in the East and the bodies he'd seen torn apart, this was still hard to take. His breakfast tried to get past his throat and he swallowed to keep it in.

Wollenstein walked to the other side of the bed. Kirn remembered his mask, and with clumsy fingers, lifted it over his mouth and tied the strands behind his head. The man in the bed moaned, hacked a deep, ragged cough, and spit a clear stream onto the floor. Kirn stood behind Wollenstein, looking over the doctor's shoulder. Wollenstein reached out—the hand trembled—and touched the Frenchman's shoulder with a rubbered finger. The man's eyelids flicked open and he coughed again. Wollenstein flinched and almost stumbled over Kirn's feet in his haste to back away.

"Tell him he's sick," Wollenstein said, "and that we're here to help."

Kirn watched the Frenchman. The man's face glistened with sweat, even though the room was cold so early in the morning.

"Tell him he's sick," Wollenstein repeated.

"He knows that," Kirn said. Instead, he told Tardif they were here to help.

"Tell him we know about the Jews, that the Jews made him sick," Wollenstein said. "Tell him to name those who freed the Jews from the trucks. Tell him we must find them if they're not to die like his wife and daughter."

"*Qui était donc avec vous quand vous avez libéré les juifs?*" Kirn asked from behind the cloth mask. He leaned a bit closer. "*Les juifs, est ce eux qui vous ont rendu malade? Nous devons avoir leurs noms ou sinon ils tomberont malade comme vous et votre fille. Soyez raisonnable, je vous prie.*"

The Frenchman coughed again, darkness in the phlegm this time, and sobbed out a sound Kirn had never heard, long and longer, like the wind moaning in the winter. Wollenstein backed away again and lost his nerve entirely; he hurried from the room. Kirn heard his boots on the wooden floor of the corridor.

"*Mais où sont donc les juifs?*" Kirn asked the *Wulewuh*. And the Frenchman finally answered.

"Port-en-Bessin," the *Wulewuh* wheezed.

Kirn knew the small port. It was four or five kilometers north and east, with a tiny harbor. A working place that stank of spoiled cod; no one would mistake it for a summer's spot like Arromanches, farther east. "*Nous les avons pris à Port-en-Bessin,*" the Frenchman moaned.

"*Maquis?*" Kirn asked. "*Vous êtes maquis?*"

"*Allez vous faire foutre.*"

Kirn smiled. "Go fuck yourself," he'd said. *Maquis* for sure.

"*Il y auraient d'autres qui ont aidé les juifs?*" he asked. He needed the names of accomplices in order to run down the Jews. The Frenchman coughed again, and as Kirn backed away, the man went still and silent. Kirn didn't want to put out a hand to see if he was dead.

"He has the typhus," said Wollenstein from the safety of the doorway. "The cough, see how it's turned to blood? And he has a fever, I don't need a thermometer to tell me. This is what you look for in my Jews."

"Your Jews are in Port-en-Bessin," Kirn said, yanking down his mask. He pulled a last Eckstein from its green package and tossed the empty pasteboard box to the floor, kicked it across the wood and watched it disappear under the bed. Kirn lit the cigarette and breathed in its smoke to cover some of the smell.

"Where?" Wollenstein asked.

"On the coast. A few kilometers," Kirn said. He was angry at being made to do this one's dirty work.

But Wollenstein didn't hear the contempt in his voice. The SS officer's eyes, the one blue the other not, stared over the edge of the cloth mask. He looked like a thief in one of the American Westerns. Wollenstein pulled down the mask. "He tell you of the others, the ones who freed the Jews? Find these men. And anyone who has been with them. But first my Jews."

Kirn nodded, tired.

"Talk to the friends of this family. Anyone who had been with them since day before yesterday, I want you to arrest. Whether they're sick or not. Find these Jews and the *maquisards* who took them."

"And what will I do with all of them?"

Wollenstein hesitated, then said, "Empty a building, anything will do, and quarantine them. Telephone me when you have them." The way he'd paused, Kirn knew Wollenstein had changed his answer before it came out of his mouth. Liars did that during questioning.

"And you? You won't be coming?"

Wollenstein's fright was past, perhaps because the Frenchman remained unconscious. He was still alive, though the man's chest rose and fell too rapidly.

"I have work to do."

Wollenstein half turned to clear the doorway, and Kirn gripped his mohair sleeve tight.

"And what about this one? He's still alive. You said you were treating the Jews," Kirn said, nodding to the man under the blanket. "Give him something."

Wollenstein yanked his coat from Kirn's fingers. "He's too far gone. I can't help him."

"You never could, could you?"

Wollenstein said nothing, so Kirn shoved by him and clumped down the stairs and out through the kitchen and into cleaner air. By the time he had reached his Renault, Kirn had pulled his anger inside. Wollenstein had too many secrets for him to get hotheaded over every one.

But as he climbed into the car and reached for the starter, a single shot rocked the morning, and Kirn flinched. The sound escaped over the wall surrounding the farmhouse and rang through the poplars.

A second shot echoed and Kirn tasted a bitterness. No one shot anyone over typhus.

"Nous sommes lá pour vous secour, monsieur," Kirn said out loud, the French words he'd said to Tardif at the start. We are here to help.

Kirn spat out the Renault's open window. SS help was a different beast, he thought, and pressed the starter.

Kirn drove the Renault a hundred meters, then pulled off the lane, through an open gate, and into a field. He turned the car around so its nose pointed back through the gate.

He only had time to smoke one Eckstein from a new package before the blue Mercedes rumbled by dragging a small tail of dust. Kirn waited a minute, then drove the car from the field and onto the lane. He kept his distance, a hundred, two hundred meters behind the truck, as it took several turns, and then onto the N13, the Caen-Cherbourg highway. From there, Wollenstein headed west.

Kirn kept his good hand on the steering wheel most of the time, only switching to pull more Ecksteins from the green package between his legs. He stayed a few vehicles behind the Mercedes. Kirn had the accelerator pressed almost to the floor, and the four cylinders in the little Renault's motor banged away to keep up. The crate wouldn't do better than sixty kilometers an hour.

Herr Wollenstein was not just a liar, but a poor one. And lies, Kirn knew, meant secrets. And secrets were something his policeman's heart hated.

Wollenstein had lied not just about the typhus—if what he'd seen in Tardif was typhus, he was Heinrich Himmler—but about everything.

What was the secret, Kirn wondered, that Wollenstein kept from the Wehrmacht? Keeping secrets from the French, that was one thing—they couldn't be trusted, not even the collaborators—but secrets from German *Landsers*, that was something else. If this disease was so dangerous, hundreds should be combing the countryside for these missing Jews. Not one half-handed Kripo. It made no sense.

Kirn flicked his latest cigarette through the open window, and flexed the thumb and forefinger on his right hand. Sometimes it felt as if the missing digits were still there, just as sometimes he still saw Alois and Brunner and Misch in his dreams. The way they'd looked before Russian shell fragments had scoured them dead.

Wollenstein's Mercedes motored west though La Cambe, Saint-Germain, and Isigny-sur-Mer on the N13, the highway never straying more than ten kilometers from the coast. Then the truck slowed as it entered Carentan. The road squeezed into the town between two-story buildings, and became a narrow street when the buildings grew to three floors. Only a small mud-daubed DKW separated the black nose of his Renault from the blue tailgate of Wollenstein's truck.

And then he lost Wollenstein.

The truck trundled through an intersection, the DKW hard on its bumper. Just as Kirn was about to follow, a *Feldgendarmerie* stepped into traffic with his white baton and raised it so that the red circle on its end faced Kirn.

He stomped on the brakes and the Renault shivered to a stop. Fuck.

The military policeman turned his back to him as a series of trucks roared across the intersection, left to right. Leafy branches were tied to the top of each. Kirn shoved the shift lever into reverse and twisted to look behind him. But all he saw out the tiny rear window was the radiator of a big Büssing, barely half a meter back. Kirn squirmed in the seat. More greenery roared past. Wollenstein was getting away. The anger smothered him, and he slammed the accelerator to push the Renault through the narrow gap. The *Feldgendarmerie* shouted something, then the edge of the Renault's bumper caught the policeman's leg and sent him tumbling, and his baton banged off the hood and cracked against the windscreen.

From the left, an immense grille came at him, and Kirn gripped the wheel hard and leaned even harder on the accelerator, fumbled with the gearshift. The Renault bucked ahead, but the truck caught its rear bumper and spun it to the left—*bang-bang* as it hit and the Renault knocked back with its front left tire against the side of the truck—and Kirn twisted the steering wheel to keep the car from leaving the street and darted through the intersection. Brakes screeched behind him, more metal on metal, and in the side mirror, Kirn saw the *Feldgendarmerie* standing, mouth open, leg bloodied, and outstretched arm pointing after him.

Driving through Carentan he breathed deeply, each breath a bit steadier than the one before, but he didn't dare reach for another Eckstein until he was halfway the twelve kilometers to Sainte-Mère-Église. It was only just as the N13 reached the town that he spotted the Mercedes through the starred windscreen. It took a left in the middle of Sainte-Mère-Église and, on pitted macadam, headed south and west. Kirn kept the Renault a hundred meters behind Wollenstein's truck, the steering wheel shivering in his hand because the front wheel now wobbled. At a place where a dozen houses clustered at the road, the Mercedes went right on a dirt lane. Kirn let it vanish, then ground the Renault into gear and followed.

A minute later he let the car stutter to the shoulder and switched off its engine. The Mercedes idled fifty meters up the lane, just past a pair of guards now disappearing into a small wooden shack tucked against the hedgerow.

Kirn smoked an Eckstein. What was he going to do, drive to Wollenstein's front door and ask about secrets? He shook his head. He could, he supposed, tramp across fields and scramble through the boscage hedges to spy out Wollenstein's home, get mud on his boots, tire himself out, and by the look of the guards on this road, likely bump into a patrol watching the place where Wollenstein lived. But there was a better way to get information.

He drew one more lungful of the cigarette and tossed out the butt. As a Kripo he could ask questions in the village behind him. He was sure he'd find out more about the guarded road and the SS at its end. Then he had a long drive back to Port-en-Bessin and the missing Jews.

As Kirn swung the Renault back into the lane, his absent fingers tingled.

Seven

The ball came at him, breaking down and in so fast that it was nothing more than a streak. It skimmed the back inside corner of the plate, missed his mitt by huge inches, and was gone, bounding for the backstop yards behind him. A man, indistinct and dressed, Brink thought, in grays and whites, thundered home from third.

The ball had gotten by him.

"Doctor," someone said, and Brink raised his head from the table where he'd rested it to sleep. "Sorry to wake you," the man said. He came to the table, and as he cleared the doorway, another man, older and thinner, followed. "Got your bearings?" the first one asked, his accent vaguely Midlands, nodding to the map spread across the table. Brink's face had been pressed against Normandy's contours while he'd slept.

There was a mug on the table and Brink reached for it, swallowed cold tea, remembering the woman who had brought it to him hours before, not long after she'd opened the door to an old building on Baker Street, the door with a ridiculous brass plate that read INTERSERVICE RESEARCH BUREAU. Brink drank again, then said, "You're the one Gubbins said knows France."

"Juniper Wickens," the man said. He brushed his dark hair off his forehead as he took a seat across the table. He didn't reach a hand out to shake. His face was soft around the edges, but he was solid in the arms and chest. He was at least Brink's age, maybe years older; the round face made it tough to tell.

"Juniper," Brink said.

"That's right," said Wickens. His hands rested on the table, and Brink saw a new, bright scar across the back of the left, three, four inches long, running from the knuckles to the wrist. For some reason, Brink thought of those boys he had hated, the ones who had beat him up until he'd gotten his height and started playing ball.

"Wot trouble have you gotten us into?" asked Wickens. No formalities. The voice was dead calm.

"What are you talking about?"

"You're one of the boffins who made these disease darlings. Just like the Huns. Playing with fire, and now we're burned, bay we?" Those words were sharp, scalpel sharp.

"Fuck you," said Brink.

The rat-face one at the door stepped from his place, but Wickens raised a hand and that one retreated. There was a long silence. Wickens broke it. "I apologize, Doctor." He folded his hands, hiding the scar, and smiled until Brink could see a chipped upper tooth. "So. Wot do you propose?"

Brink looked down at the map. All he'd done was find Port-en-Bessin, the place the girl had told him about, before he'd fallen asleep. "You're the one supposed to know," he said.

"Ours am an equal partnership," Wickens said. Definitely Midlands.

"Gubbins said you were in charge," Brink said.

"Someone said you get cross when others tell you wot to do." Wickens's smile got a bit bigger.

Brink couldn't help but give a small smile back.

"Thank you, always glad to be of humor," said Wickens. He leaned forward. "Now that the pleasantries are behind us . . ." he started, but stopped for a moment. "They say there's no cure for . . . for the darlings."

Brink glanced down at the case beside the table. Half his remaining stock of A17—fifteen small tubes—was in that case, none of it used because he'd decided that the Frenchman in Chichester had been too far gone.

"So how do you intend to fight this?" Wickens leaned back in his chair, staring intently at Brink.

"I didn't know I was." There was not enough A17 in the world to fight off an outbreak, even if he was sure it worked.

Wickens laughed, the laugh low and deep, a counter to his almost girlish face. "Right, right. No time."

Brink realized he meant the invasion. In his mind's eye he saw soldiers storming ashore some beach, the wave of them breaking on the rocks of plague.

Wickens rubbed the scar on the top of his hand. "Or so they tell me," he added.

"How long?" Brink asked.

"Doctor—"

"I want to know how long."

Wickens hesitated, but then said, "Two mornings from tomorrow's, I think. Or the next day. Or the one after that."

June 5, thought Brink. Or June 6 or June 7. Half of June 2 was already gone. He ticked off the days by touching fingertips with the thumb on his other hand. There wasn't going to be enough time. "God," he said.

Wickens nodded. "You'll know wot to look for?"

"Yes," said Brink. "I'll know it."

"And where do we start? This girl in hospital at . . . Chichester, right? She tell you where these Jews of hers came from?"

The question caught Brink off balance. He repeated the girl's tale, telling Wickens that she'd not said where the Jews had been before she and her father and friends had found them in the trucks. "I didn't know I was going to France then. I didn't think to ask."

"Pity," Wickens said. His stare was long, his eyes leaf-smoke gray. "Her name, Doctor, you got that?"

"No," Brink said. "No, I didn't ask her name."

"But she's from Port-en-Bessin? Her father came, too, both on a fishing boat you said."

"Yes," answered Brink, although he didn't remember mentioning that it was a fishing boat.

"Then we must ask her more questions." Wickens leaned forward again. "Am she sick? Am she trotting around with this . . . will she spread it wherever she goes?"

Someone had explained to Wickens how contagious it was. "She's not showing any symptoms," Brink said. And neither am I, he thought.

"Then we'll telephone Chichester and have her brought to the landing field at Portsmouth," Wickens said. He glanced down at his scar for a moment. "We'll ask this girl wot she knows before we climb onto the MTB."

"'Ow we know we don't get the sickness from 'er?" asked the man near the door. He was a Londoner, East End, Brink thought.

"Let me ask the questions, Sam," said Wickens, not turning to look at him. "Sam's his name," he said to Brink. "Samuel Eggers. He's coming with us."

"To do what?"

"I'm to watch over you. And Sam here, well, he watches over me. He's watched over me for a long time. Last of the watchers, bay you?" The smile returned to Wickens's face. "But Sam brings up an excellent question, thank you very much, Sam."

"Close contact, that's how it spreads," Brink said. "Stay a yard or two away from anyone who shows symptoms. Don't spend time with them indoors. And don't touch anyone."

Wickens and Eggers just glanced at each other.

Brink asked his own question. "What then? After we find the . . . where they make the plague. What do we do? There's just the three of us."

"We'll have a radio, of sorts," Wickens said. "An aircraft flies close to the coast, a series of aircraft, actually, to listen all hours for our communiqués. We find this place, Doctor, then chat with the aircraft. They'll chat with someone here."

"And?" Brink asked.

"And that someone calls up a squadron or two of Mosquitoes, I've been told. We'll use the S-phone to bring them on the target." He looked at Brink, letting him fill in the rest.

"Someone's been thinking about this," Brink said, remembering that Gubbins had said they'd been sniffing for the *pestis* for months. He waited for the Englishman to answer. Nothing. He wouldn't get more from Wickens—Brink had been around secrets enough to recognize the look.

Wickens glanced at the watch on his wrist; Brink did the same. Just past two in the afternoon.

"Sam and I have things to gather. I imagine you do as well. And the ones downstairs, they want to kit you out with clothes and proper papers and wot you need in the line of medical bits. I'll have one of the FANY girls show you. In four hours we drive to the airfield at Biggin Hill, fly from there to Portsmouth. I'll ring up Chichester and have them bring the girl to Gosport. We'll chat her up before we put to the MTB. That leaves at twenty-thirty, on the dot." Wickens scraped the chair back from the table, stood. "Don't worry, Doctor, Sam and I have everything in hand. All you need do is find this place for us. You'll let us know when we've found the spot where the darlings are cooked up, won't you?" Wickens's gray eyes didn't blink.

Brink nodded. Wickens stepped for the door, which Eggers had opened for him. Wickens noticed a cigarette in Eggers's hand. "You know I don't like it when you smoke," he said. Sam nodded, slipped the cigarette behind an ear.

"Wickens . . ." Brink said, and the man stopped and turned.

"Juniper, always," Wickens said from the doorway.

"Why you?" Brink asked. He waved at Wickens and the old man. "Why are you doing this?"

"Four years now—ay Sam?—almost to the day," Wickens began. "Five of us stood in warm water off Dunkirk and waited for boats. We all got run out of France. Now only Sam and I. That's why."

"We finish what we start, 'at's what 'e's sayin'," Sam said.

"Quite true, Sam, quite true," said Wickens. "And we're the experts, so to speak, on this particular thing." Wickens looked at Sam, and the two men exchanged a glance that meant something. Another secret.

Brink thought of what Wickens had said before. Bombs. They would put an end to any antibiotic. He couldn't let that happen. But telling Wickens, what good would it do?

"We'll have a grand adventure as long as you do your part." Wickens's voice was sharp again, and the smile came and went fast.

Alix twisted one finger in her hair, not knowing she was doing it until the knot tightened at her temple. She brushed against the bump there, then let her hand drop to her lap.

She stared at the door. They'd brought a tray with bread and cheese and tea and an orange, an orange, think of it, she hadn't seen an orange in four years, but they left that tray on the floor outside the door and knocked, and when she had opened the door, the policeman she'd grabbed was gone, replaced by a soldier. The boy had pointed a revolver her way from across the wide corridor.

At least the tall blond man had been good to his word. The nurse, who glared at her with old bird's eyes, had come with two men in brown uniforms and taken her to Papa. They'd made her string a cloth mask over her face and snap on rubberized gloves. He wouldn't wake up, but she'd whispered to him anyway, stroked his cheek with her rubber finger. They'd woke her at daybreak to tell her Papa died in the night.

The windup clock on the small table beside the metal bed said it had been fourteen hours since the tall blond man had come to ask his questions. He'd had good eyes, she thought. Good hands, she thought, remembering how they'd felt in hers. And he'd kept his promise.

Alix sucked the juice from the last slice of orange, drank the last swallow of tea.

Promises. Where was Juniper? She'd asked for him a hundred times, demanded they bring him here. Instead she got the tall blond one.

The door opened, and the same old nurse stood in the doorway, the cloth mask across her mouth. The soldier was behind her.

"The American doctor wants you cleaned up," she said.

The words raised her hopes—perhaps the blond man had told the truth when he'd said she wasn't sick. "I'm well?" Alix asked, the question making her feel like a child. The nurse's face was impossible to read with the mask in the way.

"A hot bath first, clean clothes, that's all I know," said the old woman.

Wollenstein laid the pretty cloth doll with the porcelain head and the movable eyes gently into the wooden drawer, pushed the drawer into the slot, and watched through the viewing glass as the little girl edged toward him. He smiled at the little Jew, crooked a finger to draw her closer. Wollenstein wished he knew French so he could tell her to come get the doll he'd found in Fougères, that lovely little place down Rennes way.

She was brave, for even though her mother shook her head, the girl darted forward, stretched on bare toes to reach, and grabbed the doll from the drawer and ran back across the testing shed. The girl turned to him and with her hand held low against her waist, wiggled fingers to him in a wave.

He put his hand near the small glass that separated him from the Jews, and waved back to the child. Through the barrier he heard the soft sound of their coughing.

"Cruel," said Nimmich beside him. He looked through the glass, too, at the eight inside. These eight were the control, the ones dusted with the *Pasteurella pestis* powder but not touched with the needles, or if they had been stuck, long after their symptoms appeared. The others, eight again, who had been given the streptomycin first thing, were in the other section of the shed, separated by the wall that split the small building. "And a waste of good money."

"Not at all," Wollenstein said to his assistant. "These Jews are selfless, remember that. Others will live because of their sacrifice."

"I doubt they care, Sturmbannführer."

Wollenstein looked at Nimmich. The boy had a narrow face, and a right eye that fluttered with a tic. "I'm serious," Wollenstein said. "That's why we take down their names. They'll be remembered, I promise you."

Nimmich nodded, but the tic twitched.

Wollenstein liked the boy—a good technician—but again he wished for a partner rather than a subordinate. He shook his head. "What strain for the others?" he asked, and pointed to the end of the shed where the eight who had received the streptomycin huddled behind their own pane of glass.

Nimmich plucked a sheet of paper from the folder he held. "Number 211."

"And?"

"Very encouraging."

Wollenstein looked through the glass again. The little girl tilted the doll's head back and forth, watching its eyes close and open. Beyond her, he could see several unmoving shapes on the floor.

"Are they still alive?" Wollenstein asked, pointing to the ones in the corner.

"Last time we asked, yes," said Nimmich. "Three of them."

Wollenstein tried to see into the shadows, but couldn't tell the color of those on the floor. The five standing were easier to see. The little girl's mother had a mouth already turning blue. "When you're finished, see me at the house," he said.

"Yes, Herr Sturmbannführer," Nimmich said.

Wollenstein stepped out of the shade beside the testing shed and into the midday sun. He looked up at the scattered clouds, white balloons against the blue blue sky. Not even one high streamer marking the path of American bombers flying east. Such beautiful weather.

He walked through the gap in the enormous hedgerow, down the dirt track a hundred meters, then through another wall of green where the huge oak towered, and onto the landing field, the long, narrow clearing he'd had his men sweep of brush and saplings and the wooden poles that the stupid Rommel had planted to rip apart Allied gliders. The field pointed east and north toward the coast, twelve kilometers away.

The Me-110 cowered under netting fifty meters to his left, the aerials for the Lichtenstein radar apparatus jutting through the web. The Messerschmitt was painted flat black, but the silvered steel of the tank and nozzles under the wing dazzled even in the gloom beneath the net. The Junkers, bigger, stood under netting beyond that.

To his right, a smaller aircraft crouched within a cocoon of its own. High-winged, with long, delicate struts for legs, it was aptly named: Storch. Tauch came out from under the netting, set his toolbox on the flattened grass, pulled a rag from a pocket of his coverall to wipe his hands. Wollenstein walked toward the engineer.

"I must mill new nozzles," said Tauch in his thick Swabian accent. Once a farmer from the Black Forest, now a magician in building things. "If they work on this one," he said, pointing a thumb to the Storch, "I'll make some for the others."

"What's wrong with those you made yesterday?"

"I thought I could get by with thinner stock, but when I pressurized the tank, they blew." Tauch pulled a thimble-sized piece of metal from another pocket and held it in the sunlight. The shaped end was shredded. "Perhaps I can find something in Cherbourg."

"I wanted to fly today."

"Not possible," said Tauch. "Tomorrow, if I can find thicker stock." He shrugged.

Wollenstein looked up again. He counted just two clouds now, both small, one evaporating as he watched. Beautiful. Invasion weather.

"No later than tomorrow noon," he told Tauch as he glanced again at the sky.

Kirn grabbed his overcoat from the old Renault and walked for the harbor of Port-en-Bessin. In a few minutes he stood on the stone quay and looked into the narrow finger of water that led to the ocean. Only one boat was tied up.

He saw nothing extraordinary, only a few Wehrmacht boys standing at posts and a pair stripping a machine gun on a blanket. So he turned at the coast road, a narrow strip of macadam that kept to the dead ground immediately behind the bluffs that fronted the Atlantic. In a few minutes, he'd left the village behind as the road climbed to the top of the hill.

The dead Tardif had told him to come to Port-en-Bessin, but it had been the old doctor from Étréham who had said to take this road south. When Kirn had stopped in Étréham to put the old man and his equally old wife in quarantine—a wretched shed was all he could find, locking it with rope over the latch and a hand-printed sign that read QUARANTAINE—the doctor told him how to find this seaport's own physician.

Jusot is his name, the old doctor said through the wide cracks of the shed's wall. He lives in a house with a green slate roof along the coast road to Huppain.

Kirn stopped to show his Kriminalpolizei identity disc and card at the concrete barrier blocking the road just outside Port-en-Bessin. The boys there, so young, only glanced at his papers.

Kirn asked, as he always did when he was anywhere between Port-en-Bessin and Grandcamp, whether they knew his old friend, Uwe Böse. Or Paul Stecker. Or what about Muffe, whose real name he couldn't remember, but whom they called "Thimble" because of the way his helmet had sat on his huge head. The boys only said "no," the same blank expression on their faces.

The 352nd Infanterie, the division these boys belonged to, didn't trace its roots back to the heady days of Russia the way he did. But there was a thin string between it and Kirn. He'd been part of the 268th Infanterie when it had marched east across the border three years ago, first for Brest-Litovsk, then marching through the summer and the months of fall as well, to end up south of Moscow in the freezing snow of December. Months later, after he'd been shipped home to Munich on the hospital train, he'd heard that what he'd left behind of the 268th had been so shrunk by losses that it had been dissolved and parsed out to build other divisions. What he'd heard, exactly, was that its remains had been sent to France and stuffed into the 352nd.

So in his travels across Normandy, he paid attention to the white-washed signs that told who in the Wehrmacht lived where. When he saw one that pointed to a piece of the 352nd, he would ask about his old friends, those he knew had been alive when he'd been carried off the muddy ground that spring two years gone. Whether they had escaped the mouth of Mother Russia, he had no clue.

As the road climbed to the top of the bluff, and Kirn climbed the road, the afternoon sun was so warm that he took off his overcoat and folded it over an arm. He stopped to catch his breath, looked down onto the beach—wide now, for it was low tide and the sand stretched for a hundred meters before meeting glass-blue water—and saw a score of soldiers. They were stripped to the waist, tanned brown.

The *Landsers* struggled under a long wooden pole. As Kirn watched, they manhandled it across the muck and laid the pole atop two logs already driven into the sand, one short, the other taller. Their pole slanted backwards from the sea; an Allied landing boat would catch on the pole and slide up toward its end, where the boys would fix a Teller mine. There were similar contraptions lined up, twenty or thirty meters apart, in a stretch that covered part of the beach between two bluffs that jutted into the ocean.

Kirn smoked another Eckstein, wiped his face with a kerchief, and squinted against the low sun's glare on the water. Across the sea was England. If they were coming, they'd come this summer. But not here. All the talk was that they'd come north, at the Pas de Calais—three hundred kilometers away. If he was lucky, he'd escape the worst and, God willing, reach home one day. Here in France, at least, that was possible—the poor bastards still in the East, they'd die in place or in some cholera-choked camp in Siberia. Kirn took a look at the hand holding the Eckstein, thinking that losing the three fingers might be the best thing that had happened to him.

Kirn left the sweating soldiers behind as the road dipped off the edge of the bluff and disappeared into the alleyway created by the boscage, the high hedgerows that divided most of Normandy into small plots of a hundred meters or so. The mounds of earth along both sides of the narrow road made it seem sunken, and the trees among the hedgerows on those mounds canopied the way. It was cooler here out of the sun, but the air was thicker because it had rained three days before and the ground was still damp in the shade. The smell was like that mud-filled bunker they'd lived in, him and Böse and Stecker and Muffe, those last days. Rats sloshing in the corners, unwashed bodies, and a slight cologne of dead things.

The buzz of an engine came up behind him and he stepped to the edge of the road as a BMW, its sidecar empty, skidded around the corner on the slick dirt, straightened, and then slowed. A *Feldgendarmerie* rode the motorcycle, Kirn able to tell because of the metal gorget, a dull silver half-moon that hung around the man's neck. The BMW hammered to a stop and the Feldwebel switched off the engine. Its echo rang for a moment in the green tunnel as Kirn wondered if this one had come to arrest him for knocking down the *Feldgendarmerie* in Carentan.

Kirn kept his hands at his side, for the sergeant had already grabbed the machine pistol that hung from the motorcycle's handlebar. The soldier used its muzzle to beckon Kirn closer.

"*Fais voire votre pièces d'identité,*" the sergeant asked, his accent horrible.

Kirn stopped two meters from the man, who still sat astride the BMW, and answered in German. "My name is Kirn. Kriminalpolizei. I'm out of Caen." He let his coat hang limp in his right hand, the thumb and finger pinching it tightly to hold it. "My identification is in my coat pocket."

The sergeant nodded and stepped off the BMW; the muzzle of the machine pistol sniffed for the dirt, not Kirn's chest. Kirn tugged his Kripo identity disc from the inside pocket, let its bronze dangle on the end of its short chain, then, still holding it, groped for his card and handed that over. The *Feldgendarmerie* looked at the card, at Kirn.

"Untersturmführer," the sergeant said, handing back the card. The soldier didn't bother to salute, though in the strictest sense Kirn outranked him.

"I'm only a policeman, like you," Kirn said, trying to smile. The sergeant didn't smile back.

"Why are you poking around?" the sergeant asked.

"I'm looking for a house with a green slate roof. Near the bluff. A Frenchman lives there who I need to talk to. A doctor."

"Cutting out the wrong ration coupons, is he?"

Kirn slipped into his coat and when his arm pushed through the sleeve, the sergeant caught a glimpse of his hand. "Russia," Kirn said.

"You were at Moscow?" the sergeant asked, wonder in his voice. The Feldwebel, Kirn realized, was envious. He'd seen this from those who thought they'd missed something glorious.

"Winter War," said Kirn, and touched his chest, as if the *Ostmedaille* with its red ribbon was pinned to the shirt. But it was in a wooden box in the drawer of his Caen desk, along with a few fading photographs, and that last letter from Hillie.

"I know the house," said the sergeant. "I could take you there." Kirn nodded, and the Feldwebel motioned to the sidecar. "You were at Moscow? What was it like?"

"Cold."

"How did you . . ." the Feldwebel began. He looked at Kirn's hand.

"Ivan artillery," Kirn answered, and made a whistling sound through his lips. The sergeant nodded and mounted the motorcycle, kicked its starter. Kirn crammed into the sidecar, knees almost against his chest, and they were off, first slow, then faster through the tunnel of brush and leaves.

The canopy disappeared as the road again climbed closer to the top of the bluff. Around a tight corner, down a slope, back up, and there was the house with the green slate roof. The BMW's rear wheel slid as the motorcycle tore through an open gate at the road's edge and up the drier dirt track that led to the house.

"What's this one done?" asked the sergeant after he'd silenced the BMW. Kirn unfolded from the sidecar.

"He's working the black market with sulfa and aspirins," Kirn lied. He was halfway to the door when the Feldwebel called from behind. "Do you need any help, Untersturmführer?" Untersturmführer now. "You have a weapon?"

Kirn patted the left pocket of his jacket. The Walther hung in there. The P38 was a child's gun, not like the Feldwebel's machine pistol, big as a cannon. "Wait for me, you can do that. You can give me another ride."

Without waiting for an answer Kirn went to the green-painted door and pounded on it with the heel of his bad hand. "Jusot!" he called through the wood. "Doctor, open the door! Kriminalpolizei!" He pounded again. Kirn put his good hand in his pocket and pulled out the Walther, used the bad hand to shove the handle. Unlocked. He pushed.

"Sir?" asked the sergeant.

"Wait here," Kirn said and stepped inside. It was the kitchen. A plate on the small table under the nearest window had been partly scraped, and a fly buzzed its edges. Flies again.

"Jusot?" he called. "Doctor?" Behind him he heard the Feldwebel's boots. "Stay out." The boots stopped.

Through the one doorway, he found himself in a large parlor, a pair of leather chairs against the far wall. "Jusot?" He hoped the doctor was only out calling on a patient, for this place was beginning to smell like Tardif's. Kirn reached across his body with his bad hand, awkward, and pulled Wollenstein's cloth mask from his coat. He pressed it against his mouth and nose.

"Did your man fly?" called the sergeant. It sounded like he was in the kitchen.

"*I said stay out!*" shouted Kirn, then pushed at a door on the right. On the floor of that room began a black trail. The smear made an *S* for a meter, and vanished around a corner. Not blood, vomit.

Kirn breathed in, breathed out, each breath shallower and faster than the last. He straightened. Pointed the Walther at the place where the trail vanished. Followed the pistol.

Another door was tucked into that corner, and the trail led under it. The latch was smeared with something, too. Using the Walther's muzzle, he shoved down the latch, then pushed open the door with a boot. The bright sunlight nearly blinded him. Across the threshold, a path led up the slope and then swept over the top to disappear, he supposed, down to the ocean below.

Back through the house Kirn heard the Feldwebel's voice again, but he ignored it. To the right, a barrow leaned against the house, on the left another path worn in the grass followed a curved line around the building. The grass was still scattered with late wildflowers, purple things that were past their prime.

"Jusot?" he called out. Here, closer to the bluff's summit, the wind was stronger and it plucked the word from his mouth. "Jusot!" he yelled, louder.

Unable to find any evidence of the black trail outdoors, Kirn took the path to the left. As he stepped past the corner, the wind nearly took his hat, and he had to use the hand holding the Walther to keep it on. When he looked up from his shoes, watching where he walked, he saw the barn sixty meters away and the big chestnut cropping grass in between. The stone barn's gable end faced him, the broad doors open wide.

Kirn went to the horse, a Normandy cob, easily a meter and two-thirds tall at the withers. The gelding raised its angular head a moment to stare at him with bright eyes, then went back to clipping grass. The cob had been bridled but not saddled, and the reins hung over its neck and dangled into the wildflowers.

There was a man at the end of the reins. He wore no coat, no shoes, only a white shirt and trousers, and he was laid out on his face. The soles of his bare feet were filthy. He'd come out of the house, Kirn supposed, walked to the barn and into its dung, back out with his mount, but made it no farther.

"Jusot?" asked Kirn. He had the wild hope that the doctor was only dozing here in the grass and sunshine. Kirn pointed his boot at the man, nudged the back of one leg. "Jusot." He put out his boot again for leverage and brought the Frenchman faceup.

A black curtain smeared the stubbled chin and cheek of the old man.

Kirn stuck the Walther in one pocket, the mask clutched in the other hand into another part of his coat. He ran his hand along the horse's neck. "Where were you going, old man?" he asked. Who cures the doctor when the doctor is too ill to cure himself?

Outdoors like this, in the sun and breeze, the dead man wasn't as frightening as the Tardifs in their stinking bedroom, or, God help him, their daughter stretched in that chair. But as Kirn looked at his missing fingers, the ones left in the mud outside a village too small to show on any map, they tingled again.

"Untersturmführer?" the Feldwebel said, behind him. The sergeant had found him finally. "Is that the doctor?"

Kirn said nothing.

"He had a nice horse, didn't he?"

Kirn kept brushing his half-hand through the horse's coat.

"You won't have any trouble finding them," the prick Wollenstein had said. The Herr Doktor had been right. All one had to do was follow the black trail.

Now he knew why the fucking SS, never scared of anything, were terrified. They were afraid the black trail led straight to them.

The aeroplane skipped across the short grass, pivoted at the far end, and returned. Alix put up a hand against the rush of the propellers when the machine rolled by her. Blades of grass blown by the false wind made a flat green rain that smelled like a just-mowed hay field.

One propeller slowed until it swung out of its blur, wavered to a halt, and the other followed. The aeroplane had a nose like a dolphin, the kind that sometimes paced Papa's boat on sunny days. Papa, she thought, just the memory aching in her.

A squat door opened in the aeroplane and a tall man jumped onto the grass. She recognized him in the dusk as he walked toward her—it was the American doctor. He extended a hand and touched her shoulder. "We need to talk," he said in accented French, and pointed to the truck that had driven her from the hospital.

More movement in the aeroplane's door caught her eye. Another man. But before he jumped down, she turned toward the truck.

The doctor made his hands into a basket and she put a foot in it to climb into the canvas-shrouded cave. She ducked—even as short as she was, the cloth roof was shorter—and found a place again on the hard bench that ran along the edge of the truck's bed. Here it was nearly full dark and all she could see was his outline against the lighter rectangle of the opening. He followed after tossing in a rucksack.

"I didn't ask your name before," he said, his voice gentle and awkward both.

"Alix. Alix Pilon," she said. "I'm well, as you told me?"

He didn't answer.

"Tell me *your* name at least." Frank Brink, he said.

"We're going to France," he went on. "We have to find the sickness that killed the Jews and your . . ." and he faltered. "It's important that we stop it, so we have to know where it began. Do you know where the Jews came from?" he asked. His French was slow and careful.

Alix swallowed hard and asked, "You'll take me home?"

"No," he said, and her hope drained fast. "But we have to know where the Jews came from." He paused again. "To make sure others don't die like . . ."

"Like Papa."

"Like him."

"I want to go home," she said, hearing a little bit of the girl in her voice again. "I must go home. There is no one to take care of Mama and no one here to take care of me."

"No," said a man at the rear of the truck. "You can't go back." She couldn't see his face—it was only a silhouette against the twilight outside the canvas—but that voice.

"Juniper," Alix whispered.

Wickens sat beside him on the hard bench inside the Bedford. Eggers stayed outside, his head turned to the water off the landing field.

"You can't go back, Alix," said Wickens. There was a softness in Wickens's voice, not that scalpel edge Brink had heard in the office on Baker Street.

"Juniper," Alix said again, still whispering.

"Yes, it's me," Wickens said. "How are you, Alix?"

"Why didn't you come when I asked for you?"

"You know each other," Brink said, feeling stupid.

"No one said you asked for me," Wickens told her.

"Liar," she whispered back. Wickens stiffened. Moments passed. Brink heard an engine, throaty and rumbling, outside the truck. "I want to go home, Juniper," Alix said, finally, in a louder voice. "Mama and Alain and Jules, there's no one to take care of them. Papa's dead."

"Tell us where the trucks came from," said Wickens.

Another long silence. "I don't know," she said.

"Junni, 'ere's the boat," called Eggers from the mouth of the canvas.

"You don't know," said Wickens, ignoring Eggers. That blade in his voice was back.

"I chased down the *boche* driver," Alix said. "When I returned, Papa and the others, they had pulled the live Jews out and loaded them in the other truck. I stood guard. I never talked to the Jews."

Brink leaned forward. "The others with you, your father's friends. They might know," he said to Alix. In the darkness he couldn't see her green eyes, only the pale shape of her face.

"Who was with you?" Wickens asked. "Tell me who was with you when you took the trucks. The rest of your cell. That's all I want. Names and where they live."

"Take me with you, and I'll tell you their names," she said quietly.

"Junni, the boys on the nanny're wavin' us on!" shouted Eggers from outside.

"Juniper, please," Alix said. She was begging now. "For what we did, you and . . . please."

"I'll say one more time, tell me the names." Wickens's voice was cold now as well as sharp. "I won't let you go back."

"Monsieur Frank, I swear I will help you find what you look for," Alix said, turning to Brink.

He knew what he should say. Same as Wickens. But they didn't have time to wander France looking for a needle in a carton of needles. He needed her help to find the plague, and if it existed, the antibiotic.

"I lost Owen last time, Alix. You remember Owen, don't you, the twiggy one? I don't have anyone else to lose, so I want it to go right this time," Wickens said very, very quietly. "Tell me the names." Wickens brought up his left hand—Brink couldn't see the scar, not in the dark, but he knew it was there—and he thought Wickens was going to hit her.

He reached out without thinking and grabbed Wickens's wrist. "Don't," Brink said in English. Wickens twisted his arm, a slight movement was all, and he was free. For a moment Brink figured Wickens would swivel and punch him, but he didn't. "You hit her and there's a chance you'll get it," Brink said. "If she has it." That was a lie, but maybe Wickens didn't know it.

"*Junni!*" Eggers yelled again.

"Take her with us," Brink said. "Get her to tell us what we need while we're on the boat." All in English.

Wickens was thinking it over. Brink wasn't sure what he'd do if Wickens beat her until he got what he wanted. He was bigger than the Englishman, but he didn't think he could stop him.

Eggers stuck his head into the truck. "Junni, they're sayin' if we don't leave now, we miss the tide on the other side and there won't be no beach, just a cliff."

"I wouldn't raise a hand to her, Doctor," said Wickens. "And fuck you for thinking I would." A long silence, then, "Take her with us."

Brink looked at Alix. She knew Wickens. From times in France, of course. It made sense now that Wickens knew it had been a fishing boat washed ashore when he hadn't mentioned fish. They knew each other, and well. He was surprised that he cared.

"We'll take you with us," Brink said in French, and she nodded. He doubted Wickens would let her step ashore, but he'd deal with that when he had to.

"Thank you," Alix said, and as she leaned forward, she extended her hand, and took his.

Brink felt her warm fingers, and next to him, Wickens breathed out a hard breath.

"Keep your hands off her, Doctor," Wickens said calmly, sharp and cold again. He climbed out of the truck and jumped to the grass.

Brink fumbled for his haversack, got it open, and pawed inside. He touched the brass syringe he'd put there, then dug under the medical things, and put fingers around one of the fifteen glass vials of actinomycin he'd packed for France. He could bring out the vial, stick the needle into its liquid, and give her an injection, himself, too, all in ten minutes. To be safe. But just like in the hospital room, he lost his nerve. What if the solution killed rather than cured? The little colored girl . . . she'd not even made quarantine.

Instead, he reached in the haversack for one of the bottles. He wrenched its lid off and shook out two of the sulfadiazine tablets. "Give me your hand," he said. He dropped the tablets in Alix's open palm and pressed her fingers around them. "I don't know for sure if you're ill or not," he said, hurrying on.

"And these?"

"They prevent the illness," he said. Lies, but he didn't know what else to say to her. He couldn't bring himself to tell her that the sulfa was a long shot at best.

She nodded, and put her hand up to her mouth to swallow the tablets dry. "You have other things in that magic bag of yours?" she asked.

"Doctor, get your arse out of that truck," yelled Wickens. *"We are leaving!"*

"No more magic," Brink said to Alix. And he waited until she dropped out of the back of the Bedford before swallowing two tablets himself.

Eight

The sea out of Portsmouth for Normandy was a metal sheet, flat and smooth as if it had been run through rollers. Even the wake, white in the moonlight, quickly soaked back into the dark water.

Brink sat at the rear of the boat, his back against the long tube that held one of the torpedoes, and wound the thin strip of white medical tape around his right middle finger between the proximal and distal interphalangeal joints. He used his teeth to tear the tape from the roll, tossed the roll into his haversack, and pressed the loose end flat. When he held up his hand and wiggled his fingers, he could easily see the three lines. Just like when he caught behind the plate, the tape helped his pitcher see the fingers to spot signals for the pitches he called. Now, though, the strips counted the days to the invasion. His calendar. Today the second, invasion the fifth.

They had all stared into the pitch of Portsmouth harbor at the blocky shapes of the ships as the torpedo boat slipped out, its engine muffled.

Eggers had whistled to himself and let out one long "gawd" after another at their number. Wickens seemed nervous from the moment he set foot on the boat, and Brink was reminded of the Englishman's talk of standing off Dunkirk four years earlier.

Alix, though, seemed as happy on the boat as Wickens was miserable. She moved around without needing to hold on to keep her balance, and one of the sailors—if you could call him that, since he wore no uniform, just a thick sweater and heavy pants—took Alix below for a short time to show her the boat's engines.

But two hours out of Portsmouth, Brink called her over. He wanted to be the one to question her, not Wickens. She tightrope-walked toward his voice, and folded her legs under her to sit on the metal deck. He could barely make out her face.

"Tell me the names, Alix," he said quietly, saying hers for the first time.

"You'll send me back if I tell you. Or Juniper will throw me over the side to see if I can swim."

She was smart, or at least clever, though maybe everyone who lived under the Germans was like this. He wondered what Wickens would do if she didn't tell.

She twisted a finger in her blowing hair. "Take me home and I'll walk you to the doors of the men you want," she said.

"We want to make sure others don't get sick."

Alix laughed, warm and throaty. "I have eyes. I saw the ships. You're not doing this for anyone French. The ones on the ships, the liberation, those are the ones you are concerned about."

"That's not true," he said. His haversack, after all, was stuffed with sulfadiazine, and the thin tubes of A17. Cotton surgical masks, two dozen. Syringes, a pair. Needles, four. A stethoscope. Scalpels and a mirror and alcohol and gauze bandages and two hemostats and rubber gloves and half a dozen morphine syrettes. He couldn't stop a pandemic, but he might be able to save a few.

"Someone must pay," Alix said. "You take me home, so I can make them pay, and I'll help you find this place where the Jews lived."

"We can't take you with us," he said.

"Because I have the Jews' sickness, is that why?"

"It's too dangerous."

She laughed again, and it made him think of Kate. "You make a joke. How do you think the Jews got to my papa's boat? We took them. How do you think we took them? We killed *boche*," she said. "I ran one down through thickets and brambles. Have you done that? I killed him with a knife. Have you?" Now her voice had the same scalpel sound as Wickens's. "I'm the one who runs the Armée Secrète in Port-en-Bessin."

"No," he said.

"No to what? You don't believe me?" She leaned close and he smelled a faint scent of soap. "You should, monsieur, it's true."

"No, I haven't killed," he said.

That shut her up, but only a moment. "Take me home. Please." Her voice didn't cut as sharp.

"What's so important?" he asked. "You're safer here. In England, I mean."

"My family."

Family, Brink thought, and her words faded for a moment.

". . . have family, monsieur?" she asked. "You understand."

He had family. He didn't have family. It depended on how you looked at it.

He had not talked to his father in almost eight years, not since he'd walked out that Sunday as the old man pounded the pulpit and shouted verses from the book of Mark about "children rising up against their parents." The sermon had been aimed at him for what he'd decided—instead of doctoring, he was going to play baseball for the Kansas City Blues. Walked right out of that clapboard-sided church caught between an Aurora Center cornfield and a dusty gravel road, and left unhealed the broken bones from horse accidents and the frostbite from the raw Dakota winters and the sawed-off fingers from vindictive farm machinery. Left for "a damn boy's game," his father'd said, the only time Brink had heard him swear.

His sister Darlene and kid brother Donnie came to see him play at Muehlebach Field in Kansas City once that season, and then April of '37 they took the train from Plankinton all the way to St. Louis when he made the roster for the Cardinals and caught Dizzy Dean on opening day at Sportsman's Park. But his father, never. And then on July 29 he broke his ankle sliding into second, in the game they'd won 5–2 against the fucking New York Giants, and the Cardinals sent him packing. He'd had no intention of crawling back to his father then, and still hated the idea of being a country doctor. Anyway, he'd always loved the lab, the clear-cut answers, yes or no, works or doesn't, rather than people who got sicker without reason and without remedy.

He'd found work with a man named Meyer who was trying to concentrate and purify a vaccine for bubonic plague. Once he figured out Meyer was brilliant and not a lunatic, he'd never looked back. Nor seen his father or done more than talk on the telephone with sister Darlene each time her birthday rolled around.

"No, I don't have family," Brink told Alix.

Wickens came out of the dark from beyond the torpedo tube and wobbled their way. The boat pointed in a new direction. He knelt close to Alix. "I've been patient," Wickens said in French. "But I want the names of your friends."

The motor torpedo boat sliced on. "Take me home and I tell you everything," Alix said. Stubborn girl.

"You think there was something between us that makes this different?" Wickens asked. "This is important, you don't know how important. And not just to me."

"I want to tell you something—"

"The only thing I want you to tell me is their names, Alix," Wickens snapped. "Just because we—" but he stopped.

Brink wanted to know the next word. "She'll take us to them if we bring her along," he said.

"Doctor, *shut the fuck up!*" Wickens shouted.

The torpedo boat swerved, a quick *S* on the water, and Brink put a hand on the deck to keep from tumbling. "Contact, zero-four-zero!" someone called from near the boat's front. "Aircraft, range one-two-zero-zero." Shoes squeaked on the metal deck as the boat's sailors ran for the guns mounted in the short turret near the front, and the one just a couple yards from them. Metallic noises came from the mount, *click/clacks*, the sounds big and deadly. And then there was a second moon low in the sky to the right. Not peeking over the horizon as if it were rising, but suddenly just there.

"Fire a flare!" screamed someone from the middle of the boat. "Green! No, white! White! *Fire white!*"

The moon came closer as if drawn down by rope, bigger still, and just as Brink understood that this wasn't a moon, the sound of engines hammered close and small winking comets sped for the boat. The evil, long-barreled machine gun in the nearby turret cracked out a string of steel bangs. A comet touched the boat near the front and yellow sparks glanced off the metal deck. The boat hesitated. It had hit a rock, Brink thought.

An airplane roared overhead, all four engines thundering. The moon had become a searchlight mounted on its belly, and its wings were no more than a hundred feet above the boat. A brilliant column of white water rose from the sea and the column fell over the deck, drenching Brink, soaking Alix, and washing Wickens toward the edge. Brink grabbed hold of Wickens's wrist to stop him from sluicing under the one-wire rail and into the sea, lost him, but had held on long enough to steer him against the torpedo tube. Someone toward the front screamed something ugly. A string of sparks raced into the air and a white light flowered at its end. The flare.

"That's one of ours," said Wickens from where he held on to the torpedo tube. His voice was so calm.

"Bloody hell!" yelled someone. "Fire a fucking green flare. It's not Jerry, it's one of ours! *Someone fire off fucking green!*"

The screaming from the front continued for one beat, two, then gurgled out. The new moon returned, still low, this time a bit to the rear and off to their left.

"Range, nine-four-zero, coming in at two-nine-zero!"

"It's Coastal Command with a Leigh Light," said Wickens, still calm. No one was listening, Brink thought, except him. The machine gun banged out another staccato. A parabola of yellow streaks linked the muzzle of the gun with the sky. A green flare popped above the boat.

"Stop firing, stop firing, it's ours!"

The searchlight grew, pinned the boat against the sea, and another hail of red comets swarmed them. Sparks and screams and shouts. Brink was transfixed, unable to move, unable to stop watching. Another flare, but this one side-slipped rather than climbed and it blew itself into green starry petals just above the water near the front of the boat. Brink's attention was held there a moment, and that's when he noticed the crewman spun in flames, twisting a moment before collapsing to the deck.

Brink stood and stumbled the twenty feet. By the time he reached the man, someone had smothered him with a coat. As he bent down, the first thing he noticed was the heat, like from a large rock warmed all day in the fall sun. And there was the smell of a cheap café, grease and old meat on a griddle.

"I need a light," Brink said.

"Contact, zero-three-five, range, one-five-zero-zero," a voice called close by. The dimmest of light spilled out over the edge of the bridge. "Range, one-nine-zero-zero, range increasing. He's running."

"Who are you?" asked someone beside him, and turned on a flashlight to pin the burnt man. Brink looked at the blackened face and missing eye and the smell, Christ, the smell.

"Turn it off, he's dead," Brink said.

"Who are you?"

"I'm a doctor."

"Gordon's bought it at the forward gun. The lieutenant caught a splinter, but he's still breathing."

Brink stood, took a swallow, another. "Show me. And bring me an aid kit," he said.

He followed as best he could, a hand out on the metal of the boat's bridge. The flashlight came on again and in the yellow-white cylinder there was another man, his back against the interior wall of the bridge, feet thrust in front of him, darkness spreading down his sweater. He was going into shock. He couldn't be older than twenty.

Brink knelt down, but pulled his hands away from the man's shoulder. Blood had saturated the boy's sweater, run across his hip, and was flooding the deck.

"Help him." Alix, not more than a yard behind him, but out of the light. "Frank?" she asked.

He probed the wound under the left clavicle. The splinter was wood, not steel, and jutted out two inches. How much was buried was impossible to tell, but by its width, nearly an inch where it dipped inside him, Brink guessed it was very long.

"Go to the back of the boat," he told Alix. Blood pumped under his fingers, between his fingers. Jesus. The knot in his gut doubled and doubled again.

"Aid kit, sir," said a young voice. A canvas bag clumped to the deck.

"Pull out all the bandages," Brink said. "Take the wrappings off."

By rights he shouldn't touch the splinter. No telling what damage it had done going in, what it had pushed aside or punctured or torn. Pulling might make things worse. But he couldn't apply enough pressure to stop the bleeding with it there.

Brink grabbed the splinter as the boat shifted and the boy under him moaned, said "Christ, Christ, Christ," and sighed. "Someone hold my hand," the boy said weakly.

Even though she couldn't have understood, Alix slid next to the lieutenant's legs and grabbed his hand. "Be brave," she said in French.

The boy sighed again, whispered "Christ," and then he was quiet.

"Give me the bandage," Brink said, and pulled smoothly, swiftly, on the splinter until it was free, all five inches of it. He tossed it aside. He took the first bandage from the man behind the flashlight and pressed its gauze against the splinter's home. "Another."

"He's dead," Alix said. She still held the lieutenant's hand.

Brink put two fingers of his right hand under the boy's jaw, the fingers slipping from the blood, moved them into the hollow of the throat to feel for a pulse. But like with Nawls, he felt nothing.

"*Goddammit!*" he yelled, and yanked the bandages off the boy's wound and threw the bloody wads into the dark.

"Frank—"

"Go to the back of the boat. Now," he said in French.

She held the boy's hand and didn't come up from her crouch.

"Fuck, now what do we do?" asked the sailor holding the flashlight.

"Wot's happened?" Wickens. It was crowded in the small shelter of the bridge.

"The lieutenant's dead, so's Jennings," said the flashlight.

"Jennings?" asked Wickens.

"The pilot. That's him port, burned to a chip when the flares caught fire."

It was Alix who asked, "What are they saying?"

"Someone else can put this boat in the right place," Wickens said.

"The lieutenant, if he was alive," said the sailor.

"Just get us near the coast," said Wickens.

"Look," said the sailor, no "sir" on the end. "Moon bright as day, Jerry waiting to blow any noise out of the water. No, we need the pilot. Or the lieutenant. They're the only ones who know the shore. And where Jerry has his guns."

"Frank, tell me what they are saying."

He leaned over the legs of the dead boy and whispered to her in French.

"I can take the boat into Port-en-Bessin," Alix said quietly. "I know the way. Even in the dark, I can find the way."

"Read it from a chart, for Christ's sake," said Wickens to the sailor.

"I'm only a rating."

"You can read a *fucking chart*, can't you? You can steer this *fucking boat*, right?"

"I'm not a navigator. Sir," the sailor said, putting it hard on that last word.

Brink took a moment to get it straight in his head. "She can take us in," he said. Wickens heard him.

"What?"

"She said she knows the way."

"You," said Wickens to Alix. "You'll bring the boat in." In French.

"Yes."

"If," Wickens said.

Alix took a moment to look at the dead lieutenant. "If you take me home."

Wickens rubbed the back of the hand with the scar.

"Or we go back," said Brink. But that wouldn't solve anything. They'd return the next night, he knew, with another pilot and another captain, and one less piece of tape on his hand. They needed all the time they could get.

Wickens nodded at last.

"You swear you will take me with you?" Alix asked. "Juniper, you swear?"

"Tell this man how to bring the boat west of the harbor. Half a kilometer west. The map says there's a small beach."

"I know the place," Alix said. But she didn't move.

"Yes, I promise," Wickens said roughly. "Jesus, Alix, yes, I swear." He stood, stepped from the bridge, and disappeared for the back of the boat.

"I was so stupid," Alix said very softly.

Now Brink understood; Alix had cared for the Englishman. "Maybe that's why he doesn't want you to go home," he said. Maybe Wickens loved her.

She shook her head. "Juniper loves many things, I think. But me? I don't think so."

"Sir?" asked the sailor, the English dragging him from Alix. "What do we do?" The sailor switched off this flashlight.

Brink realized the man was asking him. This was crazy. When had he been put in charge?

"Show her a chart, point to where you think we are. I'll translate."

"Sir?"

"She's your new pilot," he said.

Herr Doktor," said a voice in the dark. "We have visitors."

Wollenstein rolled over and stared at the fat shape in the doorway. "What time is it?" The girl next to him rustled in the sheets.

"Nearly midnight. I'm sorry, but . . ."

Wollenstein rubbed his eyes with the edges of his palms. "Who is it?" he asked. He swung his legs out of the bed and put bare feet to the floor.

"Obergruppenführer Kammler, Herr Doktor." Pfaff's voice was anxious. "And someone else . . ."

"Who?" Wollenstein stood, reached for his clothes.

"I'm not sure . . ." Pfaff started. "But I think it's the Reichsführer. It looks like his photographs."

A broom instantly swept the cobwebs. Wollenstein buttoned his shirt, and rubbed hands together. He caught himself and stopped. "How long has he been waiting?" he barked.

"Five minutes, Herr Doktor, no more."

Wollenstein stalked down the corridor, his boots slapping at the slate. A turn, then down the stairs, now carpet under his feet, and right, left, to the large farmhouse's entry. Standing there, hands behind his back, was Kammler. Beside him was a man even rounder than Pfaff, 140 kilos at least, his eyes nearly swallowed by his cheeks. It was the one who had consumed the front seat of the Horch that night at Flers. Two others stood behind them—bodyguards.

Then from the fat man's shadow stepped a middle-height, slender figure with only a slight paunch. Heinrich Himmler, Reichsführer-SS und Chef der Deutschen Polizei.

"Doktor, it is, as always, a pleasure," said Himmler, and stepped forward, hand extended not in salute but to shake. So polite.

Himmler squinted from behind steel-frame spectacles. He had no chin to speak of and his oval face looked harmless. His uniform, gray and immaculate, showed under the opened wool overcoat, finely tailored. Himmler took off his cap, gave it to the taller bodyguard. Even his thinning hair, swept to the side, was unimpressive.

Wollenstein's first thought was that Kammler had heard of the missing Jews, told Himmler, and the Reichsführer was here to punish him. The thought was reinforced by the fat man. His sail of a tunic had the black diamond stitched to its left sleeve, the letters *S* and *D* embroidered in silver. Sicherheitsdienst. The big man was SD, security police, the ones who ruled the Hebrews.

"I'm sorry to wake you, Herr Doktor," said Himmler, his voice barely carrying across the entryway.

"I was just resting, Reichsführer."

"We must talk. Can we . . ."

Talk. "Yes, of course. In here," he said, and waved his hand toward the sitting room. Himmler and Kammler and the SD followed, but the bodyguards stayed behind with the nervous Pfaff.

Wollenstein switched on the lights. Himmler took one of the two leather chairs near the cold fireplace, Kammler the other. Wollenstein and the SD Hauptsturmführer were left standing.

"Bad news, I'm afraid," Himmler said, and crossed his legs. Wollenstein's knees went soft for a second. "Göring's flying bug is useless," said Himmler. "That is the Obergruppenführer's opinion." Himmler nodded toward Kammler. Wollenstein relaxed—so it wasn't about the Jews.

"Too undependable for our purposes," Kammler said. "The A-four will be much more reliable—"

Himmler held up a thin hand and Kammler went silent. "September is a long time, Hans. Perhaps too late," said Himmler.

Kammler leaned forward in his chair. He was going to contradict Himmler. What an idiot, Wollenstein thought. He wasn't a doctor, not even one of the A4's rocket engineers. Just a builder. *Der Ofenmann.* That was how he got to be a favorite of the Reichsführer's, how he came to control the rockets, from his expertise building big things like the camps and crematoria.

"My aircraft will be ready long before September," said Wollenstein. "They can spray England much sooner than that." He kept Himmler's gaze. The Reichsführer nodded. From the corner of his eye, Wollenstein saw Kammler shake his head.

"I'd like to see your work," Himmler said.

"Now?"

"Please," said Himmler. The unimposing man stood, and with him, Kammler. Wollenstein nodded. As long as they wouldn't be talking of Jews.

He led them from the farmhouse, the bodyguards now their shadows. With an electric torch to guide them, Wollenstein took them across the walled yard and through the rear gate and on the path through the field to the culturing barn. From the safety of the doorway—he told them they would have to suit into the rubber aprons and boots and gloves and cloth masks and glass goggles if they went inside—he pointed out the wide metal trays on the nearest benches. The ones that stink like old meat, he said. Wollenstein was used to the smell, but Himmler and Kammler and the SD, the last snorting heavily from the short walk, all covered their mouths and noses with their hands or handkerchiefs.

The night shift was working the barn, but Wollenstein waved off Traugott before he came too close, his eyes wide behind the goggles. Four others were in the barn—Fresse and three Ukrainians.

Wollenstein explained it to Himmler. The culture medium is brewed in the trays, peptone and meat bouillon cooked over gas. That was what stank. Then the medium is poured into smaller stainless trays, refrigerated to make a gelatin, and those trays placed into the Ishii cultivators. Wollenstein pointed a finger across the large Norman barn to where one of the Ukrainians was stacking trays in an Ishii, the shiny box thirty-five by twenty-five by fifty centimeters. The cultivators go to the next room—he pointed to the wide door he'd had made to partition the barn—where live *Pasteurella*

pestis bacilli are swabbed across the gelatin base in each tray and the cultivators are shoved into larger incubators in a room beyond that.

"Incubators?" Himmler asked.

"A kind of oven," Wollenstein said, trying hard not to look at Kammler.
"The bacilli grow best at a specific temperature and humidity." Kammler
was nodding. An oven was an oven to him.

"All this is from the *Japsern*?" Himmler asked. His voice had some wonder in it.

"This is just as they described," Wollenstein said, "but on a much smaller
scale, of course."

"Smaller? How amazing," Himmler said. "The yellow ones really came
up with all this?"

"Crude, yes, but it works. It saved me months." Wollenstein closed his
eyes for a moment, remembering the fear aboard that blockade runner
in Bordeaux as he retrieved Seishiro's journals and papers. And the crate,
with its flash-dried bacilli secured in metal flasks.

Next he walked them all to the small outbuilding fifty meters farther,
where the *pestis* skimmed off the cultivators' gelatin was brought in bottles
and there dried in a vacuum chamber at very low temperatures. Freeze-
dry, Wollenstein said to Himmler, the process borrowed from a Nuremburg
firm's work on food storage. And from there, to the third step in the process:
another barn, not as big as the first, where the dried bacilli were blended
in mechanical mixers with a stabilizing agent and then packed into the ce-
ramic receptacles he'd ordered special from the potter in Rennes.

Finally, he led them down another path worn in the grass of the next
field—through a cart-wide gap in the boscage—to the last stop, the little
concrete house five meters square that had a door but no windows. He
freed the thick padlock with a key he drew from a cord that hung around
his neck and switched on the electric light.

"The weapon," he said, gesturing to the small wooden boxes stacked
against the far wall. "Don't be afraid. They're perfectly safe." He went to
the nearest and patted its lid, secured tight with narrow bands of tin. No
nails or screws into these boxes, not after the accident.

Neither Himmler nor Kammler crossed the threshold. Disappointed,
Wollenstein switched off the light, shut the door, and snapped the padlock shut.

"Very impressive," said Himmler. He stepped away from the door, and pulled his overcoat closer. Near him, Kammler put a hand in his pocket, withdrew a cigarette case, and spent long moments tapping the cigarette and lighting it. The moon was nearing full, and its light was enough to show everyone. As Kammler smoked, Himmler waved a hand against the cloud. Wollenstein was surprised he didn't tell Kammler to stop.

"We can go back to the house now," said Wollenstein. "I have some excellent French reds."

Kammler turned to the bodyguards, muttered something to them, and they melted into the shadows. The fat SD remained; he, too, struck a lighter, but to fire a thick cigar. "We'll talk out here if you don't mind. Fewer ears," said Kammler.

For a wild moment, Wollenstein thought Kammler had dismissed the others because he was going to pull a pistol, make him kneel in the grass, and shoot him. For sins of lost Jews.

"The Obergruppenführer has reservations about your . . . what do you call them, Hans?"

"*Grabbringer*, Reichsführer," said Kammler. Wollenstein hated Kammler's name for the *Pasteurella pestis*: grave bringers. It made what he'd done seem childish, or childishly easy. It was neither.

"Yes. I like that. Very memorable," Himmler said. "I am astonished at what you have accomplished, Herr Doktor, considering what you've had to work with. Heydrich was right to trade with the *Japsern*. You are a genius. A real genius."

Wollenstein breathed relief, unsure what to say except "Thank you." But then he saw the opportunity. "We should use the aircraft, Herr Reichsführer, to spray the *Pasteurella pestis* on England. Before they start their invasion."

Kammler snorted, but it was Himmler's opinion that mattered. He was silent for several long seconds. "Are they ready, your aircraft?" Himmler asked.

It was Wollenstein's turn to hesitate. "No, not quite ready, Herr—"

"I told you," said Kammler from inside a cloud of smoke. Himmler raised his hand again and Kammler went quiet.

"The invasion will come soon, Herr Doktor," said Himmler. "This month, that's what the SD says. If your aircraft are not ready before they put to ships—"

Wollenstein knew he shouldn't interrupt Himmler, but . . . "The anti-dote is ready," he lied. "All I have to do it put it into production. Even if they leave England before we're ready, I can destroy them here with air-craft. On French beaches."

"Every time you bring up the *Tiefatmung*," said Kammler, using his name for Wollenstein's streptomycin. "Every. Time."

Himmler shook his head. "The Obergruppenführer's right. You would foul German blood," said Himmler. "No, make them sick on their island, where it can't get to us."

"But with the antibiotic, everything changes and—"

Kammler dropped the remnants of his cigarette into the grass. "My vote is no."

"But—"

"Impossible, Herr Doktor," said Himmler evenly. Flat, his voice was. This was a change in the Reichsführer. Kammler. It was Kammler's whis-pering that had made Himmler change his mind.

"What have I done all this for? If we're not going to use it?" asked Wollenstein, letting his voice get the better of him. "Reichsführer, listen to me . . ."

Kammler stepped forward, pointed a finger. "No, listen to me. There will be no release of it here." He put the tip of his finger on Wollenstein's chest. "It's been decided."

"Precisely," said Himmler. He put his hand in front of his mouth, coughed quietly. "The air, I'm not used to French air." Wollenstein didn't know if he was supposed to laugh, and so didn't dare. Just in case Himmler was serious. "The Obergruppenführer also believes we should relocate while we have the opportunity."

"Relocate?"

"We should never have let you conduct your research in France," said Kammler. "The Americans will be here soon. And English. Moving by rail is almost impossible now, and the roads are almost as dangerous. We must take all this to the Reich for safekeeping before it's too late. I suggest the Mittelwerk. The tunnels will protect your things from Allied bombers, and the A-fours are built there, so we can marry the two before transport."

Mittelwerk. That was Kammler's hole carved into the Thuringian mountains near Nordhausen, where the Obergruppenführer's stick-thin, starving slave laborers assembled the A4 rockets. It was the place Kammler had tried to convince him was the perfect home for his project, but when he'd visited, the tunnels had been so cold, so damp, that Wollenstein had spent days in bed after.

"Move everything? Now? That makes no sense." Wollenstein started, but stopped. "Herr Reichsführer, please, if I move now . . . You said yourself they would come soon. We'll lose the chance to use the aircraft."

"Reichsführer, the A-fours, they're the only dependable method, we agreed—" started Kammler.

Himmler raised his hand again.

Wollenstein saw his opening. "A month, give me a month to make the aircraft work," he said.

"Too long. Too much chance the Americans and English will be here and the way back to the Reich blocked."

"Two weeks," bargained Wollenstein.

Himmler shook his head.

"A week, only one week. I can make it work, I swear." Wollenstein held his breath waiting for an answer. It was his, all of this, the *pestis*, the aircraft with the mechanisms he'd found manufactured in Silesia for spraying potato fields, the *Tiefatmung*. He had sweated two years making all this. To pour his soul into this and not see a reward? No, that wasn't fair.

"Not an entire week," said Himmler. "Five days. Until Wednesday next, yes? The seventh, I believe."

"No, Reichsführer, listen," said Kammler. "He'll dribble it on them, a little bit is all, and they'll contain it and find a way to defend themselves. Worse, they'll strike back. We must hit them with a torrent of rockets, all at once, only that will—"

"A few days, Hans. Only five days," Himmler said.

And then Wollenstein realized he'd underestimated *der Ofenmann*. Kammler not only wanted the *pestis* for his rockets, he wanted to be its master as well. He'd convinced Himmler that Wollenstein's work must move to the tunnels for safekeeping, but once there, Kammler would push him into a cold corner.

"The weather will turn tomorrow, or the next day, that's what the forecasters promise," Himmler continued. "No invasion. We can afford a handful of days. Kammler, your rockets aren't ready, Göring's bugs don't work, you say. If Herr Doktor makes it work with his spraying, we can douse England before they strike, stop the invasion before it's launched. That's worth five days, I think."

Kammler had found another of his disgusting cigarettes. A flame wavered, the end of the cigarette glowed, smoke rose. "I disagree," he said to Himmler, "but as you wish." He drew on the cigarette, blew some of the smoke Wollenstein's way. "But only until Wednesday. And Adler should remain. The security here is horrible. There should be patrols between the buildings, men watching over the *Gräber* all hours," he said, pointing the embered end of his cigarette at the concrete house with the crated warheads. "*Maquisards* could stroll in here anytime they wished."

"We've never had an incident," Wollenstein said, leaving out the lost Jews, which, after all, hadn't technically happened on the farm.

"I'd like to leave Hauptsturmführer Adler to help," Kammler said. He nodded to the fat SD who puffed on his vile cigar.

To spy on me, thought Wollenstein.

"A superb idea," said Himmler, of course. Adler was SD, Himmler's own security police, favorite of favorites. If he trusted no one else, he trusted the SD.

"Reichsführer, tell him the rest," said Kammler. He was close enough for Wollenstein to smell the tobacco and garlic both.

"This is difficult," Himmler said. He clutched his overcoat even closer. "You have worked miracles in this rude place, Doktor. But we cannot produce enough of your . . . *Grabbringer* . . . here, not under these conditions. And your genius is not as an administrator."

Kammler *is* stealing my work, Wollenstein realized. He's taking it. "No, that's not—" he said. "I am the one who made this."

"Your talent is in other things. Not in overseeing a factory," said Himmler. "I will find other things for you to do."

"You cannot take this from me. I've worked . . . I've worked years for this moment. *You cannot steal this from me!*" Wollenstein said. He couldn't stop shouting.

"I'm not stealing anything, Doktor, " Himmler said, matching Wollenstein's shouts with whispers. "Since this was never yours in the first place."

"You cannot," said Wollenstein softly. "This is mine—"

"Everything is the Führer's," Himmler said. "This is my wish."

"Please, don't take this from me."

"Done, Doktor. I'm sorry."

Wollenstein reached for Himmler's overcoat sleeve. As soon as he did, he knew his mistake.

"Don't touch me, Herr Doktor. Ever. Do you understand?" Himmler said, jerking away. "I don't want your little things on me."

"The letter, Reichsführer," Kammler said.

"I would like the letter returned," said Himmler to Wollenstein.

"The letter."

"You might be tempted to do something stupid. The letter?" Himmler held out his hand. "Please."

Hesitantly, Wollenstein put a hand inside his tunic, withdrew the thin leather wallet that stayed with him always, and from it pulled a single folded sheet of paper. It was too dark to read, not that he didn't have it long memorized. Centered at the top was the now-invisible embossed eagle and swastika; he felt them under his finger. Below the eagle would be a single typewritten sentence: "Give Sturmbannführer Dr. Wollenstein all cooperation."

And then the signature that leaned to the right, the line under it trailing off to the left. Typewritten beneath that, simply "Heinrich Himmler, Reichsführer-SS und Chef der Deutschen Polizei."

Himmler tugged the letter from Wollenstein's hands, beckoned to Kammler, who produced his lighter, flicked at the flint, and touched the flame to a corner. The Reichsführer tilted the paper so the flame climbed the incline, and when the fire closed on his fingers, he dropped it into the grass.

"It's all for the best," Himmler said, looking at his boot, which was crushing the blackened paper. He glanced up. "Five days, and then we move everything to Mittelwerk where the Obergruppenführer can watch over it."

When Alix told Frank that they were close—two or three kilometers from shore—he said something in English to the sailor holding the wheel. The man reached down and switched off the engine. Another motion of his hand, and Alix felt the boat push forward again. The sailor said something and Frank told her of a special quiet electric motor that would take them closer.

She knew where they were. Papa and she had sailed this a thousand times; before the *boche* forbid them to sail after sunset, they'd done it a hundred times in the pitch black. In the moonlight, it was easy to find this piece of the coast. Alix breathed in and smelled home: turned earth and cows' leavings and the full leaves of summer.

Frank had stayed by her side, turning the sailor's words into French, hers into English. Juniper had gone to the stern of the needle-thin boat and stayed there.

Stupid. It had been stupid to love him.

Three weeks ago he had knocked on the door of her home and whispered his stupid pass name "Limelight" and asked for "Bouton," the one who led the Armée Secrète in Port-en-Bessin. He was on English business looking for something very unusual. He needed help finding this thing, which was why her hidden radio had clicked and clacked a week before with the message to expect him. I am Bouton, she told him, and he looked surprised for the first, and last, time she remembered. Behind him was his rat of an old man and another, a young one who looked like he had consumption he was so thin.

He was searching for a place, perhaps a factory kind of place, he said, but one that would be watched carefully and likely not be near town or village. It would be known, Limelight said, by how it was unknown. But the *boche* were thick as the boscage, squatting like they did at every wood, field, and crossroad. Finding Limelight's one place, she had thought, without being caught was impossible. But still she took him and his two friends on borrowed bicycles to all the circled spots on his map: a patch of woods east of Bayeux and into the hills south of Caen, and even once to a clearing near Isigny-sur-Mer where there was nothing but an empty, exhausted barn and, a hundred meters away, a battery of *boche* cannon tucked under netting.

He then said they must ask all around about people who were ill, but ill unusually. They might have a fever, or not, he wasn't sure, they might have boils black as coal lumps or not. What would be unusual would be the number of the ill; there would be many all of a sudden, ten or twenty or perhaps dozens. Look for many becoming sick at once, Limelight said.

She had done what he asked because she loved his laugh and the stories he told, of a place called Afghan where the women covered their faces with cloth and the men could shoot a goat's eye at five hundred meters, he said. He spoke of the *boche* with as much ferocity as she did, and she'd loved the way his hand rested on her ankle that one time when they sat side by side, and that he talked to her a bit like Henri had before he disappeared. That was why she'd taken Limelight wherever he wanted, not that they found anything.

She had made love to Juniper—he'd told her his name in a moment of weakness—in her own bedroom. Papa and Mama slept in the next—she'd snuck him in, having to make the first move to let him know she was interested. But then he and the other two, the rat one and the thin one, went away for two days and a night, and when they returned Juniper had a gash on his wrist and the thin one was missing and the rat one was filthy and looked like he would kill anything that crossed him. Neither would say anything about what had happened.

The second time she and Juniper made love was a mistake. They'd lain on a blanket in an apple orchard on the edge of Port-en-Bessin, a romantic enough spot, but he'd been mechanical. He had finished quickly, without apologies, rolled off, and pulled up his trousers.

And then he had left, this Englishman, the only man she'd slept with since Henri had vanished in Belgium four years before. Now he was here again, but behaving even colder than he had in the orchard. She'd done wrong to risk the trip to England for him, done very wrong. Papa had died. And for that, she hated Juniper now.

Something told her this was the place. She told them to stop the boat. The swells had been getting shorter for the last half hour, and the boat rolled badly. Juniper stood behind them in the small uncovered wheelhouse. He put out a hand to steady himself as the boat moved.

"The beach is here? You're sure?" he asked.

"Right in front of us." The moonlight showed the line separating the darker bluffs of the shore from the less dark sky. Juniper talked to Frank, then to the sailor. Those two stepped out of the wheelhouse, but Juniper remained.

"You're not coming with us," he said.

"You promised."

"Doesn't matter. But you'll tell me what I need. Right, Alix?"

Dimly she felt her heart rap against her chest. If she had a weapon, anything, she wouldn't be afraid of him, but she'd not found anything, not even a knife in her search when the sailor showed her the boat's crannies hours before.

She heard something dragged across the deck, some words in English, and the sound of something light hitting the water. "You're rowing to shore from here?" she asked.

"Tell me the names of your friends, where they live, or . . ." and Juniper's voice drifted away.

"Or?"

"Don't make me do this. When I come back to England, I swear to you, we'll sort out everything."

"Everything."

"Everything between us. You and me." His voice was smooth like butter. Liar. Juniper held his hand behind his back, not out to her, as Frank had several times already.

"Did you love me, Juniper?" she asked quietly. Her voice shook. Did he have a pistol in that hand behind his back? Would he dare?

He didn't answer for the longest time, and that itself was an answer. "Alix . . ." he began.

"You're stupid, thinking you could row ashore near the harbor," Alix interrupted. "The *boche* are thick like grass there. Did you know that?"

"Tell me the names of your friends, Alix. You're safer here. Leave the work to men. You have no idea—"

"You have no idea where you are, do you?" she asked, sliding one foot, then the other, out of the hospital's hand-me-down shoes she'd unlaced earlier. She became shorter.

"What are you talking about . . ." Juniper started, but went quiet.

Alix looked to the shore again. The way the line between bluff and sky rose and fell, rose again before flattening, told her where she was. Not at the narrow, dangerous beach where the *boche* waited near Port-en-Bessin, but three kilometers farther west, near Sainte-Honorine. There was no beach at high tide here, barely a sliver at low, as it was now. No *boche* here, or at worst, perhaps a few pacing the top of the bluff.

She had known Juniper would not keep his promise. She had felt it ever since he'd sworn to take her home.

Papa was dead, his boat wrecked on the English shore because she had wanted Juniper, so now there was no one to put food in the mouths of Mama and Jules and Alain. She wouldn't shirk that responsibility. That's what she told herself, but she knew there was another truth. She was afraid, and fleeing for the only place where she wouldn't be alone.

"Where are we?" Juniper half-turned to look toward the shore, as if he could tell.

That was her chance. In a quick step she cleared the wheelhouse and two more strides got her to the gunwale. The last running step became a push with her foot against the deck, the too-large man's trousers fluttering against her legs.

And she was cutting through the water, cold enough to hurt her face. She stayed under until she couldn't stand it a second longer, afraid Juniper might shoot. But as she broke to the surface she heard no shots, only long strings of that harsh English. Angry, it was. Then a slice of French.

"Alix, come back," a voice shouted. It might be the American, but she wasn't sure.

She flung her right arm from the water and struck out for home.

———

Saturday

The coming of the devil of plague
Suddenly makes the lamp dim,
Then it is blown out,
Leaving man, ghost and corpse in the dark room.

—SHIH TAO-NAN, 1792

Nine

The swells that had seemed so long and slow when he'd stood on the torpedo boat were anything but. As the rubber dinghy scaled each peak, slid into each trough, Brink's stomach took the same ride: up, down, up, and down. He leaned over the side of the dinghy and vomited into the black water.

"Grab your paddle, Doctor," Wickens shouted from behind him.

Brink puked again.

"Paddle, you shite!" Wickens had been edgy the whole time on the torpedo boat, and now, even closer to the water, he gripped the sides of the dinghy like it was Christ's salvation.

The nearly full moon was almost down, but its light was so bright that when Brink looked toward the shore, the line between earth and sky was ink sharp. The Germans would see them plain as ants on a white tablecloth. When he turned to look for the torpedo boat, it was gone.

Brink grabbed the paddle and stuck it in the water. The dinghy rose again, skated down the swell, and seemed to move forward. Eggers did most of the work from his place at the front. Each time the old man raised his paddle, freezing water slapped Brink's face; in seconds he was drenched and his teeth chattered. He let his mind go empty while he dug into the water, lifted the paddle, dug again.

"Careful, Sam," Wickens said. He wasn't shouting now that the shore was near. Eggers pulled his paddle from the water. The boat slipped down another slope. Brink heard the sound of surf. "Nearly there, Sam. Be ready."

Eggers reached for something other than his paddle and the dinghy climbed a steeper crest. Brink scrabbled first for a handhold to keep from tumbling backwards, and then put out his hand for the haversack with the actinomycin-17 and all his medical things, but he came up empty. He pitched onto Wickens as the dinghy kept climbing and the sound of the surf got louder.

"Hold—" Wickens yelled, too late. The bottom dropped out from under the rubber boat and Brink was in the bitter water. He came to the surface, gasped for air, but another wave broke over his head and he went under. Tumbling, rolling, spinning, he lost track of up and down. It was just by luck, he thought later, that when he put out a hand he felt air, not water, and surfaced. He kicked and struck out for where the surf was loudest.

He touched sand finally. A wave pushed him up the shore. On hands and knees, he crawled until the ocean lapped at his boots and then he laid his head on the damp sand and vomited seawater.

"Get up," a dull, hollow voice said. Someone grabbed his shoulder, and for a minute he thought it was Dutch Grootvader telling him to rise for chores. "Brink, get up." Grootvader never called him that, and he opened his eyes and saw black sand. His mouth was sour.

Brink got to his knees, then to his feet, shaking from the cold.

"Doctor, haven't got all night," said the voice, clearer now. It was Wickens.

"My bag, where's my bag?" Brink asked, remembering how he'd reached for the haversack.

"Unless you had your hand 'round it, it's gone," Wickens said. "The boat capsized."

"My things—" The A17, his last resort against the *Pasteurella pestis*, as unproven as it may be.

"They're gone. You should have held on tighter." Wickens put a hand on his arm to steady him. "We must get off this beach. That raft will be washing ashore and come daylight they'll sniff behind every bush looking for us. And there's the damn moon . . ."

He disappeared into the deeper dark under the bluffs. Brink followed, and in a few steps the sand turned to clattering rocks. At sounds behind him Brink spun, his heart thick in his throat.

"Just me, you noisy turd," Eggers's gravelly voice said. "'Urry up, or Junni'll leave us behind."

"Where is she?" Brink asked, remembering the sight of Alix as she'd darted into the water.

"'At cunt? Who cares? Better rid of 'er." With that, Eggers made to pass him across the rocks. But Brink stopped him with a hand on the man's chest.

"Get out of my way," the old man said. "Said step aside or I'll give you what for, peahead."

Almost before he knew what he was doing, Brink grabbed Eggers's coat with one hand and pulled the other back, then punched the Brit right under the eye and sent him sprawling on his back.

"Don't call her that again, you little fuck," Brink said, leaning down and over Eggers.

"Don't hurt my Sam, Doctor," Wickens said. He was like smoke, the way he just showed up. The quiet was enough to hear the drip of water from Wickens's clothes onto the rocks.

Eggers stood, brushed imaginary dust from his coat, but his fingers made only wet noises on the cloth. "You bugger, I 'ave mind to cut you."

"Sam, Sam, leave be. You started it."

"Sure, Junni, sure, sorry, but 'e itched me," Eggers jabbered.

"Call her that again and I'll be the one hits you," Wickens said.

"Yer right, Junni, won't 'appen again, swear."

Brink rubbed the knuckles of his right hand and kept his distance from the both of them.

"Have any idea where she's brought us?" Wickens asked, back to business.

"Not a whit, Junni."

Brink looked up and in the moonlight saw the sheer of the bluff, and in its folds, a steep cut that sliced through to the top.

"West of Port-en-Bessin, do you think?"

Eggers glanced at the bluff, then back at Brink. His eyes were small black circles and they were aimed at him. "Maybe. Should we 'ead up, then? Take a looksee?" asked Eggers.

"Up then, Sam."

Eggers stole a last look at Brink, shrugged into his haversack, and slung his Sten over a shoulder. He grabbed a handhold and pulled himself into the draw, his boots sending down thin showers of dirt and pebbles.

"You're next," Wickens said. Brink followed the old man, or tried to. For every three feet of headway he slipped back one. But in a few minutes, the cut flattened out to a steep path through the knee-high grass.

"Stay down, you'll show against . . ." Wickens whispered, but didn't finish. Brink stiffened as he heard a voice. Not Eggers's. Not French. Brink knew German, what with spending so much time with his Grossmama from the old country. That's what it sounded like.

Wickens pushed him aside and made for the top of the bluff. Before its lip, he pulled off his pack and laid it in the grass. He removed something and handed it to Brink.

The metal was cold and damp.

"Webley. Just pull back on the hammer. There's no safety, so watch where you point," said Wickens. Wickens took several more somethings from the pack, and as Brink watched, he fit the somethings together, the metal snicking to make a gun like the one Eggers had over his shoulder. A Sten, Wickens had called it when he'd showed it to him on the plane down from London. Wickens pulled a long, narrow box from the sack and fit it to the left side of the gun. Another snick. He pulled back on a bolt and that, too, clacked as it found its home.

"Stay close," Wickens said quietly. No moonlight gleamed off the flat black of the Sten. "Pay attention, and remember wot I told you about that," he said, pointing to the revolver Brink held too tightly. "You shoot me in the arse, Doctor, and you'll have a very angry patient."

Wickens slithered the last couple of yards to the lip of the cut and slowly raised his head. Brink followed.

Wickens nudged him with a wrist. Fifteen yards to the left, two figures stood. The moon's light showed the silhouette of a helmet on one. German. That one held a long shape in his hands, a rifle, Brink realized, the shape pointed at the narrower figure without a helmet. It was Alix, her wet hair slicked against her skull.

Another shape stood to the side, a few yards from the others and closer to them. German, too, this one had his back half-turned to them and was smoking a cigarette. The end brightened and the man tossed it to the ground. Sparks flew as it hit thick blades of grass.

"*Zeig mir deine Papiere,*" the one near Alix asked. It took Brink a second to puzzle the meaning. Show me your papers.

"*Je ne vous saisi pas,*" Alix answered. She didn't know German maybe, or maybe she didn't want to.

She was the only one who could show him the way to the *pestis,* which was one thing. So she was the only one who could lead him to the trail of the German cure, which was the second. He couldn't do anything without her. Brink clutched the revolver and pointed it at the closer sentry. He was surprised that his hand was steady.

"Don't," whispered Wickens, and pushed on the revolver until its barrel pointed into the grass. "That's an order."

Wickens was going to give her up.

Again Brink didn't think or he wouldn't have been able to do what he did. He stood, and as he did, he stuck the revolver in the waistband of his pants before he put his hands in the air and shouted "*Nicht schiessen!*" The German who had tossed away the cigarette turned and struggled with the gun slung over his shoulder. The one in front of Alix spun Brink's way, too. "*Nicht schiessen!*" Brink yelled again.

"You fuckin'—" someone said to his right.

Brink felt naked standing there, but he took a step out of the draw. All he had was the Germans' confusion. He had to get closer. "*Nous faisions juste l'amour,*" he lied as he walked forward. Maybe they would believe him, that two French had been making love in the grass in the cold in the dark along the bluffs. Sure.

"*Hände hoch,*" the nearest German said. His hands *were* up, Brink thought, but he said nothing. He stepped nearer. Four yards, three. The German had his weapon off his shoulder. It was a short gun, nasty in the fading moonlight, and looked a bit like a Sten, but different. Its muzzle wavered as Brink moved closer. Two yards, one.

"*Halt!*" the German said, and Brink stopped, his hands still above his head. He stole a look toward Alix and was about to yank the revolver from his waistband.

Wickens's Sten banged a single round, another, then a string. The soldier near Brink was suddenly on his back and thrashing in the grass.

Eggers's Sten hammered from his right.

The German with the rifle shifted its barrel from Alix and toward Eggers's shooting. Brink heard Eggers cry out, the sound somehow loud over the noise.

And then the other German was up again, kneeling with that short gun in his hand. He had a hold of it like a bat, the moment slowing for Brink like it sometimes did when he stood at the plate and waited for his pitch. The bat bashed his knee. Brink went to the grass and the German was on him, hands around his throat and squeezing so tight that the moon went dim.

Brink scratched at the German, who smelled like old beer and new blood. He put his hands under the German's chin, shoved up.

The pressure loosened, and he gulped in a ragged breath, but there was still one hand on him and he grabbed at its fingers, curled one back. The man's other hand swung into view, a point glinting there. Brink used his forearm to block it, and the knife's end stopped a few inches from his eye. With that arm he shoved back, the German leaned in, and the knife waved for his face, moved closer, away, closer still. If he blinked, he'd be cut.

In the background he heard a long burst of a Sten ring out, *bap-bap-bap-bap*.

That was the moment he discovered the fingers around his throat again. He gripped two of them, bent them against the metacarpophalangeal joints, and heard the tendons rip. The German screeched and the knife was gone. Brink sucked air deep into his lungs. He rolled onto his side. The German clutched his hand and whimpered. Brink bent to pick up the knife, not really knowing what he would do with it.

Alix stepped into view, a Sten to her shoulder, and fired into the dark, another *bap-bap-bap* chasing who knows what. She raced after the sounds and was gone.

Wickens appeared from the shadows at the right with a moaning Eggers at his shoulder. Wickens had the old man's arm hung over his neck, dragging him forward. "Sam's hurt, Doctor. In the other arm, I think," Wickens said. His voice was calm, still in charge. He sat Eggers on the grass. The old man groaned a low sound. To the east, a whistle shrilled, then a short rush of gunfire, a chatter of answering shots, and more whistles. The German beside them moaned again.

Another whistle. "Fix his arm, Doctor," Wickens said.

Alix came out of the dark, the Sten in her hand. "I couldn't catch the other one," she said, breathing hard. Another whistle from where she'd been and gone. "They're coming."

The wind off the Channel rose up the draw behind them and blew Brink's coat flat against his back, wet cloth plastered against him. From the sound of the whistles, there wasn't time to tend to Eggers.

"Oh, bloody hell, shut up," Wickens said to the German, who groaned in his pain again. The Englishman left his old man's side, came to Brink, plucked the knife from his hand, kneeled at the German, and pushed the sliver into the German's chest just under the sternum. The German gasped, weakly reached for the handle, breathed out something Brink couldn't understand.

"Port-en-Bessin *c'est par lá*," Alix said. When Brink looked up from the dying German, she was pointing toward the whistles.

Wickens stood over the German. *"I know it's blocked that way! Where can we go?"* he shouted back in French. Eggers moaned, coughed. Brink saw a smear of dark on the upper arm of the old man's coat.

"I know a place," Alix said.

"Where?"

"Sainte-Honorine, less than a kilometer," she said.

"Too close," he said, back now at Eggers, lifting him. "They'll find us." More whistles. "Hurry."

"Étréham then, three kilometers across the fields, five by roads. A farmhouse. We'll be safe."

Brink had to say it. "He'll never make it that far." Eggers's stain had spread in the few moments they'd talked.

"He'll make it, Doctor. You don't know Sam," Wickens said, sounding desperate. As if in answer, more whistles, three different ones, and closer.

"Grab the rucks," Wickens went on, "and take this," he said, and held out a Sten. Brink took it, not wanting to, and went and found Wickens's pack. He dropped the revolver into it, and closed it again.

Alix came back from Eggers's hiding place with another pack. "I got lost getting to the top," she said to Wickens. "Then the guards came, Juniper—"

"Just take us there," Wickens said. That edge sounded like it had been stropped thin and sharp.

She turned her back on Wickens, but looked over her shoulder at Brink.

"Go!" Wickens yelled. "If Sam bleeds . . ."

But she was already gone into the dark on her bare feet. Whistles blew again, and now voices carried from the east.

Wickens dragged Eggers after her, and Brink took up the last spot in the short file. He gripped the stock of the Sten as hard as he could, and glanced back at the German dead in the grass. The knife once buried hilt deep in his chest was gone.

Kirn stepped out of the onion stink of the Hotel Commes and into the cobblestone street. Another fine day ahead, but still cool before dawn. He brought up the collar of his overcoat, then put his good hand under that coat to scratch. The *Wulewub* mattress had been thick with bed lice, though that had been the least of his worries. He had jammed a chair under the latch of the thin door and slept with his Walther alongside the bed, the safety off, afraid that some *maquisard* would come into the room to murder him.

Kirn lit his first Eckstein of the day.

He'd wasted yesterday afternoon by returning to Jusot's house, but all he'd done was make it a shambles as he spilled out the contents of drawers and rummaged through closets looking for clues to Wollenstein's typhus lie. Nothing. He'd covered the dead doctor with a dusty, straw-flecked blanket stolen from the barn while the Feldwebel took the cob back to a stall, fed it oats, and filled its water bucket. Then they'd ridden the noisy BMW, him squeezed into the sidecar again, back to Port-en-Bessin. The motorcycle and its leather-coated driver drew more attention in the village than his banged-up Renault, so Kirn wasn't surprised that when he stepped up to the door of the Police Nationale, the old gendarme was waiting in its frame. He dangled his bronze Kriminalpolizei disc on its chain in front of the old man's face, and for a minute Kirn thought the gendarme would run. No, the policeman had stammered in answer to his question, there are no Jews here. No, no one sick. Kirn thought about telling the gendarme about Jusot's body—even *Wulewuh* deserved a coffin—but he didn't. He didn't need gossip making things difficult.

The morning's first Eckstein nearly gone, Kirn used it to light a second. He'd woke before dawn with the realization that the Jews were likely not in Port-en-Bessin after all. If Tardif told the truth and the Jews *had* come to Port-en-Bessin, they weren't here now.

The reason had come to him when he looked out the dark hotel window and at the dim masts of the fishing boats. The village was a port. Ports had boats. Boats took things, even Jews, to other places.

Kirn stepped out into the morning, walked one street to the center of town, such as it was, and again found the Police Nationale. He made the old gendarme, Lesueur, pull on his jacket and boots and walk him to the harbor another four streets away. Although the low-tide smell was easy enough to follow with his nose, Kirn wanted Lesueur to help navigate the men who would be there.

About three dozen fishing boats were roped to the long stone quays that bordered the narrow inner harbor. No more than sixty or seventy meters wide at its widest, at places the harbor was barely forty meters across. The shuttered houses looked down over it, and at the end, where the inner harbor spilled into the outer, towered a whitewashed, six-storied building, tall faded letters across this end spelling CASINO. No card games of rami or shimmy now, however, only MG-42 machine guns in the oceanfront windows and a PAK-40 antitank gun stuffed into the cellar, its long barrel sniffing through a grating just above the pavement.

The quay was crowded with men in patched coats and soft ragged caps. Some carried nets from poles where they had been hung to dry and mended the day before. Others sat on the flat stones of the quays and smoked hand-rolled cigarettes. They were all old or middle-aged. The young were long gone; dead in the war of 1940 or taken to the Reich for labor or perhaps become *maquisards*.

"Are all the boats here?" Kirn asked. The gendarme Lesueur stared, the gray stubble on his cheeks making him seem older than yesterday.

"I don't understand."

"This is a small place. You know everyone. I think one boat is missing, or it's been gone and came back again."

"I don't know every boat."

"Ask them." Kirn pointed to the nearest boat. "I want you to ask each captain if all the boats are here or if one was gone overnight . . ." Kirn began, and then made sure he had it right, "three days ago."

"You want me—"

Kirn sighed—he was tired of the *Wulewuhs* pretending to be dim. "And don't tell them who I am."

"No," Lesueur said.

That surprised Kirn. He took in the old man, whose eyes were now large under bushy gray brows. Kirn didn't waver, nor did Lesueur glance away. God, he was sick of these games. He looked around the quay, saw a woman across the way with a small pail of paint and a brush ready to touch its blue end to a door, and went to her. He took the pail, the brush, too, with only a glare, and walked to the nearest boat. Kirn stepped onto its deck.

A man blocked his way. The fisherman was almost as old as Lesueur, but his face was lined deeper and the hair that showed under his cap thicker, with more black than gray.

"This paint," Kirn said, dipping the brush and letting the blue drip onto the deck, "means a boat doesn't sail today or the rest of the week. No fish. Hungry mouths, I expect." His French was accented, he knew, so the *Wulewuh* would understand he wasn't just some bureaucrat with a temper.

"What do you want?" the fisherman asked. His eyes took in Kirn, gauged him.

Kirn held the brush against the glass windows in the small wheelhouse. "One boat's missing. Which?" The fisherman's eyes flickered. There it was; one *was* gone, not, as he feared, gone and returned, which would make it harder to find if these *Wulewuh* kept their traps shut. "Whose boat?" Kirn asked, and when the fisherman didn't answer, he drew a thick blue line across the glass.

Kirn dropped the brush back into the pail and turned for the quay, but where boat met stone half a dozen more fishermen stood. "I hope you have a lot of paint," the oldest in the front rank said. His white skin was thin as first ice, almost as transparent. The veins were blue cracks in that ice.

"You touch me and I'll hang your cocks in the Petit Lycée by nightfall," said Kirn. He wasn't afraid, not yet, but he wondered if he could drop the paint and reach the Walther in time.

"What do you want?" the old ice man asked. Kirn didn't answer, only held the paint pail and took in each fisherman. The old man turned to the owner of the boat Kirn had just marked. "Ferre, what does he want?"

"The name of the boat that's not here," said Ferre from behind Kirn.

"Tell him, what's it to us?" yelled someone in the back of the thickening crowd. Whoever talked was hidden by men in front of him. Coward. "They're gone to the bottom—"

"Shut up. Tell him nothing!" another shouted.

The group edged nearer, the ancient one close enough for Kirn to smell the morning's wine on his breath. A pair of low voices mumbled from the back. Kirn counted—first to five, then ten—and still the oldest one stood his ground.

"Pilon," the old fisherman said finally. "He didn't sail Wednesday morning with us. I haven't seen his boat since. Nor his daughter."

"Pilon," said Kirn.

"Don't say another word, Gerald!"

"Claude Pilon," said the old man. "Always sails with his daughter, Alix."

Kirn waved the brush, now free of the pail, to shut up the old man. He didn't need a history lesson on the Pilon family. He tossed the pail into the water, and handed the brush to the old man. "Go fish, then," Kirn said, and stepped off the boat to slip through them like he imagined fish sometimes slipped through their nets.

Alix led them south, down lanes that were tunnels with hedgerows for walls and trees for the roof, all of it dark and smelling of rot, the mud in the pathways cold between the toes of her bare feet.

They were slowed by Eggers, but they knew where they were going and the *boche* didn't. Within fifteen minutes they'd left the whistles behind. It wasn't hard; she knew this ground. Henri had been from Colleville, a few kilometers to the west, and the two of them had tramped these lanes and fields those last summer Sundays to find private places where they could make love. An empty barn here, an orchard there. Even though that had been five years past, Alix remembered the ground. She smiled at the thought. Her back had felt the ground more than once, Henri pressed against her, his face both determined and absent.

Henri was gone, but the ground was still here.

Only once, when she heard a motor in the distance, did they pause. They crouched around a broken-backed wagon at the edge of a field as the light changed from black to gray. The car or truck finally puttered on its way.

They walked nearly three hours to make the five kilometers to Étréham, but by the time the sun was over the trees, they were squatting at the gate to Tardif's house. Alix held the Sten and listened to a moan behind her. Juniper let the old man slide to the ground with his back against the brick wall. "There's a barn across the lane," she said, pointing to the wall opposite, its wide wooden gate open, too, and the narrow end of the stone barn showing in the gap. "He'll be safe there."

"Where are you going?" Juniper asked as she straightened up.

"To see if Papa's friend is home."

She caught Frank's eyes for a moment. Alix didn't say anything to him or even motion him to follow, but when she ran for the door of the Tardif house, she heard his boots on the packed dirt courtyard behind her, just the slightest hitch in his steps.

"It looks like no one's home," he said as he stood beside her.

She put a finger to her lips, then pointed to the broken latch. She pushed the door with a finger and it swung inside and open. First she brought up the Sten so it pointed into the dim kitchen. "Madam? Monsieur?" she called. "Josette?" All she heard was a buzzing.

Alix stepped into the kitchen on her dirty feet. A scent, like fish guts left in the sun, smothered the room. Someone had pulled off the blackout curtain and left it a pile. She went into the next room where the smell was even stronger. Josette was slumped in a chair, head back, legs braced wide, and her dress a bundle above her thighs. She was black like an Algerian.

"Josette," Alix whispered. Flies settled at the girl's eyes. Some German did this. Raped her. Frank stepped past to look down at the dead black girl, but he didn't touch. Without a word, he headed for the doorway into the rest of the house, and then she heard the sounds of his boots on stairs. Alix looked again at Josette and remembered the Jews.

She hurried after Frank up the steps, then down the corridor. Where the stink was thick as fog, she caught up. Alix peeked around Frank's shoulder into this room where the sunlight laid a square onto a bed, and on the horrible things in it.

Two bodies lay side by side, facing apart. Monsieur was not as black as the other, who was swollen exceedingly fat, but it must be madam. A green blanket covered both, neither completely.

"Don't come in," said Frank.

"They're dead," she said. She stayed at the doorway, the Sten like an anchor in her hand that kept her there.

"Someone else has been here, looking. The girl downstairs, her, too. They were looking for buboes, dark lumps, that's why they'd pulled at her dress like that," Frank said. He turned to face her. "They had the pestilence, all three of them."

La peste. A name, finally, for what was loose. For what had killed Papa.

Alix trembled and she let the Sten fall to the floor. She slid to the floor alongside it, one leg tucked under her and the other out straight. Papa had been dark when she'd seen him last, and she wondered if he'd looked like this at the very end. She cried no tears for the Tardifs, but the look of them kept her legs weak, and she stayed on the floor. Virgin Mother.

Frank squatted in front of her. She wanted to feel his touch. Anyone's touch.

"I'm sorry," he said, and she looked up into his blue eyes. Frank put his hand on her knee. Small bandages, perhaps once white but now graying with dirt, were wrapped around his last three fingers. This man was so odd.

From her spot, she could see a small green box under the bed. Frank followed her gaze, bent to look, saw the package for himself, and gingerly picked it up. Eckstein No. 5, the label said, *zigaretten*, black on the green.

"*Boche*," Alix said. "Only they smoke those things."

"Give me your hand." But she shook her head and stood on her own. Her legs were shaky, but she made herself take the two steps to the foot of the bed. There was a dark star at Tardif's temple, and the pillow under his head wasn't black from fabric, but from blood. His skin, deep blue, was tight, as if he'd gained weight since she'd last seen him three days ago.

"It was a kindness?" she asked, her look going from madam to monsieur to madam again. Madam's face was a rotted pumpkin. She prayed Papa had not looked the same in his last moment.

"No, not a kindness," Frank said. He threw the Eckstein package into a corner. His voice was rough. "Too late for that."

Wollenstein wanted coffee, even Pfaff's horrible coffee. He rubbed at his eyes. But there was no coffee. Aspirin. He yanked open a drawer in the desk, and shoved aside the Nagant lurking there, pushed away the cold metal of the Russian revolver—Nimmich's gun, bought from one of the Ukrainians who worked in the culturing barn—and groped for the packets of aspirin powder he remembered seeing there once. Nothing.

He slammed the drawer, stared at the journal again. "All eight, are you sure?" he asked. The paper didn't answer, but Nimmich did.

"Yes, all eight. Right as rain," Nimmich said. "Strain number 211, this one works." Wollenstein looked at the beaming young man who had been with him since Sachsenhausen. A good worker, clever once he was pointed in the right direction. His word could be trusted.

Unlike Himmler's. The sourness in Wollenstein's stomach boiled again. Urged on by his lackey Kammler, the Reichsführer was going to steal everything. For a moment Wollenstein couldn't think, the pain in his stomach was so great and the ache in his head so enormous. A genius, that's what Himmler had called him, and in the next breath robbed him.

Wollenstein looked up. It was early morning, the sun over the trees showing through the window. Once a barn for farm tools and seed, he'd turned this into another workshop, had his men cut windows and add electric lights and install oil feeds for the burners scattered on the benches that wrapped around its edges. The building was ten meters long by eight wide, solid beams at its corners bracing the slate roof, rough wooden planks its siding. The joints between the planks had been plugged with mortar, and the animal and hay and dirt and dung odors sealed under the plaster and whitewash that covered the interior. Even in the winter it was warm, what with the burners under flasks distilling solutions. It was his favorite place on the farm.

If Nimmich's notes were correct, the *Tiefatmung*—the ridiculous name Himmler demanded he use in the enciphered reports—was ready. Nimmich's strain number 211 had been given to the eight Jews in half the sealed barracks in a series of five injections, one cc each, the first injection at the onset of symptoms. And number 211 had kept the *pestis* away. Amazing.

The control group of eight, however, would not live. Four of that number had not been given injections; the other four had, but not until forty-eight hours after symptoms showed. Wollenstein remembered the little Jew and how she'd waved at him through the glass. She had been one of those.

Four years he and Nimmich had spent on this, starting at the concentration camp of Sachsenhausen, with tuberculosis first. It had infected not just the prisoners but the guards, too, even struck down Achter, his assistant then. Wollenstein had devoured everything he could find on the subject, papers and journals, drove the thirty kilometers into Berlin to research there. He'd started to look for a cure in the actinomycetes found in manured soils and later, God help him, in the throats of chickens. Nimmich had been the one to think of chickens.

But he had not found the antibiotic then. Heydrich had plucked him from Sachsenhausen after the camp's commandant had suggested his chief doctor's talents were wasted on Jews and homosexuals and political prisoners. Heydrich was the one who had brokered the deal for the bacilli from the Japanese in exchange, Heydrich had told him, for five hundred kilos of uranium oxide and the technical drawings for a new type of aircraft. Heydrich had not lived to see the blockade runner arrive from Indochina—in between, the Czechs killed him with grenades in Prague—but the plan had been set in motion, and Himmler took it under his wing.

All along, Wollenstein had not given up on tuberculosis. He had brought Nimmich with him to Normandy, and together they continued, even as they worked to re-create the *Japsern* manufacturing process for the plague bacilli. Wollenstein had had an epiphany while cleaning some slides, a chore he never left to others: tuberculosis and the plague shared a characteristic. Both were caused by gram-negative bacilli. A treatment for one might be a cure for the other.

And if an antibiotic existed, the *pestis* could be used anywhere, even near German troops.

And now they had done it. The antibiotic—he named it streptomycin, after the *Streptomyces griseus* fungus from which it came—not only inhibited the growth of *Pasteurella pestis* in vitro, on the cultures placed in the glass dishes, but in vivo, in people infected with pneumonic plague. The surviving Jews were proof.

This was the ammunition he needed to keep Himmler and Kammler from stealing his work.

"What do you want me to do with the Jews?" asked Nimmich.

Wollenstein came out of his daydream. "What?"

"The Jews."

Wollenstein thought. "Don't send them to Caen like the others."

"But we don't have a crematorium," Nimmich said. "The infected ones, we've always—"

"Talk to Pfaff, he'll know what to do," said Wollenstein, pressing his temple with a finger. He didn't want to think about it—the little girl with the doll deserved better. "Tell Pfaff to do it tomorrow night. And I don't want that SD watching," Wollenstein said. Nimmich stared at him, the tic flickering in the boy's eye. From working with too many invisible dangerous things, that's what made the tic. Wollenstein caught himself rubbing his hands together and pulled them out of sight. "I don't want them digging their own pit, tell Pfaff that."

"I'll tell him."

Wollenstein looked around the shed. Only one of the burners was fired. The flask over it held a furiously boiling cloudy liquid. "Why are you distilling just one?" he asked.

"I wanted to explain the results of the latest tests before I made more."

"How many doses do we have? Of this?" Wollenstein tapped a finger on the journal in front of him.

"Not even two dozen," Nimmich said.

Wollenstein again looked at the journal, the columns and rows of numbers and times and names. Jews had names here. He wondered which name meant the little girl. Sarah? Rachael?

"Make more," he said, now looking up. "Around the clock. Bring Traugott or Fresse from the culturing barn to help. I want as much of this made," and he pointed to the bubbling flask on the bench across the shed, "as soon as possible."

"Herr Doktor," said Nimmich, nodding.

I have only four days now, Wollenstein thought. To make the sprayers work, put the Me-110 and the Junkers into the dark over southern England, and mist the encampments and harbors crammed with millions of soldiers. Or Himmler will take this from me and give it to Kammler.

Wollenstein wished he could stuff *der Ofenmann* into one of his own ovens. That would solve his problem.

Ten

Brink breathed the smell of his Grootvader's barn, and for a moment, saw the quiet old Dutchman squatting on the stool with hands pulling teats under one of his three skinny cows. Grootvader vanished but the smells remained. Manure, old straw, the sweet scent of newer hay, dusty grain. He sucked it in like tobacco and tasted it on his tongue, in his throat, closed his eyes against the moment, opened them again.

This barn lacked cows, animals of any type. But it did have a truck, tan with dark, dried mud clinging to the tires and packed in its wheel wells. Rather than the usual canvas hood, a box sat on its back.

He went to where Wickens had piled hay to make a bed in a corner and looked down at Eggers.

"Piss off," the rat-faced man said. He tried to grin, but ended up only gritting his teeth.

"Do something," Wickens said. He looked up from Eggers's side.

Brink took in Eggers's arm. On the walk from the bluffs, he'd tied gauze tight around the forearm, but it was already soaked and bloody creeks escaped the dam and ran for the wrist. The arm was broken, too, for there was a long, thick ridge where it should be smooth and flat.

"Any more gauze?" he asked.

"That's the last," Wickens said.

"Don't let this wanker touch me again, Junni," Eggers said quietly.

But he felt Wickens's eyes on him, Alix's, too, so he kneeled, lifted the gauze, and probed the entrance wound. It welled with blood. Eggers moaned, moved as he tried to get away from Brink's fingers. The bullet had passed through and through, fracturing the ulna certainly, likely the radius, too. It may have nicked the ulnar artery, although the blood could just as easily be from the tissue damage. The hole on the posterior was an inch and a half wide. Eggers was lucky the bone had deflected the bullet or it would have pierced his ribs and entered his chest. There was a rip in his shirt to show the bullet's odd path, between his arm and body, as it had twisted out.

"He's lost blood," Brink said. His hands were steady from the practice—Nawls and the boy on the torpedo boat—and it was coming back to him, what a physician did. He picked up the aid pouch that Wickens had pulled from the pack, found the sulfa in its paper wrapping, ripped it open and sprinkled the powder over the wounds, entrance and exit. He ripped up Eggers's undershirt for a dressing and tore the lining from the old man's coat, tied everything around the wound using laces from the man's boots. Wickens beat out a dusty blanket he'd found in the back corner of the barn and brought it to cover the old man.

Brink had seen a morphine syrette in Wickens's aid pouch, and pulled that out, too. But Eggers's chest rose and fell in short, too-shallow breaths; he was sliding into shock. Morphine would cut his pain, but it might kill him. Brink slipped the syrette into his own coat pocket.

He sat back on his heels and suddenly knew what was going to happen to Eggers. It wouldn't matter what he did. Without proper medical treatment, Eggers was going to die. The wound and the long walk would be too much. It might take a few days, but Eggers wouldn't make it. Either the shock would take him, or infection.

"Do something." Wickens sounded almost frantic.

"Everything was in my bag."

"You should have held on to it, you fuck," snarled Wickens. He reached for Brink's coat, grabbed its dark cloth in a bunched fist, and jerked him from his crouch. "You're worthless, Brink, you're bloody worthless. You stood up, you stupid arse, and got Sam shot, didn't you?" Spit flew from his mouth.

Brink wondered if Wickens was going to punch him.

"Do something!" Wickens shouted. He drew Brink closer, yanked at the coat so their faces were level.

Brink put his hands on Wickens's chest and gently shoved back. He wasn't afraid of Wickens. Not when he had other enemies, much more murderous ones, running through his body. "That's the best I can do," Brink said.

"Junni," whispered Eggers, pale as a twice-boiled sheet.

"Sam, shut up, please," Wickens said lovingly as he bent down again.

"Fuckin' frogs, Junni," said Eggers softly. "Tol' you they'd be death of us."

"If we can get him to a doctor who has proper instruments, I might be able to stop the bleeding," Brink said. "He needs blood. A transfusion. I may need to amputate—"

"Don't let that fuckwit take me fuckin' arm, Junni," Eggers whispered. His voice was like a dreamy echo it was so faint. "Please."

"I won't let him," said Wickens. "He won't touch you, I swear." The anger was almost drained from his voice.

Eggers hadn't heard him; he was out cold.

Brink went to the truck and sat on the dirt floor, his back to the muddy wheel. Alix turned to him from her spot on an upturned wooden bucket, carefully peeling an apple with a long-bladed knife, the steel six or eight inches. It was the knife Wickens had pushed into the German on the bluff. The peel curled off the apple in a long spiral. *"Il va mourir, n'est-ce pas?"* she asked calmly.

In the sunlight streaming through the broken window, she was pretty, although the tone of her question made Brink shiver inside.

"He'll die?" she asked again, biting into the bare apple. Brink rubbed his right ankle above the short boot top, where the break from '37 ached. "I think he'll die," Alix said through her chewing. The flatness of her voice gave Brink the creeps. He closed his eyes and heard the apple core land in the dirt somewhere far away. "Where is your bag?" she asked. "With your doctor things?"

He kept his eyes closed. "At the bottom of the ocean," he said.

A moment passed, then, "The tablets you gave me, the ones to keep the sickness away. They are gone?" Alix asked.

"Yes," he said, still with shut eyes. That and the A17, the syringe and its needles, and everything else, including things that might save Eggers.

"Comme lui, je vais mourir," Alix said.

Brink opened his eyes and looked at her. It hadn't been the paint on the hospital walls that had made her eyes green. Brilliant green, like cornfields at dawn in June. Her hand was in her hair again, twisting it, but she didn't look afraid.

She was like Kate that way. Kate had been fearless, never afraid to be smarter than the men around her. It was the thing that drew him first. But Kate had had a flaw: that fearlessness had gone too far. She'd tested the actinomycin on herself because she didn't have enough fear. He'd had his doubts about that strain and told her, but she hadn't listened.

He hoped Alix would listen when it mattered.

Yet this woman was not Kate. Kate might have been prettier—that dark red hair of hers turned heads—but Alix had dived off the MTB and swam to shore, stood up to Wickens, who smelled of menace more than any man he'd met, and ran after Germans. Peeled apples with a knife that had killed a man. For all her courage, Kate wouldn't have dreamed of doing those things.

"You're not going to die," Brink said, got up slowly, and went back to the corner with the silent Eggers and Wickens. He picked up the canvas aid pouch and shook out the white cardboard box, half the size of a package of cigarettes. SULFADIAZINE, 8 X TABLETS, the print said on the flat box.

"Is there another kit?" he asked, and Wickens turned from the unconscious Eggers.

"No," the Englishman said. "Wot you doing?"

"Taking these."

"Sam needs them."

"She needs them more," Brink said, and nodded toward the upturned bucket where Alix sat, unable to understand their English.

Wickens wrapped his fingers around Brink's and the flat carton of sulfa-diazine tablets. His hand was like a clamp.

"Give them over," Wickens said.

The pain jumped as Wickens squeezed harder, but Brink didn't drop the carton. "They won't do him any good. By the time infection starts, he'll be dead," Brink said.

The pressure on his hand built to a peak, then vanished as Wickens released him. "Wot kind of doctor bay you? You can't even help a man with a simple wound."

"A good one," Brink said quietly.

"Then be one, for Christ's sake."

"You want me to sit with him, I will. I can set his break if you want. But there's nothing else I can do."

"Get the fuck away from us, then," said Wickens.

Brink walked back to Alix, tore open the flat carton, and shook out two tablets. He dropped the sulfadiazine into her palm and put the carton in the pocket of his worn coat. Alix looked at the tablets, and asked, "How many more of these?"

"Six."

"Enough for . . ."

"I don't know."

Alix swallowed the first tablet dry. "What are you doing here, monsieur?"

"Frank," he said. "Just Frank."

"Why are you here?" She grimaced as she choked down the second tablet. "You're here to heal those with the . . . the pestilence?" She answered her own question. "I think not. Not without your bag."

"I'm looking for a medicine," he said, keeping his voice low so Wickens wouldn't hear. The truth, sometimes that worked, although he'd used it so rarely the last years that it felt like a stranger. "The *boche* . . ." he stopped. Those green eyes ate at him. "I think the *boche* have a medicine that cures the pestilence."

"And this medicine . . ." She picked up another apple from the crate beside her, rolled it idly in her hand a moment, then tossed it. His hand went up automatically and the apple smacked into his palm. "Where is this medicine?" she asked.

More truth was necessary. "I don't know. But your friends, they may know."

She shook her head.

"The one who makes the pestilence," Brink said. "He makes the medicine."

"You know this, or only think this?"

Brink shrugged. "I think this."

She looked at him for several seconds, her head cocked to the side, then she nodded. "I'll take you to Clavette," she said. "He's another in my Armée Secrète. He may know where the Jews come from. If what you say is true, we are both looking for the same *boche*." She plucked another apple from the box beside her and bit into it.

That moment, Wickens spoke from his place next to Eggers. In English. "Just so you know, Doctor, when this is over, if Sam dies, I'm killing you," he said.

"What did he say?" Alix asked.

Brink thought of Alix's father breathing in his face, and didn't answer. Instead he peeled the strip of tape from the little finger on his left hand. Two days. He squeezed the tape into a dirty white pebble and threw it under the truck.

The Pilon house was near the small central square of Port-en-Bessin, a plain stone house with red flowers in two wooden boxes on either side of the steps. Like all the houses on this cobbled street, it was hard by its neighbors.

Kirn saw a woman with a shawl draped over her shoulders step from a doorway three houses down, a short white dog hard on her heels. The terrier saw them first, braced its front legs, and as if it was a fierce thing, barked. The sounds echoed up and down the street. The woman turned, stared. Kirn tugged at the brim of his brown hat in greeting and smiled, but she saw through that—word was out who he was, he thought—and glared back. The little dog stayed where it was, kept barking.

The gendarme didn't come up the steps of the Pilon house. Kirn tugged the Walther from his pocket with his good hand, and rapped its butt against the door. Chips of peeling red paint flaked like snow from the door. He banged the pistol against the wood again for another scarlet snowstorm.

"They may not be home," said Lesueur lamely.

Someone was. Kirn could hear noise beyond the door. He pointed the pistol at the step, but kept his finger near the trigger. The safety was off.

The door opened a crack, and part of a face showed in the gap. A woman's face.

"Yes?" she asked, looking first at him, then past him at Lesueur.

"Open the door," Kirn said. She saw the Walther and the crack between door and frame narrowed. Kirn pushed against the door with his foot, then his shoulder.

"What do you want?" she asked, retreating. She was short and solid, with dark hair pinned up, wisps loose at one ear. Late forties at least, with the face careworn enough to match the age.

"Your husband, where he is?" Kirn asked. Inside the house, a child cried. He followed the woman as she backed away, but was careful not to get too close. If this woman's husband had found the Jews and taken them to England, she might be harboring Wollenstein's pestilence.

"I . . . I don't know where he is," she stammered, still looking at the Walther.

"Your husband's boat has gone, you know that, don't you? Gone since Wednesday, and here it's Saturday."

The child yowled. Kirn waved the Walther to tell her to move farther into the house, and Lesueur followed. Madam Pilon led them down a short corridor and into a kitchen. One boy, perhaps ten years old, sat at the long, battered table in the room's center, slowly chewing at a thick-crusted slice of bread. Another boy, a few years younger, sat on the floor in a corner by a door, hands wrapped over his head, crying, snuffling, crying again. He looked up at Kirn through reddened eyes. None of them looked sick. The kitchen smelled clean, of bread baked not long before.

"I hear your daughter is also missing," Kirn said.

"I haven't seen them since Wednesday. They went fishing with the rest and they haven't returned."

"Where are the Jews they found?"

It was as if he'd slammed the Walther against her face. She reached out a hand for the table.

"So it's true, they found Jews," he said. "Sick Jews, I hear."

"I don't know what you're talking about." The boy at the table kept at his bread and stared at him with lifeless eyes. Kirn glanced at the one on the floor. The little one shivered, frightened out of his wits like his mother. But this older boy, he'd be trouble someday.

"Don't lie," Kirn said.

She reclaimed her courage. "I don't know where my husband is. He sailed and he's not returned."

Kirn was tired of this. He wasn't Gestapo, but he had been a policeman too long to have much patience. He went to the corner and with the claw of his right hand pinched the youngest boy's collar and yanked him to his feet. Kirn squatted with the boy's face pointed away from him, just in case. He scratched the Walther against the boy's earlobe. The child whimpered once, twice, then sniffed at tears.

"Where did your husband go with the Jews?" he asked, not able to look into her eyes, using her little one like this.

The woman's face became red and her hand against the table trembled. "Please, please don't hurt him," she whispered.

Lesueur muttered something, but Kirn ignored the gendarme. "Your husband. His boat. The sick Jews," Kirn said. He rested the edge of the Walther's barrel against the boy's skull. The child squirmed, but Kirn tightened his one-armed grip.

"England," Madam Pilon said quietly. Short sobs broke from her. Between them she mouthed, "Wednesday" and "Alix" and "England" again.

"You're certain?" Kirn asked.

She nodded, whispered, "England."

England.

The child roped by his arm squirmed, twisted to face him, breathed dampness on his face. He released him, and the boy folded against his mother's plain blue dress. Kirn rubbed at his face with the sleeve of his overcoat, then pointed the Walther again, this time at the woman. "Damn you, and your damn Jew-loving family," he snarled, "poisoning everyone with the pestilence . . ." and he pushed the Walther into her face, the muzzle stopping centimeters from her nose. Her eyes got huge, but she didn't beg. Kirn wiped at his mouth once again.

The older boy at the table said *"boche,"* quietly but plainly. Kirn twisted to look and they locked eyes. If the war went on long enough, he would grow up to be a *maquisard*.

At first Kirn thought about reaching across the table and slapping the boy for the insult, but instead the word gave him pause. It wasn't the Jews' fault, was it, that the little one was sick. It was Wollenstein's fault. *Boche.* Yes, indeed. Wollenstein was the enemy. He looked back to the mother again. "Who helped them?" Kirn asked. "They didn't take these Jews and send them off to England by themselves, did they?"

"I don't know, I swear to you, I don't know anything," Madam Pilon said, her words astride hiccups.

"You know something."

"No, Claude tells me nothing, he would never tell me names. I didn't want to know—"

Kirn looked in her green eyes and knew she was lying. He wanted a cigarette to chase the bad taste in his mouth, like when he'd looked into the back of the Daimler. He hated this, but sometimes a policeman needed to be a madman. "I'll have to hurt you, or them, if you don't tell me," he said.

The woman pulled the boy closer to her.

"Alix," said the older boy at the table.

"Alix," Kirn said back. The mother shut up her hiccuping.

"Alix is the one you want. She's the one who runs the Armée Secrète here." The boy's eyes remained dead. Perhaps not a *maquisard*, Kirn thought, the way he betrayed his sister. Perhaps he had other plans.

Kirn lowered the Walther and nodded for the boy to continue.

"Don't say anything, Jules," the mother barked.

The boy brushed a hank of hair off his forehead. "Papa is dead, isn't he? Drowned with Alix."

"Jules!"

"Mama, shut up," the boy said, his little voice hard. That and his eyes gave Kirn a moment of nervousness. This one would be evil one day. But the mother, she did what her little son said, and stayed quiet. "I know the friends of Alix and Papa," the boy said. "They play *Belote* together, all of them."

Kirn turned to Lesueur, who mumbled, "A card game."

"She doesn't know anything," said small Jules, and those dead eyes darted for his mother. Kirn wondered if Madam Pilon realized what her son had become. "I do. I know where Alix buried her radio in the garden, I can show you if you want." Kirn shook his head. "I followed them, I know where they play *Belote* and who is in their little *armée*."

Kirn moved the Walther so it pointed to the boy. He should shoot him now, he thought, before his mother's heart was broken.

"I'll take you to them," the boy said. He didn't blink at the pistol. "For a thousand francs."

"*Jules!* Don't say another—"

"For a thousand francs, I'll take you to them."

"*Jules! No!*"

"How does bread get on the table now, Mama?" Those hateful eyes stared at her. Back to him. "A thousand francs."

"*Jules!* Don't say another—"

"Papa's gone, Mama, Alix, too. Her mooning over that blockhead Henri all this time," Jules said. "She got Papa drowned, didn't she?"

Kirn shook his head at the little collaborator. "I don't have a thousand francs," he said. He put the Walther in his pocket. He wouldn't need the pistol to make this family do what he wanted, only money. He felt sorry for Madam Pilon.

"Eight hundred," the boy said. "For these men who took Alix's Jews."

A light blinked in Kirn's head. If the fisherman and his daughter had sailed for England, they must by now have either reached it or sunk, for they hadn't returned.

And no Jews meant no problem. All that was left was to tell the SS shit. First he'd do that, then he could look for the card-playing friends of Pilon.

"My Claude," the woman said softly as she held her good son closer to her. "Alix."

Kirn pulled aside Lesueur and told him that the woman and her boys were not to leave the house. Then, without a word to Madam Pilon or Jules, he left, slammed the flaking red door behind him, and lit an Eckstein.

The white terrier waited for him three doors down. Its mistress was gone, but the dog ran to Kirn and braced its stubby front legs like before and barked at him as if it knew what had gone on inside the Pilon house.

"Go away," Kirn growled at the little dog, but it barked back, with each yap edging closer. "Go away," he said again, this time in German, but the dog was as dense in that language as its own, so Kirn flicked the Eckstein at the creature. The cigarette caught the dog on its blunt wedge of a nose, and amid the sparks it yelped, turned, and with its tail low, ran back to its doorway.

Even the *Wulewuh* dogs hated him.

The Normandy countryside slid beneath the Storch as if it were painted on a long, unwinding roll of canvas. A stone barn with a high-pitched roof, a farm's house enclosed by one of the ever-present rock walls, wriggling green hedgerows surrounding small fields dotted with black-and-white milk cows. The little aircraft bounced in the morning air but remained low enough for Wollenstein to count the cows.

He looked over Sillmann's shoulder and out the windscreen. The propeller was less than a blur, its circle barely hiding what was in front. The Storch bounced again.

"Higher!" he shouted into the pilot's back.

Sillmann's head shook, he shouted something in return, then jabbed a finger up. Wollenstein craned his neck to look through the glass canopy above them, but there was nothing except blue sky interrupted by the occasional lumpy cloud. The weather was brilliant. What were the Allies waiting for?

The Storch banked left, left again in a quarter-circle, and took the Merderet River for a course north and west. Usually just a few meters broad, the Merderet was now flooded a kilometer, two kilometers, wide. Some bright mind had decided to open the La Barquette locks at high tide to let the ocean roll up the Douve, and then close them again at low tide to keep in the water. The flood backed up the Merderet, too, and would drown any paratroopers who tried to land, they said. The bridge at Chef du Pont, and the raised road above the marshes, was one of the few ways over the new lake.

It was risky testing in daylight like this, but he had no choice, not with Himmler's deadline only four days away. He would have to be very unlucky for someone to see the Storch, wonder what it was doing, and start asking the kind of questions that could lead back to him. The flooded marshes were the most isolated part of the Cotentin.

"Slow down!" Wollenstein yelled and Sillmann's hand went to the control at his left and the rattle of the engine quieted. "Slower!" Wollenstein said after peeking over Sillmann's shoulder and seeing the needle at eighty. Sillmann throttled back until the needle pointed to sixty. Below, the bright water of the too-wide Merderet glinted in the sunlight.

"Switch on the tank!" Wollenstein shouted, and Sillmann moved his hand to the wired controls bolted beside him. Wollenstein twisted in his seat—he'd not bothered to buckle the harness—so he could look through the circular panel at the rear of the canopy. At first he saw nothing, but as the seconds ticked by, the air behind the Storch turned faint red.

The red dye grew into a thin cloud trailing the Storch, its curves and billows twisting in the wash of the propeller. Good.

"Lower!" Sillmann nodded and the nose of the Storch dropped. The aircraft rattled and bumped, but every time Wollenstein looked, the mist remained. Far behind, it had spread into a ribbon a hundred meters wide and was drifting onto the water. Excellent.

Over Sillmann's shoulder, he saw the railroad causeway as a straight line above the flooded meadows, and beyond, a speck of a village to the north and west. Wollenstein glanced at the map on his lap. La Fiére.

He'd blended the dye with silica and some clay, ground into a powder that he thought approximated the *Pasteurella pestis*. It showed that the sprayer worked and gave him an idea of dispersion. Wollenstein twisted in the seat one last time to check the color, and caught the first interruption in the stream, a clean swath of air twenty meters long. Perhaps the tank had run dry.

"Is it empty?" he shouted. The pilot looked at a dial they'd mounted, and shook his head.

"Quarter full!" Sillmann shouted back.

Wollenstein looked back again and the red dust was there, then not. The Storch bobbed and weaved. He slumped in the seat. The finer he ground the powder the more the particles clung together, like talcum on hands, and stopped up the nozzles. But this spray was the longest yet, eight minutes by his watch. That was something.

One last twisting look, and Wollenstein saw that the red ribbon had returned. The nozzles weren't clogged after all.

"Back to the farm?" Sillmann shouted.

"Yes!" yelled Wollenstein, and turned to face forward again. "Close the valves!"

Sillmann said nothing, but the Storch banked, its nose sliding right, the left wing up, the right down. Wollenstein stared through the propeller's blur looking for landmarks, searching for the landing strip near his farm. There it was, a long, narrow slash through the irregular walls of the boscage.

"Lower!" he shouted. The Storch dropped and his head knocked against the ceiling. But he blinked against the sharp pain and reached for the flare pistol under the seat. Wollenstein broke open the breech, checked for the fat flare, then pushed at the small window beside him. Air rushed into the cockpit. "Back to sixty!" he yelled at Sillmann, and the engine's sound went from rattling to jarring.

Ahead he could see the landing strip, now just a kilometer away. The sun glared from one spot in the field, then another and another. The glass plates he'd set out on wooden stands in the grass. He couldn't see the men who were supposed to be on the strip, but they'd be there.

Wollenstein stuck the wide mouth of the flare pistol out the open window, thumbed back the hammer, and pulled the trigger. The flare sparked away from the Storch, trailing a line of brilliant green. That was the signal for those on the ground to look up.

"Switch on the valves!" Wollenstein yelled, and turned to watch the red ribbon return just as they approached the strip, too high to land but almost brushing the topmost leaves of the oak tree at its south end. He turned to the side window and tried to see if Pfaff had the men positioned properly, but he couldn't crane his neck far enough. "Turn off the valves!" he shouted. "And take us down, all the way. Sillmann, do you hear?"

Sillmann yanked the Storch around, its nose rising, then falling, Wollenstein's stomach doing the same. Sillmann pulled at levers and set the little aircraft on the grass. It rolled toward the oak, braked. As soon as the tires stopped turning, Wollenstein raised the door and jumped down.

One of the glass plates was just ten meters away. He plucked it from its stand, the plate held so it lay flat a meter above the grass. He tilted the glass so the sun would pick up the red dust. He thought he saw faint shadow, but wasn't sure. He'd forgotten his magnifying glass, but he couldn't wait. He spat on the plate, rubbed it with his fingertip in a wider circle on the glass. Pink, no question. Excellent. Excellent.

Pfaff came toward him and stopped a few meters away. Wollenstein looked around the field for the first time, counting the men arranged in the grass. Sixteen, as he'd ordered.

"Sturmbannführer" was all Pfaff said. His machine pistol was slung over a shoulder.

"Do you have the cloth?" Wollenstein asked. Pfaff nodded, a quirky movement. The Unterscharführer pulled a square from his pocket, dazzling white in the sun, clean because it had been cut from one of Wollenstein's own linen bedsheets.

"Now?" Pfaff asked. Wollenstein nodded and Pfaff put the cloth to his nose and blew.

"Again. Harder this time," Wollenstein said. Pfaff blew his nose again.

Wollenstein beckoned for the cloth. "Now spit," he told Pfaff as he took the square. Pfaff brought a new cloth to his mouth, hawked and spat into it.

Wollenstein looked at the first cloth. Mucus centered in the square, but it was clear with only a trace of yellow. He looked at Pfaff. "There's nothing here."

Pfaff shuffled his weight to the other foot, stared down at the cloth he'd spat into. When he glanced up, his eyes, small in the fleshy face, wouldn't hold a stare.

"Pfaff?"

"Sturmbannführer, I'm sorry, but I held my breath," Pfaff said, each word treading on the heel of the one before. "I couldn't help it, I'm sorry."

"I told you this was just a test," Wollenstein said. What a coward.

"I know what you said. But we could have used the Jews, don't you think?"

Wollenstein shook his head and walked for the nearest man, Ribe, who sat in the grass twenty meters off the center of the landing strip. The Jews wouldn't do. The control Jews were too sick to move, and those who had been touched with the needles wouldn't ever willingly take a deep breath again, he guessed, not after the powder had come out of the ceiling of their wooden prison and panicked them into beating their hands bloody against the walls.

"Blow," he told Ribe when the man had the white swatch to his nose. The pear-shaped man blew and handed him the cloth by its corner.

Red. The mucus was stained. Wollenstein looked into the linen. Not nearly like a bloodied nose, but pink, like the ears of a white cat perhaps. Ribe spat into the second cloth and Wollenstein looked there, too. The same. The saliva carried enough of the dye to make it one shade rosy, and if the Storch had had the *Pasteurella pestis* powder in the tank under its belly, more than enough, much more than enough, to turn Ribe black within one or three or six days. Excellent, extremely excellent. The sprayers worked.

For a moment he thought about walking to the house and telephoning Berlin—to the long gray façade at No. 8 Prinz-Albrechtstrasse, where the Reichsführer had waved him and Heydrich into his office that day years before—and demand to talk to Himmler. Everything is ready, he'd say. The next moonless night, he'd tell Himmler, the Me-110 and the Junkers would poison southern England.

But he didn't. Instead he walked to each of the others in the field and looked at their cloths, seeing enough pink to satisfy him. Although the quantity varied by the wind, it was enough to make them all into Ethiopians.

It would do the same to the damn Americans and English, whether they were in their camps across the Channel or struggling out of French surf.

Wollenstein felt like celebrating and went back to the Storch, where Sillmann lounged in the shade of his aircraft. He told Sillmann to climb in. Wollenstein followed to sit in the rear seat like before.

As Sillmann cranked the starter and throttled up the engine, Wollenstein unfolded his map, pulled a thick pencil from his tunic, and drew a line from Chef du Pont north to Quinéville, then east and north along the coast as far as Le Havre. He held the map in front of Sillmann. "Fly this course!" Wollenstein yelled against the surging engine. "I want to see the beaches between here and there."

"That's hours each way!"

Even Sillmann's arguing couldn't stifle his euphoria, and he shouted at the pilot to take it up. Sillmann turned the Storch in a tight circle, pulled out the throttle, and the machine leapt into the air. In a few minutes, Quinéville was below them. Sillmann banked the Storch over the coastline, its grass-held dunes rippling beneath them, and pointed the aircraft south and east, following the shore.

The sandy beaches, with their wire and obstacles—poles and tetrahe-drons of welded rails—rolled under them. Farther back, the outlines of trenches and gun emplacements could be spotted. The Storch was low, no higher than a hundred meters—low enough for him to see soldiers waving from those trenches.

As the Storch jounced in the warming air, Wollenstein kept an eye on the shoreline, and at each beach large enough for a landing, he made a cir-cle on the map.

Perhaps the *Pasteurella pestis* could keep them in England. But if not, he wanted to be ready when they jumped out of their boats and into the surf.

Kirn stepped out of the stone house and nodded to the guard at the door.

The captain who commanded this company of the II/916th, 352nd In-fanterie was still absent from his command post—this plain house facing the inner harbor—but his adjutant, an officer younger than this sentry, had let him place his telephone calls once Kirn showed his Kripo disc.

The connection crackled and spat in his ear, telling him it was passing through several switchboards. The man who came on the line the first time said he was Pfaff, an Unterscharführer, and in a wheezy voice told Kirn that the Herr Doktor was away. Out, leave a message. Kirn didn't. He wanted no confusion over what had happened to the Jews, and told this Pfaff that he would telephone again. He did, several times each an hour apart, the second and third calls broken by a meal of watery wine and old bread and a very good Pont l'eveque cheese at the Hotel Commes, the third and fourth separated by a nap in his room, boots left on and the Walther under his left hand.

He could have driven to Wollenstein to tell him this news, but if he did, how would he explain how he'd found him?

With Pfaff's raspy voice from the last conversation still in his ear, Kirn walked past the harbor and breathed the salt in the air. The fishing boats were still out, all except the same one left behind the day before, the one that leaned against the quay even lower in the water today. The fishermen who had crowded the flagstones near dawn had disappeared along with their boats, and the only *Wulewub* were two women sitting in chairs in front of a house near the corner. A clutch of *Landsers*, helmets off in the late afternoon sun and propped against a low wall, listened as their sergeant shouted at them to get off their lazy arses and march back to the beach for another work detail.

He glanced at his watch. He should go to little Pilon, he supposed, to see if the boy would tell him where his father's and sister's *maquis* comrades lived to wrap up the loose ends. He could promise the boy a few hundred francs.

Kirn came around a corner, the stone church, Port-en-Bessin's next biggest building after the casino, ahead and on his left. His old flat-faced Renault was where he'd left it, down the street on the right.

There was a crowd in the open space between the church and the row of shops. Mostly women, but a few old men and a scattering of children, were bunched near the door of the Police Nationale office. He couldn't see Lesueur over their heads, but he guessed the old man was there somewhere. Not watching the Pilon woman and her two sons as he'd been told.

Kirn stopped at his Renault, leaned against its radiator, felt it sag under his weight. He was close enough to the crowd to make out their voices, but not too close. He put his good hand in his coat and left it there, fingers touching the Walther as he listened to the first words.

"Lesueur! What did the *boche* say?" a woman yelled.

"It's Jews they're after." An old man that one.

"Jusot's sick?"

"*Jusot's dead, you imbecile!*"

"*Gestapo!*"

It was Babel. While Kirn watched, the outer edges of the crowd frayed as a few drifted past him back toward the harbor and its quays. A woman walked by, a little girl's hand tight in her own, almost dragging the child. A small gnome of a man, cane in hand, hobbled past as fast as his shuffling feet allowed.

Kirn wanted to push his way through the crowd and put the Walther against the gendarme's head. It wouldn't change things, but it might make him feel better. He wondered how the talk had started, thought about it a moment, and decided someone had found old, dead Jusot under the horse blanket outside his barn. And Jews? Lesueur had heard him speak the words *sick Jews* in the Pilon house, and the rest, like the talk of Gestapo, well, that was just the *Wulewuhs* jumping to conclusions.

Shit.

Kirn retreated up the street toward the harbor and the house with the company's command post. From the looks of things, the village was getting ready to run.

Kirn turned and jogged for help.

Alix stopped and put a hand over her eyes as a shield from the low afternoon sun. From this spot, this very spot beside the tall, knotted apple tree with the goiter on its trunk, she could see the green-streaked gray roof of Notre Dame des Flots in Port-en-Bessin. She'd come up this road countless times, but she'd never felt so eager to take the last few steps.

"Home?" Frank asked. He tugged at the straps of the old man's rucksack and wiped sweat from his face with the back of his hand.

"Home, yes," she said.

"There'll be no stopping," said Juniper. His ruck held a Sten broken into its pieces and tucked there, and like Frank he was dressed in the clothes and boots of a laborer. "I want to find Jusot," he said, looking at Notre Dame's tower above the trees.

In Tardif's barn, Juniper had asked if Port-en-Bessin had a doctor who might have the necessary things to treat Eggers, and she had told him about Jusot, who lived on the bluffs west of town. They'd left the unconscious Eggers in the barn after noon, Juniper not willing to abandon him before that. He'd set food and water by Eggers's side, a heavy black revolver as well, then had touched the man's hand tenderly. He'd never touched her that way.

The five-kilometer walk to Port-en-Bessin had been uneventful except for when they'd met a line of *boche* marching toward them, one of the patrols that always curried the lanes and fields and woods near the coast. They'd hid in a hedgerow easily enough.

Alix looked up at the sound of an engine. To the west, barely over the treetops, a little aeroplane droned from Port-en-Bessin, making first for the point where their road left the village and then taking the road as its guide. Square black crosses were plain on the underside of its narrow green wings. She craned her neck as it rattled overhead for the south, and as she turned, she noticed that Juniper had stepped off the road to take shelter under the shade of the apple tree.

"You look suspicious when you do that," she said.

"Did you see that?" Frank asked. He'd stayed in the road and still gazed after the aeroplane, which brushed over a line of alders a few fields to the south.

"See what?" Juniper asked as he came out from his hiding place.

"The tank under it. Did you see that?"

The aeroplane circled over the alders in such a steep spiral that one wing pointed at the ground.

"He's looking for a place to land," Juniper said quietly.

"Is he looking for us?" she asked.

Juniper shrugged.

"I don't think so," Frank said. "There was a tank of some sort under it, and something under its wing, too." The aeroplane ducked behind the alders and didn't reappear; it must have set down like Juniper said it would.

It didn't matter, Alix decided, and set out, letting her steps lengthen as long as they'd go, each step nearer home, the men following. Just past the line of willows that edged the last field, the road became more like a street—houses sprouted suddenly on both sides, the line between town and countryside razor sharp—and the street bent just enough to the left so that as she cleared the angle, she could see the square facing Notre Dame des Flots. It was packed with people.

It must be Sunday, Mass finished and people leaving. She had lost track of the days, tell the truth. She kept walking. Frank clutched her forearm and pulled her beside the stone facing of the second house into Port-en-Bessin. "It's only Mass letting out," she said.

"No," Frank said quietly, "it's Saturday," and she looked again into the square and saw that, indeed, people weren't coming out of the church. Lesueur, the old policeman who was afraid of his own shadow, had his office there. He stood on a box in front of his door, his head and shoulders above the crowd.

". . . the pestilence." Lesueur's voice bounced off the stone walls of the church and reached the doorway where they stood.

"I heard of reprisals!" screeched a woman.

"I . . . I don't know—" Lesueur began.

"Is Jusot truly dead?" another woman, this one unseen, shouted from the middle of the crowd.

The voices rose until they were a roar like surf. She could no longer pick out words among the noise of everyone talking and shouting and yelling.

The crowd blocked her way home, and Alix prepared to shove through. But Frank still had his hand on her arm and gripped it.

"Didn't you hear?" he asked. *"La peste."*

Eleven

Y ou can't," Brink said, his hand full of Alix's coat sleeve. She wriggled, but he held tight. "You promised to take us to Clavette. He has to help us find the *boche* who might have the medicine," he whispered. He nodded to the crowd in the square from which *la peste* was shouted still.

She looked up at him, those green eyes of hers cold as the country he'd come from.

"My mama . . ." she said.

"A few minutes won't matter." From the expression that flashed across her face, he could tell it was the worst thing he could have said. Bottle that look, he thought, and he could sell it for poison. "A few more minutes might make all the difference to us," he continued carefully, and nodded to Wickens.

"This way, isn't it?" Wickens asked. He pointed ahead and to the left, where the first side street angled away. "To the bluffs, where Jusot lives, isn't it?"

Alix squirmed one last time and Brink let go of her.

"We're going straight for this Jusot," Wickens said. "Then right back to Sam."

"Can't you hear, they just said Jusot's dead," Alix said.

"What?"

"Jusot is dead! Listen to them!" she yelled, waving an arm at the crowd forty yards away. Wickens backed off.

"Take us to Clavette," Brink said. "If he tells us what we need to know, we'll go to your mother." Time was slipping away. Brink glanced at his taped fingers. "I promise."

The wind blew at her short hair. She pushed it back into place behind her ears and looked at him as if she'd noticed the way his eyes had lingered on her face. "Yes," she said. "I do what I promise." She glanced at Wickens, who stared back at her.

"We have to find the plague, isn't that what we're here for?" Brink asked Wickens.

"Brink . . ." Wickens started, but stopped. He seemed like he was searching for words. "You're right. But as soon as we have wot we came for . . ."

Alix led them back the way they'd come. Brink followed, feeling Wickens's eyes on his neck. Twenty yards later, Alix turned left onto a dirt lane that cut behind a line of round willow trees. As they put the last house between them and the church, the noise of the crowd faded. They made another left a hundred yards farther, followed it until it became a narrow street where two-storied buildings loomed over the cobblestones, and kept to Alix's heels as she took them through more small streets.

Brink sniffed the air. It was going to rain soon, despite the brilliant morning. He glanced up at the clouds that were thickening into a single sheet. The wind began to pick up.

They passed a house where a twitchy young woman backed out of her door dragging a small carpet piled with belongings—a radio, a brown satchel, two cloth sacks—that she stacked onto a handcart. She pulled the empty carpet back to the house for more.

Port-en-Bessin was scared.

Alix took them closer to the harbor—Brink got a glimpse of the stone docks and a bit of slate-colored water—and although he knew the church and its square was behind him still, he couldn't see either.

Alix stopped and pointed to a simple stone house with a small garden out front. A stand of trees blocked any view of the harbor, but he could still smell the salt. "Clavette lives here," she said.

"Introduce us," Wickens said. He had a revolver, the black Webley, in his hand, his arm loose alongside his leg. When had he pulled that out?

Brink couldn't tell if Alix saw the gun, but she acted like she hadn't. "I did what I promised," she said. "I brought you to Clavette. *You* ask him your questions, Juniper. I'm going to my mama."

"You're not going anywhere until we find a doctor for Sam," Wickens said tightly. She noticed the revolver then.

Alix took a deep breath. "Who are you, Juniper?"

"Someone's worried about losing his friend, that's who," Wickens said. "We talk to this Clavette now that we're here, but then we go look for a doctor."

Alix glanced at the revolver again and without acknowledging Wickens, she approached the door. She tried the latch, then rapped at the wood. "Monsieur Clavette," she said. "It's Alix." Lowering her voice, she said, "It's Bouton."

Nothing. She led them to the back of the house, which faced a narrow cart path and, across that, a line of bushes half again as tall as he was. No one could see them back here. The door on this side was unlocked. Alix pushed it open, but Wickens stepped around her, the gun now up and pointed into the house.

"Clavette!" he said and went inside. Alix followed, and Brink kept close to her. *"Clavette!"* Wickens shouted. Brink shut the door. For a moment, the dim room was all black, but as he stood there, his eyes adjusted. Wickens was almost through the room and into the next when someone coughed from the corner.

"What do you want?" asked a rough voice. The voice coughed again, a long stretch of hard, hacking sounds, then spat. "God, my chest hurts." The hairs on Brink's arms stirred.

Wickens moved toward the corner and the direction of the voice.

"Wait," Brink said in English. The man hacked again, groaned, and retched. "He has it."

Wickens shrugged out of his pack, fumbled with it, and switched on a flashlight. He shone it on a face; the man lifted his hand to shield his eyes.

He sat on the floor in his corner. Both pants legs were flecked with vomit. His skin was flushed red—a hot fever, Brink knew—but there was a wash of blue around his mouth and on his lips. "Ahhh," Clavette said, his hands on his stomach. More coughing. "Shit."

"It's Bouton," Alix said. She was smart enough to keep her distance.

"Damn you and your father," Clavette said, wheezing. "I hope you both burn in Hell." He coughed, just a single sharp sound, like a dog's distant bark, then moaned again.

Brink stepped closer, obscuring the light for a moment until he stepped aside. "I'm a doctor, monsieur," he said. "I have some questions."

Clavette coughed several times, each time that hoarse bark. He groaned again and stretched out a leg. "Jusot was no good to me, was he? Go away, let me die in peace."

"The children and Madam Clavette, where are they?" Alix asked. She'd come up behind Brink's shoulder.

"I sent them away," Clavette said. "To my mother's." More coughing. "In Longues."

Brink knew this man's family might be carrying the plague, infecting more French towns. But there was nothing he could do about that. There wasn't time to run down every case.

"We must know where the Jews came from," Brink said. He pulled off Eggers's pack, dropped it beside the door, and came to Clavette. He stopped at six feet, and squatted. "It's important."

Clavette shivered in the flashlight's gleam. "Fuck the Jews. It was one of them that gave me this, wasn't it? I helped them out of the truck and that hag put her arms around me and I smelled her witch's breath, didn't I?"

"Did they say where they came from?" Brink asked. Clavette's fever wasn't the only symptom he presented. The man had chills. Nausea. Abdominal pains. And the coughing. And he stank. Not from the vomit, but as if he was going rotten inside. A smell a bit like cheese. Gangrene?

"If you're a doctor, make me well," Clavette said.

That got a snort out of Wickens. Brink kept his eyes on the dying man. "I can't, I have no medicine," he said. The two remaining sulfadiazine tablets in his pocket wouldn't do Clavette a bit of good.

"Is your father sick?" Clavette asked as he looked with red eyes at Alix.

"Yes," she said softly.

"Good," he said. "Good." He coughed up a watery stream of sputum that he wiped on his worn corduroys. "Tardif? What of him? Did he—"

"Dead," Brink said.

"I told Claude to leave them. Look what's happened . . ." Clavette's voice faded, and for a moment Brink thought he'd passed out.

"*Clavette!*" Wickens shouted and the man's eyes snapped open. He squinted against the light and his head moved back and forth as if he searched for something familiar. "What did the Jews say?" Wickens asked.

Clavette spat up again. There was red in the sputum now. "Ah, dear Mary, mother of . . ." the man whispered, moaning. He shivered.

"*Clavette!*"

His head rose at the shout and his eyes focused again. "Bouton, you bitch," he said to Alix. "Why didn't you just shoot us all, it would have been kinder than what you did."

Brink looked at Alix, whose face was frozen in a rictus of shock.

"*Clavette!* The Jews?" Wickens asked.

"Jews? Yes . . . the Jews." Clavette coughed some more, moaning again the sound of an animal. "One . . ."

"One what?" asked Wickens.

"Is he—" Alix began.

"Wake him," Wickens said.

Brink turned to the Englishman and got a face full of light from the flashlight. He put his hand up. "He doesn't know anything."

"Fuck." Wickens snapped off the flashlight. "This is bollocks," he said. Wickens stepped to Clavette, and the arm with the revolver extended and pointed down. He pulled back its hammer.

"What the hell are you doing!" Brink yelled, and stepped toward Wickens.

"If he has nothing to tell us, I'm going to put him down, for one, then I'm going to walk to the next bloody village to find another doctor, and then . . . then I'm going to march that doctor back to Sam. That's what I'm doing." Wickens pushed the revolver nearer Clavette. There was just a foot between muzzle and temple.

"You can't shoot—"

"Orders, Doctor, orders from on high. Very high." Wickens was almost whispering, almost talking to himself. "This is the only sure way to stop it, isn't it?"

"Wickens, don't do this."

For a wild moment, Brink thought Wickens was bluffing, but then the muzzle touched Clavette's temple.

Because Wickens's back was to him, he took the Englishman by surprise. He struck Wickens in the back of the neck, inches right of the spinal column where neck met shoulder, and the man stumbled. The revolver skittered over the wood floor. Wickens fell into the unconscious man in the corner, their two bodies a heap.

Brink stood, his hand still curled into a tight ball, panting almost as fast as the sick Frenchman. Alix went for the gun, picked it up, and came back. Without saying a word, she handed him the revolver. Its grip was damp.

Wickens kicked himself free from Clavette until he sat a yard away, his back against the wall.

"No one's shooting anyone, goddammit," Brink croaked.

The soldiers had piled hard-backed chairs, a ratty settee, and a rolled carpet in the far corner of the room when they'd taken this house for their company's command post. One rickety table was crowded with radio equipment, a wood-boxed cipher machine, a black telephone plugboard. Another table, once from a kitchen by the looks of its greasy surface, had been dragged here for maps. A cold iron stove sat near the one window, atop that stove was a gramophone. The room smelled of unwashed men and cabbage, a good smell, and from the gramophone Edith Piaf quietly sang "L'Accordéoniste," a good sound.

The Hauptman standing behind the map table wasn't much older than him, Kirn thought, looking at the captain who commanded the garrison.

Grau, that was his name, spoke. "I heard what you said. Why you need my help, that's where I'm not clear." He glanced at Kirn's ruined right hand.

"There's a—" and Kirn stopped. Wollenstein had ordered him to keep the secret. But that made no sense. The news should have been shouted from one end of Normandy to the other. The hell with Wollenstein. "There may be a disease here. And the *Wulewuh* are getting ready to run."

In the short walk to this house, he'd seen two old men loading a cart with pots and blankets, baskets of food, and, of all things, an accordion.

Farther, a woman screeched from a window at her three children to hurry inside, they were leaving for Bayeux.

"So?" Grau asked, twisting the wedding ring on his hand. Kirn looked at his ringless finger, Hillie months buried under rubble from British bombs fallen short of Munich.

"This disease, Hauptman, is contagious. Very."

"Like influenza?"

Isselmann had told him to mind Wollenstein, the Doktor had said to keep his mouth shut. Orders were, always, orders. But these orders reeked. "Yes, yes, exactly like that," Kirn said, the words fast. "But no, not exactly." Grau's face went confused again. "I've been looking for these sick, Hauptman, under orders from the SS," said Kirn. Grau grimaced. "It was explained that the illness is a kind of typhus, but . . ." And he struggled again.

"Typhus. Really." Grau looked at Kirn's hands again. "You're the one who still asks for friends from Russia, aren't you?"

That caught Kirn by surprise, but he managed a nod.

"I've heard talk of a Kripo who stops and asks of friends from the 268th," Grau said. "That's you."

Kirn nodded again.

"I was there, too, you know. The 321st. But after Kursk . . ." Grau's voice dissipated. "They took what was left and put us here, and then gave me this bunch of children." Grau gestured to the three young soldiers.

"It's not typhus, Hauptman," said Kirn. He liked this Grau, trusted him. Grau's eyes didn't blink, but they weren't dead either.

"No?"

"I don't know what it is exactly," he said, "but it's . . . I've found four dead since yesterday, and none of them . . . they didn't die well. None of them."

Grau took this in. He played with his wedding band again.

"There's not time to think too long," Kirn said.

"Me and the children, we're in danger?" Grau asked. Piaf finished her song and the gramophone's needle scratched in the final groove, over and over.

"Yes."

"Shit," said Grau. One of the boys went to the gramophone and lifted the needle off the shellac to silence the hissing and popping.

"I don't know that anyone else is sick with this," Kirn said, hurrying on. "But if only a few are, and they run . . . they could carry it to others."

"I don't care about the *Wulewuhs*."

"Others of ours, that's what I mean."

Grau nodded, seemed to think, for his eyes went to the small telephone plugboard at the table along the wall and the boy in front of its wires. "I'll need orders before—"

"There's no time. Half the place will have flown by then."

"Shit," Grau said again. He turned to the boy at the plugboard. "Kift, go to the detail working the beach and bring them back. Leutnant Peninger's bunch. Hurry, fast as they can come."

The boy stood, gave a "Yes, Herr Hauptman," and grabbed his cap. Kirn heard his boots on the cobbles outside the open door, the sounds fast and fading faster.

"That's the best I can do," Grau said, sounding apologetic. "The rest of the company . . . it's scattered up and down the shore, and the *Feldgendarmerie*, they're off chasing partisans who killed one of mine along the bluffs last night."

Kirn felt the weight release, not just of the secret but of the convincing. "Block the road south and the one west to Huppain and the other east," Kirn said. "They'll stick to the roads with night coming. They won't want to take it across country." He remembered the cart piled with possessions.

Grau tugged on his ring a third time. "And where will you be?"

Kirn thought for a moment. He should ask to telephone Wollenstein again, but the telephone boy was gone now. "There may be one or two sick who I can find," Kirn said, thinking of the little Pilon's promise of treachery in return for eight hundred francs.

Grau shook his head. "And I thought Russia was strange."

Kirn nodded. Very strange.

Frank's hand wasn't shaking. That was what Alix noticed. Juniper said something quiet to Frank, but he used English and she understood none of it.

"Alix," Frank said, "go find some soap. And alcohol if there is any." The revolver stayed steady, its hammer pulled back from when Juniper had been ready to murder Clavette.

She left them, Juniper sitting with his back to the wall, Frank a meter or more from Clavette, Clavette still unmoving. She knew where the kitchen was and found soap and a cloth fast enough, and after banging around, a bottle of Calvados, quarter-filled, as well. She filled a pan of water from the pump at the sink, and brought that, too.

The scene hadn't changed, but it had. Juniper still sat on the floor, Frank still held the revolver. But Frank was relaxed now and they spoke in quiet words.

"Soap, and Calvados," she said. Frank nodded to Juniper. She set down the yellow bar and the cloth and the pan of water and the bottle of dark brown apple brandy. Juniper grabbed the first, dipped it in the water, then quickly washed his hands. With the cloth, he rubbed his face and the front of his coat where he'd pushed it against Clavette. After Frank made a drinking gesture by tipping a thumb at his mouth, Juniper reached for the Calvados, unstopped the bottle, and drank a swallow, then another, and spit out the second. He dropped the bottle and it rolled toward Clavette, drawing a wet, looped line that smelled of apples and oak.

"What now?" she asked Frank.

No one answered her. Juniper got up and went to Frank, held out his hand for the revolver, but Frank shook his head. Juniper shrugged, yanked his rucksack off the floor and carried it out the front door. It slammed shut in the far room.

"Is he going to—" she began.

"No. He's just going outside to . . ." He looked at her. "To talk with an aircraft. He brought a special radio, but it won't work inside." He released the revolver's hammer, stepped toward her, and gave her the gun. "He needs to tell the aircraft what we found so far."

The light outside was dying. Dark within thirty minutes, sooner perhaps. Alix couldn't see Frank's eyes, but she remembered them as blue. He brushed blond hair from his forehead and scratched at his scalp.

"What pact did you make with Juniper?"

"He won't kill Clavette."

"And he agreed?"

"I told him I wouldn't help him if he did."

They had secrets, he and Juniper. They looked for the Jews' home, to find the illness, to find the special medicine, so Frank said. What they hadn't told her was what they were going to do once they found these things. And besides, Juniper wasn't the kind who gave in to anyone.

Alix found a lamp on a shelf near the door and lit it with a match from the box on that same shelf. She turned up the wick until the lamp smoked, turned it down again, then set it in the middle of the floor. Stared at Clavette. He had almost given away her secret, that it had been she who had urged the others to take the Jews to England. She didn't want either Juniper or Frank to know. Not because she was ashamed, although there was plenty of that to last her the rest of her life, but because she didn't want Juniper to know she had killed Papa for him. And because she didn't want Frank to . . . to know the same thing, strange as that felt. For a moment Alix wished Clavette would die now, in his sleep, but then she wished she'd never thought such a thing. Who was she becoming?

As if he had heard her thoughts, Clavette stirred, moaned. His head snapped up and he coughed, coughed again. He groaned.

"Help him," she told Frank. "Do something."

He shook his head. "There's nothing I can do."

"You're a doctor."

"It doesn't matter." But when she said nothing, only looked at him, he went to the kitchen and she heard the sound of the pump. He came back with a new, wet cloth in his right hand, that hand dripping water, and another cloth in his left, that cloth dry.

Clavette muttered, swung his head back and forth.

Frank went to him slowly, at the same time pressing the dry cloth over his own mouth and nose. But when Clavette coughed, Frank hesitated. He stood a meter from the moaning, dying Clavette, the wet cloth dripping water, one-two-three drops to the wood floor.

Alix went to Frank and took the watered cloth, then crouched beside Clavette.

"Don't," Frank said. She ignored him.

Alix pressed the cloth against Clavette's forehead and held it there. Clavette leaned into the cloth and her hand, sighed. His mouth moved and she bent closer.

"Jews," he whispered.

"I know, I know," Alix said. She brushed the cloth over his eyes, his nose, dabbed it at his stubbled cheeks, wrung it out, mopped Clavette's mouth, cleaned the vomit and blood from the corners of his lips. Every moment felt a month, every movement was a struggle against the terror that if Papa hadn't given her the sickness, Clavette would. But she stayed at his side, hoping it would wash away the shame of wishing him dead.

"I'm sorry, Bouton," Clavette said, so quietly she was sure Frank couldn't hear.

"Did they say where they were from?" she asked.

Clavette's eyes were open, barely blinking.

"Rémi, tell Bouton," she said. "Bouton orders it."

And he so so softly told her. One of the Jews, he said, had told him they had lived on the dark farm. Clavette said words in German—*der dunkle Bauernhof*—and told her to repeat them. She whispered them back.

"Where is *der dunkle Bauernhof*?" she asked Clavette, but he didn't answer. He breathed too fast, that breath brushing her face, but his eyes had closed. Alix stepped back and dropped the cloth into the pan of water Frank held. Frank's other hand gripped the brandy bottle.

"What is this thing?" she asked. "This illness."

"The Germans made it," Frank said, staring at the closed eyes of Clavette. "Black death," he said, the words *la mort noire* not making sense at first. "Like bubonic plague, but not. Pneumonic plague." *C'est pareille à la peste bubonique, ou mieux la peste pneumonique.*

"What did he say?" Frank asked, nodding to Clavette. Alix wished he wouldn't ask questions. She felt the pestilence inside her, felt it as if she could mark the moment in the future when it would make her like Clavette. God would punish her for what she'd become. In her eagerness to go to Juniper, and in her wish for Clavette's death, she'd sinned. God punished sinners.

"The name of the farm where the Jews lived," she said.

"And . . ."

She looked into his blue eyes, their color clear. He might be a good man, but she didn't trust anyone.

"Where?"

"He didn't say."

"Tell me the name of the farm."

"No."

"Alix—"

"No."

"You said you want the medicine, but I don't know . . ." She held her breath for a moment, looking into those eyes. "I'll help you find the medicine because you say the man who makes it made this." She pointed a finger at silent, sleeping Clavette. "But I own the name of the farm." No matter what he said to her, she would turn it aside. He could promise her anything, but she would not tell him of *der dunkle Bauernhof*. "You'll do what I say now, won't you? We're leaving as soon as Juniper returns. I want to see my family, Frank. Now."

He stared at her. She thought he was going to put down the pan and bottle and try to get Clavette to repeat what he'd told her. At least she held the English revolver, so he couldn't use that to threaten Clavette.

From the kitchen side of the house, they heard the door open. That would be Juniper, come back from his conversation with the mysterious aeroplane. They would go to Mama, her brothers, now, like she'd told Frank.

But when she looked at the doorway to the kitchen, it was not Juniper standing there.

"*Wer bist du?*" the man asked, and pointed his arm into the room.

Twelve

Brink just stared at the German in the loose overcoat, big, much bigger than he. Another one, half tucked behind the big man, was sizes smaller. It was a child.

Brink looked down. A pan of water in his left hand, the heavy empty bottle in the other.

"*Hände hoch,*" the German said.

"*Frank, get out of the way!*" Alix shouted behind him.

"*Alix!*" a thin voice called from behind the German.

Later, he thought maybe he stepped aside to give Alix a clear shot like she asked, but at the time it was automatic. Rather than raise his hands, impossible with both of them filled, Brink moved to the left, gripped the bottle tight, and hurled it at the man's chest as if trying to gun down the bastard stealing second.

The German was a lot closer than second base, but he had good reflexes and pulled the trigger just before the bottle glanced off his arm. The bullet went into the wall behind them, and then the German's pistol spun into the corner where Clavette lay. Brink threw the pan of water, and the German twisted away, tripped, and fell, exposing his smaller companion.

Alix's gun went off as an echo to the German's.

The moment went to slow motion as the German fell to the wet floor and the boy was thrown backward under the impact of Alix's bullet.

"*Oh my God!*" Alix rushed across the small room and pointed the revolver at the two on the floor, and Brink thought she was ready to put a bullet into the big German. "*Jules!*" she screeched.

Brink got to her before she dropped the revolver. On the floor, face up and legs tangled, one twisted under the other, was a boy, ten or twelve, with surprised eyes and dark hair not hiding the new tunnel in his forehead. Brink took the revolver from Alix's stiff fingers.

"*Jules!*" she screamed.

Afraid of more boots banging into the house and the memory of whistles chasing them from the bluffs, Brink dragged a kicking Alix away from the dead boy and through the door out into the dark.

It had been absurdly easy to lose three hours. When the Storch had bounced over Port-en-Bessin on its way home from the sightseeing trip of Normandy's beaches, Wollenstein had seen beads of black that looked like gathering people. So he'd told Sillmann first to put the Storch in a tight circle for a better look, and when he was convinced something was wrong, he'd ordered the aircraft down. Port-en-Bessin was where the Kripo was looking for the Jews. A crowd meant trouble, and perhaps the trouble involved his Jews.

Sillmann put the Storch down all right, but the little aircraft got stuck in gluey mud and it took the two of them an hour and a half of pushing at its landing struts and digging into the muck with bare hands to free the wheels.

He'd ordered Sillmann to fly back to Chef du Pont and tell Pfaff to come with men. Then he'd left the field for the village, though he'd immediately gotten turned around. Idiotic. One lane looked like the next, each stretch of hedge identical to what he passed minutes before. Three times he'd come upon farmers, but they acted as if they knew no German and he, of course, couldn't understand their squawking. Even his Walther didn't help, though he waved it in the face of the last man. Finally he'd stumbled upon one of those thickets of white signs, and in the thicket was a board that read "2 KOM/II/916 PT BESSIN." He'd followed it.

The small square was filled with people when he finally reached it. He elbowed his way through them hearing the panic although he couldn't understand a word. Where was that Kripo? He should be here somewhere.

A knot of soldiers came around the corner and into the light spilling from a shop's opened door. They were led by an officer too young to shave. The wind gathered dust from the gutters and sent it billowing down the street, and Wollenstein stopped to both block the way and rub his eyes.

"What's going on?" he asked as the officer stopped. The boy's men noisily huddled behind him, sweat on their faces under the helmets even though the wind was growing cold. One, two, five, eight soldiers, Wollenstein counted.

"Who the hell are you?" the boy asked, looking at Wollenstein's mud-caked boots, his filthy trousers, and once-clean mohair overcoat, now clay-covered.

Wollenstein pulled aside the lapels to show the collar tabs of his tunic and the SS runes. "Wollenstein, Sturmbannführer. I want to know what's happening."

"Major," the boy said, and he barely saluted. One of the soldiers behind him, an older one with a nose bent to the side, turned his head and spat onto the cobbles.

"What's going on?" Wollenstein asked again. He couldn't help himself, and babbled on. "Jews? Looking for Jews?"

"There are no Jews here," the officer snorted. "We're blocking the road south from town."

"Block the road? Why?"

"Leutnant Peninger, we should be—" said the spitting soldier in a heavy voice. He shifted the strap of the rifle on his shoulder and stared at Wollenstein.

Peninger waved his hand to shut up his man. "I was told to block the road, that's all I know. Not let anyone out."

The wind rolled down the street and plucked the hem of Wollenstein's dirty coat. "Have you seen a policeman? A Kripo. He's missing part of a hand."

Peninger shook his head. "No, and if you don't mind . . ." He began to push his way past.

Wollenstein grabbed the boy's sleeve. "Where's your commander?"

Peninger stopped and turned. The light from the open door put his eyes in shadow. "Back up the street to the harbor. On the left-hand side. Fifth house. It's posted, you can't miss it."

"Show me." Wollenstein tried to keep his voice level as he let go of the boy's tunic. If there were no Jews here, it must be the *pestis* upsetting things.

"I don't have time—"

"Have this one show me, then," Wollenstein said, pointing to the *Landser* who liked to spit. "I insist."

Peninger shrugged, nodded. "Show the major, Matthius."

The *Landser* stepped forward, hawked again. The wind caught the spittle and splattered it across Wollenstein's muddy boot. Wollenstein looked into the man's face, trying to memorize it.

"Yes, Lieutenant. Of course," the man rumbled.

"Come to us after, Matthius," the boy said over his shoulder. He was already taking his men through the French crowd, which flowed aside like an ebbing tide to give them room.

"Major, this way," the *Landser* said, beckoning with a hand. His tongue moved inside his mouth; Wollenstein saw the muscles twitch alongside his jaw.

Wollenstein stepped closer, and said, "You spit on me again, and I'll have your head on a stick."

The *Landser* didn't spit. He grinned instead. "Major," he said, sweeping his hand in a grand gesture, taking half a bow.

Wollenstein glanced one more time behind him at the crowd, which had swallowed the boy and his men. He thought he heard someone in the crowd cough.

By the time Kirn found his pistol near the *Wulewuh* in the corner and had wiped it dry, there was no one to shoot. The tall man who'd pitched the bottle and the short one, a woman by voice, had vanished through the door that led out the back of the house. It swung open still and the wind tried to snuff out the lamp set on the floor.

He stumbled to the door and held the gun on the dark. No footsteps, no voices, just the wind in the bushes across the alley behind the house. He stood at the threshold, and rubbed his right arm with his good hand. Not broken from the bottle, but there would be a bruise under the coat. He realized he made a perfect target, silhouetted as he was against the light, and he slammed shut the door.

The little Pilon traitor lay on the planked floor. Kirn went to him, touched his cheek to turn his head, but there was no use to ask the child how he was. The boy's open eyes were already milky. A coin-sized circle in his forehead, just above the left eye, was barely bloody, but there was a dark pool spreading under his head and Kirn knew if he lifted Jules he would find the back of his skull pulped by the bullet. Someone would have to tell Madam Pilon that her boy had been shot and killed.

He should have left well enough alone, he thought. But no, he'd gone back to the Pilon house and its door snowing red paint and told Madam to bring her oldest out to the steps. Neither she nor Jules looked sick with fever, neither of them coughed, the symptoms Wollenstein had told him, but he was careful and didn't stand too close. Instead, he handed a hundred francs to the boy, all he could beg from Hauptman Grau and his men, the notes folded into a thin sheaf, and told him he wanted the names of the men who played cards with his father. The rest, another seven hundred francs, I'll give you later, he promised the boy.

Jules didn't say the man's name—Clavette—until they stood in front of this house ten minutes later. In case it was a trap somehow, Kirn made the boy open the door, step into the first dark room before him. But when he saw it was empty and he heard words from the next room, he made sure the Walther's safety was off and had the boy stand behind him.

Now he wouldn't have to pay him the other seven hundred. Kirn thought about digging in the little boy's pockets for the money to give back to Grau, but he couldn't make himself do that. It smacked of perversion, pawing through a child's clothing. All he did was finger the boy's lids closed.

Jules wasn't the only dead one in the room. There was the one in the corner.

No, not quite dead, Kirn discovered when he took the lamp there and held it over the man slumped on the floor. His chest quickly rose and fell.

The long tongues of bile down his shirt told the only story Kirn needed to know. Tardif. His wife. Jusot. Wollenstein's fucking typhus that was pestilence.

This must be Clavette. Kirn imagined that the air around Clavette was thick with whatever small things had made this scourge, and he backed away.

So he carried the lamp along the edges of the room, shining its light into the corners. Water stains on the floor, a small overturned table. And in its shadow, near the door now closed—how had he missed it?—he found a ruck, vaguely military, made of canvas. He'd seen a hundred, a thousand like it.

Kirn knelt and set the lamp beside him. He touched the leather and buckles, fumbled a minute with his half set of hands, then reached in and began pulling out the evidence.

First some clothing, a rolled white shirt and a pair of gray socks. But then more cloth, and in each scrap a piece of metal. Kirn let the pieces clunk to the floor. Half a dozen that, he bet, would puzzle into a weapon. He dipped his left hand into the ruck again and again, and came out with four box magazines for the weapon. He dropped them into a pile.

More still. Three small blocks of what felt like clay, wrapped in thin brown paper, for when he pressed on the paper, it gave and left a dimple. A handful of long things like mechanical pencils, small pins in the ends of each. A spool of wire, another of yellow cord. An electric torch and a pair of spare batteries. A hand-turned igniter, not much bigger than his palm. A bundle of one-hundred-franc notes, damp under his fingers. And a map.

He spread that on the floor and looked at the Cotentin and Calvados, from Cherbourg to Caen. The paper was oiled and waterproofed, but unmarked. He pushed it aside and put his hand in the ruck again to feel at its empty bottom.

And found a small book, its pages damp like the francs. Kirn ran his fingers over the clothing and the cloth that had wrapped the weapon. They were clammy as well, as if they'd not had time to dry. But it had not rained for days.

The book was blank, but then at the very back, between the last page and the cover, he found a photograph.

He held it close to the lamp's smoky light. The photograph showed a woman, plump and smiling, and beside her a man, pinched-faced, in his forties. It wasn't the man who had thrown the bottle. In front of the man and woman were two girls in summer frocks, the oldest perhaps fourteen or fifteen, the other three or four years younger. It was loved, this photograph; all its corners had been bent and unbent and there was a well-worn crease across its middle. It had been in more than a few pockets.

Kirn turned it to look at its back. In a woman's loopy hand, blurred a bit by water, were inked words. He traced them with the one finger of his right hand.

P-l-e-a-s-e c-o-m-e h-o-m-e t-o u-s s-a-f-e l-o-v-e L-a-n-a

English.

Whoever once owned this ruck had been foolish. Until this moment, Kirn had thought its carrier was *maquisard;* everything was explainable. The weapon would likely fit into a Sten, one of those British machine pistols the English spread across France. The clay was explosives, with fuse cord and time detonators and wire and an igniter to blow rails out from under trains. He'd seen it all one time or another. But now . . .

He'd heard of English saboteurs who came by parachute to lead *maquis,* but he'd never seen one. Commandos were like the nightmares under a child's bed.

Kirn pulled an Eckstein from inside his overcoat and lit it by leaning over the lamp's chimney until the tobacco caught. What were English doing here? he wondered, as he looked at the things arranged on the floor around the ruck. They'd come by sea; the damp cloth and water-smeared letters told him so. Up to any number of mischiefs. But why here, why Clavette? Because Clavette was *maquisard?* Because the English were told to make contact with the *maquis,* and Clavette was that contact? Perhaps.

But Kirn mistrusted coincidence. Chance lived, he didn't deny that. A centimeter farther and the Russian fragment would have missed him. The way his hand had been cupped at his ear trying to hear what Stecker shouted through the barrage, a couple centimeters nearer and it would have carved out a piece of his head. But coincidence was not the same as chance.

Then the Englishman had come for the same reason he had.

Because Clavette might be sick? No.

What is at the heart of it, what does it mean on its own, he thought, remembering the lessons knocked into him by his first partner, Simon Vogel.

He was here because there was a connection between Clavette and Pilon, the fisherman who had stolen the Jews. And the English must be here for the same reason.

Pilon had sailed to England with the sick Jews, so said his wife. English were here. One led to another. Pilon had found his way to England, and the English played it back by coming to France. For what? The typhus-that-wasn't, of course. That's what joined Pilon and Clavette and the Jews, what brought the Englishman to France. The English was trailing the pestilence, just as he was.

But why? What did they care if it laid low a thousand French, or a hundred times that many Germans?

Kirn closed his eyes and breathed another lungful of the Eckstein. Did they want it, the pestilence? To steal it? No, that made no sense. Who would want it? The SS, of course, they were mad enough to want a disease. But only the SS were insane like that.

He slipped the photograph into the pocket of his overcoat, looked at the stack of francs for a moment before putting them in the same pocket. Also the torch and batteries. What was left he jammed back into the rucksack. Kirn dropped his cigarette and stepped on it with a boot.

Clavette. He might slap the man awake if he dared touch him. But the *Wulewub* would tell him nothing even if he woke. Sick, the man was; he knew that. English had been here; he knew that, too. Kirn put his whole hand in his pocket to touch the Walther P38. It would be a mercy to pull it out. But although a finger brushed the pistol, he left it in the pocket. He was not Wollenstein; he was no SS using bullets as aspirin.

He left the lamp lit to give Clavette company if he woke, and Jules comfort because he never would. Then he grunted one strap of the ruck over his right shoulder, and gave both the boy and the man a wide berth.

They ran, but it wasn't more than a hundred meters before Frank dodged from the alley to hide under the eaves of the Lussier house, where they were sheltered by the dark maple overhanging the roof, its leaves beating in the hard breeze. Frank breathed in great gulps. She pressed a hand on the stitch in her side and listened. No footsteps followed.

He asked her something, but she didn't hear. He moved closer and she smelled him, sweat, damp clothing, and faint, it seemed, of cigarettes. He was a dark shape in front of her.

"I shot Jules," she said, hearing her voice flat like the sea that night on the way to England. A gust of wind plucked her words away and she wasn't sure Frank heard. Jules dead on Clavette's floor, the hole bored through his face by her revolver. How could she tell Mama? "Jules," she said again. Frank moved a half step closer.

The wind bit through the thin coat she'd taken from Juniper's wounded old man, and she crossed her arms over her breasts. Closed her eyes a moment, but that didn't help. The picture of Jules was painted on her eyelids in exquisite detail. His face, his mouth open after calling her name or at the surprise of her shooting him, the image so fresh she could see the edges of the shadows in the corner and Clavette slumped there. Like a photograph postcard. The big *boche*'s coat had not been buttoned. Jules wore the shoes that were too tight to lace. There was a pool of water on the floor in the shape of a goose taking wing.

For the rest of her life, she would lie awake each night, damp on the sheet and staring into the black, and see Jules every time she blew out the lamp. She saw an endless rope of those nights.

"I just killed my little brother," she said. "I don't know what he was doing there. I shot the *boche* but he jumped when you threw the water. I saw him, I saw him, his eyes—" She stopped, the last word a cliff and the silence the ocean below. "I killed Papa and now I killed Jules," she said to keep from crying.

Frank touched her sleeve and perhaps because she didn't pull away, he grabbed her arm and squeezed hard. "Alix" was all he said.

That broke her, and she sobbed. "Oh Mary, oh God," she cried, and she stepped closer to Frank. He folded her into his arms and wrapped her tight into his chest and held her as she cried into his coat.

Frank combed her hair with his fingers, over and over, kept his arm tight on her back. He didn't say anything, which she found comforting.

How long she cried she didn't know, but she spilled both the tears for Jules and the ones that had been kept in the cistern of her heart. Cried for

Papa and herself, cried for Henri, and Juniper's betrayal on the boat, and for everything. But finally her shoulders shook a bit less, and she felt her head tap a slower tattoo against his chest. She wormed a hand between them and wiped at her eyes.

The wind picked at her hair, and Frank loosened his arms. She stayed there a beat longer than necessary, caught his cigarette scent again. For a moment she thought he would bend down and kiss her, but that would have been wrong, and he was smart enough not to.

"I have to tell Mama what's happened," Alix said. She put a finger into her hair and twisted there, used that hand to wipe again at her eyes, and blew her nose into the cuff of the ragged coat.

"Where's the pack?" he asked.

"I forgot it," she said. They'd left it near the door. All they possessed were the clothes on their backs, the revolver in Frank's hand and its five bullets, and the knife she'd wrapped in a scrap of barn blanket and stuffed through the belt of these trousers.

"The *boche* was a policeman," Alix said. Her voice was still flat. "He was there for Clavette. Like us." She took a deep gulp of the chilling air.

It began to rain and a few wet needles of spray penetrated the leaves above them.

"He'll look for us when he finds the rucksack with Eggers's things," she said quietly. Her voice sounded far away even to her.

"Let's go," Frank said. He was thinking of a clock, she decided. There was a clock in his head, and this task must be completed before that clock showed a certain time. He held out something. "Take this," he said. The revolver.

"You keep it," she said.

"I don't know anything about guns."

The rain got quicker, larger, but not fat drops yet. It was going to be miserable. She took the gun.

Kirn put his identity disc and card in the light of the sentry's torch and when the boy waved him on, he stamped his feet to shake loose the rain on him and stepped into the lamp-lit house near the harbor. The room was even more crowded than before, with five men around Hauptman Grau.

Worst of all, Wollenstein was there, his back to the door. The thing that Kirn noticed first off was that the doctor's boots were muddy halfway to the knees. And the doctor's once precious mohair looked like he'd rolled in a plowed wet field.

He had been thinking of Wollenstein as he walked through the confusion of Port-en-Bessin, and now Kirn wondered if his thinking had somehow brought the SS. No; even those bastards couldn't read minds.

Grau looked up, although Wollenstein still hadn't seen him.

"There is nothing wrong here, no matter what he told you," Wollenstein said to Grau.

Grau looked over Wollenstein's shoulder, caught Kirn's eye. "Really? The Kripo was very convincing. He said my men were in danger."

"No one is in danger," said Wollenstein, his voice heating. "He's an idiot. He's not a doctor."

"Only doctors know the truth, is that what you mean? Or is it because you're SS?" asked Grau.

"I'm the only one who knows—"

"You're not the only one who knows things," Kirn said as he moved into the room. Wollenstein turned and the man's mouth made a circle of surprise. "I know this isn't like any typhus I've seen. I know I've found two here with whatever it is."

"You—"

"Yes, I told him about the sickness," Kirn said. He locked looks with Wollenstein, watched those disquieting eyes of gray and blue.

"I'll have you shot," Wollenstein said. The words were said like any other words, but everyone heard and even the boys at the telephone plugboard and radio and cipher machine went quiet.

"So there *was* a secret," Grau said softly.

Kirn's missing fingers itched. "The illness is here," he said, rapping his good left hand on the greasy tabletop. "If the people run, they'll spread it."

Wollenstein's mouth opened, then shut.

"I was acting out of concern for Hauptman Grau's men," Kirn said. "Perhaps I was wrong. If you want to take this up with, say, someone higher, fine." He waved his itching hand toward the telephone. Wollenstein said nothing, looked again at Grau. "See, Hauptman, there *are* secrets here," Kirn said.

"That's enough," Wollenstein said.

"What exactly is going on?" Grau asked, his voice rising closer to a temper. "Is there a danger or not?"

Wollenstein said nothing.

It was time to face the devil. Wollenstein not only didn't care that he had let loose a killer, but he didn't care if the fucking *Wulewuh* gave it to his own kind. "Tell him or I will," Kirn said.

The doctor rubbed his hands together another time or two, then stuck one in a pocket. "We must talk. Privately." He straightened in his muddy overcoat.

Grau glanced at the uniforms in the room and after a long pause—Kirn could hear the rain against the window above the stove—Grau told his men to leave. They tramped out of the room and Wollenstein went to the door and closed it behind the last.

"He's right," Wollenstein said as he stared at Grau. "There is danger. And it isn't typhus. I told him that because I don't know what it is. It's the—"

"Not the truth, Hauptman. He knows what it is," Kirn interrupted. "It's the pague. *Die Pest.*"

Grau's eyes widened.

"That is a state secret," Wollenstein hissed. "I *will* have you shot."

"What if the English knew your secret?" Kirn asked. "Who would the Gestapo shoot then? Not just me."

"English? What are you talking about?" asked Wollenstein.

"Commandos," said Kirn. He picked up the English rucksack, upended it over the table and its maps, and let the contents spill out. One chunk of the Sten fell to the floor. Grau bent for it, fingered the black metal. Wollenstein touched a brick of the explosive.

"Commandos?" asked Wollenstein.

"I've seen them, one man, one woman," Kirn said. "They're here for your secret, that's what I think. Not so much a secret then, is it?"

"I don't understand," said Grau, who put the machine pistol piece back on the table.

"Herr Doktor lost track of some Jews, Hauptman, and those Jews ended up in Port-en-Bessin. Then someone took them to England. And now the English are here." Kirn plucked the photograph from his coat and thrust it toward Wollenstein. The doctor looked at its face, turned it over to look at the writing.

The man is smart, he'll figure this out quick enough. His mouth moved as he read the letters on the back. Wollenstein's face went white. "England?" he asked. Yes, he was understanding.

"A fisherman took them there on his boat three nights ago."

"They're after my . . ." Wollenstein said quietly. "They mean to steal the *pestis*."

"The . . . what?" Grau asked. Confused. "The . . . the pestilence?"

"That's what was in the box from the yellow bastards, wasn't it?" Kirn asked. The thought had passed through him days before when Wollenstein first lied about typhus, there beside the truck. Then it had only been a suspicion—the way Wollenstein had looked frightened—but now Kirn was sure. Whatever had been in the crate somehow became this serpent that ate innocents. The feeling when the littlest Pilon had breathed wet in his face returned.

"Shut your mouth," Wollenstein said softly, still looking at the photograph.

"No accident. The pestilence, it's yours," Kirn said. "You made it from what was in the box."

"I said shut your mouth." Wollenstein gave him a look with the gray eye that put a chill on Kirn.

The hell with him. He'd never been afraid of criminals before, and he wasn't going to start.

He put this together in his policeman's mind. Cause and effect. Motive and crime. It was no different from when he pieced together wrongdoers, their reasons, and the events. "A weapon, is it? Like mustard gas."

"*I said shut your mouth!*" Wollenstein bellowed, losing control and stretching out a hand for Kirn's coat. Kirn slapped it away and used his bulk to lean into the doctor, made sure Wollenstein felt his breath. He wished some of the little Pilon's wetness was still in his mouth. Wollenstein retreated a step.

"I've breathed some of it," Kirn said, "from a little boy no older than six. And if I get sick from it, I'll make sure we talk one last time, Herr Doktor. And then I'll cut out your fucking SS heart and feed it to *Wulewuh* pigs."

Kirn's look didn't swerve from Wollenstein, but he heard Grau say, "Christ," and "Christ" again.

Wollenstein's face was still white, but whether from the realization that the English were here to steal his sickness or the rage at his words, Kirn wasn't sure. And didn't give a damn. Wollenstein didn't seem to know what to do, someone bullying him like this. So the doctor did what the guilty did: made excuses.

"We would never use it here, there's too much chance it would spread to our own," Wollenstein said, more to Grau than to him. "That's why I had to find these Jews. I told you we couldn't let it infect us. Ours. Yours."

"But you had only me to find the Jews," Kirn said. "You should have been telling everyone. The Hauptman, for one."

"I said this is a secret of the state. At the highest level. The very highest," Wollenstein said. "You can't go spreading talk of something and still keep it a secret, can you?" Anger crept back into his voice.

"I don't care if the Führer himself said never to whisper it," said Grau. Kirn glanced at Grau, and saw fear. This was the first time the Hauptman had been frightened since he'd left Russia, Kirn bet. "I want to know if my men are in danger."

"This changes nothing," Wollenstein said, his courage returning.

"*It changes everything!*" yelled Grau.

"No, no it doesn't," said Wollenstein. "What we must do is keep the illness from spreading." He paused a moment. "To your men."

"And just how will you—" started Grau.

"I've already sent word for my men to come," said Wollenstein. "Two dozen will be here soon."

"That's not enough. I have that many blocking the roads now, and when I pull them out—"

"No, leave them in place. My men will go house to house. Clean out the village. Everyone into quarantine." Wollenstein glanced at the map and jabbed a thumb on its center. "The church, it's large enough. Once they're collected, I'll sort them out. Those who are sick, I have a medicine. The others, they can go back to their homes."

"Medicine?" asked Kirn. "You mean what you wouldn't give Tardif? I thought you said you couldn't save the sick."

Wollenstein stayed calm. "I said no such thing." The doctor looked at Grau again. "I have just perfected a medicine. It's been tested on others— Jews, naturally—who were sick, but they only now recovered."

"Jews . . ." said Grau slowly. "Naturally."

Liar, Kirn thought. If there was a medicine, he was a *Japser* monkey.

"In a few hours, I'll have this cleaned up and you can go about your business."

Grau said nothing as the rain hammered the windows. Finally. "Take care of it," he said.

"Hauptman, don't believe—" Kirn began.

"I'll see to everything," Wollenstein said.

Grau nodded. He was eager to get back to what he understood. Not an invisible sickness for an enemy, but men who came at him with guns. "See that this place is scrubbed clean enough that you'll eat off its cobblestones, Doktor," said Grau. "Or hope the weather does the cleaning for you." He gestured to the windows from which they could see the windblown rain, then opened the door, and disappeared.

Wollenstein looked at Kirn, saying nothing at first. "I'll remember this," he finally whispered.

"I'd hope you would," Kirn said, "or this was all a waste, wasn't it?" He raised his maimed hand.

———

Sunday

'Tis certain they died by heaps, and were buried by
heaps, that is to say, without account.

—DANIEL DEFOE, 1665

Thirteen

Twice they backtracked when they stumbled on Germans going door to door. Both times Brink and Alix tucked behind a corner or stepped into a side street to watch. Bullying the townspeople, yelling in a strange mix of a little French and a lot of German, the soldiers turned everyone outdoors. One shoved a heavyset man from a backlit doorway, then raised his rifle and banged the big man on the face with its butt to send him falling into the rain-slick street.

The strange thing was that the Germans all wore rubber aprons and had masks pulled over mouths and noses. They're afraid the town's sick.

Brink wasn't afraid, but he was worried. If the Germans feared the plague, it meant that for all the needle marks on Jews, they must not have a working antibiotic. If they did, they'd be pricking people. But Alix didn't let him linger on it, since she kept moving down the narrowest of streets and squeezing through greenery between buildings. And eventually, she got them to her house, the only place he could think to hide until they figured out what they should do next.

The rain was cold and solid now and he was soaked. He took off the flat cap, wrung it out as he stepped into the narrow shelter of the doorway. He brushed the water off his forehead and out of his hair. Alix was at a door, this door at the rear of the small house, the house jammed against others on both sides. She tried its latch, and stepped out of the rain.

It was a kitchen. Light from the hall, another wick lamp like at Clavette's, shone into the room. "Mama?" Alix called. The house was as quiet as the back of the truck behind St. Richards, but it smelled of Grootvader's and Grossmama's, like baked bread. It was so warm inside that his face itched.

"Mama? Alain?"

There was a heavy plate on the table that filled the kitchen's center. A thin crust of bread was the only thing on that plate. It could have been home; his kid brother Donnie had always left a scrap even when he was hungry, like he was set against clearing his plate.

"Mama?" Alix called, and moved into the short hallway. That blocked the light. At the same time Brink heard a knock, the sound like a heavy foot on the floor above. He wiped his forehead with his cap. Alix ran down the hall and stamped up stairs he couldn't see.

"*Mama!* It's Alix! *Mama!*"

Brink trailed her upstairs, hoping not to find her mother blue like Clavette or black like Tardif. He took two narrow steps at a time. Alix stood in the doorway of the room on the right of the landing, hands pressed against its jambs. An outline of water spots on the wood floor marked her place.

Brink peered over her shoulder. They were alive. Her mother sat in a red cushioned chair beside a window. A little boy, six maybe or seven, was on her lap, head against her shoulder, dressed only in a long shirt. She stroked his hair. The bed a few feet from them was unused, but it had been slept on, for the blanket over it was pulled into the center.

The boy woke himself by coughing, and Brink knew. He looked at Alix's mother again, this time only at her face. Even in the yellow light of the oil lamp on a small stand beside the bed, her skin looked flushed. There was a sheen of moisture above her lip and when she brushed her hair off her forehead, he saw sweat there, too. The boy drew his head from her shoulder and coughed into her chest. Once, twice, both with wet edges. He moaned, a homesick dog's sound, coughed again.

"Alix," the mother croaked. She had to catch her breath after the one word. "Where is Papa?"

Alix didn't answer. She stayed in the doorway, her hands, Brink noticed, pressing against the jambs so hard that her splayed fingers went white. The sound of her dripping coat, his, too, punctuated the silence with a regular ticktock. Like a clock counting.

The boy coughed again.

"Don't—" Brink began.

"I know," Alix said.

Brink breathed in, held it, waiting for her to step across the threshold and into the bedroom. But she didn't. He let out his breath.

"Papa's dead," Alix said to her mother.

The boy coughed. Almost straight into his mother's face, not that it mattered.

"Mama, did you hear?"

"I told him he was foolish," the woman said from her chair. "And now . . . now I'm so hot. Open the window, Alix." Her voice was slow and absent any affect.

"Yes, Mama." Alix stayed in the doorway. The window *was* open, for that moment a wind pushed at the drawn blue curtain and the sound of rain got louder.

"Dr. Jusot couldn't say what was wrong with Alain," her mother said. She held the boy closer as he moaned again. "He thought influenza. Clavette had something like it the day before, Jusot said. Yesterday. No, the day before that."

"Mama," Alix said, and she trembled in the doorway. Brink was ready to grab her sleeve.

"Don't come closer, *bouton*," her mother said, and the last word caught Brink off-guard. *Button?* "I'm sick with it." She blinked and looked around the room a moment. "Jules, where is Jules?"

"Yes, Mama . . . Jules . . . he . . . I . . ."

Her mother started to cry, tears filling her eyes and then running down her cheeks. All Brink heard was her rough breathing and that of the boy on her lap. "Jules. . . . You must leave, *bouton*. Now."

"Why Mama?" Her voice caught, choked.

"Jules . . . he is . . . he is a collaborator, *bouton*." The mother's tears continued. "He left with a *boche*, a policeman. He's led the *boche* to Clavette, I think, or Papa's other friend, that one near Étréham, I never remember—"

"Mama."

"Run, *bouton*, before the *boche* find you." Her mother sobbed and the shaking startled the boy on her lap. He weakly tried to raise his head from her chest, but couldn't. "God have mercy," she said. "Pray for Jules, *bouton*." She shifted the boy to a different spot on her lap, but held him just as close. She had been looking at Alix, but now her eyes darted away to an empty corner.

Brink knew what was coming. He reached a hand for Alix's shoulder to give her some comfort in the moment because he knew what was coming, and he touched her, put a hand on the back of her rain-wet neck.

"Mama. Jules, he's dead, Mama," Alix said quietly. "Mama, did you hear?" Her mother's eyes came back to Alix. "I shot him, Mama. I shot Jules."

Her mother simply stared. She was an empty bottle with nothing left to pour out. Even the tears had stopped. "Jules?" She patted the top of the boy's head with her free hand.

"It was an accident," Alix said. "I didn't mean—"

Brink hated hearing the pain in that voice, and made a mistake. "Come downstairs," he said. "There's nothing you can do."

She whirled on him, her hands tightened into fists, and she pounded them into his chest. *Goddamn.* He staggered across the landing and she followed him, her face filled by fright and hate and then fright again, each face framed by wet hair slick at her temples and droplets on her eyelashes that caught the lamp's light.

"*Do something!*" she shouted. "*You wretched man, do something!*" She came at him again, her face iced in that look and her fists leading. He backed up and his right foot stepped on air.

Automatically, he reached for her and she did the same. Their fingers touched, but because those fingers were still wet from the rain, they slipped and missed. He felt nothing under his shoes as he fell.

Brink opened his eyes and stared into the darkness. How was he supposed to see the baseball in the dark?

He wasn't in a ballpark, he was somewhere else. France. Port-en-Bessin. He started to sit up but lay down just as quickly when a pain stabbed the center of his head, a flash of white light inside his skull.

Standing in the doorway was Alix, holding a lamp. "You're awake," she said, putting the lamp on the floor and kneeling beside it. She had changed out of the wet pants and shirt and coat, and into a dress. Her best dress, church clothes, because it wasn't mended like the one he'd seen in St. Richards. He saw pretty legs under that dress before she kneeled and hid them.

He lifted his head enough to see her face, let the pain wash up like a wave at a lake's edge, then wash back out. He sat up slowly to manage the ache and looked at the cluttered room. Wooden crates, a tangled net in the corner, empty bottles on a shelf, carpenter's tools on another. The room was small: eight by eight maybe.

"How long?"

"More than an hour." She shifted in her spot, but only to fold her legs, Indian-style, and he caught the flash of thigh for a moment before she smoothed the dress.

The rain beat against the house.

"At first, I thought you were dead," Alix said, but she wouldn't look him in the eyes, instead gazing at the floor between them. She glanced up. "I'm glad you're not." She smiled, the pretty smile that showed no teeth but still lit her face. He wished she'd laugh, that warm and throaty sound he'd heard once.

Instead, Brink listened to the rain, hearing the wind curl around the house. "Your mother?" he asked finally.

"Sleeping. Alain, too." She stared at the floor again. "They're very sick." She looked up. In the background the rain's noise rose, fell, rose again.

"Yes."

"I'm afraid I have it inside me," she said. He expected tears again, but there were none. She was tough. She didn't cry for herself, only for her brother stretched out on Clavette's floor with a hole in him.

He was going to tell her he had the same fear, tell her about her father and what had happened in the hospital room. He wanted to tell her about Kate, too, but she broke the spell by standing. She towered over him, and when he looked up he got dizzy again.

"I'll find us something to eat," she said, and took the lamp with her and left him in the dark.

Alix sat on a crate near the door of the storeroom and used that long, sharp knife stolen from the German to slice into a half loaf of bread. She used the knife to cut a chunk of sausage into pieces, too, the same to a wide wedge of white cheese, each time holding the food against the front of her dress and cutting toward her. Her hands were sure and steady and the pieces came out even. They ate without talking, taking turns to gulp warm cider from a cream-colored crock she'd brought from the kitchen. Brink had never tasted anything so good.

The weather rattled the house again. Rain ran hard fingers up and down the walls, then across the roof above them. In the corner, Brink heard a leak *drip-drip-drip*. But even with the shrieks under the eaves outside, the room, so small and close, felt good. The lamp smoked and its yellow light couldn't penetrate the corners, but the room felt safe. Alix was just far enough away that he couldn't see the green in her eyes, but he watched her twist a finger in her hair.

"You said that . . . outside, before . . . you said you killed your papa," he said. At first he thought she hadn't heard him, because she reached into a pocket of her dress and pulled out a wrinkled package of cigarettes. She drew out one and tossed the pack his way. A plain wrapper, with a winged helmet on the front. "Gauloises Caporal Ordinaire" the printing read. Alix lit her cigarette by holding the lamp's chimney under the cigarette's end until it went red. She got off the crate and carried the lamp to him and he did the same. He hacked hard at the first harsh lungful.

As she took the lamp away, its light fell on her face and he saw by the way she looked at him that she'd heard. "And Clavette said it would have been better if you'd . . . if you'd killed everyone. What did he mean, saying that?" he asked.

When Alix exhaled, the smoke curled out of her nostrils like a fog and it obscured her face. She stared at the ember end of the short, thick cigarette for long seconds, a minute maybe, then told him. It sounded like the truth.

"It wouldn't have made any difference," he said. "I think he got it when you found the Jews. Once that . . . It didn't matter where he went. Or Clavette. Or Tardif. They were going to . . ."

She crushed her cigarette on the floor.

"It didn't matter where your papa went, Alix. He was going to die. Here or in England. Do you understand?"

"I wonder where he is," she said. For a moment he thought she meant her father, but then he understood she meant Wickens.

"He's back at Tardif's barn by now," said Brink.

"To his old man," she said. "He loves that old man." She sounded almost wistful.

"Maybe we should go to the barn," he said after several more moments of listening to the wind. "If he's there . . . And it's safer."

"No."

"Alix—"

"I won't leave her and Alain. They're not going to die like Papa."

The Germans should be here with teams to sweep the village for those presenting symptoms, like the two upstairs, and pricking skin with syringes to keep the plague from spreading. They weren't. Maybe there wasn't an antibiotic. But they wouldn't know unless they asked.

They couldn't sit here. They needed to find the men who had tamed the *Pasteurella pestis*. "We must find the cure," he said. "Or they'll die." He looked at his watch. It was past midnight, and now the fourth. He looked at his right hand, the two strips of tape there, and picked at the end of the tape, now only vaguely white, on the ring finger. Brink unspooled the tape, rolled it into a ball like before, and let it curve across the floor into the dark of a corner. Now there was just one.

Alix watched him, but didn't ask. "You're right," she said. "We won't give up. I won't. I have no one but them," she said softly. She gestured for the cigarettes and he slid the package across the wood. She lit another from the lamp like before, and scooted closer.

"I lost my Henri to the *boche* four years ago. I lost my Papa to the Jews. I lost Jules . . . I'm not losing any more," Alix said as she sat in front of him, drawing on the cigarette and letting loose a stream of smoke. "You must know what I mean."

That moment he wished he did know. As the rain drummed against the windowless room's walls, he envied Alix for what she had, even though what family remained was sick and likely soon dead.

"You have a woman in England?" she asked. She coughed on the cigarette.

He sucked a last breath of his Gauloises, stubbed it out on the floor between them. "No," he said.

"Once you did?"

"Once."

"And . . ." She leaned forward and he couldn't help but look where she hadn't buttoned the top button of her dress, how the white skin below her throat swept up to a neck that was beautiful. She noticed his glance, and she smiled but said nothing.

"She's dead," he said finally.

"See, we have something in common, you and I. Mine, he's dead, too. Or disappeared."

Henri, the name she'd mentioned twice.

"What happened to her?" she asked.

"I made a mistake," Brink said finally.

Alix nodded. "I see." She seemed to think for a moment. "Like my mistake with Papa? Like my mistake . . . with Jules?"

He took another cigarette, too, and looked up. They were close enough for him to see the green of her eyes. "More like Jules."

"Life is mistakes, I think. Mistakes are what make it life," she said.

He looked at Alix. "I don't like mistakes," he said finally.

She closed her eyes a moment, opened them, took a drag from the cigarette. And smiled. It was a false smile, but it was still the best thing in the room. "We have to accept what happens. Live with the mistakes, yes?" She flicked ash onto the floor. "It's still my fault, my papa, and I will pay for it. But I think if I didn't talk Papa into England, I would not have met you, and so Mama and Alain would be without a chance. At least now there's a chance."

"Jules?" he asked.

It took her a long time to answer this one. She stubbed out the cigarette on the floor even though it was only half-smoked and her hand trembled as she plucked another from the package and lit it. "His mistake, collaborating with the *boche*," she said quietly. "He knew better. I don't know what made him do that. So . . . Papa, yes, but Jules . . . no, I don't think so."

He stared at her. If she told the truth, she was so much stronger than him, or brutal, he wasn't sure. He couldn't put Kate behind him, or what he'd done before meeting her, working up the anthrax.

Brink looked at the cigarette he hadn't really smoked and crushed it on the floor.

"We'll find them," she said, sounding so sure.

Brink leaned his head against the wall and closed his eyes to try to forget all he couldn't. So he thought of Alix's top button unbuttoned. *Bouton.* He thought of buttons and how *they* couldn't remember, and fell asleep with that thought fresh in his mind. He dreamed of a ball corkscrewing into the dirt alongside the plate and hitting his shin guard and ricocheting into the dead corner near the visitor's dugout and the crowd on his back and Warne putting his head down and kicking the dirt on the mound, mad because the tying run scored from third. He couldn't breathe.

It was Alix, swimming in front of him so close her breath warmed his face. She had a finger pressed against his mouth.

"Shsss," she sighed. "Listen, There." She cocked her head to one side. A creak of wood, too long lasting to be caused by the storm, and the sound of wind came through their door louder. Alix leaned for the lamp and blew out its wick. The creak again, and the wind sound dropped. A footstep, another, in the kitchen. A third and fourth. Large shoes, heavy feet. The silence drifted on, and he felt Alix's hand on his. He folded his fingers around it.

From the front of the house *"Aufmachen!"* came shouted over the wind, and fists slammed on wood.

Kirn tugged at the brim of his felt hat and pulled at the collar of his overcoat, but there was no meeting of the two and the back of his neck was a river. The rain ran down between his shoulder blades. Fucking weather.

As they walked up the cobblestoned street and into the wind, he looked past the three SS in front of him and saw that the red flowers in the boxes on either side of the Pilon's door were drowned and blown flat. The little white terrier that hated him was gone, too, barking at him from its warm home, he supposed.

The flaking red door had new paint on it since his last visit: a meter-high *P* in black, the edges of the letter already fading under the rain. *P* stood for *peste*, he guessed. Angry neighbors, or neighbors afraid, or both. The Pilon secret was out.

"Give me a minute or two," he shouted in the ear of the SD, the fat Adler, who nodded. Kirn stepped quickly for the break between houses back the way they'd come, four down, and groped through the gap to the lane behind, tracing the path in his head to the rear of the Pilon home, counting dark shapes to his left as he went—three, two, one—and finally stood before the back door of the Widow Pilon. If the commandos were inside, he didn't want them escaping again.

The door was unlocked, but it stuck—the rain had swelled it—and it took a good push to get it open, and when it did it creaked loud in the quiet between a gust of wind and some distant thunder. He came into the kitchen, closed the door behind him, and the damn thing creaked just as loud again.

He groped for his lighter and spun the wheel to strike the flint. There was a lamp on the table, also a plate with its crust of bread where Jules had left it, and Kirn pulled off the lamp's chimney to light the wick. With the lamp in his good hand, he couldn't very well hold his Walther, too, so he left the pistol in his overcoat pocket. Kirn stepped around the table for the short corridor that would lead to the front of the house, made for the door there and stopped near some stairs that led to the next floor. The front door was just a couple meters away, and he listened as the heavy Unterscharführer whom Wollenstein had called Pfaff, the one Kirn had talked to on the telephone, pounded with his machine pistol. "Open up!" Pfaff shouted.

Try the door, you dolt; it's likely not locked.

But instead boots took turns shattering the latch. Simpletons. The SS rushed in, boots thundering like a herd of cows, and Kirn held up the lamp in his good hand, waving the maimed one to make sure they didn't shoot him, the idiots. Adler squeezed through the door, then Pfaff. The Unterscharführer switched on an electric torch and pointed it aimlessly.

Kirn took off his hat and swung it to fling off the water. Adler opened his immense overcoat, pulled a thick cigar from somewhere, and lit it.

A half hour earlier Kirn had watched Adler claw himself free from the cab of the Mercedes truck that had pulled up in front of the Norman house near the harbor. Thinner men with weapons, some in helmets and others in the green-and-brown cloth caps favored by the SS, jumped out the back of the truck.

Adler was big. No, huge. One hundred fifty kilos, no question. He wheezed like a broken accordion when he walked, he was so big. "Don't say a word to him," Wollenstein had ordered. "Not a word, you understand? I'll do all the explaining."

Kirn had only lit another Eckstein.

Minutes later, when the three of them talked in the dry corridor just inside the door of Grau's command post, the SD said he had come to help. The smile on the fat man's fat face was a fraud. "You want to help?" Wollenstein had asked. "Put your nose to the ground and root out the English."

He was making fun of the way *Wulewubs* used pigs to sniff out truffles. But Adler's smile remained, and politely he said he would do whatever the Sturmbannführer wanted.

Kirn said then that he was going to visit the Widow Pilon with more questions. He didn't bother explaining why to Wollenstein or the SD, but he'd remembered Jules shouting out a name and the woman shouting *"Jules!"* back. They knew each other. He couldn't pull from his memory the name Jules had yelled, but more thinking made him hear the talk of the fisherman at the wharf who said Pilon had sailed with his daughter. Perhaps that woman was the daughter. If so, she might head home.

"He can help me," Kirn said to Wollenstein, pointing his Eckstein at Adler then. If the SD hated Wollenstein, Kirn wanted to find out why. Perhaps they could be allies, he and the fat man. So as they walked the twisted way from the harbor past the square to the Pilon house, he told Adler about the English commandos, why he thought they'd come, even about the Jews. Nearly everything.

"No one's in the kitchen," Kirn said, now back in the moment and in the Pilon home. He pointed behind him. Adler took another puff on the cigar, stared up the staircase instead.

"Upstairs," Adler said, taking charge, and the three enlisted men stomped up the narrow, steep stairway at their left. Rather than follow them, Kirn returned to the kitchen, where there was another door he'd noticed seeing his first time in the house. He had put the lamp on the stove and was reaching for his Walther to try this new door, when the SS upstairs shouted.

"They're up here!" they yelled. Kirn heard voices, low and incomprehensible, then a woman's scream and the sound of furniture shoved aside. More footsteps on the stairs, and as he looked back up the corridor, Madam Pilon and her little boy, him in her arms, stumbled the last step or two and nearly into Adler's big belly. The SD, now with his own torch, put its light on their faces. Adler motioned the woman toward the kitchen, and Pfaff used the barrel of his machine pistol to slap her shoulder.

They all crowded into the kitchen and she laid the boy on the table. He was asleep. No, he couldn't be asleep, not in this noise. Kirn looked hard at the boy and tried to remember exactly what Wollenstein said about the signs of typhus. Fever he remembered, chills, that, too, and a cough. Kirn went to the table and put his hand close to the boy's face, but didn't touch. Like a coal-fed furnace. He could warm his hands over the boy, the skin was so hot.

"Mais qu'est ce qu'ils font ici les Anglais?" he asked the widow. In the light from the wicked lamp her face was flushed. Her eyes were half closed almost, but then they came wide open.

"I don't know anything about English," Madam Pilon said.

"Make her tell," Adler ordered. He stood near the door, the glow of his cigar lighting the cloud of smoke around his head. He understood French at least.

"I'm no Gestapo," Kirn said. He looked at the little boy, then back to Adler. "Not fucking SD either." The little boy breathed like the dying Clavette.

"I'll take care of it," Pfaff growled, and made to step toward Madam Pilon.

"Stay where you are," Kirn barked. Pfaff glared a moment but obeyed.

"Alix came back," the woman said softly.

Alix. That was the name the fisherman said at the wharf. Jules's sister. She had to be the one at Clavette's. "Where is she now? *Madam!* Where is Alix?"

She shook her head as if to clear it. "She came back, her and . . . I don't know."

"Is she still here? She and the English?" Kirn asked. Pilon said nothing. "Where is Alix? The English?"

But it was Adler who lost patience with the widow, not him. The SD stepped to the table and touched the boy with his hands, the hands probing the boy's chest as if he was nudging him awake. The boy moaned. "Tell me," Adler said to Madam Pilon from around the cigar he'd stuck in his mouth. Adler brushed the bread's crust from the heavy plate on the table, picked up the plate, and placed it on the child's chest, the rim tucked under the boy's chin, its edge pressing on his throat as the fat SD pushed. The boy gurgled and his eyes snapped open.

"*Mais qu'est ce qu'ils font ici les Anglais?*" Adler bellowed at Madam Pilon. But she didn't hear. She screamed, the scream filled the kitchen, and she clawed for Adler. Pfaff grabbed and held her arms and she kicked and flailed at him while Adler killed her boy. Kirn lunged for Adler, but the SD was huge enough that he pushed Kirn's hand away with one of his own while he pressed the other on the plate. He grimaced around his cigar.

"Let him go!" Kirn yelled.

Too late. The little boy's eyes nearly jumped from his face and he was as blue as India ink, even after Adler plucked the plate from his throat and tossed it against the wall, where it shattered. Madam Pilon fell to a heap, arms still held by Pfaff, and she shrieked and shrieked. Kirn closed his eyes against the high-pitched sounds.

"*Tell me about the English!*" Adler boomed at the woman.

Kirn opened his eyes, caught the look of the other two SS, whose faces showed shock at what Adler had done. Every thought he'd had about allying with Adler evaporated. The fat man was worse than Wollenstein.

Adler looked at the hand he'd used to press on the plate, and the blood there that had been squeezed from the little boy's mouth and nose in the early seconds. He wiped it on his trousers, pulled the cigar from his mouth, brushed a blood-flecked hand against his lips as he did.

"You prick," Kirn said. "You didn't have to kill him."

"You have a problem with my methods?" Adler asked, his voice barely audible over the screaming that flooded the kitchen. Ash fell from the end of the cigar now in his massive paw. "You wouldn't complain if you knew." He smiled, what the SD surely thought was a sly smile.

"Know what?"

"Take her out," Adler ordered, voice now sharp. "Get her out of here!" He looked at Pfaff, and the Unterscharführer seemed confused for a moment, but he dragged the woman, still screaming but in shorter gasps, from the kitchen to the hallway and the front of the house. The two SS followed. The child they left stretched on the table behind Adler.

"We must find the English," Adler said. "I need them as proof that what Wollenstein's doing is wrong." He put the cigar into his mouth, rolled it there, sucked on it as he put a new match to its end, now out.

Kirn said nothing, only looked at the little boy.

Adler breathed out smoke. "Wollenstein means to put his sickness on the beaches when they come, the English and their friends."

Kirn made himself look away from the boy and at the SD. Wollenstein's pestilence *was* a weapon, but let it loose here? It would kill everyone. Not just the English and Americans, but men like Grau. Men like Böse and Stecker and Muffe, if they were alive still. Every *Landser* up and down the beaches.

"I work for someone who wants control of the sickness," Adler said. "If I find the English, it shows Wollenstein cannot be trusted. He's already lost Jews, yes, like you said." More cigar smoke.

"If you want this, you're as mad as he is," Kirn said finally.

The SD grinned. "But less so than the Herr Doktor."

Less so? Kirn looked at the dead boy, at the spots of blood on the SD's hand. They loved the bullet, these men. And now they had something much much worse to love. My God.

"If you have the . . . the pestilence . . . what will you do with it?" Kirn asked.

Adler shrugged his shoulders, wiggled the cigar from one side of his mouth to the other. "That's not up to me. The one I work for, he decides."

"What cracks do you people hide in?" Kirn asked. If Adler was more evil than Wollenstein, and he was, Kirn knew, looking at the boy again, then the SD would do darker things with the sickness than even the doctor.

A small bump behind him, and he turned. Adler had heard it, too. The kitchen was silent. "What was that?" Adler asked, his cigar now out of his mouth.

Kirn went to the door he'd not opened before.

There's no key," Alix said in the dark. "I can't lock it." Brink moved to where he remembered the door and bumped her shoulder.

"Where's the gun?" he whispered.

He heard the Webley's hammer snick back.

The sounds of boots on stairs and shouting, then someone moving again in the kitchen. A feeble crack of light appeared at the bottom of the door. More voices, more feet on the floor, and then the clear sounds of others entering the kitchen. Brink put his ear closer to the crack under the door.

A man's voice, barely audible, and before he understood it as German he had missed the words.

Next another man, this voice stronger and in French. *"Mais qu'est ce qu'ils font ici les Anglais?"* Why are the English here?

Christ. They'd come looking for him and Alix.

Alix's head was down to the floor, too, listening like he was. He smelled the cigarettes on her breath, she was so close. Brink caught her eye in the light under the door and she nodded, then stiffened as a woman's voice answered. Alix's mother.

German again, two voices, *Gestapo* the only word he caught. The voices grew and the shouting started, next the screaming.

Brink felt Alix move beside him and he knew she was reaching for the door's latch. Her mother's sound went to a shriek, the sound spearing the door. "No," he said, and grabbed for her, missed the first time, touched her wrist the second.

"Let me go," she hissed.

He wrapped his arms around her to hold her close and keep her from the door. They wrestled in the dark and her fist struck him on the cheek, but he clutched her tighter. In the storage room, where until now the only sound had been his panting and hers, something fell to the floor—heavy, the revolver—and the next moment the intertwined two of them tipped against a crate.

Hinges creaked.

Kirn aimed his torch on the floor of the storage room and found a revolver. He swung the beam to the faces, both turned to him now.

The man. The woman. From Clavette's. Alix, Jules's sister. And the Englishman.

"What is it?" the killer Adler called from the kitchen behind him.

It was that moment, hearing Adler's cigar-thickened voice, when Kirn understood. It didn't matter who owned the pestilence, Wollenstein or the SD or the Gestapo or the fucking Führer himself. It didn't matter. All of them would put it into people. Jews and gentiles, *Wulewuh* and English and German. The pestilence didn't know who it took, and it didn't care.

He'd killed. Even a pair of women once, partisans. But he was no murderer of children or the old, and certainly no killer of his own.

The two in the light on the floor were here to steal the pestilence, Wollenstein had said, but when Kirn looked into their faces, he didn't see thieves. They had brought explosives and fuses in the rucksack he'd found. They were here to ruin, not to rob. They were here to destroy the sickness.

The woman's hand snaked for the gun, and Kirn followed her hand with the torch. Her friend pulled her hand back just before it reached the revolver. Kirn looked into the man's eyes, blue in the torch's beam, and put the single finger of his right hand to his lips. A long, long moment passed between them and the English put a finger to his own lips, that finger marked with a white line that showed nicely in the torch's light.

"Nothing," Kirn said, loud so Adler could hear. "There's nothing in here. Just an open window."

He switched off the torch, stepped back, and slammed shut the door.

Fourteen

Across the street, two aproned *boche* banged on the door of Madam Aiton's house with their rifles, shouting at the old widow who lived inside, though they couldn't know it was only her and that she was ninety and hard of hearing. Alix stepped back into the shelter of her own doorway to get out of the rain. Frank did the same.

Mama was gone by the time she and Frank reached the street. The *boche* who had closed the storeroom door, he was gone, too.

Alix was numb. She'd touched Alain laid out on the kitchen table where her family had eaten for years, not imagining it would be her littlest brother's deathbed. A few days ago Papa and Jules and Alain had lived in this house. Now all three were gone, just because she'd thought Juniper loved her.

It had been so quiet in the kitchen. Alix had turned her head to listen to the four walls of silence, and watched as the walls raced away to grow the room four times its size, the kitchen expanding as she watched, her in its center all alone. When she breathed, she had heard an echo from the house made so large. This house was never quiet.

Frank had gently pulled her hand away from Alain. When he did, she heard the rain come harder against the house and the thunder rumble closer.

"Come on," he had told her, and tugged her from the kitchen. He'd opened the front door and Alix saw the black *P* painted over the red, and knew she'd never return. She didn't even bother to shut the door behind her.

There in the doorway, Frank said they had to find the *boche* policeman; he said the policeman knew something. That was why he'd not dragged them from the storeroom. What did she care about the policeman? But she'd nodded because she was following Mama, and Mama was with that policeman. Alix tucked the revolver and the knife wrapped in cloth into the old black coat of Papa's she'd pulled over her dress. As the *boche* pushed the Widow Aiton into the rain, she darted across the street, then led Frank through the narrow alley—no wider than the width of outstretched arms—and turned left down another and twisted left again before finding the small yards of the houses facing the back of Notre Dame des Flots. They carefully edged along the garden walls until they looked down the flank of the church and into the open square between it and the shops across the way. Alix crouched against the church's wet stone to make herself small, hardly noticing the rain that slicked her hair. Frank squatted beside her.

The *boche* had put up a metal tripod at the edge of the square, and on its roost were four electric lights that pointed into the square's center. Cables snaked across the pavement and into the doorway of the police station. This was a good spot, for although the square was only thirty meters away, the *boche* had to look into those lights to see their way.

Alix wiped the rain from her eyes and stared into the lit square. Mama was there somewhere. But the space was thick with people, all keeping close like boats do when it storms. A few *boche* paced the outline of the crowd, packing it tighter.

And the noise. The thunder cracked again, sharp, but it wasn't loud enough to smother the shouts and screams coming from those jammed in the square. They weren't going quietly, nor were the *boche* staying silent, for the ones in gray yelled back, sometimes darting in to lash with the butt of a weapon.

It looked like the whole village. One hundred, one hundred fifty; it was impossible to count the mass. Each minute or two, a pair of soldiers came into the light herding another knot of people. Neighbors were being slowly pushed out of sight to the right; Notre Dame's door would be there. The *boche* were shoving everyone into the church. "Look for the policeman," Frank said.

Alix looked, but one *boche* was like another, and she couldn't remember what he looked like. But as she looked, she found mama. She recognized her first by the way she stood, then by the long hair, now wet and draped along her face. She was close to disappearing beyond the stone corner of the church.

She didn't intend to do what she did, but when a *boche* slapped mama with his machine pistol, making her stagger, Alix's mind went as clean as the rain-washed cobblestones.

The next thing she knew she was running for the lighted square, shouting "Mama!" and "*Mama!*"

Don't leave me, she thought.

Just as Brink picked out the big policeman from the crowd, Alix took off like a rabbit. By the time he understood what she was doing and had straightened from his crouch, she was halfway to the lights.

Goddammit.

It was like that moment at the bluff when all he knew was that he needed her, and he'd done the first thing that popped into his mind. Same here. So he ran after her.

Brink was fast, but she had too much of a lead, and as he splashed across the cobblestones alongside the church and then onto the square, he gained ground but not enough. Ten yards between them, then five. In a dim way he thought of her as a base and figured to slide, reach out a hand to tag safe.

She pushed past the loose cordon of Germans—they were spread yards apart and none of them could touch her—and shoved into the crowd, using her arms to plow toward her mother. Brink reached out to grab sleeve or collar and drag her back.

It was a mistake.

Before he'd done more than snap out an arm for her coat, fingers gripped his wrist and spun him around to face a boy under a metal helmet, that boy's mouth open in surprise and anger, his words almost drowned by some faraway thunder and muffled by the mask he wore over his mouth. *"Wo kommst du her? Geh zurück!"*

Brink struggled against the boy's grip, looking the ten yards to the policeman, who stared back at the scuffle. The boy shoved him toward the wet bunch of French and Brink spotted Alix again, now stretched on the cobblestones. A German, fat-bellied with a nasty gun, stood over her, ready to swing it onto her head.

Brink shoved aside the one old Frenchman between him and Alix, lowered his shoulder and bulled the German to the ground in an embrace. He flailed at the man's face with his fists, connected just once, the rest of the blows glancing off his chest or helmet. Then something struck him in the back. Pain shot through his hip and into his leg.

"Steh auf!" someone shouted over him, and hands dragged him off the German and onto his feet. The fat man stepped so close that his spit rivaled the rain for a second as he bellowed about killing him, then he pulled back a gloved fist and punched Brink in the jaw. Brink went down again.

Puffing like a locomotive, the fat man loomed over him, the gun in his hand aimed at Brink's mouth. *"Steh auf!"* he screamed through his mask.

Instead, Brink got to his knees, dizzy there for a moment, and then slipped his hands under Alix. He stood up with her in his arms. Her bare legs dangled against his, her head lolled back. But she was alive.

Brink staggered with the French as the Germans fed them into the mouth of the church.

Brink let the wet crowd sweep him along. Ranks of pews stood at either side of a narrow aisle leading to the altar, where a priest leaned his hands against the long wide table. Even in the dim electric lights on the walls Brink could see the old man's white collar. The church had the Catholic crucifix at the far front wall behind the altar, the Jesus hanging there with bright red splashed at his palms and ankles, a creek of it down his side.

Carved fish ended each pew and on the walls high above the tall, narrow windows were yard-long stone reliefs of fishing boats. A heavy wooden plaque to his left held names, lots of names. *PERDU EN MER*, the top line read. Lost at sea. One Pilon was carved in there already.

It was so different from the stark church by the county road where his father ministered every Sunday, his sister as pious, him along for the ride, Donnie not yet decided. But so much the same. The keening and shouting out in the square were gone, replaced by hushed tones, a calm now that they were out of the storm of rain and Germans. Brink felt a bit of the same calm settle on him, the feeling stronger than any moment he'd had in his father's church. Water dripped from the clothes of those around him.

He looked down at Alix's face wet with the rain, her short hair glued to her head. He carried her toward the front of the church and laid her out on a pew after stepping over a little girl crying on the floor. Behind him, he heard Germans shouting, and the sound of the big wooden door slamming shut.

As he wiped away the water from Alix's face with his hand, the priest called out, the old voice carrying. Brink understood only a little because it was Latin, and Brink's only Latin had been meant to teach him anatomy. Brink heard *"In nomine Patris, et Filii, et Spiritus Sancti, Amen,"* the sudden sound at the end louder than the thunder that shook the place that same moment. "Alix," Brink said quietly, touching her shoulder, then her cheek. Behind him, the French stirred and he felt cooler air on his neck.

He twisted to look toward the door again. The German policeman standing there took off his hat, wiped his forehead, replaced the hat. The church door shut and with a fumble in his pocket, he pulled out a cigarette and lit it.

It was no coincidence. The man was looking for them.

Everyone in the church had gone mute except for a child screaming in a far corner.

Kirn stood in the dim nave, the square wooden door at his back, and tried to light a cigarette. He jammed an Eckstein between the thumb and finger on his right, and fumbled the cartridge case lighter from a pocket and spun its wheel. It took him several seconds to put the flame and the tip of the Eckstein into the same spot. He breathed in the tobacco smoke and felt calmer.

The high ceiling, with its dark recesses, was much the same as how he remembered Hillie's church, Alter Peter. The ceilings here were lower and the walls much less ornate, but the darkness was the same as Munich. He drew the darkness to him and felt it like a warm blanket. With the hand holding the cigarette, he crossed himself.

Port-en-Bessin was small enough that everyone instantly recognized him as a stranger. He caught the eye of a man five or six meters away—the fisherman from the harbor, the one whose boat he'd brushed with blue paint.

He'd not been this afraid even those days crouched in the snowy trenches south of Moscow, waiting for the howling Mongolians to come out of the blizzards again like angry angels, their white coats flapping like wings. Even months later, when he'd lost his fingers and almost bled out into the mud, he'd not been so scared. And now, he wasn't afraid of the *Wulewuhs*—he had his Walther, still in its pocket—but afraid of what he was about to do. It was treason.

Kirn scanned the crowd, looking for the tall English who had slammed Pfaff to the cobbles out in the square. But he didn't see him.

A girl, no more than fifteen, came forward. She had pleasant eyes, but a flat look on her narrow face. He didn't know what to do. Put up his good hand to shield himself? Bring out the Walther? So he drew another breath from the Eckstein, waited, and tried to keep his bowels tight.

"I know who you are," she said in a high voice. "I saw you with the other, the SS." She spat at him and the rest of the *Wulewuhs* moved closer.

Brink patted Alix's coat for the hard shape of the Webley. She stirred at his touch and moaned quietly. She'd wake in a bit.

Brink took the revolver and, holding it near his leg, stalked down the aisle. He shoved past the French as someone shouted *"Boche!"*

Brink thumbed back the hammer of the revolver. He shouldered between a teenage boy and a gray-haired crone. "Get out of the way," he said as he reached the thin ring of Frenchmen—hard-looking men who smelled like fish—around the German. He raised the revolver just when the biggest Frenchman knocked down the German with a hand to the face—pop, the sound like a ball in a mitt—and then others were leaning down and swinging fists. One kicked, and the German's head snapped to the side.

"*Stop it!*" Brink shouted, but the Frenchmen kept up the beating. If the German died, they'd never know why he'd let them hide in the storeroom. Brink moved behind the closest Frenchman, and pressed the barrel of the gun against the man's left temporal bone. "Stop . . . right . . . now," he said, each word deliberate.

The Frenchman's fist froze. One at a time, the others straightened. Brink stepped back, but when the Frenchman turned, Brink kept the gun on him.

"Who are you?" the fisherman asked. "*Boche?*" Brink shook his head. The church was quiet, quiet enough to hear the rain beating the roof far above their heads.

"*Je suis Américain,*" Brink said. "*Je suis médicin.*" The Frenchman's eyes opened wide.

"Then what do you want with this filth?" the fisherman asked.

Brink glanced at the German. He wasn't the one who had killed Alain; he was the one who had pretended not to see them. Rather than try to explain all this to the French, he told a lie. "He's sick, like some of you."

"Doctor?" the fisherman asked. "You are a doctor?" The rough fisherman's eyes were nearly hidden by deep crow's-feet. He wants me to tell him what to do, Brink realized. "I thought we would be safe in here," the fisherman said.

Safe. Brink looked around. Church was meant to be sanctuary. It had never been that for him, with so much rage in his father's sermons, but it could be for the fisherman. At the least this place could be safer. He told the fisherman what he wanted, and although the man argued at first, remembering the Webley shoved against his head, no doubt, he agreed because Brink reminded him he was the doctor.

First Brink pawed at the German's overcoat, found a black pistol, and pocketed it. He told the fishermen to drag the policeman to the same pew as Alix, had the men lay out the German. Next Brink stood on a pew and shouted "*Votre attention!*" until they listened and then called out for any who felt a fever or could not stop coughing. Just four raised their hands.

For these sickest he made a quarantine area, the space between the back of the altar and the hanging Jesus. Anyone who lived with those who had raised their hands, they sat in the fourth and fifth rows, the vacant pews at the front enough of a buffer. All the rest went to the rearmost rows.

Once he'd separated the clearly ill from the possibly ill from the unlikely ill, Brink examined those of the middle group. Without instruments, it was guesswork and perfunctory. One girl, a waif of seven or eight, breathed too ragged and had a touch of cyanosis at the edges of her ears; one of the fishermen felt too hot under his hand when Brink rested the back of it against the man's forehead. He sent both to join those beyond the altar. They went, looking fearful. But despite the horror he saw in their eyes, Brink felt braver knowing he was able to doctor like this. It was different from looking through a microscope, so far from what he'd done at Porton Down that he had a tough time believing he'd called himself a physician then.

He would need that courage. The canvas-topped Bedford had been bad, he thought, but it had only been filled with dead people, the plague run its course on them. Here he'd see the pestilence at work—hour by hour, face by face.

Until it touched him, too.

For a second Kirn thought he was still in that Munich hospital and Hillie would be waiting beside this hard bed when he opened his eyes. No. And this was no hospital. As he struggled to sit, the ache in his ribs caught short his breath. Then he touched his face with the finger of his right hand and felt the flesh tender and swollen. The fucking *Wulewuhs*.

"You are feeling how?" a man asked. The man sat on the pew beside him. His German was clumsy.

"You almost broke my arm with that bottle, English." Kirn moved slowly and rubbed his arm gently.

The man smiled as if he was about to laugh. He shook his head. "English? No." He went quiet. Smart, and used to keeping secrets. Most criminals couldn't help but talk to fill the air.

"You're here for Wollenstein's pestilence, aren't you?" Kirn asked. This was not like any questioning he'd ever done, for he was in church and as he put a hand on his overcoat, he realized he was without the Walther. And as he looked closer, he saw that the English had a revolver, blocky and black, tight in his hand. Still, Kirn wanted answers.

"*La peste,*" the man said, stealing a glance to the woman sleeping on the pew at his side. Jules's sister.

"I found the ruck you left behind," Kirn said. "You've come to destroy it. I saw the explosives."

This one gave nothing away, not an errant blink of the eyes or a dart of a glance elsewhere. Kirn kept on. "You're not here for them. A few sick *Wulewuh*, what's that to you? And Germans? No, I think not. The Jews . . ." and Kirn stopped for a moment because something registered on the man's face. "Yes, I know about the Jews. They reached England, didn't they? That's how you found this out." A bit more on the man's face. "I let you live in the storeroom," Kirn said. "You owe me answers, don't you think?"

The English stared back.

Kirn pulled a half-empty package of Ecksteins from his coat. The man watched him carefully, looked hard at the cigarettes. "Would you like one?" Kirn asked, and shook a cigarette free. He handed him an Eckstein, lit it with his cartridge case.

The English coughed behind a hand. "You know Tardif," he said. "You *knew* Tardif. But he's dead now."

Tardif? How did this one know of that one?

"You left an empty cigarette package like that, in their room," the English said, pointing to the black-and-green wrapper. "You shot him." He drew on the cigarette. His blue eyes cut into Kirn.

He's traveled far, this one. England to Tardif to Clavette to here. "Not me," said Kirn. "It was Wollenstein. He's the one who cleans up like that. Me, I'm only Kriminalpolizei."

"Gestapo."

"No, *not* Gestapo. Kriminalpolizei. Different."

"Wollenstein killed the boy in the kitchen?"

Kirn shook his head. "Another one. SD. Security police. Adler, very fat. He choked him with a plate, if you can believe that." Kirn met the man's gaze and held it.

"Why didn't you arrest us?" the English asked.

The man would make a good policeman, always asking more questions than he answered. Kirn drew deep on the Eckstein. He looked up into the darkness at the peak of the ceiling, the shadows above the tall windows. Hillie had loved Mass in Munich's Alter Peter. "I want the pestilence destroyed," Kirn said. "Like you. That's why I said nothing."

"Why?" The single word—*pourquoi*—was barely loud enough to make it the meter between them.

Kirn turned to look into the pews behind them, at these people trapped. The uncertainty and fear he saw in their faces would be repeated in uncounted places if this sickness got loose. At first only a handful would be sick, then another and another, each handful bigger than the one before until it spread through the church and into the countryside and across the borders between France and Germany, jumped the line between civilians and *Landsers*. He had little sympathy for the *Wulewuh*, but the faces would look the same when they were German.

"The man who did this must be shot," Kirn said. In his mind he saw Wollenstein. But then he looked at the English, who wouldn't meet his eyes, and his policeman's mind churned a moment, two, and something fell into place. "You make these diseases, too, don't you?" Kirn asked. "For the English."

The English said nothing.

"You've come to steal it, haven't you? Steal the pestilence so you can use it. Wollenstein was right."

"No." The English eyes met his now. "No." The man swallowed, glanced at the pews filled with *Wulewuh*, like Kirn had. "We've come to destroy it."

"You're lying," Kirn said.

"No. I worked on something like this once," said the English. "But not anymore."

"I don't believe you."

The English shrugged. "I'm the one who has this," he said, lifting the revolver. "So it doesn't really matter."

Kirn wished he still had his Walther. "Wollenstein means to put the pestilence on the beaches when your people come." That got a reaction from the English, whose mouth twitched. "Wollenstein says he has a treatment, but I don't believe him. So if he does this, it won't only be yours who die." The man's mouth opened, closed. "Mine will, too. That's why it must be stopped." Kirn thought of the men who had crouched beside him in a bunker far to the east, now perhaps along the beach somewhere.

"A treatment? A medicine?" the English asked. Kirn studied him. The medicine, *that* was what the English wanted.

"I've told you my secrets," said Kirn.

The English said nothing. He's wondering whether to trust me, Kirn thought.

"You should never lie in God's house," Kirn said, waving the Eckstein a moment, then dropped the cigarette to the stone floor and let it smolder there. "I could be shot for telling you these things." He paused. "My name is Kirn, Willi Kirn, and the Reds did this." He held up his disfigured hand. "I'd like to take what's left of my fingers home someday."

"I'm not English," the English said. "American. My name is Brink."

Kirn waited.

"We've come to destroy it," this American said.

"You said that."

"I want the medicine, if there is one," Brink said.

"Why?"

The American hesitated a heartbeat.

"Why now? Why here?" Kirn asked. But he didn't need an answer from Brink. The fisherman Pilon took the Jews to England on Wednesday, Kirn counted, touching one finger on his good hand with the thumb of the other. By Saturday, Brink had come to France, looking for the pestilence, finding it in the houses of Tardif and Clavette. Another finger. If the English were here, it must be for reasons other than to help, for why would they care if *Wulewub* and Germans fell sick? A third. The only reason that made sense was that this part of France was important. Very important. Kirn took the thought the last step, not believing it, but knowing it was true. This was where they planned their invasion. They feared that the pestilence would upset those plans. And they wanted the medicine to keep themselves clean of the sickness. He ticked off a last finger.

"*Es ist soweit,*" Kirn breathed. He found another Eckstein, lit it.

Brink stayed silent.

"I know where Wollenstein lives," Kirn said, feeling the tobacco calm him. Or was it being in the church? "I can take you there. I can get you out of this place and take you to him."

Brink's blue eyes went wide.

"But you must tell the truth," Kirn said, aiming the Eckstein at Christ on the wall. "Tell me why you're here," Kirn said, and tapped the pew. "Why now. Swear on it and I'll help you."

Tell or don't tell?

It was the best-kept secret of the war. He couldn't. Think of the hundreds, the thousands, who would die on the beaches if he blabbed.

But it was a secret that wouldn't matter if he didn't find the *Pasteurella pestis*. Kirn said the bacilli would be cast on the beaches, and if that was right, the invasion would die there, or soon after. If he didn't tell, he'd never get his hands on the antibiotic.

It was treason, he figured, to do this. But he had to.

"Here," Brink said, rapping on the pew. "Monday."

Kirn looked hard at him. "Tomorrow?"

"Tomorrow," Brink said. He scratched the tape on the middle finger on his right hand.

"I'm here to burn it," Brink added. "I swear I'm going to burn it out."

Fifteen

Wollenstein put his hand on the massive wooden door. It was wet from the slanting rain. But he stepped away, said to his assistant, "You first."

Nimmich's nervous eye ticked, but the boy pulled a cloth mask up over his nose and pushed at the door. Wollenstein moved aside until the four others—helmets, machine pistols, rubber aprons, masks, and gloves all—slipped inside. Only then did Wollenstein walk into the church.

It was beautiful and dim, with a high ceiling of arched stone overhead and ornate carvings at the walls and, he noticed, on the pews. Fish, of all things. But so odd. Not as alien as that Paris synagogue on the rue des Tournelles he'd toured, empty because its Hebrews had been carted away, but the Catholics cloaked everything with such strangeness—from the mannequin on the cross up front to the candles burning in stepped ranks far off in a corner—that it left him feeling as if he didn't belong. And he hated that.

But God was here all the same. Wollenstein may have been a lapsed Lutheran, but he felt Him now as he walked into this church. He was in the solidness of this place and the clarity of its air, in the faces of the French who rightly feared Him, even in the black satchel he carried. The moment was fleeting, for the sound of glass on glass inside the satchel was all it took to jar him back to normal.

Wollenstein hefted the doctor's satchel, brass fasteners long tarnished, that he'd taken from a Jew physician in Sachsenhausen years and years and years before. He set it on the flagstones so he could tug on rubbered gloves.

Wollenstein had expected pandemonium or at least confusion, but there was neither. Where was the chaos he'd seen in the streets? The townsfolk sat in the pews as if they waited for a priest to tell them what to say. Several rows were filled nearest him, then several rows empty, the pattern repeated. And farthest from the door and the rest in the church, a small group sat beyond the altar.

"Get them on their feet," he said to Nimmich's back. He remembered the crew of the ship in Bordeaux whom he'd made form a line and remove their clothes. How he'd burned a hole in his stomach that morning looking for buboes. Now his stomach was fine because he knew what to expect. "Have them stand against the wall where I can get a look at them."

Nimmich nodded. "Yes, Sturmbannführer," he mumbled through the mask.

"Have some respect," Wollenstein warned. He glanced toward the crucifix. "This isn't Sachsenhausen. Not the farm either."

Nimmich shouted in his thin voice, *"Up, get up!"* the reedy noise ricocheting off the tall stone walls. Nimmich and his four cleared out the rearmost pews, herding the French from their seats to stand, then shuffle down the pews to the left wall. The others, those in the pews nearer the altar, they stood, too, uncertain if the shouting was aimed at them or only the unlucky at the back. The noise grew, the keening rose. This wasn't what he had intended.

And then he looked toward the altar and saw the Kripo. As he watched, Kirn stood and came toward him. For a second, Wollenstein thought the Kriminalpolizei meant to murder him. Wollenstein groped under his tan overcoat for the holster, but only managed to put a hand on the leather by the time Kirn reached him.

"News, Herr Doktor," Kirn said. Suddenly he was Herr Doktor again.

"Really?" asked Wollenstein, breathing again. The moment had passed and he knew Kirn didn't intend to kill him. Wollenstein glanced over the Kripo's shoulder at the blond man who'd been sitting beside him. He didn't look French.

"Yes, news. The invasion, Herr Doktor, it's starting Monday morning," Kirn said.

The six Germans swept into the church, bringing the wet smell of rain with them. The first five carried guns and the sixth, a tall, thin man in a mud-streaked overcoat, gripped a black briefcase. The wind kicked the door wide and the damp breeze reached all the way to where Brink sat next to Kirn. Brink glanced at the Webley revolver but knew there was no way it would get him out of here. If he was lucky, he might shoot one before he was full of holes on the stone floor.

Kirn stood a moment later, as one German screamed at everyone to get up and move next to the wall. The big policeman approached the one in the tan coat. Brink rose to follow.

"Invasion . . . Doctor . . . Monday," Brink could hear Kirn say as he got near.

Brink's stomach cramped at the words and next he felt a numbness start in his chest and creep toward his throat. No. God, no. He'd gambled the lives of thousands of men on the sharing of the secret, and he'd crapped out. For a moment, his knees went soft.

"I want to take this news to Caen," Kirn was saying.

He'd given Kirn his great secret and now the policeman was turning him in, the son of a bitch. Brink tried to say something, but his throat was too tight and all that came out was a grunt, so he pulled the Webley out of his coat pocket and hid it as best as he could behind the other hand. Stepped closer. The one in the overcoat called out a name, and when Brink stole a look, he saw a skinny one near the wall turn this way.

"Herr Doktor, did you hear?" Kirn asked. "I know when they'll come, and where. The commando, he told me. I want to take him to Caen for questioning."

So this was Wollenstein, this Herr Doktor. The one behind the *Pasteurella pestis* that had sickened Alix's father and in all likelihood him. And Brink changed his mind in that instant. Shoot him, not Kirn. Shoot him, Brink told himself. Shoot and put an end to it. He raised the revolver and pointed it at Wollenstein, aiming over Kirn's shoulder. The secret won't be out, the plague will be stopped, and the antibiotic . . .

Brink hesitated. He looked at Wollenstein's strange eyes—one blue, the other gray—and he thought of the needle marks in the elbows of those Jewish women. They needed Wollenstein alive if he'd found an antibiotic.

The godless best know Satan, his father had said from his pulpit. Brink might be one of the few in the world who understood, really understood, this man Wollenstein. It was the kinship that made him take pause.

A sound snicked behind him. The skinny boy had come up on him and now held a pistol at his head.

"I must take this man to Caen," Kirn was saying.

"No, I don't think so," said Wollenstein. "No, I don't think you're going anywhere."

Nimmich tugged the revolver from the Englishman's hand, then called for two more SS. In a moment they were hard on either side with their machine pistols leveled at the commando and the Kripo.

One of the SS patted the coats of both Kirn and the English, and came away with another weapon, a Walther P38, from the second's pocket.

"What the fuck do you think you're doing?" Kirn asked.

Wollenstein didn't answer, only looked at his watch. Quarter past two in the morning, so it was Sunday already. Monday, Kirn claimed. Here. That meant the English and Americans must be aboard ship by now. Out of their camps and likely out of port, sailing into the Channel wrapped in steel. Not enough time before daybreak to prepare the Messerschmitt and Junkers; without the cover of dark, they'd be shot to pieces long before they got close to England. He couldn't launch an attack today.

But tomorrow, he'd catch them on the beaches.

"Let me go," Kirn said, puffing up, trying to act like he was in charge.

Wollenstein thought it through. The Kripo created the same problem as had the SD, Adler. He'd tried to solve that problem by sending Adler on a useless errand to search the Tardif farm for clues, the only thing he could think to do to keep him from a telephone. If Kirn sounded the alarm of the invasion, the news would flash from here to Berlin as fast as a teletype banged on paper. Himmler might lose his nerve or Kammler would lose it for him, and the Reichsführer would demand he abandon the farm before the boats landed. Today, he'd say. And Wollenstein would lose all chance of holding on to what he'd created.

"I have all I need to stop the invasion myself," Wollenstein said. Kirn's face was blank. He was an idiot.

Kirn tried to get to him by using his bulk, and there was a flurry of arms as the Kripo swung his big fist. But Wollenstein's SS protectors were nimble; one danced aside, then slammed his machine pistol into the Kripo's stomach. Kirn fell to his knees.

Wollenstein stood over him. "I told you I'd remember."

Kirn rolled to his back, still gasping, and his eyes squeezed shut.

Wollenstein wondered if he should have the Kripo shot now—take him into the rain and put a bullet in him—but he doubted Nimmich would do it and he wasn't certain if even the SS would follow the order. It was one thing to shoot a Jew, quite another to shoot a Kripo. That was murder. Wollenstein wished Pfaff were here; he always did what he was told.

Wollenstein pointed to the front of the church and told the SS to drag Kirn there.

The English hadn't moved. He was older, thirty or more. He certainly didn't look like a commando. But then, Wollenstein had never met one.

"I'd like a cigarette," the English said, but the accent was American. His blue eyes were steady.

Wollenstein nodded to Nimmich and the boy fingered a cigarette from a white-and-red pasteboard box, gave it to the American, lit it with a cheap chromed lighter. He cupped his hands around the flame, though there was no wind in the church, and sucked in smoke before looking up.

"So it's you who made the *Pasteurella pestis*," said the American as he exhaled.

It was just him and Wollenstein as far as Brink was concerned. Inside that bubble, he heard voices only as a deep buzz in the background, and the church itself faded to a blurry watercolor. Only Wollenstein had sharp edges and a vivid tint.

Wollenstein said nothing as the rain dully beat on the windows for a moment. Brink waited.

"Yes," Wollenstein said slowly, clearly, and surprisingly, in English. "Yes, the *pestis* is mine. What do you say to that?"

"Your English is good, that's what I'd say."

"Milwaukee."

"What?"

"I was born Milwaukee. You're American, you know where Milwaukee is, don't you? Until 1924, when my father took ill with the influenza, we lived there," Wollenstein said. "Then we come back to the Reich, my mother and sisters and myself."

"You're an American."

Wollenstein shook his head. "Never." The gray and blue eyes stared. "Who are you?"

"I'm the one who quarantined the sick at the front of the church," Brink said, pointing his cigarette. "I'm a doctor. I know the *Pasteurella pestis*."

Brink saw he'd piqued the German's curiosity.

"A doctor. Really. Where have you seen this?"

"Dakar," Brink said, and put the cigarette to his lips again. He was surprised that his hand didn't shake, for his stomach was still knotted tight. "Also England." He forced out the words. "And in your Jews."

Wollenstein's face gave it away. He *was* the one who pricked Jews with needles.

"I am not a sadist," Wollenstein said, confirming it with his words. "They weren't meant to die like that." He glanced at his watch.

"You have a treatment, don't you?" Brink asked. He didn't have much time.

Wollenstein's eyes seemed to shrink in their sockets. "You're a thief." He rubbed his hands together, the rubber squeaking just loud enough to be heard. "The Kripo said you'd come to steal this."

Brink shook his head. "I found the needle marks on some of the Jews. You used the Jews to test the treatment."

Wollenstein smiled. "What did you come for? The disease or the cure?" He glanced at his watch again. "It doesn't matter. You won't get either."

Brink stared at the leather case. Just a look inside, that's all he wanted. "How did you do it?" he asked.

Wollenstein reached for the case and their bubble broke as Brink heard the sound of glass on glass. The rain knocked against the windows. "How close have you come?" Wollenstein asked finally.

I didn't have your Jews, Brink thought. All I had was Kate, and she was crazy. "You found an antibiotic, didn't you?" Brink asked.

The German leaned forward just the slightest, held the case handle even tighter, but his odd eyes betrayed a nervousness. There *was* a medicine, Brink thought.

"You didn't answer my question. How close?" Wollenstein asked.

He and Kate had worked so hard and all they'd come up with was the actinomycin that killed her and maybe killed the colored girl. But he wasn't going to answer the German. Not yet. Instead he asked the one question he wanted answered. "Does it work?"

"You didn't get far, did you?" said Wollenstein. His eyes narrowed. "That's why you came to steal mine."

"Does it work?"

"Yes, it works," Wollenstein snapped. He'd struck a nerve. "The Jews you found? They were the last failure. The ones at my farm now, they're alive. Now I have—" and he headed for the front of the church. Brink grabbed the overcoat sleeve.

"How did you do it?" Brink asked. He held tight.

Wollenstein pried Brink's hand from the material, then put a finger alongside his own nose. "A secret." He smiled thinly. "The Jews." He looked at the case he held. "They may be animals, but without them, I wouldn't have this." He rattled the case again.

Brink remembered the smell that had slapped him when he'd lifted the canvas cover of the Bedford in St. Richards's gravel lot. The little girl with the blood goatee. Now was the time.

"I did it without killing anyone," Brink said to Wollenstein, lying. Brink made himself smile, as if gloating. "Four months . . . and six days ago. January 29," said Brink. The day when Kate poisoned herself.

"I don't believe you."

"I used it on a real plague in Dakar, not one . . ." and Brink waved a hand dismissively, "not one in a laboratory." He had to convince this German that he was worth talking to. Only then might Wollenstein take him out of here and give him a chance to escape so he could find Wickens and hunt down the pestilence before it was too late.

Wollenstein looked at him carefully. "How did you find it?" the German asked finally. Testing him.

"Soil samples," he answered. "A lot of soil samples."

Wollenstein nodded, but looked at his watch again. "I must take care of the sick," he said, hefting the case and taking one step toward the altar.

"You're going to murder them, like you did Tardif?" Brink asked, desperate, and Wollenstein stopped, turned.

"No."

"You're a doctor," Brink said. "You swore like I did. *Primum non nocere.*"

Wollenstein returned and pushed one of his gloved fingers into Brink's chest. "The only harm I'll do is to my enemies."

Childess had said they had to be as evil, but he was wrong, Brink thought. "Even if you didn't have enemies, you'd still use the plague," said Brink. "That's what I think."

Wollenstein stared. "If you had this," he said, jangling the case again, "then you would use the pestilence, too. Why else did you make it if not to cure what you planned to sow on us? We're no different." He spun and strode up the aisle then, the skinny boy at his shoulder.

By the time the pair reached the three stone steps that led up to the raised space, two SS soldiers had joined them. Brink followed, close enough to see but not close enough to make the SS with the machine guns do more than watch him.

Wollenstein had his mask pulled over his mouth and nose now, and bent low to look into the faces of those in the quarantine. Alix's mother, sitting on the floor, her shoulders against the stone wall, and six others. Wollenstein looked at them all.

As Brink watched from the steps, the German opened his black case and pulled out a syringe, already needle-tipped, and a glass bottle with a rubber stopper. He upended the bottle, stuck the needle into the stopper, and withdrew some of the clear liquid, peering closely at the marks on the syringe. Brink was too far to see the dosage, but it was short, a cc or two.

All seven got the needle. The German swabbed arms with alcohol on a cotton cloth, then gently stuck each with the needle and pressed the plunger home.

"Move these," the Germans said to his boy. "Put them in the gendarme's cell until you find another truck to bring them to the farm."

"Of course," the boy said. He motioned to the two SS, and they chose four big Frenchmen to haul the seven to their feet and help them wobble down the steps and aisle and to the door at its end. One Frenchman cradled the little girl in his arms, another struggled with Madam Pilon in his.

Wollenstein was the last down the steps, with the boy and the four guards following now, their gun swiveling from side to side as they retreated. But the doctor stopped as he came even with Brink. "You made this medicine, too? Truly?" the German asked. Again the black leather case rattled. There was a pistol in his free hand now, although it pointed at the floor.

"I'm the same as you," said Brink, using the German this time. *Ich bin so wie du.* He looked at the pistol, the case, the pistol. "We should talk, you and I. I can tell you how it worked in Dakar." It was the last bone he could think to dangle in front of Wollenstein.

"No, I think not. We are not the same, not in this. *I* have it," and Wollenstein shook the case and raised the pistol, "while you have nothing." Brink held his breath. But Wollenstein only turned and made for the door, the nervous boy at his shoulder, the soldiers pointing their weapons left and right as they backed down the aisle. And then the door slammed shut.

Wollenstein took shelter in the doorway, yanked off the mask to let it hang around his throat, tugged the gloves to remove them from his too-wet palms. His hands trembled.

He'd wanted to shoot the thief but he'd not known how to pull the trigger. Pfaff took care of such things. Pfaff had put Tardif out of his misery, Pfaff dealt with the Jews too sick to make the truck ride to Caen and its crematorium.

What he couldn't decide was whether he wanted to kill because the American lied or told the truth. Had he been baiting him with the talk of finding his own antibiotic?

The American had been right about one thing. Wollenstein had wanted to talk, discuss the hows and whys, because there was no one else—not Nimmich, not *der Ofenmann*—who understood. This American may be the only other in the world who understood. Wollenstein glanced at his watch. But there wasn't time. It was already nearly three in the morning. Twenty-four hours, a few more, a few less.

A black rain swept flat past the doorway, and brought Wollenstein out of his dream. The weather was scrubbing the street like Grau had wanted. The SS boy with the bad lip stood across the street, bright in the glare of the electric lights, water cascading off the back flange of his helmet as he guarded the door to the police station and the seven given the medicine. Nimmich came out of the station and ran to him, newspaper held over his head. When he reached shelter beside Wollenstein, Nimmich tossed the paper aside.

"Where's Pfaff?" Wollenstein asked.

"He's not returned with Adler," Nimmich said. "The rest are there." He pointed to a doorway three down from the police where the word *Boulangerie* was painted on the plate glass. "They were hungry," Nimmich said, shrugging.

Wollenstein did a count. Issmer and two others were with Adler in the Mercedes truck. Pfaff was on his own in the Kripo's Renault, following those four to make sure the SD didn't find a telephone and raise the alarm. The droop-lipped one guarded the seven French. That left seventeen packed in the bakery.

"Find a car," he told Nimmich. "We need to return to the farm."

"A car? I don't think there is one. Klein couldn't find another truck like you wanted." He waved a hand to the boy in front of the police station. Klein, that was his name.

"Go ask the Hauptman. Grau. He runs this place, that house up the way." Wollenstein pointed toward the harbor. "Tell him I've taken care of his problem, and I need transport. Anything with an engine. I'll return it later today, promise him twenty liters of petrol for the trouble."

Nimmich looked at him, the tic returning.

"I'll tell you on the drive back," said Wollenstein. He looked at his watch again. Another minute.

But Nimmich had more questions. "What of them?" he asked and glanced at the gendarmerie.

"Klein stays," Wollenstein said. He pointed to the SS standing in the rain. "Have two watch the church. I'll leave orders for Pfaff. Go on, find something with wheels." Nimmich hesitated, then nodded and ducked his head and ran back into the storm.

Wollenstein groped for his notebook, pulled it from inside his tunic and using the pencil buried in its pages, wrote in thick block letters: "Kripo and doc. require special handling." He let the pencil waver over the notebook a moment. What else to tell? Wollenstein looked at the time. Three more minutes forever gone. He couldn't spare Pfaff for long—he might need him at the farm, him and his fat, blank face and the hardness it disguised. "Bring Fr. in gendarmerie to farm . . . watch Adler. *No telephone.*" He signed it with a quick scrawl, tore the page from the notebook, folded it. He shouted to Klein, and at the second call the boy came trotting. "Give this to Unterscharführer Pfaff when he returns. As soon as he returns." The boy nodded.

An engine clapped up the street, and around the corner slid a muddy Kübelwagen. It lacked windows on the sides and there was a long rip in the canvas top. Nimmich drew up to the curb a few meters away. It would be a long, wet ride, thought Wollenstein as he stepped around the blunt nose of the little car and climbed in. Nimmich shoved the lever into gear and it began to jump over the cobbles. Wollenstein's teeth clattered together.

Another look at his watch. Ten past three. The minutes ticked by as fast as that nervous eye of Nimmich.

Brink woke at the peal of thunder, his head snapping up and banging against the long altar at his back. Gray light filtered through the tall windows. He looked at his watch: half past ten.

Christ. He'd been asleep for hours.

He stood and put one hand on the flat top of altar. This had felt like a sanctuary the night before; now it was the same prison as Porton Down. He'd gone to work there confident in the cause and glad he had a part, but the clots of sheep dead from *Bacillus anthracis* had given him nightmares that wouldn't be calmed no matter how much he drank. So he'd begged Childess to set him free. But for all he loved Kate, the work on the A series was just as much a jail as the anthrax, for it was all marching to the same end. He had tried to tell Kate, but she'd never understood. And then she was dead in the prison they'd built out of their delusion.

There was no better proof than the view from here. Most of the townspeople had fallen asleep, heads on others' shoulders, or stretched out on the pews. Only a few of the men were awake, those in the middle rows, who were talking in low voices and sharing a cigarette. None of them were safe, even though the most clearly ill had been dragged away. The *Pasteurella pestis* could be in any of them—maybe in him, maybe in Alix—and might not show for days. Let loose, those here in the church could make another truck's worth of dead, then another. An endless convoy.

What had they been thinking, him and Paul Childess and Katherine Moody and all the others at Porton Down? Once they'd spawned the darlings, they'd never be able to keep them in the petri dishes. Nobody had thought this through, not really. And now look.

The rain swept hard on the tall windows and knocked harder against the roof, and thunder banged in the distance and the wind shrieked. Maybe the weather would buy him time. Surely the clumsy boats he'd seen in Portsmouth harbor wouldn't launch in this. Brink peeked at his hand. Time was nearly gone.

He looked for Alix. Found her in the second pew, overlooked before because she'd had her head down. Now she stared straight ahead, not at him, Brink thought, but at the Christ figure behind him. Her hands were folded in prayer, wrists over the edge of the pew in front of her. The old priest sat beside her.

They put their heads together, she and the priest, hers almost on the narrow shoulder of the gray-haired man. The old man put his hand on Alix's head, Alix crossed herself that Catholic way.

To have someone between you and God, something in Brink rebelled against that. Yet he couldn't help but feel a bit of envy that Alix had someone to share her prayer with, someone to tell her that it would all be fine. Someone to give her the end of her story.

Alix rose from the pew and wound her way to the altar and him. "How are you feeling?" he asked. She touched the back of her head.

"People told me that the *boche* came last night and took mama," she said. "The *boche* have it, the medicine you talked about?" Brink nodded. "She's safe," she said. He nodded again. Her shoulders relaxed and she seemed at peace for the first time since he'd met her in the hospital. She looked toward Kirn, who sat alone in the first row at the far left. "I want to ask him about Jules."

"Not now. We need him. He said he can take us to the place where the pestilence and the medicine are made."

She stared at Kirn a moment longer, then at the priest, who now had another parishioner at his shoulder. "You won't lie to me, will you?" she asked, the question catching him off guard. She leaned toward him, touched the altar with one hand and rested the other on his chest. "You're certain that the medicine cures this?" Alix asked. "You are very, very sure?"

He believed Wollenstein. "I'm sure," he said.

Alix nodded. She pushed her hair behind her ear. And she moved closer—the altar was at his back so he couldn't retreat—and put both hands to his face, her callused fingers rough on his unshaven cheeks, then she leaned in and kissed him on the lips. He let it happen, smelling her hair and smelling apples as he closed his eyes, and didn't push her away. She broke the kiss. He could feel her breath hot on his throat, and opened his eyes as she looked up at him.

"If I'm sick," she said, "you're sick now, too."

He didn't bother telling her it didn't matter, that, like her, he'd been exposed through her father.

"We're like family now," she said. She gestured toward those still in the church. "You'll make sure we find the medicine, won't you, for us?"

He looked at her, not at the others. "I'll find it," he said.

Brink didn't bow his head nor close his eyes, but prayed all the same. That moment, he wished to feel his father's hand on his shoulder, but there was nothing, not even a ghost of a Jew or two. Just him and God.

Brink looked around the church, sick and tired of being alone.

Kirn watched as the Pilon woman leaned toward Brink, kissed him.

I'm an ass, Kirn thought. "I've got all I need to stop the invasion," Wollenstein had said. Kirn had used the news of the invasion as a test, and the doctor had failed. Wollenstein would rather spread the pestilence across France than raise the alarm. The fat SD had told the truth.

If Wollenstein had passed my test, he would have let me take the English . . . the American . . . Brink. He would have let me go to Caen to tell Isselmann of the invasion, Kirn thought. And then I would have driven the dirt road to Wollenstein's home, and Brink and I would have burnt out the pestilence.

What an ass I am.

Kirn, his stomach still uneasy after taking the blow, stood and wound his way down the row, up the aisle, up the short steps to the apse, and then to the altar. Brink and the woman both turned as he came to them. The woman, she hated him with all her heart—that was plain. Because of her little brother, he supposed, the one she'd shot. Brink, however, was impossible to read, like before.

"You told him about the invasion," Brink said. "That wasn't part of our arrangement." His voice got louder.

Kirn spoke quietly. "I thought he would let me take you out of here if I told him."

"Liar."

Kirn shook his head. He had known there was a chance Wollenstein would not let him go. But he'd thought that no matter what, the SS doctor would shout out that the invasion was coming.

"How do we get out of here now?" Brink shouted. Kirn thought the American might come at him with his fists. He made his good hand into one.

Kirn didn't have an answer, so he asked his own question. "What did you tell Wollenstein?"

The Pilon woman surprised him. She jumped forward, her hands on the front of his overcoat, and she reached for his face and scratched a finger toward his eye, shouting out *"Jules!"* like in Clavette's house. But before Kirn could push her down, Brink was between them, trying to separate them. Kirn thought the American meant to hurt him and he grabbed Brink by the throat with his one good hand.

Behind him, he heard the big wooden door bang open, a gust following that brought the humid air and rainwater all the way to the apse. It wet the back of his neck.

"*Let him go, Kripo!*" yelled someone from that open door.

Kirn didn't release the gasping American, but twisted to look over his shoulder to see who ordered him. The fat one, Wollenstein's Pfaff, was the one who called; the fatter one, Adler, the SD prick who wanted the pestilence, stood next to Pfaff, hands in his overcoat pockets, looking pleased with himself. Perhaps he'd murdered another child to put that grin on his face. Two other SS crowded at the SD's shoulders.

"Let him go, Kirn," called Adler. "I want to talk to him."

That's when the pounding walked toward them.

Brink heard a rumbling squeeze through the thick church walls, and at first thought it was just long thunder. Kirn let him go and stumbled off the altar's platform, fell, then on hands and knees crawled for the shelter of the first pew. The stones under Brink shuddered and Alix tripped, then crawled closer. The noise was deafening, a hundred times that of the roar from the largest crowd he'd heard that summer of '37 playing for the Cardinals. Dust drifted from the high ceiling. He tried to stand, not even remembering falling.

Another hammer pushed him to the floor. He put out his hands to catch himself, and felt the flagstones scrape his palms. More loud cracks came, just like that, and bounced him against the altar.

The sounds rolled the church. Brink twisted enough to see that Alix was now beside him, her mouth open wide but with no sound coming out. She opened her arms and he pulled her close.

The bomb punched through the upper panes of the middle window and buried itself at grave's depth between the aisle and the north wall. Then it exploded, pushing pressure waves through the ground and air to shatter the nearest pews into impossible, dangerous jigsaws. It blew a gaping hole in the roof above, and shifted most of the wall into a landslide that filled the nave.

For Brink, it was as if the world ended.

Russian artillery had never rained like this. But Kirn had heard aircraft overhead a time or two, been under bombs twice—once under the fucking Luftwaffe's own, some idiot pilot lost and confused. More important, he'd heard their distant pounding during his time in France. His reflexes were still quick enough to let go of the American and dive for shelter without him.

This was the last thing Hillie had heard, he thought, as the bombs came fast and close enough to shove him hard against the enclosed back of a pew, making his space a long coffin with only one open side. He folded his hand over his head and pressed his cheek against the flagstones and prayed fast that the next one landed past them.

No. It blew into the church, snuffed out the light with its sound, tipped over the pew so it covered him completely, and clattered fragments off the wood above his head.

Kirn never lost consciousness, but it was several seconds before he could worm out from under the pew and come to a knee to look at the bomb's work. The middle of the church was gone, he could see that much through the swirling dust. Most of the *Wulewuhs* were buried under the rubble, made thin by the thick stones and timbers.

In the other direction, the altar stood, but its cloth and candlesticks were missing, brushed away by the concussion. The bomb had tumbled the crucifix off the wall. It lay facedown on the stone floor.

There was no sign of Brink, nor the Pilon girl.

No door now to block his way, Kirn stood on unsteady legs and headed for the street. In the mid-morning's dim light of the street, he saw fat Unterscharführer Pfaff knocked flat on his back. Kirn walked to him. A wooden shard half a meter long speared the man's big stomach like a signpost, a wash of thin red on the cobbles beside him ran like paint in the rain. The wood that staked Pfaff to the cobbles wavered as Pfaff breathed. Kirn bent down, letting the rain patter against his bare head, wanting to say something, but the man's eyes were closed. Pity. Instead, he simply put his hand on the end of the splinter and thought about pushing.

Pfaff's eyes fluttered open, and blood leaked from his mouth. No, better to let this one wither on his own, Kirn thought. He leaned close enough so that Pfaff could hear him if the fat man's ears still worked.

"You should have kept Adler from killing that boy," Kirn said. "We both should have." Pfaff didn't seem to understand, and Kirn gave up.

Instead, he looked to his left where the way was clear. To his right, a mound of rubble—a slice of the church's tower that had collapsed into the street—blocked the way toward the harbor and Grau's command post. Beyond the mound was a wavering line of dust and smoke where the bombs had landed. He wondered if he'd be able to see all the way to the water when the air cleared. Across the square, a dust-covered man crawled on stumps of wrists from the wreckage of a line of shops and collapsed facedown. A bakery had been there, he remembered, but it was nothing now, just splinters in the street and in this fat fuck. Kirn looked down at Pfaff again; the arrow in him still moved, faster now as the man got closer to death.

The gendarme's station had disappeared, too, a pile of ripped lumber and cracked masonry. An SS moved slowly in the street, ten meters from where it had stood.

Kirn felt the raindrops beat his head—where had his hat gone?—and tried to decide. Turn left to run alone toward Chef du Pont to destroy Wollenstein's sickness? Or go to the right, to Grau, to report the invasion?

Perhaps it was the ghosts of his comrades who told him the way, Kirn didn't know. He went neither left nor right, but instead turned back to the church to search for Brink.

Brink came awake with the hearing of an old man, fuzzy and far away. He reached up to the altar for purchase, failed, and once he'd found some strength, put out his hand to pull himself upright. His sight faded for a moment, vision tunneled, but he held on to the massive wooden table with both hands and the dizziness passed.

The bomb had brought down stones and columns and roof tiles and rafters to smother everything from just this side of the door to the third row of pews. A small fire flickered against the wall in a corner. Rather than a crater there was a heap of rubble and, beyond that, the street.

The noise in his ears slowly faded and was replaced by cries and moans, a single loud, long scream and a choir of shifting, slipping stones. He turned from the ruin. Alix was a gray blanket stretched on the floor face-down in the shelter of the altar, covered in dust that made Brink think of the DDT-powdered Jews in St. Richards's morgue.

He bent over her, chest hammering, but when he touched her she moaned.

Brink rolled her over, then pulled her into a sitting position. With hands under her arms, he hauled her off the floor to clutch her tight. She made another sound, low and long. He swung her arm over his shoulder, and stooping, dragged her down the short steps. The old priest lay at their bottom, his eyes open to the ruined roof.

Brink turned to look for Kirn at the place where he'd crawled for protection, but all he saw was tipped pews. Down among those pews, he helped Alix over the mounds of broken church, around bodies that showed under the wreckage, over the few living who sat stunned. One man—it was the fisherman against whose head he'd rested the revolver—sat talking to his own shattered foot.

Brink reached the door. The rain washed out of the clouds, and although the sun had been long up, it seemed like dusk. Beside him lay a pair of Germans, one with a bright slash across his forehead and a blood-ied stone nearby to tell the story; the other moaned, then twitched. Yet another was trapped under that one; Brink saw a thick leg and boot that didn't belong to either of the first two. The leg and its boot moved. Brink bent slowly so as not to lose Alix from his shoulder, and picked up a gun, a German gun, and straightened.

He stepped into the street with the gun in one hand, the other arm wrapped around Alix, and looked up to see Kirn in front of him.

"We're going to Wollenstein," the German said. "But once we finish with him, I'm raising the alarm."

"After Wollenstein, I don't care what you do," Brink said.

"Mama," Alix said weakly. She struggled against him, but he held tight and she was too weak to escape his grasp.

Brink headed for the nearest corner and the street that would take them away, southwest, he knew, and in the right direction. The mouth of the street swallowed them, and they stayed close to the walls and doorways.

Brink could hear their footsteps over the shouting of more Germans reaching the church.

It was only after they'd trudged a street or two, Brink's sense of direction holding true, that they met him. Wickens stepped out of a doorway, his hand holding a Sten, the pack on his back, and earphones—like what a telephone switchboard operator would wear—curled around his neck. He pointed the Sten, nodded to the weapon Brink held.

"You're alive," the Englishman said. He sounded disappointed. "Give me the gun, Doctor. We're going to see Sam."

Sixteen

Tardif's barn smelled some of the same—hay and old dung, grain dust and dirt dust—but there was a different odor over all that. A woody, tobacco smell that at first was not unpleasant, but the deeper into the barn he went, the more it was just the harsh stink of cigars. Wickens sniffed it, too, for he'd stiffened as soon as they'd stepped into the dry barn and no one had answered his call of "Sam."

Eggers hadn't died well. His own belt was around his neck, the buckle cinched beyond the last punch, the leather nearly swallowed by the flesh folded over it. His tongue was a fat slug between his lips, his eyes bloodshot, a deep red. Blood covered his arm and the dressing that had been wound around it lay in the hay; a small shovel nearby was smeared dark on its blade from the pressing or the banging on the swollen wound. There were more bloodstains on Eggers's pants at both knees, and something white in the dirt caught Brink's eye. A fragment of a tooth. There were four cigar butts mashed into the dirt in an arc a few feet from Eggers. Someone had taken a lot of time doing this.

Eggers's eyes were open and Wickens knelt and fingered the eyelids down.

The man had died not long before, maybe a few hours or so, for rigor mortis had not begun to stiffen the fingers that Wickens took hold of. Wickens sat in the hay beside the old man and touched his shoulder, let a hand rest there for a moment. "He'll go rank for certain."

"Let me help you bury him," said Brink quietly.

"Like Christ you won't," Wickens said without any anger. "Go away, just go away. Leave me alone."

The three of them, Brink, Kirn, and Alix, moved nearer the door, and then Alix left the barn. In a few minutes she returned with a bundled blanket and spread that on the beaten dirt. Inside its folds were apples, a loaf of bread, and a small, chipped crock the size of her hand. She pulled off the lid and sniffed, put the cover back.

Brink took two apples and a torn chunk of the bread to the open door where he wouldn't have to see Eggers. Alix and Kirn stayed beside the truck.

He glanced at his watch. Quarter past four.

It had taken them hours to slink from Port-en-Bessin to Tardif's barn, hiding in stands of trees under dripping leaves or kneeling behind the short walls that edged from silent houses, getting wet there, too. They met a clump of Germans heading into the town and later hid from two patrols wandering the roads and lanes. The last bit he'd limped on an aching ankle.

He threw the second apple core into the rain and stepped back into the barn. Alix, her back against a mud-thickened wheel, glanced up but said nothing. Other than to give directions, she'd kept quiet since they'd left Port-en-Bessin. She'd looked over her shoulder once as they cleared the village, but there was nothing to see except a thin line of smoke in the rain, no sound once they cleared the town other than the hard noise of the rain on the leaves in the trees above them and in the hedges beside them.

"It was the fattest one, the SD," Kirn said from his spot next to Alix. He pointed at Eggers. "Adler. He killed your youngest brother by choking him, too. It must be a habit."

Eggers had been tortured, killed when he talked or murdered when he didn't. Brink wondered what Eggers had said, if anything, but then he remembered it didn't much matter because he'd already told Kirn the most important secret. Kirn, in turn, had told Wollenstein who might have spread the word to Paris and beyond by now.

He glanced at his watch again. Twenty-five past four. Dawn, and the invasion, was just thirteen or fourteen hours away. What chance did they have of finding Wollenstein's hole in that time? Brink glanced at Alix— she was talking to Kirn, their heads close together—and wondered if the bacilli were incubating, multiplying in her. Or in him. If so, it was too late.

But there was still a way to put an end to Wollenstein's *pestis*. It would stamp out the antibiotic at the same time, but that couldn't matter now.

Brink went deeper into the barn and to the pack that Wickens had carried, flung back its flap, and started pulling out things. Long metal magazines for the Sten, a tight bundle of dry clothes, one can, then another—Spam he recognized, the other didn't have a label—and several small paper-wrapped blocks. A spool of wire, another of cord, a map that he unfolded on the dirt. He looked into the pack and saw Wickens's Webley. He reached in and almost touched it.

"Wot the hell you doing?" Wickens's voice made him jump. "Get away from that."

Brink straightened from his crouch over the pack. "You said you had a radio," he said, and pointed to the earphones still wrapped around Wickens's neck. "What happened to the radio? We can call the bombers. He knows the location of the lab." He pointed to the map. He'd told Wickens on the long march that the German was along because he knew where the *pestis* was made, but that was all. He'd of course said nothing about the secret he'd spilled, or even that Kirn said he wanted it destroyed. He didn't trust Wickens. "Maybe the bombers can hit it."

Wickens plucked the earphones from around his throat, tossed them into the hay piled behind Eggers, then stood. "The S-phone's under a lot of stone, I imagine."

Brink ran the image through his tired mind. If he'd had more sleep, he could figure this out.

Wickens helped him. "That's how I called them onto Port-en-Bessin," the Englishman said. He reached for the things Brink had yanked from the pack. "They didn't do a bloody right job, did they?" Wickens asked. He closed the flap on the pack.

Wickens was supposed to use the S-phone to blow the Germans' laboratory to smithereens; Brink remembered that much of the Baker Street plan. Now he understood. Or thought he did. Wickens had used his S-phone to shepherd the bombers to Port-en-Bessin. He thought he knew why.

"How did you know the bombs would set us free?"

The Englishman laughed. "You *are* thick. I wasn't trying to break you out—I didn't know you were in there. The church, I mean. I just snuck up and set the S-phone against an outside wall and the Mosquitoes rode in on the signal."

It took Brink a minute to understand. "You're crazy."

"I told you I have orders, orders from on highest," Wickens said. "Told you in that frog's house."

"To stop the plague from spreading." All those in the church. Christ.

Wickens nodded and smiled thinly, his chipped tooth showing only a bit. "Time was up. The first bunch will be dropping out of their Dakotas in"—Wickens looked at the watch on his wrist—"less than eight hours. Not enough time to find the darlings. So I decided."

He didn't find us at Clavette's when he came back to the house, so Wickens had watched while the Germans pushed everyone into the church. They'd made his job so easy, collecting everyone for him. Then he'd called in the bombs.

"But we have to destroy its source, where they make the *pestis*," Brink said quietly. He looked at Alix again, anywhere but at Wickens, because if he did he'd lose it. He'd take on Wickens for trying to murder them, him and Alix and Kirn. Only this time Wickens didn't have his back turned, and the Brit would kill him.

"We're out of time. I've done best I could," Wickens said, looking straight at Brink. "We'll sit tight," Wickens went on. "Wait for the lads to come ashore or the paras to find us." He pulled the Sten, which had been slung over his shoulder on a canvas strap, into his hands. The barrel aimed for the dirt floor, but that was just for show. "You and her and him," Wickens said, the Sten's muzzle weaving a bit as it seemed to search for the others, "you're not going anywhere. You were all in there, bay you? Sick by now. When the lads come I'll find a way to get a message home. They can decide wot's to be done." He glanced at Eggers for a second, back toward Brink. "Especially you. You're not going anywhere."

If there was no way to call in more bombers, they had to reach

Wollenstein on their own. Each second that ticked away was another that they might need to get to wherever Kirn took them. They couldn't just sit here.

Brink looked into Wickens's eyes and knew what he had to do. Stay calm, he told himself. Don't look at the gun. "I told the policeman about the invasion," Brink said.

Wickens flinched and the muzzle of the Sten drooped. "You bloody—"

"I told him it was tomorrow. Here," Brink said, tempted to look at Wickens's hands, how they were wrapped on the gun. "I had to tell him so he'd take us to the disease."

"You'll swing for this, so help me God," Wickens said. He motioned with the gun for Brink to back away.

"We don't have time to waste, that's what I'm telling you," Brink said, not backing up a step.

"It's too late," said Wickens.

"We have to try," Brink said.

"I said it's too late."

"No, we have half a day yet and—"

"*It's too late!*" Wickens shouted. "*Too bloody fucking late to find him! Wot don't you understand? Fuck!*" A vein stood out on Wickens's forehead.

At first Brink thought he'd heard Wickens wrong. "Him?" he asked.

Wickens stared back.

How could I be so stupid? thought Brink as the bits went together. "You've come for Wollenstein. You want to take him back to England."

A small moment of shock registered on Wickens's face, but he recovered and made his expression go flat. "Is that his name?"

"Jesus."

"Don't be so surprised," said Wickens.

Brink didn't ask the why; that came to him as pieces assembling like Wickens's Sten. Wollenstein had figured out the secrets of *Pasteurella pestis*, something Porton Down had never uncovered. Porton Down wanted that secret, ergo they wanted Wollenstein.

"You can't take him back," Brink said. Wollenstein in England meant that the *Pasteurella pestis* only switched sides. He'd risked his life a dozen times so they could burn it or bury it, not just so it could pack up and move across the Channel.

"Do you know wot's funny? That's exactly wot Childess thought you would say."

"This was always about Wollenstein," Brink said. "Wasn't it?"

"Sam and I and Owen been looking for him and his darlings for months, and the last time we lost Owen, Sam and I did, and now I've lost . . ."

Wickens had been told to find it. Not to destroy it, not to burn it, not to wipe it out. But so Porton Down could have it.

Paul Childess had told him over and over that the anthrax wouldn't be used without cause. Each time he and Kate made more progress, he'd gone to Childess to hear one more time how if they got the antibiotic to work, it would only be used if the Germans strewed something on English or American heads. The antibiotic would never be insurance for their side firing first with tiny, killing things.

But all that time Childess had coveted Wollenstein.

"He was in on it from the beginning, you know," Wickens said. Wickens knew exactly what he was saying; he was enjoying how this was hitting Brink.

Childess wanted Wollenstein's killers. He had the *Bacillus anthracis*, a fine enough toy, but he wanted the German's *Pasteurella pestis*. It was such a better weapon, wasn't it, the way it struck fast and direct. Anthrax could take weeks to work its way through the food supply and then might kill just a quarter, certainly no more than half, of those infected. Pneumonic plague killed in days, killed everyone. Brink saw all these things in one flash after another.

Secrets, Brink understood secrets. But lies, lies on top of lies . . . The duplicity put a heat at his temples, and in the rush he wanted a cigarette, stupid as that was. The betrayal was an empty hole in his chest, the lies coming not from just a friend, but family almost. What had *ever* been the truth with Paul Childess? When had he *not* lied? All Brink could do was pull fragments of conversations, one separated from the next by weeks or months, until it was just a jangle of Childess talking in his head.

Liar, liar, liar.

"The old man didn't trust you, did he?" asked Wickens. Nearly laughing at him now. "He had other orders for me, too. Said if I found the Hun, I wasn't supposed to bring you home. Do you understand?" Wickens put an index finger to his temple, his thumb making a revolver's hammer.

Brink felt the barn's temperature drop, until the cold chased down this throat and invaded his heart.

"Not enough space near the darlings for two geniuses, was that it?" asked Wickens, who grinned.

No, that wasn't it. But he knew why in a short, bright flash, an actual flash that shorted out his vision. Kate, it was Kate. Childess blamed him. He'd loved her once; Brink had stolen her. This was how Childess put teeth in that blame.

Wickens told the truth, Brink knew. He remembered Childess's last words outside 10 Downing. "Good-bye, Frank," Paul had said. Not "good luck" or "Godspeed." The finality of good-bye.

I will kill this Judas when I get home, Brink swore.

"How do you know his name?" Wickens asked, the turn in conversation bringing Brink back. "The German doctor?"

Slowly. "I talked to him."

"You talked to him," Wickens said. "Wot did you tell him?"

Brink looked at Wickens. He had to focus on the here and now, not the future and what he would do to Childess.

Brink had to push more, make Wickens even angrier so he could make a grab for the Sten. "The policeman told him about the invasion, that's what."

"You fucking fool," Wickens whispered. "Do you know wot you've done?"

"I'm trying to finish what we started. Didn't Sam say that's what you did?" Using Eggers's Christian name, maybe that would send the Englishman over the edge.

"Sam and I, we lost Owen looking for him," said Wickens, the words rising in volume as each came out, "and now Sam's dead because of *you!*" Wickens caught his breath. "He'll bray it all the way to Berlin and the fuckin' Huns will be all awake tomorrow morning, won't they? *And Sam's dead for nothing!*"

"Juniper," Alix said behind him.

"Mind your business, Alix," Wickens said in French.

"I'm not going to let you take him back," Brink said, looking at how Wickens's hands were on the Sten.

"Not going to let me?" Wickens shouted. He laughed. "You've never had a say, you stupid shite."

"Childess didn't tell you everything, did he?" Brink asked, keeping his voice so low that Wickens stepped closer, which was what he wanted. "I didn't come here just to take you to your damned darlings." Wickens edged nearer. Brink played his last card. "I came because there's an antibiotic, a medicine, you ignorant piece of shit, and I'm gonna find that medicine because *she has the sickness.*"

He went softer with each word and then Wickens's eyes got wide as Brink told him the truth, or the lie, whichever it was, of Alix. The Englishman came within arm's reach and the Sten's mouth slipped a bit toward the dirt floor and Brink took his shot, stepping forward with his right hand down and out to grab for the barrel and his left, awkward, but that was what he had, arcing toward Wickens's jaw.

He didn't have a prayer. Wickens gracefully leaned back as if he was expecting it and Brink's fist caught air. The Sten came up too fast for Brink to snag, and the hole in its end looked as big as the barn's door.

But Wickens didn't pull the trigger.

"Juniper, don't hurt him!" he heard Alix yell. Pleading, like. *"Juniper!"*

The mouth of the Sten disappeared, and instead Wickens's fist came up to meet Brink's jaw. He was down and done as if he'd taken a baseball to the head.

It all made perfect sense to Wollenstein.

He stood under the large oak that dominated the south end of the landing field—the rain fell slower in the shelter of its leaves—and squinted at the lights set around the black Me-110 thirty meters away. The ground crew he'd had quartered in Chef du Pont came and went in the light, appearing one moment from beneath a wing, the next disappearing under the radar antlers at the nose. The two broad propellers were motionless, bright, and the three wet blades on the nearest gleamed in the light. The aircraft had been old four years before, but with the Lichtenstein in its nose, it had been given new life as a night-fighter, and had brought down six British bombers; the stenciled shapes painted under its glass canopy said so. The Me-110 had been his since March, when The Letter had pried it away from the Luftwaffe.

His watch read quarter to eleven when he put his torch to it.

"What if they don't come?" asked Nimmich. Wollenstein pointed the torch at the boy, and Nimmich shielded his eyes so Wollenstein couldn't tell if the tic still flickered. He switched off the torch.

"They will," Wollenstein said. He was certain Kirn told the truth, not because he trusted the policeman, but because of the American doctor. By now both Kirn and the English were dead, killed by Pfaff. He regretted only the American's death. If circumstances had been different . . .

"But if they don't. It's not exactly invasion weather." Nimmich cupped his hand to catch a few drops.

"No one knows but us," said Wollenstein.

"Adler, what about Adler?"

"Count on Pfaff. He's never let us down."

Someone came from under the Messerschmitt. Wollenstein switched on the torch again to pin Tauch in its circle. The Me-110 was ready, the Swabian engineer said, and the trimotor Junkers beyond would be refitted with the newest nozzles in two hours. Tauch wiped his wet forehead with a cloth, looked nervous. And the powder, the powder has also been loaded, he said.

The best news all day. Wollenstein told Tauch to get back to work and the engineer moved through the fat raindrops showing in the electric lights to the night-fighter.

Once he was out of earshot, Nimmich piped up. "We won't be able to keep it a secret if they don't come in the morning."

"Don't worry so much."

"No matter what, some of ours will get sick."

"Second thoughts?" Wollenstein asked. "They can't have this. This is ours—yours and mine—and they want to take it, or worse, hide it in a cave when it should be used now. We need to show them it works, that the *pestis* and the streptomycin, both together, work."

Nimmich found a cigarette in a pocket and lit the thing. "Now that we're close, I'm not so sure."

"Nimmich," said Wollenstein. "Relax."

The boy dropped the cigarette, barely smoked, into the wet grass. "We'll hang for this," Nimmich said. "And then they'll hang our families, too." He turned and walked across the landing field, back to the farm.

———

Monday

They died by the hundreds, both day and night,
and all were thrown in those ditches and covered
with earth. And as soon as those ditches were filled,
more were dug. I, Agnolo di Tura . . . buried my
five children with my own hands. . . . And so many
died that all believed it was the end of the world.

—AGNOLO DI TURA, 1348

Seventeen

Awake in one instant, Brink sat up. And immediately regretted moving, for the ache in his jaw, a final ache laid over all the other accumulated aches, split his head. He gagged at the pain and tasted apples, but didn't vomit.

"Lie still," said Alix, putting a hand on his shoulder to keep him down. Brink closed his eyes and breathed.

"What time is it?" Brink asked. He could hear the rain sheeting on the barn's roof back and forth, and the wind rattled glass in a window.

"I don't know," Alix said. She moved in the dark and he smelled hay as she crushed it shifting her place. Grootvader's barn had smelled that way when he'd played in the loft, and he wished he was there now. "You slept for hours. Past midnight," she said. Alix struck a match and brought it to him, her hand cupping the light. He squinted at his wristwatch. Half past one. The match fluttered out, but not before Brink saw Kirn a yard away, his broad back to them, stretched in the hay. The big man grunted quietly and shifted on the hay before taking up snoring.

"Where's Wickens?" Brink asked. He sat up again, this time slowly, breathing shallow and then deep as the pain rose and fell. He wished he had some aspirin.

"Stay still," Alix said.

The rain on the roof slackened, faded, died, returned as a shadow of itself for a moment, then was gone altogether. Brink listened, heard nothing, and that nothing gave him hope. No noise of airplane engines, no guns going off, nothing that meant paratroopers. The rain swept the roof again.

"There's no invasion," he said. He slowly looked around for Wickens.

"He's still sitting next to the old man," Alix said. "He hasn't moved in hours."

Brink used a hand against the barn's rough interior wall to steady himself, stood on shaky legs, traced the planks for a foot or two. "Wickens," he hissed. "Listen. Do you hear anything? There's nothing. No invasion!" No answer but for the short echo of his own voice and then a cough from Kirn.

"I told you," Alix said.

Brink followed the wall until he sensed the truck near him, not seeing it but just feeling it there in the dark, then cut left, his hand guiding him along the back of the vehicle to where Eggers lay. "Wickens," Brink whispered, but again no answer. Alix struck another match and the light showed only the closed eyes of Eggers, his terrible face, and the German gun Brink had found in Port-en-Bessin. "There it is," she said, and picked it off the hay. The match died and put Eggers in darkness again, thank God.

Brink groped his way along the other flank of the truck to the barn's door, which was open just wide enough to let a man slip out. The rain, horizontal now from the gusting wind, slapped his face and he wiped it away, stepped back into the barn. As he listened for sounds other than rain and wind, Alix put a hand on his shoulder. "He'll come back," she said.

Another reason they should hurry. They'd been given the gift of another day and he wasn't going to waste any of it on Wickens.

He felt his way around the hood of the truck, stepped over the sleeping Kirn, found the left-side door and its latch. Alix kept at his heels. He heard her toss the German submachine gun into the hay beside Kirn. Brink yanked open the truck's door, the hinges squeaking for oil, and climbed behind the wheel. Alix scuttled around the front of the truck again to scrabble into the cab from the other side and settle onto the hard seat beside him. Brink fumbled for the starter, but Alix grabbed his wrist.

"I'm so sorry, Frank," she said.

"What?"

"I said I was sorry. In the house when I pushed you down the stairs, I'm sorry. I never said I was sorry."

Because it was pitch black, he could only listen to her. Her breathing was regular and unlabored. She didn't cough. He waved for her until his hand touched her forehead and he laid the back of it against her skin, then held the same hand to her cheek. It didn't feel like she had a temperature.

"We'll need the *boche*," she said. "I'll wake him." She put her hand on the door.

"No, wait." He touched her again. He wanted to tell her how she was stronger than anyone he'd known, and how that made him feel safe when he was with her, and in a way, stronger himself. How in the church he'd prayed not to be alone anymore. But he couldn't put that into words.

She took his silence the wrong way, or maybe the right, he wasn't sure anymore, and in turn touched his cheek. She stroked his face, and as her hand moved to his jaw, her fingers scratched over his stubble. He could smell her in the dark. Apples again, and damp clothes and the salt tang of dried sweat.

Brink touched her face, this time drawing her closer across the bench seat of the truck. He let his fingers slip to her neck, caressed that with fingertips, listened to her breathing, no less regular, no more rapid, than before. He leaned into her and brushed his lips against the spot below her ear, felt himself grow hard instantly. Brink kissed her neck, breathed in the apples and kissed her neck again, tasting salt. She stretched back to expose more of her neck and she moaned very very softly as his heart pounded.

He shifted on the seat and raised his head and now his lips brushed hers. Their tongues met a moment, met again.

But then a hand was on his chest, first only holding him in place, next pushing him away an inch, two. "No," she said, her voice low. "I don't want you sick."

All those years in church, when his father had exhorted him to get close to God, accept Christ's love, he'd never felt anything no matter how hard he tried. But now, with that one small gesture, he felt as if he was smothered. He heard a worry in the words and felt it as she shoved him away, the worry not for herself but for him. It was like a warm bath, the moment, enough that he thought it might be love. But he wasn't sure, since the only other time he'd felt this was when Kate had done the same, pushed him away from breathing her illness.

"It doesn't matter," he said.

She had her hands on either side of his face and she drew him back to her and he opened his mouth and they kissed, deep and warm, so warm in this cold place, and he used his hand against the back of her neck to hold her to him.

"Life is mistakes," she'd said in that storeroom. Maybe she was right.

Her breath was moist on his face as they broke the kiss, and it felt like the kiss beside the Catholic altar. Brink unbuttoned the top buttons of the dress—*bouton*, he remembered—and slipped his hand inside the cloth, put fingers on the so-smooth skin between her breasts. Alix shivered, maybe from his cold hand. He touched her breast, rode his finger up its inner swell to her throat, then back down again, brushing the nipple.

She tugged at his hand to pull it from its place, held it in hers, and brought it to her mouth. She kissed the palm of that hand. *"Monsieur,"* she whispered. *"Aller! Hâte!"*

Before Frank reached for her in the dark, all Alix could think of was how alone she was.

Alone. Like after Henri vanished into the squall of May four years before. Like after she'd killed Papa with her silly dream of finding Juniper, as if he had loved her ever. Jules shot by her own hand and staring from Clavette's floor. Alain dead on the table. Only Mama was alive and she was gone to the *boche*. Alix hated the vision of emptiness that stretched out in front of her like a calm ocean.

She had fixed Frank to her with that first kiss in the church, and he had promised that he'd never leave. It had been a trick then, a grasp at keeping the loneliness away. Now she wished she could have done things differently. She imagined a courtship where she laughed with him when he made jokes, brushed away his eager hands on warm August nights, let him finally fumble under her dress.

He was not angry like Juniper, perhaps not nearly as brave as a consequence. But he was as much a hero. And Frank had been kinder than any man she'd known.

She held him tight, as tight as her arms let her, her hands in his hair pressing him against her neck. When he moved his mouth to kiss her and then his hands found her breast, the warmth, like a summer day out on the water, the deck of Papa's boat giving back the sun, started at her thighs and went to her throat. She clutched him closer.

It is a mistake, loving this man, she thought as the warmth grew. She was sick, perhaps, and even if she wasn't, whoever she touched died. But she didn't care. She didn't want to be alone.

Wollenstein pressed the heavy black handset hard against his ear and tried to understand what came through the static in the wires.

"I said, Major, that the church has been destroyed," Grau's voice scratched over the wire.

A raid, Grau said, a heavy air raid without any warning, English Mosquitoes sweeping low under the clouds from the Channel and scattering bombs from the harbor to the church. Half the village was rubble and ruins. Scores of his men were injured, dead.

"I've been trying to reach you for hours," said Wollenstein. "When did this happen?" He fingered the wire that ran into the telephone plugboard in the small room under the staircase of his farmhouse. The room smelled like Pfaff's bitter coffee, of cabbage and unwashed men. A stink, this room.

"What did you say? I can't hear you," Grau said.

Liar, thought Wollenstein, but instead he shouted into the handset, *"When did this happen?"*

"Yesterday, about noon."

"And you didn't tell me?" Wollenstein yelled. The static faded for just a moment, then came back as a grating buzz from a lightning strike between here and Port-en-Bessin.

". . . lines were cut by the bombs, we only just patched them together," Grau said as the buzz faded.

"My men, what about my men? Put Pfaff on the line!" Static filled his ears. "What did you say?" he shouted.

". . . dead."

"What?"

"The corporal of yours, he's dead," Grau said, his voice loud now, too.

Wollenstein's heart went cold. Pfaff was dead? The fat one was his hammer. "How many of mine alive?" he finally asked.

"Four, and the fat SD, but they left hours ago," Grau said in his ear. "Two more, but they won't see daylight, I think."

"The French, all of them dead?"

"No, we pulled out a few from the church."

"Those at the gendarme's?"

"Dead, yes, all of them. Can you hear me?" Grau asked.

Liar, Wollenstein wanted to shout into the handset, hearing the lies in Grau's voice and feeling his command of things slip away. His plan was in shambles. Pfaff dead and Adler alive meant there was no one to keep the SD from the telephone. He would squeal like the pig he was to *der Ofenmann*, Kammler would ring up Himmler, and that would be it.

"What about the doctor, the American, in the church?" he boomed into the telephone. "And the Kripo? Are they alive?"

Static, more static. ". . . what doctor?" Grau asked. "I don't know of any doctor. And the Kripo, I don't know."

More lies. "Who have you told?" he asked.

"What? I couldn't hear you."

"Who have you told?" Wollenstein screamed. He wanted to throw the black telephone across the room.

"Told? About the raid? My battalion commander, naturally," said Grau. His voice was slippery in Wollenstein's head.

"About the sickness! *Who have you told about the sickness!"*

The static grew loud and louder.

". . . no one, Major. The danger is past, isn't it?"

Wollenstein rubbed his hand against his trousers. The captain was lying with each word.

"I want my men to return immediately!" he yelled into the telephone, which was suddenly clear of noise, a perfect connection.

"By all means, but you'll have to find them. The SD and his four, they left on foot last night. The truck your men came in, it's still smoking."

"Where did they go? Where did the SD go?" Wollenstein shouted out, not having to because the line was perfectly still.

"He didn't tell me, Major."

"I'm sending a man this very minute. And if he finds—"

"Bring my Kübelwagen back, Major, like you promised," said Grau, and the line went dead. He'd hung up.

Adler didn't care that the ground was muddy, and plopped down beside a poplar tree. His overcoat had let in more than enough rain to soak him from neck to toes, and the wind had taken his hat, so his head was drenched. Even the bandage on his throat was soaked in something, what he didn't know, and he kept his hands away from it. Adler breathed hard, his ribs aching from the effort.

"This is the farm, Hauptsturmführer," said the dimmest of his SS dimmed wits. Issmer. The boy was barely huffing. None of the boys were.

Of course it was the right farm. He'd never forget the stink of the thing in the chair inside the farmhouse, and he'd smelled the killing pits in Russia, hadn't he?

Another SS fidgeted with his rifle. That one was Klein, the one with the sagging mouth and the new wound in his arm from the raid. The hell with them. Adler knew they would have been here hours ago if not for him, but they could wait another moment so he could catch his breath again.

From his first visit here, Adler knew the windows on the second floor of the house showed above the wall, but when he peered into the dark, there was no light. So no one was in the house, as if ever anyone would live there again with that smell steeped into the plaster. To the left, across the road, was the barn where he had worked on the old English commando.

He knew Wollenstein had sent him here the first time only to keep him busy, but the SS doctor had made a mistake: They'd found the old Englishman and he'd talked a little. Enough that when he drove back to

Port-en-Bessin he went straight to the church looking for the American doctor. But then the bombs fell and it had taken forever to pull himself from under the unconscious Issmer and have his own wound tended to, and then walk all the way back to this farm because the truck they'd driven before was just twisted metal under rubble in the little port.

"Should we go look?" asked Issmer.

No, let's just sit in the rain a bit more, you stupid boy, Adler thought. But he only extended an arm. Issmer knew by now what that meant, and grabbed hold to pull him up.

Issmer led Klein and the other two SS to the dirt lane, crouching like animals. Adler had no intention of bending over and only thumped through the mud after them.

If he'd marched these endless kilometers for nothing and the commandos weren't here, the first thing he would do was beat the shit out of Klein, who swore he'd seen the Kripo scurry from the church with a tall blond man dragging a woman, all heading south. Adler had known they must be running back to the barn, and the tall blond must be the American doctor.

Issmer stopped at the gate to the barn, held up a hand, like he was some front fighter, and everyone knelt. Adler let himself slide to the wet grass along the wall and breathed again. If the rain wasn't pouring down he would have tried to light his last cigar.

Issmer pushed at the wooden gate, and disappeared. Adler heaved himself to his feet, wished one last time that the old man in that barn had told him more.

Just as Brink heard Alix whisper "Hurry," the door beside her squealed open. She flew out of his arms, everything happening so fast that it was as if she simply vanished.

"You fuckin' cunt!" Wickens shouted outside the truck's open door. "I smelled it, Christ, after what I did—"

Alix screamed.

Brink scooted across the seat, put hands on either side of the door's frame, ducked his head, and pushed with his legs to launch himself at the dark. He slammed into the Englishman and they went down in a heap. Something that Wickens held went flying to the dirt floor. Brink felt in the dark, put a hand around it, and only then realized it was a shovel handle.

Wickens's fist chopped on the hand holding the shovel and it spun out of Brink's grip. He pushed at Wickens and scuttled on all fours across the dirt and dung in the direction of the shovel, but the Englishman snaked a hand around his ankle.

Brink kicked that leg, kicked both his legs, and felt a foot connect. He was free. And then he had the shovel and next he was on his feet. He raised the shovel, searching the dark for Wickens.

"You got my Sam killed," snarled the thing near the floor, and the hairs on Brink's arms stood. "Not bad enough, that, but then you fucked her. When I told you to keep your hands off her." In the dark, there was the clack of metal on metal, the sound so familiar now. Wickens had that Webley and he'd just pulled back its hammer—Brink didn't need light to know it.

"*Juniper!*" Alix called. Then, from her direction, he heard the same sort of sound, metal on metal, but bigger. *"Don't hurt him, Juniper!"*

A burst of gunfire filled the barn that moment. But the blinding flashes didn't come from where Wickens crouched or even near Alix's silhouette at the truck's fender, instead from the far front corner of the barn. Kirn stood at the one small window on that side of the door and shot at something outside. *"Da drüben!"* he shouted. And started shooting again.

The shouting from the barn told Adler his guess had been very lucky, and that the commandos *had* returned for their dead comrade.

Issmer led the way, the two SS next, then Klein. Adler came last. He had his pistol out of its holster and it was wet, like everything else. Adler thought they had been quiet, but suddenly there was the sound of glass smashing. A short licking tongue of yellow lit the yard, and a gun fired and fired and fired.

Issmer jerked in place and flopped backwards. The next two dropped for cover straightaway, but Klein was shot down, too. That gave Adler time to get down into the muck. A second gunman joined the first, but at the black crack where the door must be. The bullets cut through the rain and shattered against the brick wall behind him. Adler wiggled deeper into the mud, chest pounding. He prayed for God to make him thinner.

An electric starter whined, an engine caught, a throttle opened, closed. The door to the barn swung out and open. The snout of a truck sniffed into the yard. It was the Opel he'd seen earlier in the barn. He raised his head to look as the truck butted against the gate. The gate held as the driver put foot to throttle and he heard its wheels slinging mud back into the barn. The monster was trapped.

Why didn't the last two SS boys get up and shoot? Get to your feet and shoot, he wanted to shriek, but he was too afraid to even whisper. He raised his pistol, but didn't find the strength to pull the trigger. Then one SS got up from the mud and fired a short burst from his machine pistol and was sliced the next second by a flicker that lanced from the Opel's running board. In the flash all he saw was someone standing with an arm wrapped over the door and into the truck for purchase. Adler squeezed shut his eyes and pulled the trigger of his pistol one-two-three.

The Opel's engine shouted for mercy and the gate gave way with a squeal.

Juniper was in her face—she smelled him, remembering how he'd smelled when they made love that first time—and he took the Sten she'd picked up from the dirt. "Get Sam in the truck," he shouted as he sprinted for the barn's door. The *boche* fired his machine pistol again in the corner and the barn was briefly lit as if by a dozen oil lamps.

Frank went with her to the back of the truck, fumbling like her along its flank, to where the dreadful, dead old man lay. Alix didn't want to touch him, but she grabbed his feet while Frank pulled his shoulders. Together they carried him to the rear of the truck. In the dark, Frank got the door unlatched somehow—the *boche* and Juniper both firing their guns now at the other end of the barn—and he clutched at the old one's arms and tossed him in, pushing his legs in after. The door slammed.

"*Get in!*" Frank yelled.

The shooting paused a moment. "*Don't waste any time!*" Juniper called from the door.

Alix dragged the ruck through the straw and dirt back to the cab where she and Frank had been about to make love. The door was still wide open, and as she heaved in the ruck and followed it up and in, first the policeman, then Frank slid in the other side. The *boche*'s machine pistol smelled of cordite and scorched oil. Frank leaned out his door and screamed something in English.

He pressed the starter and the engine coughed, caught. He pulled at a switch and the truck's headlamps put Juniper in their glare. He glanced back at them, squinting, and shoved open the great wood door.

Frank put his foot to the accelerator, the truck jounced once, almost stalled, but shuddered forward. Juniper, who leapt to the running board, rapped on the window with the barrel of the Sten. She understood, and cranked down the window glass. Juniper wrapped an arm inside the frame to hang on, the same hand that had yanked her from the truck, the one with the scar on it.

The truck slid through the mud toward the gate, Frank wrestling the steering wheel. He butted the truck's bumper against the gate, thinking to shove it open, but Alix remembered the Tardif gate swung inward. Frank pressed harder on the accelerator. The truck bumped forward and spun its wheels.

A gun rattled from the yard and Juniper, his free hand still gripping the Sten, shot back. The noise swamped the cab and Alix shrunk away, pressed her shoulder against the *boche*. Lightning lit the yard and in its hard gray glare she saw Juniper's face surprised as his arm loosened its hold. Alix reached, cried out his name, but she only caught the front of his coat with two fingers. He disappeared just as the gate gave way and the truck bulled into the lane.

A heartbeat later, Frank grabbed the gear lever and ground it, once, twice, before the truck swerved a moment, straightened, then flew down the tunnel of the road. She closed her eyes against the crash she was sure would come. But Frank was a good driver and kept the truck on the path. She opened her eyes to the dark again. *"We must go back!"* she shouted.

The steering wheel vibrated under Frank's hand as the truck bounced through the ruts at an unmarked crossroads. He had heard her, she was sure of it, but he wasn't turning around.

Alix put her hands in her lap, wove the fingers together as if in confession, and hated herself for not forcing Frank to stop the truck.

Adler listened to the Opel accelerate down the lane. He lay still until the noise faded into the weather.

"Hauptsturmführer," someone said, and Adler looked up to see an arm extended. He grabbed it and let the boy—he would have to learn this one's name, he supposed—pull him up. Adler slapped at the mud on his overcoat, pried it from his nose and spat it from his mouth.

"What now?" the boy asked. His voice was strange and high.

But Adler dared not talk himself, for he thought his fright would strangle his voice, too. Instead, he stumbled toward the one who had dropped off the truck's running board.

The man lay facedown, and Adler grunted to the boy, who turned him right side up. Adler pointed the pistol, but rather than shoot he asked for a torch, and the boy flicked on a light. The man was alive. Shot through the wrist, a lucky bullet for me, Adler thought. The man's eyes fluttered open and he croaked something, perhaps a name.

One of the commandos. Here was the proof Kammler needed that someone was out to steal the *Gräber*. But without a truck, there was no way to haul the commando to Kammler. He would have to find his way from here to Étréham, where that shit Grau said there might be a telephone.

"*Saujude,*" Adler said in an even voice. He stepped on the commando's smashed wrist with his mud-balled boot and listened to him scream like a child.

He told the SS boy to drag the English into the barn and try to keep him from bleeding out; also tend to Issmer or Klein or the other one if they were still breathing. He would return soon.

His feet aching, Adler trudged to the gate, stopped to catch his breath, and then swayed through the mud, one boot after another, in what he hoped was the right direction.

Eighteen

Brink shoved on the brake and the truck shuddered and slid to a stop, its right front wheel on grass along the snake of a road. He switched off the engine and it caught one last time before dying. In the quick silence the only sound was a brief pinging on the roof as water dripped from the sheltering tree. The headlights, still on, showed yet another stretch of muddy lane and, twenty yards ahead, a spot where it dipped between ten-foot-high walls of green foliage.

"Where are we going?" Brink asked the German. Kirn had his big hands wrapped around the gun that smelled too hot, and seemed lost in thought.

"We must go back for Juniper," Alix said quietly. It was the first thing she'd said in the ten minutes since Wickens had dropped off the running board.

"No," Brink said quickly. Not in a million years.

"We must."

"We can't," Kirn said. "Who knows how many are there." Kirn shifted the gun. "Wollenstein's men, they must have been. No one else knows that farm."

"The same who killed the old man," Brink said.

Kirn squirmed. "I have to get out."

Alix opened the door on her side and slid out. Kirn was hot behind her. Brink listened to the engine tick as it cooled, then dropped out, too. Kirn stepped around the front of the truck and, without embarrassment, unbuttoned his pants and pissed a long stream into the grass. He moaned as if he'd been holding it for ages, then lit a cigarette, gave one to Alix, too. Her face was yellow in the flare of Kirn's lighter.

"Where is your invasion, Doktor?" asked Kirn. "I don't hear any gunfire."

"Maybe it's the weather," Brink said. He looked at his right hand. The fifth or the sixth or the seventh, that's what Wickens had said. "The weather turned, maybe that's the reason." Brink started to tear the tape from his middle finger, but stopped. He smoothed down the end to make it stick again.

Kirn smoked his cigarette. "Perhaps you lied," he said.

"No. They'll come tomorrow, or the next day." He smelled the tobacco and wanted a cigarette of his own. An ember glowed in front of Alix's face. He wished he could see her eyes. "I thought you might run," Brink said to Kirn. "To warn your . . ."

The cigarette in Kirn's mouth moved up and down as the German nodded. "I killed some of my own," he said slowly. "It won't be easy to go home." He tossed the butt into the mud and it sizzled there. "But I'll hold you to your promise. That prick Wollenstein, he's the danger now. When we're finished with him . . ." Kirn held out something, pushed it at Brink, and as it touched his chest, Brink went cold. "Take it. I'll drive," Kirn said, and Brink took the gun, wanting it now. He'd learned a few things the last two days.

Kirn brushed by and climbed in behind the wheel. The starter whined and the big truck's engine turned over and roared.

When Alix dropped her cigarette, Brink went to her. He laid the back of his hand against Alix's forehead. Warm. Warmer than before. He touched her cheek, then her forehead again. Cool, almost cold.

"Am I sick?" she asked.

He hesitated. "No, you're fine," he lied. "I have to check every few hours, that's all." He told himself it could be anything, this low fever. Fatigue, even.

He touched fingers to her hand this time, not her cheek, and even that was warm.

The *boche* twisted the steering wheel to avoid a hole in the road. Frank's shoulder touched Alix's, but she got the idea that he would slide away if there was room.

The truck was hot. She had asked Frank to let down the glass a few centimeters, but even the cool morning air didn't help. Perhaps the *boche* had moved the lever to let in the engine's heat, that was why it was so warm.

Alix laid her head back to rest it against the hard seat. She felt light, as if she'd stood up too quickly from a night's sleep. Small flashes of yellow in the corners of her eyes made her close them. With her eyes closed, she felt with her right hand for Frank. She found a corner of his coat, and she twisted her fingers into its cloth.

A cough tickled in her throat. It was only from the *boche*'s hard cigarette, she told herself.

But she wasn't stupid. She knew what it meant.

The truck rattled down the cobblestone street that split the place labeled "Vouilly" on the map Brink had spread across his lap. Kirn downshifted to take a corner, and on the rain-slick street he almost hit a woman standing alongside a shop. She first made a face of confusion but then terror as the truck bumped onto the sidewalk. Kirn wrestled the wheel and got the vehicle back on the road. "Christ that was close," Brink said, but in English and Kirn didn't even glance his way.

This was crazy. With daylight, someone would see that they weren't German. They'd already had close calls. Twenty minutes before, Kirn had hissed between clenched teeth and Brink had looked up to see two long lines of black shapes marching up the road. Kirn turned right, at the first road before they reached the marching men. The turn had led them north to this flyspeck.

They passed the last house of Vouilly and as the truck picked up speed, its tires hummed as cobbles gave way to pavement. This wasn't good. All the roads were dangerous, but even Brink knew the paved roads would hold the most Germans. The policeman glanced in the mirror mounted outside the cab on the driver's side, then back to the road, again to the mirror.

"What?" Brink asked.

"Nothing. I thought I saw something, but it was nothing."

"Get us off this road," he said to Kirn, and looked again at the map. Up ahead there was a thinner line that peeled off from the highway, Brink saw, using his finger as a ruler and changing kilometers to miles. Another mile or two. "The next left, take it," he said, his eyes on the map. He leaned toward Alix as the truck rounded a slow curve.

"Shit," Kirn said, and stepped on the brake.

"What—" Brink said, and looking up, shut up.

They'd cleared the curve, but as the road straightened, a motionless snake of vehicles blocked their way. The column was long enough to hide its head around another curve far in the distance. Tires sliding on the wet pavement, they slowed and then stopped, their grille not more than twenty feet from the tailgate of the last in the line. It had a green canvas cover, that truck, and the back of that cover had been tied off to the sides, showing the cave inside. Something moved inside the cave. A leg in a boot. That leg was connected to a German soldier, coal bucket helmet and all, who jumped down stiffly, and walked to the side of the road to piss. The rain dappled the windshield as the single wiper slapped back and forth.

"Back up," Brink said quietly.

"We can't, they'll think something's wrong," Kirn said, and then looked into the mirror. He let out a long sigh. "Shit and shit. Too late," he said. His big voice sounded tired now, soft, too, as if Kirn was afraid the German taking a leak out there could hear him talking French. "A motorcycle behind us. The rear guard for the convoy. Hide the weapon," he said, nodding to the submachine gun at the still-sleeping Alix's feet. "He's gotten off his motorcycle." Brink slid the German submachine gun under the seat.

The German in front of them was climbing back into his truck and small clouds of exhaust huffed out of the truck's tailpipe. Down the column, other clouds rose behind other trucks. Kirn jammed the gearshift into first. Faces peered out from the canvas cave; they were close now, close enough to see the dark stubble on the cheek of the one who had taken a leak. The Germans stared blankly back.

And then the truck, following the others, moved forward. Kirn kept theirs tight on its tail. Seconds fell off Brink's life, then a minute, and another, and still the convoy rolled on. Every moment he expected the Germans to begin to shout and point.

"He's back on his motorcycle," Kirn said, talking to the side mirror again.

"The turn should be just ahead," Brink said.

"We take the turn and he'll follow. He's there to bring up stragglers."

Kirn kept pace with the truck ahead, staying ten or fifteen feet off its tail. Brink waited for the men in its cave to notice that they didn't belong. His stomach soured, his mouth went to sand, and he couldn't wipe the sweat from his hand fast enough. He wasn't cut out for this.

It got worse, because there was another bend in the road, this time to the left, and he could see the column accordion as trucks at the front slowed. One stopped, another, each truck's tiny taillights brightening as its driver applied the brake. Kirn took his foot off the gas and let their truck almost coast to a stop. He kept looking in the mirror. The rain swept the hood of the truck one last time and was done.

Alix opened her eyes to the quiet and swung her head back and forth as if she didn't know where she was. Brink brushed her hand with his finger, and the touch made her look his way.

"Where are we?" Alix asked, confused still by sleep or her fever or maybe both. The truck's wheel clicked slowly, a rock stuck in its tire. One of the Germans in front of them put a hand on the canvas to steady himself as that truck jerked and stopped.

Alix stared at Brink and whispered, "I don't feel well." The words were quiet. "I'm going to be sick," she said, another whisper.

Kirn brought their truck to a stop. Brink started shoving at the door, but Kirn reached across Alix and grabbed his coat at the elbow. "They'll see her."

"She can't be sick here," Brink said. Alix was ill with the plague, he didn't doubt that. But he might not be; Kirn neither. But let her puke inside this cab and they would be. She'd hack and cough, and put enough invisible droplets in the close air to make both of them blue-skinned in a few days.

"My God," Kirn said, understanding. "Get her out of the truck, then. *Get her out!*"

Brink kicked open the metal door and, with a hand on Alix's arm, pulled her from the truck, and she fell against him as her legs went soft, but he held her by the waist and walked her toward the back of the truck, putting his back between her and the Germans to shield her face from their eyes, even though they would have to see her bare legs below the hem of her dress. Once they got around the truck's rear corner, he saw the motorcycle slowly approaching. He had his arms wrapped around her, and although his idea had been to let her drop where she could be sick on her own at a safe distance, he couldn't let her go but still tried to disguise her by standing with his back to the motorcycle. She bent over and vomited. Again. And again, each retch like a death sentence.

"I have to sit," she said finally, and he moved her away from the pool of brown and lowered her to the dark, damp asphalt. Brink stayed between her and the motorcycle, which had stopped a few yards away, its engine roughly idling. In his imagination, there was a fog around her that spread in the light breeze.

Alix put her head between her knees, wiped what remained from her lips and onto her dress, then breathed deeply a time or two. "Better. I'm feeling better." She raised her head and looked at him. She tried to smile that smile of hers. She knew.

She'll die unless I find Wollenstein's antibiotic.

The sound of boots stopped, close enough that the man might reach out and grab him by the coat collar. Brink refused to turn around and kept looking at Alix. *"Du siehst nicht gut aus!"* said the German.

Kirn stepped out of the truck and thought how easy it would be to walk to the *Landsers* looking at him from under their canvas, tell them his story of commandos, and let his burden lift. Tell them that the invasion might be coming soon, get ready for it, for he had looked in the American's eyes both in the church and in the truck, and known he was telling the truth. Perhaps not today, but the invasion would come.

Yet he only waved at them with his bad hand. If he told about the invasion, and was believed—not thought mad, which was likely—he'd be explaining for hours. The *Landsers* could handle the Americans and English when they came ashore, but not the pestilence Wollenstein would spray on them.

He cleared the corner of the Opel just as the BMW popped to a halt. Its rider, his sidecar empty, lifted himself from the machine. Only as he approached did the rider pull down his goggles. Kirn recognized him immediately: the *Feldgendarmerie* sergeant who had taken him to Jusot.

"Feldwebel," Kirn said.

"Untersturmführer Kirn," the sergeant said. He looked confused.

"I'm taking them to Carentan," Kirn said quickly, nodding to Brink and his sick woman. The sergeant still looked unsure. "The *Wulewuh* doctor? With the horse. Remember him? These are some of his friends," Kirn said.

"That doctor died of typhus, I heard," the soft-faced Feldwebel said. Kirn wasn't surprised; rumors flew faster than a telephone call in the army. The sergeant pointed to Pilon, still on the ground. "She looks sick. Does she have it?"

Kirn didn't answer, not certain which was the best way to put the Feldwebel's mind at ease. Brink stepped up, the idiot, and answered for him.

"Yes, she's sick," the American said, his German obviously accented. "Not with typhus. Only the influenza."

"I . . ." the sergeant began. He looked at the pavement, seemed to ponder a moment. "I'm sorry, Untersturmführer, but you're traveling with a military convoy, that's not allowed. And with her . . ." He aimed a thumb at Pilon. "You should . . . you must come with me, I think. We need to put this all in order."

"Feldwebel," said Kirn, trying to fix Brink's mistake, "the *Wulewuh*, he's right. It's influenza, not typhus." He pulled his identity disk, dark brown in this poor light, from his pocket. "I have to get to Carentan. To a doctor there and then make them talk and—"

Pilon hacked out a cough, her head falling to her knees again. She spit. The sergeant's eyes widened. "No, I am sorry, but we must—"

Kirn heard a sound then, a drone like a housefly from across the room. Brink's mouth moved and he said something, but Kirn concentrated on this new sound. Out of the thick cloud cover to the west, an aircraft swung for them. It was a dot just visible over the Opel, but in a second it was a fingertip, then suddenly larger than a fist, and as he stared, lights winked on its wings. A second shape followed the first.

It took him a moment to put straight what he saw. *Jabos*. Both fighter-bombers winked at him.

A hundred meters up the highway the macadam erupted in thin black and gray geysers and the sound of the *Jabos*'s engines were drowned by the noise of the road coming apart and a truck up the column disintegrating into a yellow ball that thinned as it climbed. The aircraft howled overhead just above the trucks, close enough for Kirn to see the round painted rings—red within white within blue within gold—on the bottoms of both wings. RAF.

Kirn scrabbled for the ditch and tugged at Brink's coat, who in turn dragged Pilon off the pavement. They slipped into the ditch the three of them, one after the other, Brink last, their heads near the road, their feet in the water at the bottom of the slough. Brink pressed an arm into Alix's back to shove her into the weeds. The housefly sound was replaced by a whirlwind of heavy, howling wasps. Kirn tucked his one good hand under his body—he wasn't going to lose more fingers—and tried to make himself become the mud.

When the second *Jabo* screamed overhead, Kirn heard the sound of hammers on tin and men shouting and another explosion that first shook him and then peppered the road. Something sizzled into the water at his feet and he smelled hot tar.

He stole a peek over the edge of the road. Soldiers sprinted from the convoy into the brush. Their own truck was smoking, the one in front of it completely in flames—the canvas cover already flapping into long strips that one by one peeled off and floated away as ashes. One *Landser* hung out the back of the truck, caught by his heels, his gray uniform darkened by soot and his arms dripping blood to the macadam. Several others trapped inside it screamed.

The *Feldgendarmerie* had not had the sense to follow them into the ditch, and he stood, weaving a bit, near the rear of their truck. Kirn saw him stare at his stomach, at the blood escaping through the fingers clasped over his belly. The Feldwebel took one step, ever so slowly, leaned, then pitched onto the road.

Nineteen

As soon as the fighters swung back into the clouds, Brink got to his feet and ran toward their truck. Its cab was smashed; the guns had peeled back the hood and fenders like a badly opened can, its windshield pierced by round holes with spider lines reaching for the edges. Dark smoke poured from lazy flames licking the wooden box on its back.

He pulled at the door, had to yank twice to free it, and the door shrieked open. The seat was shredded, and then the smoke blew into the cab and he couldn't see a thing. He pawed at the floor, found the pack and swung it out the door, tossing it to safer ground. He stuck his hands under the seat, and as the heat stung his face, he found the gun and threw that after.

Brink backed away from the burning truck and wiped at his eyes to clear the smoke. He grabbed the pack's strap in one hand, the German submachine gun in the other. The convoy was chaos, men stretched out on the asphalt, others straggling out from the greenery along the road. The German truck fifteen yards away was consumed by flames and missing its canvas cave. No one paid any attention to him as he staggered toward Alix and Kirn.

They were only now climbing from the ditch, Kirn holding Alix's arm. The German helped her sit, crouched down beside her—too close, Brink knew, but he didn't say anything—and whispered to her. The other German, the one from the motorcycle, lay in the road, facedown.

Brink knew what he had to do. He dropped the pack and gun onto the grassy shoulder, and without a word went to the wounded man.

He kneeled, rolled the man over, and began twisting the buttons on his heavy leather coat and then his tunic to get at the blood underneath. The man's shirt was like new red paint, slick and sticky under his fingers. Brink ripped at the shirt and found the raw, ragged opening in the hollow along his belt, below the fat of his belly.

"*Was machst du?*" someone asked. Brink glanced up; Kirn, of course.

"Look around, find some bandages," Brink replied in French, turning away from Kirn and looking at this other German. "Go on. Hurry." Brink tore at a dry part of the man's shirt, and wadding it, pressed the makeshift dressing against the wound.

There was no one to bring back, Sturmbannführer," Sillmann said. Wollenstein stared from the workbench at the ranks of beakers over gas flames, boiling cloudy liquid in each. The smell reminded him of Sachsenhausen and the watery excuse for soup they brewed for the Jews.

"Did you hear me?"

"I heard," Wollenstein said, watching a flask on the bench across the workshop. The liquid inside had almost boiled down to the line drawn near its bottom.

"I left behind two of our wounded. The *feldgrau* said they'd look after them. Of the French in the church, they'd pulled only a handful alive from the rubble. The rest . . ." Sillmann began, then shrugged. "And the ones you said to look for in the gendarme's place, I couldn't find them. They're gone, Sturmbannführer."

"Gone where," Wollenstein asked. "Where did they go?" He still had not looked up at Sillmann.

"Just *gone*, Sturmbannführer. The whole street, the gendarme's, was nothing but rubble," said Sillmann.

Wollenstein reached for the green-bound notebook, flipped it open, and paged through Nimmich's handwriting to check the numbers one last time. Wollenstein rubbed his temples.

"That's not all," Sillmann said.

"I know, Pfaff is dead."

"No, not Pfaff."

Wollenstein finally turned to the door where Sillmann slouched.

"The *feldgrau* pulled bodies from the church, but none were this Kripo with a mangled hand like you described. Either he's buried under the worst of it, or he escaped."

What with his luck, and mine, the Kripo lives, Wollenstein thought.

Worse, the policeman's talk about invasion had been nonsense. Wollenstein had rushed to prepare the Me-110 and the Junkers, had his pilots sit in the aircraft past dawn. But he'd heard no guns and been told "No, nothing unusual, Sturmbannführer," each time he'd telephoned the garrisons at Isigny and Vierville and Courseulles. Finally, he sent the Luftwaffe boys back to Chef du Pont. Wollenstein closed his eyes again.

He looked up. "What other bad news?"

"I asked about Adler, as you told me, but all I found out was that he took four men on the south road. On foot. No one knew where he went."

Wollenstein caught himself rubbing his hands together, the friction making them warm. Nothing had gone right. He glanced at the flasks distilling his antibiotic. Adler could be anywhere by now. To a telephone at least. He'd managed to talk to Kammler by now, certainly.

"What do you want me to do?"

Wollenstein didn't answer, only rubbed his hands together again. He stopped, and rested them on the bench over the notebook to keep an eye on them.

Alix watched Frank help the wounded *boche*.

She felt better. Light-headed still, and her mouth tasted terrible, but better. She took a deep breath. It was still hard to get one. Another, deeper, she forced her lungs to pull in as much of the wet air as she could, but it still didn't seem enough.

Alix edged toward Frank, who huddled over the *boche*, his hands busy at the soldier's waist. "Frank, it's time we go," she said to his back. The *boche* were finding their wits. One or two up the road glanced their way past the burning trucks, theirs fully caught now by the flames, its tires sending clouds of black smoke into the air. Inside that furnace, hot so hot on her face, was the body of Juniper's old man. He'd be a small black pebble and a few chalky bones soon enough.

But sooner than that, the *boche* would come for a closer look to see why a Frenchman tended one of theirs, why a woman stood in the road. Even the policeman wasn't dressed like a *boche*. This time Frank turned his head, his face looking up at her.

"We can't stay here," she said, and his eyes locked on hers. She was sick, she knew, and all that was left was revenge. She had places to go before she died, and a devil or two she'd like to see.

Alix glanced up the road as movement caught the corner of her eye. A *boche* holding tight on his rifle walked toward them.

What do you think you're doing?" the *Landser* said, shifting his Mauser so that he held it with both hands. The barrel made a small circle in the air. Kirn gripped the MP-38 that Brink had dropped, but kept its muzzle pointed at the road so as not to alarm this soldier who'd come sniffing.

Beyond this *Landser* were more, clustered around the first undamaged truck in the column forty meters away. They had their heads again—it had been ten minutes since the RAF *Jabos* stormed overhead—and others would soon follow. Kirn stepped around the Feldwebel Brink was trying to save. He slung the MP-38 to free his good hand, reached inside his coat, pulled the identity disc from the pocket, and let it dangle on the end of its short chain.

"Kriminalpolizei," Kirn said, and the man was already nodding.

"Who are they?" the *Landser* asked, waving the rifle's barrel at Brink and Pilon.

"Mine," Kirn said. He made sure to keep his eyes on the *Landser*'s. "This one," Kirn said, and he gestured toward Brink, "is a *Wulewuh* doctor. He's been stealing medical supplies for the black market."

Kirn paused, wondered if the *Landser* would live to grow older. If so, would he ever know my name, Kirn thought, and the treason I'm committing? "I must get them to Chef du Pont," Kirn said. "They've promised to turn on their friends."

The boy nodded, satisfied with the story.

"Who are you with?" Kirn asked.

"Second battalion, 914th," the man said. No, another of the many boys. His accent was odd, Volksdeutsche, perhaps Baltic.

"I may have friends among you," Kirn said, "from my time in the East." He raised his right hand to show the missing fingers. He asked this boy of Böse and Stecker and Muffe, the habit impossible to break. But as he questioned the Balt, and half-listened to the answers—no, no, and no again—Kirn could not keep another thought from filling his head.

He was sick, like the *Wulewuh* woman. Kirn brushed damp hair from his forehead, felt the heat at his brow as his fingers touched there, the ache in his chest when he breathed deep. From the little Pilon boy who he'd clutched close that first visit, most likely. Though who gave it to him was not important, because in the end it all led to Wollenstein.

Kirn glanced behind him, where Brink labored over the *Feldgendarmerie*. The doctor had a hand under the Feldwebel's neck to lift his head, and he leaned in to whisper something. The sergeant wouldn't live; his shoulders trembled and his knee jerked and he moaned. But Brink wasn't giving up. He kept talking, the words too soft to hear. Kirn had done the same in Russia with friends. Brink would be telling the *Feldgendarmerie* to stay awake, that he would be fine, there was nothing to worry about, help was on its way. Lies. But good lies.

"My truck," Kirn said, nodding to it still burning. "I have no way to Chef du Pont."

The boy glanced at the smashed truck, looked back at Kirn. He nodded. "We're going north of Sainte-Mère-Église somewhere," the boy said. "I'll ask my sergeant if you can ride with us that far."

Kirn wanted to reach out his left hand to give an awkward handshake in thanks, but knew he couldn't. Wollenstein spread the pestilence; he would not.

Where is Adler?" asked Kammler's voice from the telephone.

"I have no idea," Wollenstein said finally, slowly. "Last I saw him was yesterday afternoon." True enough. The silence on the line went on so long Wollenstein wondered if the connection had been cut. He toyed with the wire that went into the plugboard. "Are you still there?" he asked.

"Where is Adler?" Kammler asked again.

He doesn't know, Wollenstein realized. Not about the invasion that wasn't. Not about the disaster in Port-en-Bessin. Not about his Jews who had run to England. Not even about the commandos and the American doctor come to steal the secret. "I don't know. I last saw him here, on the farm." He listened to his first lie and thought it sounded fine.

More silence.

"You've lost him? On that tiny farm of yours?" Kammler asked. "Hard to believe, Herr Doktor."

"I've . . . I've been working in my shop. I slept here last night, in fact. I haven't been to the house since . . . yesterday. That was the last I saw the Hauptsturmführer."

"I would like you, Herr Doktor, to have *someone*," and the last word *der Ofenmann* nearly hissed, "look around your *speck* of a farm and put him on the telephone."

"I will," said Wollenstein. "I will have him telephone you."

Still more silence.

"Is that all?" Wollenstein asked.

"How goes your potato spraying, Herr Doktor? It's Monday. Wednesday is the Reichsführer's deadline."

"It's going well." He wasn't about to tell Kammler how well. The Me-110 and the Junkers were fueled and ready. Tonight, just past midnight, he would send them over England, bound for Portsmouth or Southampton or Bournemouth, he hadn't decided yet. Someplace near the water, where the Messerschmitt and goose-slow Ju-52 could get in and get out before dawn.

Only then would he telephone Himmler to tell him the news, when it was too late to recall the aircraft.

"Don't do anything stupid, Herr Doktor," said Kammler.

A mind reader, this one. "Never," Wollenstein said.

"How about the packing? Are you packing for the move to Mittelwerk?"

Baiting him at every step. *Der Ofenmann* never gave up. "Yes, of course," Wollenstein lied, a second time. The line was quiet; Kammler didn't believe him.

"If I'd been able to convince the Reichsführer, we wouldn't be having this conversation," said Kammler. "I'd arrest you in an eyeblink. You're a very dangerous man, Herr Doktor."

Wollenstein felt a slight chill on his neck. "A good thing he doesn't listen to you," he said into the telephone. *"Ofenmann."* He said that one word very softly. Again there was a long silence on the wires.

"It's a mistake to overestimate your importance, Herr Doktor," Kammler said quietly, but the voice came over the line clearly. "The Reichsführer thinks you a genius, but he changes his mind like the wind blows."

"Don't threaten me," said Wollenstein. He twisted the cord from the handset, tighter and tighter.

Kammler laughed; the tinny sound over the wire made the hairs on Wollenstein's arm stir.

"Oh, you'll know when I threaten you, Doktor," Kammler said.

The line clicked faintly and he realized the connection was gone.

Brink tried to keep his eyes on the floorboards of the bouncing, rattling truck. Anything not to look in the eyes of the Germans packed under the canvas with him. Look at them and they'll know.

Brink stole a look at Kirn, who sat across from him, closest to the opening where the canvas had been tied back. The policeman stared at the floor, too, looking through its cracks at the slowly passing pavement and smelling the exhaust seeping through. They were lucky to be moving. The convoy had stopped five times already, dissolving into chaos as the trucks jounced off the highway to hide from real or imaginary airplanes.

Before they'd all climbed into this truck, he and Kirn had moved the dead man to the side of the road, and covered him with his long, leather coat. Kirn had almost missed the ride, for he'd knelt at the dead one's body a moment too long before jogging over. Brink had to hold out a hand to pull Kirn in.

Kirn still hadn't caught his breath from his run for the truck and his big, square face remained flushed. Brink wondered if the policeman was sick, but couldn't come up with a way he'd caught it. Even if he'd been exposed in the church somehow, it wouldn't show so fast. Not the *pestis*, surely not, it couldn't be.

Alix leaned against Brink's left shoulder, while on his right sat a soldier, a grim-faced man who might be twenty-five, but looked forty.

"How are you?" Brink asked Alix, speaking low and in French. Even if some around them understood, he'd not said anything dangerous. He put his hand on her forehead. Warm.

"Better. Much better." She smiled wanly.

"We'll be there soon," he said.

"How much longer?"

Brink wasn't sure whether she meant their destination or how much time she had. Then he realized the answer was the same. "I don't know." She laid her head against his shoulder again. At least she wasn't coughing.

"The woman's sick?" the German beside him asked, but he spoke to Kirn, not him. "You don't look so good either."

Through tightness on his face, Kirn nodded and made a kind of smile, like a grimace. "Never better," he said.

The soldier next to Brink leaned forward and held out a cigarette. Kirn took it, went through his routine of jamming it between thumb and forefinger, and lighting the cigarette with that lighter that looked like a bullet.

"Where?" the soldier asked, pointing his own cigarette to Kirn's hand.

"Russia," Kirn answered. He drew a breath from the cigarette, looked out the back of the truck at the green scenery reversing. "I always ask for friends I knew there. They might be in the 352 now," Kirn said, looking now at the one next to Brink. "Uwe Böse and Paul Stecker and one called Muffe." The smoke from his cigarette was pulled from the truck even faster than his voice.

But someone heard. "I know Böse." That soldier was closer to the front of the truck. He leaned from the bench and into the space where legs and knees jostled for room. "He's in 5 Kompanie. Tall, a bad face, a gunner. Works an MG-42."

Kirn's smile now was real, a broad grin. "That's him! How is he?"

"Somewhere up the column, I would think," the soldier called back, mistaking his question in the noise of the truck.

Kirn reached inside his overcoat, pulled out a small notebook and pencil, and scratched on the paper for a bit. He tore it from the book and folded it, held it out. "If you see him, give him that," he yelled. The note went from hand to hand to reach the soldier who said he knew Böse. He took it, nodded, stuck it inside his tunic.

"I told you," Kirn said, still in German but looking, Brink thought, at him. And grinning like it was Christmas and he'd just unwrapped his first present.

Brink had tried to save the motorcycle rider because Kirn knew the man. It had been pointless from the start—too much blood, wounds too deep, and nothing to work with—but he'd kept at it even when the motorcyclist himself gave up and let death come.

For his part, Kirn had gotten them this ride.

They were in it together now, Brink thought.

What else?" Adler asked, and leaned over the English commando who smelled of shit. The man shook his head.

Adler straightened the kink in his back, felt his belly rub against his belt, wiped sweat from his forehead, and flicked it onto the dark-spotted floor. He went to the small table against the wall of the schoolroom, poured a glass of water, tipped his head back, and swallowed it by gulps. The room on the second floor of the Petit Lycée was hot; the furnace for some reason was at full steam. He found a cigar in the pocket of his tunic and lit it. He tossed the match under the table, let the smoke fill his mouth, breathed it out to make three rings, each larger than the last. Then he returned to the English sitting in the boxy schoolboy's desk. Caen's Gestapo used what they had handy.

"Limelight," Adler said, calling the Englishman by the only name he'd admitted to. "What haven't you told me?"

The man slowly raised his head; his eyes tried to focus. He opened his mouth and showed broken teeth—they were somewhere on the floor—but said nothing. He shook his head.

Adler clenched the cigar in his mouth and hit the English on the cheekbone again. The man's head rocked back. Adler leaned closer, close enough to see the ragged edge of the torn ear when he'd hit this Limelight with the broom handle he'd found in a corner. "You told me about Jews. And swimming to France, I heard that. Two men and you and a *Wulewub* whore, yes, that, too. Even that traitor Wollenstein you've come to steal from us. And your own you were to kill. But what else? Anything else in there?" He flicked at the man's temple with a finger, and the English flinched.

"Go to hell," the English said slowly, his German flawless except for the effect of the missing teeth.

"Do you remember what happens when you say things like that?" Adler went to the table and set the cigar on its corner so that the ash end wouldn't burn the wood, then picked up the length of dirty rope. It had once been white as a virgin's teat. Adler let the rope uncoil and held it so Limelight could see it. "I've heard commandos are very very brave. How did you slip in?" The man's eyes wouldn't leave the rope.

Three hours they'd been at this, but Adler still felt there was more in the English. A few more secrets. He could let it go, he supposed, sit and rest—the endless walk to a telephone through the rain from the farm, the wait for the car to drive from Caen to fetch him and this English, the ride to the offices in this schoolhouse, all had tired him beyond tired—but he wanted these last bits. Who knew what else was in Limelight's head?

Adler tied a sliding knot in the rope again and grabbed the Englishman's right arm, the one that ended in a filthy dressing around his smashed wrist, and eased the hand and wrist through the loop. Limelight blubbered, saying *bitte bitte bitte*.

The man had been so brave through the beating and the hitting with the stick, but once Adler had thought of the rope, not so much. Everyone had a weakness, and Limelight's was the rope and wrist.

Adler got a grip on the rope, let his hand climb up it, and tugged, a short sharp tug just to set the noose, and Limelight yelped as the rope tightened around the smashed wrist. Adler yanked, hard this time, and the English screamed, breaking into a sob.

"Tell me the rest," Adler ordered. He jerked the rope again, but got nothing but more screams.

Adler gave the rope slack, breathed hard—I should shed a kilo or two—and planted his feet and pulled out the slack. "Wollenstein is part of this conspiracy, isn't he? Wollenstein let the Jews escape, didn't he, to get the message to you? Lead you to him?" Limelight raised his head again, shook that head back and forth. Adler held the rope tighter and pulled, leaning back on it, seeing it bite into the Englishman's wrist, seeing the arm extend and the wrist stretch, but didn't hear any bones against bones through Limelight's shrieking. *"What haven't you told me!"* Adler shouted over the noise.

Enough, Adler thought, changing his mind. Enough is enough. He walked the rope back to Limelight's wrist, gently picked at the loop to loosen it, and pulled it off. He went to the table, took a puff, then two, on the cigar, poured himself another glass, drank it quickly, then folded the rope on itself once, twice so it was a strand thick as three fingers.

"Nothing more?" he asked the English from behind. The man sobbed quietly. Adler swung the rope over Limelight's head and drew it across his throat and pulled back hard as he could. The English struggled, tried to get fingers under the rope, but he only had the one hand worth anything. Adler let the rope slacken, just enough. "Tell me what else."

"Soon," Limelight gasped. "Soon."

"Soon what? What is soon?"

Limelight said nothing and Adler pulled again, straining on it. He'd break the Englishman's throat and get nothing else, but that was what it was.

"You don't want to be killing him," a voice called from the door. He looked up to see Kammler. "I'll want him as evidence, won't I?" Kammler came into the room, followed by an SS with a thin scar that wriggled across his chin.

Adler let go of the rope and Limelight gulped for air.

"This is the one who came to steal our doctor?" asked Kammler. "The one you telephoned about?" Kammler came to the desk and the Englishman. He touched Limelight's cheek, saying quietly, "You know all about it, do you?" Adler wasn't sure if the general wanted an answer from him or the English.

Adler went for his cigar and blew more rings of smoke. "We had better leave now," he said, looking at his watch. Nearly six. "Something's happening soon."

"What?"

Adler shrugged, pulled the cigar from his mouth, spat on the stained floor. "All he said was 'soon,' that's all. But it's about Wollenstein. It has to be."

"We must hunt down every English," said Kammler, grabbing hold of Limelight's chin and raising it to look into the man's glassy eyes. "None of them can get away. Kill them all."

Twenty

There were signs at nearly every crossroad. None of the white arrows spelled out "Chef du Pont," but his electric torch found the one that told Kirn the way: 9 KOM/III/1058 in black paint. That was the bunch holding the bridge across the Merderet and garrisoning Chef du Pont.

"This way," he said. He pointed to the south and west.

He put the torch on Brink first, then Pilon. Kirn held the light on her the longest.

"What are you looking at, *boche*?" she asked.

Kirn gripped the MP-38. She was the one to watch. In her washed-out face Kirn saw another and searched for the name. Her name . . . her name . . . Kirn stared at Pilon until it came to him. Leesa Pulsnach. She'd schemed with an alcoholic physician in Munich, the two of them selling disabilities to men avoiding conscription before the war. But they'd gotten into an argument, the whore who sold the papers and the doctor who signed them, and Pulsnach had beaten the old man to death with a clothing iron. Pulsnach didn't stop there, though, but killed one more that night, stabbed a man who once pimped her. Early morning, Kirn had found her sleeping, the whore stupid enough to go back to her apartment and drink herself into a stupor.

Pilon made him think of Leesa Pulsnach. Not because she was stupid like Pulsnach, but because Kirn saw that this one had the same fury. Unfinished business. Her brother, of course, the collaborator Jules. He'd told her Jules had believed she was dead; if the boy had known she was alive, he would not have done what he'd done, he told her. She'd listened, but still blamed him.

Kirn lowered the torch's beam and switched it off. The moon was rising and full, and showed through a gap in the clouds. Pilon's labored breathing pinpointed her spot. Brink was beside her, as he'd been the two kilometers they'd walked from Sainte-Mère-Église, since the *Landsers* had dropped them there and driven on in their trucks. His hand was on her arm when needed, or around her shoulder.

This was as good a place as any to talk. He guessed it was another kilometer to Chef du Pont. And he needed rest. Kirn wiped sweat from his eyebrows, held his good left hand against his cheek to cool his face. He wished it would rain again, cold rain, to damper the heat. But the rain, it appeared, was over. The weather looked like it had broken.

"I know the name of the farm," Pilon said. She sounded tired, but her breathing, quick while they'd walked from Sainte-Mère-Église, was slower now. "The Jews said it was called the Black Farm," she said. *"Der dunkle Bauernhof."*

"I told you, I know where Wollenstein lives," Kirn said.

"Yes, yes, I forgot," Pilon said with a sad tiredness to her voice.

Kirn pulled an Eckstein from a pocket and lit it. But the breath of smoke clogged his lungs, and he coughed and couldn't stop. Neither of the others said anything, but Kirn knew they knew. Kirn dropped the Eckstein, coughed again. He had given up covering his mouth, for he hated the wetness that his hand caught. He spit the phlegm from his mouth, breathed deeply of the night's humid air.

"How can we do it?" asked Brink. He, at least, wasn't sick. He, at least, could be trusted. Kirn felt that, just as he felt Pilon's rage.

"Wollenstein won't have enough men to properly guard the farm," Kirn said, hearing his breath rattle in his chest. "Not after losing so many at Port-en-Bessin. We'll find a way to creep close." God, what he'd give for a clear breath of air.

"The medicine first," said Brink. He was thinking of Alix.

"No, not the medicine," Kirn said, even though that was foremost in his mind, too. "We stop the pestilence first. Then we look for the medicine."

"No, we must find the . . . antibiotics . . . first," Brink argued. They'd had this disagreement twice since Sainte-Mère-Église.

"Where will he be?" Pilon asked. "Wollenstein."

"Wherever he works on his pestilence," Kirn answered.

"Then that's where we should go first," she said. "The medicine can wait." She paused and Kirn was tempted to turn on the torch again to look at her. "Frank, the medicine can wait." Brink said nothing. "That's how I vote," Pilon said.

She was the one sickest, Kirn thought, and so she should decide. Brink remained silent for a time, but finally murmured agreement.

"How, then?" Kirn asked. "How do we destroy it?"

"He'll have a building, or more than one, where he makes the *Pasteurella pestis*. The tiny thing that causes the illness," Brink said. "This building will be separate from where he lives, him and the guards. They won't want it near. We must burn that building. We must destroy the equipment he uses to make the pestilence. And burn any papers we find."

"Is that all? Just the three of us, only one weapon . . ." Kirn began, but couldn't finish. It was absurd. Even in Russia he'd never faced absurdity like this.

"Someone needs to occupy the guards," Brink said.

Yes, thought Kirn. Like in Russia, when Muffe would hammer at the Reds from behind the MG-34, Böse feeding the belt, while the rest of them took the brown-shirted shits on the flank.

"I'll do it," Brink said.

"What does a doctor know about fighting?" Kirn asked. The clouds swept across the moon. Nothing more than the breeze in the leaves for sounds. "You know the pestilence. You'll know what to do. Let me do what I know."

Kirn stood up, and his head, quickly light, required him to stay still for a moment. He wanted an Eckstein, worse than he ever remembered, but knew only coughing would follow.

"Yes," Brink said.

Decided, then. Kirn switched the torch to his watch. Five minutes to ten. It had taken two long hours to walk the two kilometers from Sainte-Mère-Église, where the Baltic boy had pointed the road to Chef du Pont. It would take them another hour, perhaps longer, to reach the village. And then find the farm . . . and then . . .

Pilon stood with Brink's help. "The doctor, he's my part." Her voice was strong. "You, *boche*, have yours, Monsieur Frank has his. The SS is mine."

Wind and leaves were the only sounds again.

"Agreed?" Pilon asked.

As if to answer her, thunder rolled under the clouds to the east, near Carentan perhaps, or even farther. The noise, long and low, faded and grew stronger, faded again. It kept on, not dying like thunder made from weather. Bombs. Kirn listened, but couldn't pick out the sounds of aircraft. He looked above the trees in the direction of the noise and thought he saw small bright spots on the underside of clouds. Searchlights, he thought, or flak. Someone, somewhere, was under those bombs. They listened, all of them then, to the thunder.

Though his bedroom was tucked into the far corner of the house, the noise from the yard woke Wollenstein. He rolled over, put his feet on the floor. His head was still blurry with sleep, and as the deep bass sounds rumbled through the farmhouse, he tried to remember what he'd dreamt. He turned the switch to light the room.

Fists pounded his door. The whore from Chef du Pont stirred in the sheets and sat bolt upright, clutching the linen to her throat, her eyes bright and wide. "No one's coming to get you, girl," he said, but she didn't understand much of his German.

"Sturmbannführer!" someone shouted through the door. The noise outside the house grew, low and throaty, until it became heavy engines. Wollenstein opened the door. Nimmich shifted his weight from left foot to right, right foot to left. His eyelid ticked fast. The girl and Nimmich made a couple, both so scared.

"Trucks in the yard," Nimmich stammered.

Wollenstein's stomach tumbled but he kept his voice calm. "Trucks, at this hour?" He glanced at the small table and the silvered clock. Five minutes to midnight. He'd overslept after the hour with the girl.

"Call for Sillmann, tell him to bring in the guards."

"He's at the landing field. Ribe's the one who came for me."

"Who's out there?" Wollenstein asked. He ducked back into the room to pull on shirt and trousers and yank his tunic from a chair. Nimmich said nothing. Wollenstein pushed by the boy and padded through the dark house to the front door, fumbled for his boots, buckled on his belt, and pulled the Walther from its holster.

It was brighter outside than in. Two trucks filled the yard between the front door and the gate. Their engines idled and their narrow headlamps put beams in his eyes. Wollenstein put up a hand for shade and saw a low sedan creep into the yard, too. Its rear door swung open. The trucks' engines stuttered off, the car's, too, and the quiet rang out loud.

"Herr Doktor," said a voice from beside the car. The sedan's door slammed shut.

That was the same voice Wollenstein had heard in his dream. The slim, short shape walked toward him. The man's peaked cap jutted at an angle.

"Kammler," Wollenstein said.

"You can put down the pistol," Kammler said. The general brushed by Ribe, the pear-shaped soldier who was supposed to guard the gate.

"No—" Wollenstein whispered, ready to ask more questions, or point the Walther and pull the trigger. But of course he couldn't. Coward, he cursed himself.

"Perhaps you should let me have it," Kammler said. "You might hurt yourself. Doctors don't carry guns, do they?"

"I had to let them in . . . he's an Obergruppenführer—" Ribe got out.

"You did right, boy," Kammler said. "I'm sure you were only following the Sturmbannführer's orders. Not to let anyone steal the precious *Grabbringer.*"

Kammler held out his hand. There were others just behind him with guns. Wollenstein put the Walther in Kammler's palm.

"Why are you here?" Wollenstein managed. He remembered what Nimmich had said at the landing field. Ropes. He touched his neck.

Kammler's men, with shouts from sergeants, grouped around each truck. Three dozen or more, all armed with rifles or machine pistols, few with helmets, most with cloth caps. Not combat soldiers, then. Barracks troops.

"Better to talk inside," Kammler said as he motioned to the farmhouse.

"What's going on?" Wollenstein asked. "Why you are here?" He worked up his anger. "This is my facility and only I decide—"

"It's obvious, isn't it? I've come for the *Gräber*." Kammler looked up at him, his face in the darkness because of the headlamps against his back. He waved a black-clad arm at the farmhouse door. "I don't want to talk out here in the dark."

Wollenstein shivered, but led the way through the door, down the short corridor, and into the first room on the left, the one where he and Kammler and Himmler and the fat SD Adler had talked three nights before. Kammler found the light switch and waved to the room's two chairs. Through the open door to the corridor came the noise of boots on the stone and then on the stairs to the second floor. Kammler's SS were searching the place.

From his chair, Wollenstein tried to think. He was too valuable, too important, for the rope, no matter what. Himmler would not let Kammler throw him away.

Kammler paced to the desk, leaned against it, then set Wollenstein's Walther on its scratched wooden surface. "It doesn't look like you've done a thing to get ready for the move."

"No," admitted Wollenstein. Kammler would find out soon enough. None of the documents in the house or his workshop had been boxed, and the culturing barn was still operating. Nimmich was distilling more of number 211. Nimmich. Why had he been the one to wake him? He should be in the workshop.

"Why haven't you packed up?" asked Kammler.

"Adler. I assumed he would tell me when it was time to pack." Wollenstein shifted in the chair.

Kammler slowly tapped a cigarette onto a polished metal tin he pulled from a pocket, and lit it. Smoke drifted for the ceiling. "Adler, yes. Our lost eagle." He called to the open door and a soldier stepped in. "Bring them, the both of them," Kammler said. He smoked another breath. "Sometimes lost things are found. Without the help of a Kripo even." Kammler smiled.

Wollenstein was confused. Who was coming? How did Kammler know of a Kripo? "Some of us are better at finding things than others," Wollenstein said quietly.

"Very true." Kammler flicked ash from the cigarette.

Boots in the corridor again, and the sound of something heavy being pulled along the floor. Adler's bulk blocked the doorway until the SD stepped sideways into the room, a lit cigar pinched in his lips. After him, two SS dragged a man wearing only baggy trousers and a filthy, bloodstained cotton shirt, no coat. The SS pair dropped the man into the remaining chair.

It was the face that drew Wollenstein's eyes. One eye was so swollen shut it was invisible. Blood drew a line from the left ear to his neck, his nose was broken, and his cheeks were bruised yellow. Around his throat there were thicker, wider bruises, purple and blue. His right ear was attached by just the barest strip of fat-white cartilage. At some point, he had been tended; the man had a bloodied dressing around his right wrist.

Wollenstein managed to take his eyes away from the ruin and looked to Kammler, Adler, Kammler again, waiting for one to say something. But both only smoked, Kammler his cigarette, the fat one his stinking cigar.

"Who is he?" Wollenstein asked, trying to dredge up the last bit of cold annoyance he could.

Adler took the cigar from his thick lips. "English, Herr Doktor. One of the thieves brought here by your wayward Jews." The fat one grinned a toothy grin. Wollenstein noticed that one leg of Adler's trousers showed a rip and the uppers of his boots were coated with dried mud.

"I've never seen this man before," said Wollenstein. He heard the desperate flatness in his own voice.

"But you knew," said Kammler. "Adler says you knew commandos were here, but you didn't telephone. Instead, you sent him on a chase to make sure he couldn't tell me about this."

"I . . . I only had suspicions, the Kripo, he was the one who said there were commandos. But he had no proof, he—"

"Liar," said Adler. "There was another English in the church, that's what this one says. And you put him there with the sick *Wulewubs*."

"What in God's name does that have to do—" Wollenstein said.

"Keep your mouth shut," said Kammler.

"This commando was sent to bring you back to England, that's what he says," said Adler. "Weren't you?" The man didn't respond. He wasn't sleeping—that one eye was wide open—but it stared at a place outside the walls of this room. Adler went to the Englishman and asked again. "Haven't you? Come for the doctor, isn't that what you're here to do, take him to England?"

The English stared, still not at Adler, and after a moment the SD gently untied the wrap at the man's wrist. It was shattered, dark and swollen, from the looks broken carpals, perhaps the metacarpals as well. Adler took a step to the desk and put a big hand on the black telephone there, yanked its line by the roots as he snapped the Bakelite off the desk. He carried it to the English, the man's eyes following him.

Adler slammed the blocky base of the telephone on the English's wrist and the man screamed. Only when the scream exhausted itself into a series of racking sobs did Kammler drop his cigarette and grind it into the carpet, then come to stand in front of Wollenstein's chair. "You've ruined everything. Cost us surprise," said Kammler. "Now that they know about the *Gräber*, they'll be ready for my rockets, you shit." Spit launched from Kammler's mouth. "You know, I think you conspired with him. You let the damn Jews escape and you helped them flee to England to get your message that you'd turn. All because we forbid you to spray men like potatoes. Because *Himmler said you were fit for more than running a fucking factory*!" Shouting, he had leaned in to put hands on the arms of the chair, his breath smelling like cigarettes and garlic. Then Kammler straightened, and his voice dropped to a whisper. "Treason."

"I did not conspire! That's a lie!" Wollenstein yelled back, beginning to raise himself out of the chair.

"Sit," Kammler barked. Wollenstein let himself fall back.

"Make him say it," Wollenstein said. "If it's true, make him say it."

Adler looked at Kammler, Kammler nodded, and Adler pounded the telephone again. The Englishman screamed, shorter this time, caught his breath—in the hesitation, Wollenstein heard the word *promise* in English—and then he screamed again.

"Tell what you told me before!" Adler shouted.

The Englishman stayed conscious and started talking, in German of all things. His speech sounded like a child's in places, because of his broken front teeth. He told of Jews lost and found, of swimming ashore from a foundered boat, of coming with a man, no, two, and a woman, of how he came to sniff out the pestilence and whisk its maker back to England. But he said nothing of Wollenstein plotting anything. And nothing of the *Tiefatmung*.

Kammler heard the same words differently. Once the Englishman sobbed into silence, the Obergruppenführer turned to Wollenstein and said, "You heard. Treason."

"All I heard was that he came to kidnap me," said Wollenstein.

"Then you haven't heard everything," Kammler said. He made for the door, opened it, shouted, "Bring in the next one." He stepped aside to make way for Nimmich, the boy escorted by an SS close to his shoulder. The SS shoved Nimmich, who sprawled on the carpet at Kammler's feet. Then he stood again, his legs trembling.

Kammler went to Nimmich, put a hand on the boy's shoulder. Kammler, short as he was, had to reach up. "Herr Nimmich called me . . . today, was it?" The boy didn't answer, only trembled. Kammler smiled, removed his hand from Nimmich's shoulder. "Didn't you telephone, Nimmich?"

The boy mumbled.

"Talk of traitors," Wollenstein said, looking at Nimmich. "I took you into—"

"I'll speak for him, it seems," said Kammler. He tapped out another cigarette. More smoke joined the cloud already floating under the ceiling. Wollenstein looked down at his hands. Kammler blew smoke Nimmich's way and the boy recoiled, his eye twitching.

"He felt guilty," said Kammler. "Can you imagine? Someone who makes the *Grabbringer* feels guilty?" Kammler laughed, the sound out of place, and Wollenstein paid attention to his hands.

Wollenstein looked up. "You can't stop my work," he said, hearing his voice even and without anger. As he spoke he stole a look at the Walther on the desk. It was only a few meters away. "If you let me, I can show you what we can accomplish," he said, giving Kammler back his stare. He'd found a last reserve of courage.

Kammler shook his head. "You're mad *and* dangerous. An unhealthy combination, Herr Doktor."

"We can melt the Allied armies like candles." He stared at Kammler to keep his eyes from the desk and its black pistol, from Nimmich's frightened face and the English's broken one.

"*At what cost?* Nimmich told me everything. How you swore to use the potato sprayers on the beaches if the English come. You'd sicken Frenchmen *and* Germans. Or Frenchmen first, then Germans. We cannot use this here, don't you understand? Do you want us dying of this in Köln and Munich and Nuremburg, from one end of the Reich to the other? That's what would happen. You'd turn Europe into our graveyard. Put it in my rockets, yes. Drop it on their pygmy island, yes. *But not here!* Can you understand that, you halfwit?"

"But—"

"Enough," Kammler said, waving his hand and stepping away from Nimmich. He looked toward the door, where the three SS who remained stood. "Take the boy out and shoot him."

Two of the soldiers reached for Nimmich's arms, and pulled him back across the carpet to the doorway.

"You . . . you said . . . you said—" the boy cried, as he vanished into the corridor.

"I promised to save you from the rope," Kammler called after. "Believe me, this is better."

Kammler walked to Wollenstein's chair. "And you. You have another future."

"Not like Nimmich."

Kammler shook his head. "We'll fly back to the Pas des Calais and you'll meet some people from Prinz-Albrechtstrasse. You'll tell them everything, you'll explain the processes, I'm sure, in exquisite and intimate detail."

Wollenstein looked at the Englishman a moment. He felt the air around him close in, press on his temple and throat and chest, and grow cold as if a winter's wind had crept into June.

Kammler smiled again.

"You won't dare—" Wollenstein began. "I demand to talk to the Reichsführer."

Kammler placed the cigarette in his other hand, reached into his fine gray wool coat, and pulled out a flimsy sheet of paper. A teletype signal. Kammler waved the paper. "This is his order for your arrest. You've run out of friends, Herr Doktor . . ." Kammler paused, cocked his head as if listening to something.

Wollenstein heard it, too. Aircraft engines, low, dozens, scores of them. They sounded like a train of goods wagons trundling over rails, close enough to touch. The window rattled. Whole railyards full of goods wagons.

Kammler stared at the ceiling for a second, then suddenly turned and left the room, Adler right behind. The one SS still in the room glanced at Wollenstein and the English, then toward the open door and the corridor beyond, and he, too, stepped out. Wollenstein was alone with the Englishman and the Walther. The sounds banged against the window. It wasn't a raid; raids were thunder in the distance or a drone high above the clouds. Aircraft didn't fly this low for a raid.

He stood, picked up the Walther, checked that its magazine remained, and pulled the slide. Next he went to the door, put his hand on the frame, and glanced into the corridor. It was empty. The fearsome roll of engines vibrated through the house. A painting's frame rattled against the wall in the corridor that led to the entryway.

"Help me," a voice behind him croaked. Wollenstein turned to stare at the English. "Help me and . . . I'll take you to England. Safe." His German was without a hint of accent.

Wollenstein looked into the corridor again. How far could he run before Adler found him? A kilometer at most before the fat eagle swooped down and crushed him.

The English stirred in the chair, as if he wanted to rise, but wasn't able. "Help me," the man said a third time. "You'll live."

Wollenstein wondered what time he could make with the man. Fast enough, perhaps, to reach the landing field. Sillmann and the Storch were at the field, the Me-110 and Junkers and their pilots, too.

Wollenstein slipped the Walther into a pocket and helped the English from the chair. The man stank of sweat, dirt, feces, and a taint of bile or infection; the odor smelled, Wollenstein thought, like the color green. Kammler would let him live only long enough to have the gangsters from Prinz-Albrechtstrasse make him smell like this. It was England and keeping alive his work, or this stink and the death of everything. The smell made up his mind.

Wollenstein put an arm around the waist of the Englishman, and helped him to the door. Down the corridor, left, right, through the empty kitchen, and to the back door.

They stepped into the night. Here the sound was loud enough to shake in his chest. Dozens of engines, hundreds. Toward Chef du Pont, languid lines of yellow and red scored the night sky. Tracers. From the Luftwaffe flak guns south of the village. The lines waved, like thin limbs in a slight breeze, as they searched for the aircraft.

A bright arc streaked through the clouds, and as Wollenstein watched, the arc turned into an aircraft with wide wings and two engines, its tail ablaze. It vanished below the trees of the near woods. He waited for an explosion, but heard nothing, only more engines.

In the light of the tracers and in the moon, which had just peeked from the clouds, Wollenstein saw flowers open, pause as if suspended, then begin to drift down. The wind carried the flowers east. Parachutes.

Kirn had been right, Wollenstein thought, only a day early. "Invasion," he said.

"Fuck the invasion," the man said. "I want to go home."

Wollenstein stared at the falling flowers. Yes. But only after he'd waved his aircraft to the same destination and let them blanket England with his own invisible parachutes. Make a thousand, ten thousands of them sick and they would have to welcome him with open arms.

JUNE 6, 1944

———

Tuesday

. . . what we learn in time of pestilence: that there
are more things to admire in men than to despise.

—ALBERT CAMUS

Twenty-one

The three of them crouched in boscage north of Chef du Pont, and from a small hole in the hedgerow they watched the two trucks and the one car squirm on the narrow mud road.

"Reinforcements," Alix said, her voice just loud enough. The moon gleamed on the roof of the long, low car as it disappeared around a corner with a last flash of taillights. Frank shoved through the branches to slide down the short earthen bank to stand in the road. She followed, and the *boche* did the same. Frank pulled a cigarette from his pocket—the *boche* had given them his cigarettes because he couldn't smoke anymore, his cough worse than ever. Frank lit one, the flame illuminating his unshaven face, which was darkened by a wide swipe of dirt. "What now?" he asked.

"I don't know," the *boche* said. "Two trucks. There could be thirty or even forty men in two trucks."

In the distance, the sound of bombing drummed under the broken clouds. The thunder had been their constant companion as they'd walked from Chef du Pont to where the *boche* said they'd find Wollenstein's *dunkle Bauernhof*. Now that thunder drew closer and grew louder.

"How can we fight forty men?" Alix asked. She let loose a cough. Each step of the long walk had nibbled at her strength, and she didn't know how many more steps she could take. And now, seeing the *boche* so thick, she felt an emptiness. She would never find the one who did this to her, to Papa and Jules and Alain. She felt hope expire a bit, with each miserable breath.

"Perhaps the trucks are empty. Perhaps the trucks are here to take the pestilence away," Frank said. The red end of his cigarette glowed dully, and he coughed. Alix wished for the *boche*'s torch, so she could see Frank's face. Was he sick now, too? That would mean all three of them had the pestilence. A small army, all ill.

"This is madness," the *boche* said, and then coughed and spat.

Frank said nothing, but Alix heard him step once, twice, in the muddy road, and she realized he was heading after the *boche* trucks toward the dark farm. Alix pulled in a breath, deep as she could make it, and followed. The *boche*, now behind her and carrying their only weapon, muttered something to himself, but he, too, came along, his shoes sucking at the mud.

One step was for Papa, she told herself, the next for Jules, the third for Alain. The fourth for her. And she counted over again, Papa-Jules-Alain-me, Papa-Jules-Alain-me, to take her there.

And after a hundred, two hundred of those, she bumped into Frank.

"Listen," Frank whispered.

Alix did, and heard aeroplanes. Their engines were first only in the far far distance to the north and west, but then closer, and in a moment, directly overhead. She looked up but saw only clouds.

The noise multiplied, doubled in a second, tripled the second after that. The sound thrummed in her ears, in her head, in her too-tight chest.

Gunfire rattled next. Behind them in the direction of Chef du Pont came sharp cracks like a horse whip, each its own, but to the east rose a ripping noise, a fast, steely *rap-rap-rap-rap*. A few colored dots, yellows and pale reds, appeared over the hedge. She spun there in the road and saw lines of those dots, and even more colors, weaving along the underside of the clouds.

A massive aeroplane, like the one at the airfield in England, dropped out of the clouds above them, its engines shouting. Her mouth hung open.

Wonderful, wonderful, she thought, and couldn't help herself: she clapped her hands together.

"Look there!" Frank shouted. To the north she watched as the moon, suddenly back, silhouetted shapes in the sky. One, two, three, four, five, six—and she lost count. They swung from side to side in the air.

"*Fallschirmjäger!*" Kirn yelled.

Gunfire, closer now, a few hundred meters down the road perhaps, started and swelled. More pastel lines streaked for the parachutists.

The noise of the aeroplanes and the guns grew and grew and grew until Alix put her hands over her ears. Invasion, she thought as she watched the parachutes drift down. Liberation. The sounds that came through her hands drowned out the world.

She felt a cramp, and wondered if the pestilence would strike her down now. But the pain in her stomach passed and Alix uncorked her ears. She reached out one hand to Frank. She gripped his and squeezed.

Stop shooting! Stop shooting!" Kammler shouted from the doorway of Wollenstein's farmhouse, where he'd stood in shock watching the parachutists.

Slowly, the packed dirt yard went back to black as the gunfire from his men petered out. Still excited, they chattered, but the waves of aircraft had washed over them and disappeared, taking their sounds to the south and east and even north. Replacing those sounds were new ones. A distant *pop-pop-pop* echoed, followed by another string of shots nearer, then a long saw's sound of a machine gun farther away. The most persistent came from the northeast.

Kammler closed his eyes and opened them again. He had no idea what to do. *I am a builder, a maker of labor camps and crematoria, not a soldier.* Kammler glanced to the men around the trucks, then at the horizon, where tracers still arced as nervous Luftwaffe gunners fired at nothing. The moon remained free of the clouds that had covered it just minutes before.

"What do you think?" he asked Adler.

Adler stared up as if expecting still more parachutists. He chewed on his cigar, which had gone out, and talked to the sky. "I'm not the one to ask."

"*Oppel!*" Kammler shouted, and a uniformed man came at the run, then stiffened to attention. His head, topped by a field cap, was too small for the rest of his body, and his face owned a wriggling scar that ran over his chin. Kammler knew he was lucky to have this one, who at least claimed he'd fought in Russia.

"What should we do, Oppel?"

"Do, Herr—?"

"I want this place protected long enough to load the trucks."

Oppel glanced at the ground. "Most of the men, they're not . . . they're new." He looked at Kammler, cleared his throat. "Put patrols to the north and south and east, where we saw the parachutes. Find and fix them in place, so they can't infiltrate to the farm. And keep a reserve somewhere central, where it can react."

"Do that, then," Kammler said. "But leave two with me. And take that one with you. He knows the farm. Make him show you where they keep the *Gräber.*" Kammler pointed to the pear-shaped man who had tried to keep them out of the yard.

"The what?" Oppel asked.

"The canisters. Make him show you where Wollenstein stores them. It's a small block building, like a bunker. In the next field, I think," said Kammler. "Take a truck and load the canisters. I want them safe before anything else is done." He wasn't going to let anything happen to the *Grabbringer.* He couldn't let the English and American take it. He would haul it to the Mittelwerk and stuff it inside his rockets and come September . . ."Hurry, do it now," he told Oppel.

The man saluted, pulled the pear-shaped one by the sleeve toward the nearest truck, and began barking orders. Two men separated and edged near Kammler, while the rest climbed back into the trucks. Oppel pulled himself onto the running board of one. The truck's engine whined and caught, and its headlamps lit the place where there was enough room to drive past the house. The second truck started its engine, too, and twisted its way out the courtyard to the road beyond the gate. It turned left and headed south toward Chef du Pont.

"What about him?" an SS man called from closer to the farmhouse door. He was the one who guarded Nimmich.

Kammler thought a moment, shook his head. "Not yet. Put him in the house, watch him."

Adler took the moment to light his cigar. "Where's that shit Wollenstein?" he asked.

Kammler jerked, turned and counted the figures left in the yard. Himself and Adler and the two SS that hovered near. "No," he said. " No." He stalked for the door of the farmhouse, Adler huffing behind him.

The SS who had dragged Nimmich inside met them at the door. "The doctor's run off," the man sputtered.

"Go find him!" Adler shouted behind him. *"Find him!"*

"The English one, he's gone, too," said the SS.

"Find them!" Adler yelled. The fat one's heart would give out one day from that, Kammler thought.

"Bring Nimmich to me," he said to this SS man. To the other pair, behind him, he said, "Go after them. They can't go far, not the shape the English is in." The two disappeared into the house to find the trail at the room and follow it through the corridors and out, he supposed, a rear door somewhere.

Gunshots popped in the middle distance.

Down the dark lane, walking at its edge to keep from the worst mud, they were a single file, Brink at the front, Alix behind, and Kirn bringing up the rear.

The C-47s were gone, but the boys they'd dropped made lots of noise. Gunfire to the right, that was north by east, more straight ahead, some off to the south and west. This was the diversion they needed to close on the farm just ahead.

Brink lifted his foot, boot slathered in mud, and put it down again. Slow going, and not all because of the road. Alix sucked in great gulps for breaths—she might not make it much farther—and tucked at the end, Kirn was gasping, too. Sick, the both of them.

And Brink had to stop as well. He slowly inhaled, feeling that, even as he kept bringing in air, the lungs weren't filling. He bent over. Alix's hand was on his shoulder.

Thank God she didn't say anything, or he might have missed the thud that came through the hedge. "Tip, you clumsy shit, get up," an American voice whispered.

Kirn coughed uncontrollably, a long *ack-ack-ack*.

The Americans didn't hesitate, but just opened up. The hedge erupted in flame. Brink flopped into the mud, pulled Alix with him, and the bullets rained down leaves and twigs from beside and behind and above them.

"*Goddammit, who said to shoot!*" another voice called. It was loud enough for Brink to hear the accent—sounded like Texas or Oklahoma. His roommate second year at Minnesota had been a doctor's son from Waurika, a small town down near the Red River, and this voice sounded like that. "*Flash!*" that same voice yelled.

Brink didn't understand. Flash?

"*Flash, goddammit!*"

It was a sign, a password, Brink realized. And he didn't have its mate.

He got up on one knee. "I don't know the goddamned—" But he heard metal on metal, a *click-clack*, and stopped talking. He ran through the choices, decided on the one that seemed least likely to go wrong, and yelled, "*Five-oh-five, Dog Company!*" He might have been their ringer, but most of the boys who played ball on the parachute regiment's team came from Dog Company.

One word through the dark: "*Jesuschrist.*" Then three more shots, winging through the brush, still wild and high.

"*Knock that off!*" the accent from Texas or Oklahoma shouted.

"Don't shoot, don't, I'm an American, I catch for the Five-oh-five, Mitchovsky plays second, he's from Dog, Ives, he's from Dog, too, he pitches—"

"I'm comin' through, don't shoot, goddammit," said the Texan. A man pushed through the hedge, a dark line in front that had to be a weapon, and he squatted at the edge of the road. Others followed, three in a rush shoving into the lane side by side, then a last one on his own. "Addison, Five-oh-five, Easy. Now who the fuck are you?" asked the Texan.

"Brink. But don't come any closer," he said, and punched out the next words as fast as he could. "Stay clear, five or six feet's far enough."

Brink brushed mud from his face and started telling Addison the short version of the story. He thought he would have trouble convincing the paratrooper and worried that he would be forced to use his useless rank to make Addison help them. But once he said there was something that would kill hundreds or thousands of the men in the morning's boats, Addison only had one question.

"I heard you caught for Dizzy Dean a few times, is that right?"

Brink crouched down in the road and listened. Already he was able to filter out the constant nagging gunfire in every direction and concentrate on what was important.

"What?" Addison asked.

There. Someone grinding through a gear.

"Get outa the fuckin' road," Addison said. He slipped into the narrow ditch between the lane and the hedgerow, the depression not even a foot deep and barely three wide, but the moonlight didn't reach into its shadows. The other four paratroopers did the same, Alix and Kirn, too, and finally after Addison hissed at him again, Brink dropped in beside the Texan.

A noise growled up the road from the north. It was dark down that way, even in the moonlight. Lining the road were huge hedges that reared out of dirt mounds as high as a man and more.

The headlights crawled around the bend in the road sixty yards away, then came on, the truck struggling with the soft surface. Its wheels spun in the mud.

Addison pulled back the bolt of his Thompson. The *click-clack* wasn't loud enough to mute the thumping in Brink's chest.

The truck drew near and the driver clumsily shifted to a lower gear. Ten yards away, five, and Brink wondered when Addison would shoot, but he was afraid to speak. Then it was beside them, so near all he'd have to do is stand and take a step to touch the fender. The front wheel turned toward them and it looked like the driver would put it in the ditch and crush them all, but it straightened and Brink pushed his back into the hedge. The truck trundled on. Addison was going to let it go.

But once the truck passed by, Addison scrambled out of the ditch to stand with legs braced wide in the middle of the road, where he raised a Thompson submachine gun. Two other troopers joined him, while the last two kneeled in the ditch, rifles up. Addison started, and the rest joined in, the Thompson tearing out a stream of shots, empty cartridges flying in an arc over the lane, the Garands of the others firing so fast it was just a moment before the exhausted clips sprung up with a tinny clang.

The canvas cover was pocked with black dots as the bullets punctured it. From under the cloth, unlike the Bedford, screams and shouts rose to a choir.

Something round like a baseball left Addison's hand and bounded under the truck, and the grenade went off with a yellow-white flash and a bang. The truck slowed. Another flash-bang and the left rear tire shredded and caught fire.

When the Germans came tumbling out of the truck, Addison and the others shot them down, each one, little puffs of brown and black opening on their backs as they ran for the hedge at the other side of the road. None got farther than a few feet.

The truck leaned into the ditch on the left beyond Kirn, its front left wheel mired and its fiery back left tire flickering. The engine coughed and died. Far off, the rattle of other weapons was the only sound.

The paratrooper beside Addison said "That was dumb" in a school kid's high, reedy voice. "The way they tried to get away, that was dumb." He walked toward the black window of the back of the truck, stepping around bodies in the mud, some quiet, more moaning, one trying to crawl away.

"Watch it, Tipper," Addison said. He pulled out the Thompson's magazine and tossed it aside, snapped open a pouch hung on the webbing around his waist, and clicked a new one into place.

Another paratrooper rose from the ditch and stepped to the nearest German, toed him with a boot to roll him face up. "Hey, these guys are SS. Look, ain't they?" He lightly kicked the leg of the lifeless man. "Not so tough."

Brink went into the carpet of bodies—five, six, seven, nine all told—and leaned over to pick one of the dropped weapons. It was cold, and hadn't been fired.

When he straightened he saw the boy at the back of the truck, Tipper, Addison had called him, and a few yards away, Alix. She was just pulling herself out of the ditch. The blur behind her must be Kirn. What did Kirn think of all this, Brink wondered, them shooting his countrymen down this way?

"I said be careful, Tip, check out the truck, goddammit," Addison yelled.

As Tipper turned toward Addison, Brink saw a shadow move under the canvas. He raised the German gun to point it at the truck.

A man with light, close-cropped hair and no hat dropped from the truck behind Tipper. His uniform was dark and his face was, too, so was one arm—blood, Brink thought. He held a pistol in a trembling hand and pointed it at the back of Tipper's helmet and shot. Tipper went down face-first.

The German twisted to his right, faced the ditch so close to the back of the truck, and made for it, maybe thinking he'd climb into the hedge's leaves and branches and scramble up its muddy rise to escape. But Alix was in his way.

She raised her hands to surrender or fend him off, Brink wasn't sure, but he didn't stop to think and instead pointed the gun's short muzzle at the German, who must have seen the movement because his head swiveled for Brink. The light was not nearly enough to show the blond boy's eyes, but Brink imagined them as blue marbles, cold and smooth with a small light that glinted from within. He pressed the trigger. Nothing. A Thompson muzzle nudged past Brink's shoulder and its shots banged against his ear and the German boy went against the truck's tail, more of those puffs of black and brown spurting from his jacket. The boy collapsed like a house built from Rider Back cards.

Addison wrenched the gun from his hand, looked at it. "The safety's on." He clicked something on the weapon and handed it back.

Alix came to him but said nothing. It was Kirn who spoke, in German this time, not French.

"Ich dachte, Ärzte sollen Leuten helfen und sie nicht umbringen," he said quietly. Addison heard. The Texan wanted to know what the hell was going on, a Kraut with them.

Brink didn't answer. He was too busy trying to come up with an answer to Kirn's question.

I thought doctors were supposed to save people, too. Not kill them.

Wollenstein pulled clumps of pasteboard folders from the cabinet, shuffled through them, stuffed one into the satchel at his feet and dropped the rest into the pile on the floor. The new folders slid down the flank of the heap.

"Hurry," the Englishman said. Wollenstein glanced over his shoulder to the desk and chair where he'd left the commando. Wollenstein stole a look at his watch; it had been just sixteen minutes since they'd started through the grass, nine since he'd pulled the key from around his neck and opened the padlock on the workshop's door.

He had the files he needed. The electric refrigerator at the back beckoned, half hidden behind a thicket of glass beakers and a rack of pipettes. He dropped a final folder, heard it slip, too, and started for the white enameled box and its cache of 211. Holding open the scratched leather satchel with one hand, he filled the space free of papers with vials of the clear liquid from the refrigerator. Glass clinked as he pulled the vials off the racks inside and laid them carefully into the bag. Wollenstein had counted to fifteen, plucked the final bottle, held it in his hand. But the sixteenth slipped, bouncing first off a boot and shattering on the floor.

"What are you doing?" the English asked from behind him.

He turned to face the commando, who leaned back in the chair, his head a mess—it would never really heal properly, he thought—but Wollenstein's eyes were drawn not so much to the face but to the big, black revolver in the English's good hand. Nimmich's Russian Nagant, found in the desk drawer. The man steadied that hand on the desk's top, the wretched hand limp beside it.

"What are you doing?" The Englishman's voice was bold and loud. He must be a beast, this one, to have survived such a beating.

"The antibiotic." The English didn't understand. "A medicine. For the pestilence." He snapped shut the satchel's brass latches.

"Medicine . . ." the man said quietly from across the workshop. "The fool was right, wasn't he? It cures the sickness, does it? Then we'll want that, too." The barrel waved a bit to mean he was to move from the refrigerator. Wollenstein came to the desk. He had little choice; the Walther was deep in his overcoat pocket, on the wrong side, too, what with his right hand holding the satchel.

"Yes, you'll want it," Wollenstein said. More than want it, he knew; the English would do anything for it. They would need him for his expertise and for what was in the satchel. They would have to let him live, wouldn't they, even though he was setting out to hurt them.

He would not simply hand them number 211. When he reached the landing field he would order the Me-110 and Junkers into the air. He might run to the English to save his neck, but he was not about to see his work untried. The aircraft would still spray the *pestis*, if not over the beaches, because the beaches were yet empty, then over a city as he'd decided before. Then the English would need him and the 211.

"Bring me the case," the Englishman said. He waved the Nagant again.

"No." This was his passport, his writ of safe passage.

"We must trust each other, Herr Doktor," said the commando. "We both want the same thing. You, in England."

But what trust was there when the Nagant was between them?

"Give me the case," the Englishman said.

Wollenstein shook his head. "No. It's in here," and he pointed a finger at his own temple. "Not here." He shook the satchel enough to let the glass vials inside chime.

They stared at each other a heartbeat or two, the English with his Russian revolver, Wollenstein with the satchel. Then the door made a small, gentle noise, like a creak of a thin, old tree in the wind. Wollenstein heard it. So did the English, for he pulled himself out of the chair with surprising grace and limped to the wall beside the door.

The latch bent toward the floor a centimeter, stopped, and the door opened. As it did, it masked the Englishman, who now stood in the unseen space between the door and the wall. A pair of SS entered, one with a helmet that hid his head, the other with a boat-shaped overseas cap so clean Wollenstein wondered if it had ever seen the outside of a barracks. The first had a machine pistol, the second a rifle.

"Here you are," the first SS said, his nose a flattened Slavic thing.

Wollenstein tried to keep from looking at the door.

"They said to bring you back to the house," the Slav said, his voice thick with an accent.

"I still have papers to find," Wollenstein said, stretching out the time to let the English act. But the seconds ticked by and nothing happened and Wollenstein began to wonder if he was on his own.

"They didn't say nothing about papers, only to come get you and the English," the hoarse-voiced SS rumbled. "Where is he, anyway? The English."

"He took my pistol and escaped."

"Escaped? Looking like he did?" asked the other SS, the one with the soft cap. He was younger. "I don't think he could take a step without help, the way he looked." His voice was higher.

A hole punched through the door from behind it and the higher-voiced SS pitched to the floor. Only then did Wollenstein hear the gunshot. The older SS was fast and spun at the sound, but all that did was let him grab the second bullet in his chest rather than his back. Wollenstein noticed a curl of smoke from the edges of the new peepholes in the door. The SS gurgled and collapsed, the machine pistol clattering to the floor, splinters in the man's shocked face.

Wollenstein reached for the machine pistol with his free hand, and was straightening when the door swung from the wall. The English came from behind the door, the Nagant leading. He used the revolver to put down the groaning second SS, a shot through the man's tipped helmet.

The English smiled, the roots of his top teeth showing. Each breath must be an agony, the air on those nerves. The commando stepped closer. "You see, Doktor," said the English. "Trust." He looked at Wollenstein, his eyes like light smoke. "I'm not going to leave you or shoot you. That's the last thing I'd do." He waited for some kind of answer.

There was no turning back now, Wollenstein thought, glancing at the dead SS.

He went to the nearest workbench, turned on a gas burner, lit it with a flint sparker, and brought a sheet of paper to its flame. It caught, the edge browning and curling, finally breaking into fire, and he tossed it onto the pile he'd made. The files caught slowly, and as the flames gained ground, a small eager fire fingered the edges of the bench's leg.

Wollenstein slung the machine pistol over a shoulder, then wrapped an arm around the English's waist, and they hobbled toward the landing field.

Twenty-two

Brink found an opening, pushed through the scrawny line of brush, and held a fistful of prickly branches so Alix could scramble through. The others, Addison and his remaining three paratroopers, Kirn last, followed her onto the field.

"Which way?" Addison asked.

Brink had no idea. Why was he in charge now?

The men from the 505 looked at him. One scratched under his field jacket. Alix had gone to the grass, exhausted. Kirn stood with the German submachine gun cradled in his arms. He snorted, spat, but when he exhaled, Brink heard the man's lungs rattle like stones in a bucket.

Brink stared into the dark again and, after a moment of searching, found the dark mass that he and Kirn had decided was a farm. Like so many Norman farms, it was surrounded by a fortress wall. It must be Wollenstein's farm, Kirn had said. They'd swung around it and now were coming at its east side. There should be a gate here in the wall to reach the farm's fields,

Kirn said. Over the trees to the north Brink saw a line of sparks ascend, then break into a bright bulb. A flare. It hung in the air for a minute, floated down, and vanished as if snuffed between fingers.

Addison came out of his crouch and pointed. At first, Brink thought the glow he saw was the flare's afterimage, but as he squinted he saw it was real light. Just a flicker.

He grabbed for Alix's hand and hauled her to her feet, then led her and the others toward the light. They swished through the ankle-high grass and got close enough to see the fire licking under the eaves of a small barn fifty yards away, close enough to see the silhouettes of four men against the flames, one uselessly throwing a bucket of water into an open, smoking door, another with his hands up to shield his face from the heat, the others simply watching at a distance. One of those was big, huge.

"That's the SD," Kirn wheezed in French. "The fat one there on the left." To Alix, he said, "He's the one who killed your little brother."

She spoke a quiet *merci* and touched the submachine gun slung over Brink's shoulder, tried to get her fingers around its barrel. Brink shoved her hand away.

"I don't think any of them are Wollenstein," Kirn said.

Brink looked again. The barn was too small to be where they made the *Pasteurella pestis*. But it could be where Wollenstein cooked his antibiotic; Kate's lab hadn't been even that big. As he watched, flames broke through the high roof and a gust sent a yellow finger ten or twenty feet up and out. In its sudden light he saw burning papers pushed into the air, like feathery embers. One lit gently a few feet away, balanced atop leaves of grass. Its edge glowed a moment, but then went dark, and when he touched it, small black flakes crumbled at his touch. He stuffed what remained inside his shirt.

Papers. It *was* a laboratory. And the antibiotic was gone. Brink held up a hand to see the last piece of tape by the firelight. He should tear it off now.

"We'll want to be as evil as them," Childess had promised him, but Brink hadn't believed him. Childess had been right.

"Let's go," Brink said in English, touched Alix's elbow to pull her from the barn's fire and its disappointment. He took them back through the thin barrier of bushes, turned north, and walked into the next field.

There they found a small shed, no bigger than a car's garage, dark and abandoned. When he had Kirn press the flashlight against a window, he saw two large metal mixing machines bolted to the floor.

The smell led him to the next field. The familiar odor of overcooked soup traveled far and he put his nose to it and followed it into and out of a shallow ditch, water in its bottom. He splashed down the draw, his nose taking him finally to another, even bigger barn.

The soup smell was the same stink as at Porton Down when the wind blew from the three low buildings were they grew the rod-shaped *Bacillus anthracis*. It was from the broth that became the jellylike agar, on which the bacilli fed and grew. Like in England, the smell here couldn't be contained.

He told Kirn what he thought was inside—the pestilence—and the German policeman nodded and raised his weapon and drew back its bolt while Brink pulled on the tracked wooden door, rolling it aside so they could all see into the brightly lit place. The stench made Brink blink his eyes and Kirn coughed, spat. "Jesus," one of the troopers behind him said. Alix backed away.

The rotted smell came from the wide, shallow metal tubs. They rested on five workbenches that each ran for twenty, twenty-five feet into the barn. In front of one of the workbenches was a beast in a long green rubber apron that stretched from its chest to below its knees. It wore gray rubber boots and yellow rubber gloves, and its face was disguised by a white cloth mask over its mouth and nose and clear glass goggles over its eyes. It couldn't have been less human.

"*Raus!*" the thing yelled, the word muffled like one bubbling up through water.

One of Addison's men stepped up, raised his Garand, and *pop-pop*, shot the beast. It flailed backward and then spun so that it stumbled to the bench and, with arms outstretched, fell into the tub filled with brown crap. The tub upended, spilling the thick soup onto the concrete floor.

The wide door at the end of the barn squealed open—it was on tracks, too—and another rubber-clad beast stood there. Brink shouted not to shoot, but the same trooper, now joined by Addison, fired anyway. The reports banged off the concrete and ricocheted against the wood walls and ceiling, and the bullets shredded the man.

"*Stop it, goddammit, stop it!*" Brink screamed. "We need them alive!"

He was about to step across the threshold, see if he could find a survivor who could tell him where Wollenstein was and where he kept the stocks of *pestis*, but Kirn laid an arm across his chest.

"It doesn't matter if I go, does it?" he asked, and when Brink nodded, not knowing what else to say, the German stepped into the barn, meandered down the aisles to the door at the end of the room, disappeared through it. The rest of them waited on the safer side of the door. Addison told one of his paratroopers to stand watch around the barn's corner, make sure they weren't surprised. A minute ticked by. Another.

"Doc, we can't wait here—" Addison began.

"Just a little longer," Brink said. The clock in his head had no second hand, but he counted to himself, ticking off the tens by sticking out a finger. He got to four fingers and seven seconds when Kirn reappeared, his hand around the neck of a small man wearing the apron and boots, but no mask or gloves or goggles.

Kirn pushed the man toward Brink, but Brink stepped aside and the man slumped to the packed ground just outside the door. He glared up at the tall American paratroopers, babbling in a tongue Brink couldn't figure.

"He's Ukraine, he says," Kirn said, "but he speaks German, don't you?" Kirn kicked the man, now crouching, in the backside. The Ukrainian flattened out in the mud again. "Don't you?" Kirn booted him again.

"Wo ist Wollenstein?" asked Brink. He leaned over the prone man and yelled in his ear. *"Wo ist die Pest?"*

Kirn put a boot on the man's neck and Brink stepped aside. He watched the Ukrainian's head press into the soft earth under Kirn's weight. "Wollenstein? Tell me where Wollenstein is or I'll flatten your fucking head!" Kirn shouted.

"The house," the man slobbered out in German. "Under arrest."

"Where's the pestilence?" Kirn asked, putting more weight on the face. "The pestilence?"

"Please, please, I don't know. They made me work—"

"Where?"

"Please!" *Bitte, bitte, bitte,* the Ukrainian chanted.

"Damn you," yelled Kirn. He leaned even more on the leg holding down the Ukrainian.

The man gagged, gasped, and Kirn lifted his boot. "The landing field, the aircraft," the Ukrainian croaked.

"Where?"

"Zwei hundert Meters nördlich von hier. Bitte, bitte, bitte." Begging.

"Get up," Kirn ordered. "Stand up. Take us there." Kirn grabbed the straps of the rubber apron and pulled the Ukrainian to his feet. He spun the man around and slapped the back of the man's head.

"Kamerad," the Ukrainian mumbled hoarsely. *"Bitte, Kamerad."*

"You're no comrade of mine," Kirn said, coughed and spit, the phlegm spattering the Ukrainian's back. He shoved the man away from the barn.

Brink took the time to help Alix back to her feet and stuck close to Kirn so he wouldn't lose him.

The landing field was dark—someone had switched off the large electric lamps—but Wollenstein caught glimpses of the black Me-110 in the wavering lance of a torch. The Ju-52 would be beyond that. He let go of the Englishman, who sagged to the grass near the wall that bordered this edge of the field. With the waist-high stone wall between himself and anyone who might shoot at the first sound, he called out. *"Sillmann! Tauch!* It's Wollenstein. *Sillmann!"* Several torches turned his way and the beams crisscrossed as they searched. Finally, one touched his face. He put his hand up to wave off the light.

"Sillmann! Here!" he called. A figure jogged from the left, where the Storch would be. The pilot came to the wall, a torch in his hand. He put it on Wollenstein.

"Sturmbannführer! I thought you'd . . . the *Fallschirmjäger,* they're everywhere. I sent two of the ground crew—"

"Is everything ready?"

"I sent a runner to the farm, did he find you? The shooting, the *Fallschirmjäger,* I didn't know whether to send them—"

Wollenstein broke in a second time. "No, I didn't see your messenger." Sillmann knew nothing of Kammler coming here, or his fat SD hyena either, or even of the threat Kammler'd made to hand him to the monsters of Prinz-Albrechtstrasse, so his plan was safe this far. But he couldn't let the pilot babble of the Me-110 and Junkers and their destination in front of the Englishman.

Which enemy to deal with first, Wollenstein wondered. Sillmann would not want to fly the Storch to England, and the Englishman would want to stop the aircraft from leaving if he knew what they carried. Both would need convincing, but he only had one gun. The English first, he decided, and he put the satchel atop the flat stones of the wall, the vials ringing softly again, so he had both hands free to pull the machine pistol from his shoulder. He held it, still not knowing how it worked.

"Who's that, Sturmbannführer?" Sillmann asked, the torch swinging past Wollenstein's shoulder. "My God, what happened to your face?"

"What are you doing?" the English asked in his perfect German. "Trust, Doktor, I thought we had agreed to trust each other."

Wollenstein looked across the wall at the black oval where his pilot's face would be. "Go, Sillmann," he whispered. "Give the order. Start the aircraft."

Sillmann hesitated, and when Wollenstein turned, he saw that the Nagant was in the Englishman's hand.

"What are you doing?" the English asked Wollenstein; he had heard the whisper. There was a long silence, just sounds at the Me-110, conversation between its pilot and ground crew, perhaps, by the shine of a pair of torches under its wing. For a moment, the light glinted off the stainless steel of the spraying mechanism. "What is that under the Messerschmitt?" asked the English.

"Sillmann, go," Wollenstein ordered again. "Give the order."

"He's not going anywhere," said the English. There was a click: the Nagant's hammer.

"Go ahead and shoot him," said Wollenstein. "He's the pilot, neither of us will get away."

"Sturmbannführer? What is he talking about? Who is this?" Sillmann asked.

"Go, Sillmann, do what I said."

"Don't move, boy."

"Sturmbannführer, what's this about?" Sillmann's voice was loud.

"Go."

"Where's the fighter flying? What's that under the wing?"

"Sillmann, go!"

Wollenstein turned back to Sillmann, who didn't move. Wollenstein laid the machine pistol on top of the flat stone wall, climbed over, one knee on the wall, then another, then down the other side, and grabbed the satchel's handle.

"We saw a Storch over Port-en-Bessin with something under its wings," the English called to his back. "What is that under there?"

Wollenstein didn't answer, but took one step from the wall, another, another yet, toward the Messerschmitt. With each step he expected the English to pull the Nagant's trigger and put a hole in his back. The Me-110 came closer—to him it seemed as if the aircraft moved toward him, not the other way around—and each step was one step away from the bullet.

"Doktor! Stop!" the Englishman shouted, but even with the lisp in his voice he sounded uncertain. It was as if he didn't know what danger the Messerschmitt posed, and so was unwilling to risk killing what he had come so far to claim. Wollenstein counted on that and kept walking.

Only when his hand was on the cold metal skin of the Me-110 did he realize he'd held his breath the entire journey from the wall. He ducked under the wing, skirted the motionless propeller, and called up to the cockpit. The pilot, young Hintz, leaned over the lip of the cockpit and flicked a cigarette into the dark. Do you have your charts, do you know where you're to go? Wollenstein asked, his head craned back to see. Yes, yes, yes, and yes, Hintz said flatly, then told him to get out of the way and shouted a few other words to the ground crew before he slid the glass canopy forward and snicked it closed and locked.

Wollenstein stepped away and the right-side propeller turned ever so slowly—a quarter revolution, half, three-quarters—something whining loud in the engine until a cylinder fired, thick oily exhaust gushed from its rear, and the blades spun up until they were invisible. The far engine followed.

The Messerschmitt with the *Pasteurella pestis* tucked under its belly rolled through the short grass, as two dark figures darted out and ran down the field. Each held sizzling red flares that wafted smoke behind them as they raced for the place where the machine had to lift wheels to clear the trees at the far end.

The aircraft stopped, its engines now shouting at full throttle, then it jerked forward. A blue flame stretched from the exhaust for a moment, and reflected on the stainless-steel tank.

Kammler put a hand on Nimmich's thin shoulder to force a stop. They had to wait for Adler, who huffed and puffed behind them. Adler's torch bobbed, reached them finally, and the big man sighed and made as if he was going to sit.

"Not again," Kammler muttered. But Adler sat anyway, his fat arse sinking into the damp grass. Kammler turned on Nimmich instead. "How much more?" He put his own torch on the boy's face, watched his eye flicker. After they'd found the burning workshop, all Kammler had had to do was promise Nimmich that he would live if he told where Wollenstein would run. The boy had spilled everything in a river of words.

"A few more minutes," Nimmich said. He pointed to yet another line that marked an end to yet another field in this jumbled, confusing country. Behind them, back toward the house, there had been several gunshots a few minutes before, and before that, a longer, heavier rattle to the south, but now it was reasonably quiet.

"Are you ready?" he asked Adler.

"Another minute."

It would take them ages to reach the landing field at this rate.

Boots tramped the lane behind them. Kammler thought it best to keep quiet—the enemy parachutists were everywhere—but Adler, the sow, called out. Shapes crashed through the thickened brush and thundered toward them, boots and weapons and webbing and helmets making a cacophony. It was Oppel and his men, a dozen of them. Thank God.

"Obergruppenführer?" Oppel asked, stepping forward.

"Yes, it's me, Oppel." Kammler brought out his metal cigarette case and was ready to snap open his silvered lighter when Oppel put a hand out.

"Don't. The light."

"I think they know where we are," Kammler said. "You made enough noise." He lit the cigarette, sucked in the smoke, and felt calmer than the moment before. "You didn't find my doctor, did you?"

"No, and not the canisters, either," Oppel said. Oppel told how he'd taken a truck to the bunker like Wollenstein ordered, and found it empty. "They're all gone, Obergruppenführer. I returned to the house," Oppel said, "found men shot and dead inside the biggest barn, a smaller one burned to the ground, and made Wollenstein's man tell me where you might have gone. There was an airfield this way, he swore it."

Kammler smoked more of his cigarette, wondered how to explain to Himmler that he'd lost the *Gräber*, worse, explain how he'd lost the genius Wollenstein, and worst of all, how he'd let the English steal the Herr Doktor. Himmler would not be pleased. Even an Obergruppenführer wasn't safe from Prinz-Albrechtstrasse. Kammler tossed his cigarette aside.

An engine cranked and howled beyond the line of dark that Nimmich had pointed to. Another engine. The sound spilled over their heads and washed against the hedgerows encircling them.

Wollenstein was getting away.

Kammler started running.

Brink heard the airplane engines cough, and pushed aside their Ukrainian guide. He hobbled the length of the field, scratched and clawed up the brush-choked mound between them and the sounds, crawled over its crest, and slid down the other side. There was a rock wall thirty yards away and he made for its cover.

In front of him was a small airplane, a high-legged thing with a wing mounted atop. It looked like the plane they'd seen circling Port-en-Bessin. But its propeller was still. The noise came from the right, and he ducked behind the wall and scurried that way, popping up every few yards until he saw the other plane, big and black with two spinning propellers. At its nose was a thicket of radio antennas, slung under its belly a thick tank that nearly brushed the grass. It began to move.

"What the hell?" Addison said. The other three paratroopers slipped into place at the wall beside Addison. Kirn dropped at Brink's left, and Alix was there, too—he heard her coughs. The Ukrainian had vanished.

Brink didn't have time to explain. He braced the German submachine gun on the top of the wall, felt along its cool metal, and pulled back the bolt. He was rewarded with a satisfying click as he drew it back and another as it locked into place. He pointed the gun at the airplane, the machine moving ever so slowly yet, its graceful bulk just forty yards away. Brink pressed the trigger.

The gun banged out shots, and he struggled to keep his grip, to hold the sight on the plane. Sparks whipped off the metal and the plane rolled faster. Addison fired, too, his three paratroopers joined, their rifles barking quickly, and on his left, Kirn put his weapon on the wall and opened up. But the plane kept going.

Then, down the wall far to the right, more flashes licked for the plane. Kirn climbed the wall, stood on the flat stones, aimed his gun and let loose.

A spot of red glowed on the nearest engine, but the plane was sixty yards away and rolling faster. Kirn wrestled with his weapon, yanked out an empty magazine and slammed a fresh one home. He jumped down and walked through the grass firing at the plane.

The plane drifted right, toward the guns along the wall, but it didn't slacken speed. The glow on the engine became flame finally, short tongues on its cowling blowing backwards. Kirn kept walking, shooting.

A wheel came off the grass, then touched down again. The engine's sound became metal grinding against metal, and the propeller quivered. Brink couldn't figure out how to pull the magazine from his gun. The plane veered right some more. For a moment, Brink thought it would leave the ground, gunfire or not, but it only took a hard right, straight at the wall a hundred yards down the field. The guns that way hammered at the plane, and in the moon's light Brink saw pieces fly off the antennas and canopy. Kirn fired again, and the plane, one engine still revved high, struck the wall, metal screeching and one propeller spinning off wildly into the woods. The plane bulled its way to the stone until it was consumed by a rush of yellow and orange and red that started at its nose and worked its way back, the fire churning past the tail.

Embers swirled up in lazy spirals. A man screamed and tried to claw his way out of the canopy, but fell back into the burning wreckage. Was that Wollenstein? Brink flinched as the gas *whoomped* in a hollow noise, and a perfect ball enveloped the plane and the wall, rose quickly on a stem of yellows, immediately darkening into reds.

The tank hung under the plane had been full of the *Pasteurella pestis*, he was sure. The black smoke that now climbed from the smashed plane was thick with the *pestis*, and each breath they took of that cloud was as good as sucking death inside.

He shouted to Kirn to warn him off, but the policeman didn't hear or didn't care, because he began running for the fiery wreckage.

Frank tried to make the parachutists stay, Alix saw, but they had caught the scent of *boche* and seemed determined to kill them wherever they could. The Americans slipped into the dark toward the wrecked aeroplane, running hunched behind the wall, their weapons out and ready to use.

She touched Frank's elbow. "What if the medicine is in the fire?"

He turned to her, one side of his face lit by the moon, the other by the flames. Shots rang from down the wall again.

"I don't know if the medicine was on the aeroplane, but the devil's still alive," she went on. She put her hand over her heart. "Papa tells me." She paused. "Help me find him."

Before Frank had a chance to answer or even nod, another black monster started its engines in the shadows under the trees and the machine crawled from hiding. It was a bigger, clumsier brother to the first, with three engines, one on each wing, the third at its snout. Frank jumped the stone wall and limped across the grass.

This second aeroplane faced far fewer guns; the Americans were busy flushing out the *boche* far to the right, and Frank's machine pistol had an empty magazine.

The pilot of the second machine had also learned his lesson watching the first, and so he didn't hesitate. Once he swung the aeroplane on the grass and straightened to line up with the field, the engines howled and it began to move to where the red flares still flickered. Only the *boche* policeman stood between it and escape; Frank was still meters away.

Kirn lifted the machine pistol to his left shoulder and fired a short burst that struck the nose of the beast, and sparks curved gracefully along its flanks and over its wings.

Get away, Alix whispered as she looked at Kirn. Stay, she murmured. Get out of the way. Die there. She couldn't decide what she wished for.

Even as Frank churned through the grass, Kirn stood his ground and the aeroplane, its tail not yet off the ground, rolled over him. Its thick nose and the engine out front cleared him easily, and Kirn ducked to let the wing pass safely above him, firing his machine pistol into the engine and through the underside of that wing. As soon as the wing passed, he stood to shoot again, sparks glancing forward and blown aside by the propellers. But Kirn didn't see the short wing jutting from the plane's tail behind him, and it caught him at the shoulders and knocked him tumbling so he came out from under that tail bounding and rolling through the grass.

With a roar, the machine lifted its tail. Frank picked up Kirn's machine pistol and he raised it to his shoulder, letting loose a long burst. A single flame shot backward from that right wing's engine, a long dragon's tongue that licked toward the tail. The aeroplane leaned to the left. It leveled quickly, and skimmed over the trees at the far end of the field. The flame at its engine was like a score of shooting stars for a heartbeat, then those flames extinguished. The aeroplane didn't explode into slivers or fall like a shot bird, but flew on unharmed. In a moment, all that remained was a dim, blue speck from an engine's exhaust and then that, too, disappeared.

The aeroplane's low rumble lingered and when that was gone there was a quiet as deep as any Alix had ever heard. One shot, two, three broke the peace, but then it was still again.

She listened to her heart and asked Papa if the devil had been on that one. No one answered. In the quiet she thought she heard something nearby and turned.

Out of the shadows thirty meters away, Juniper limped into the moon's light.

The clouds crossed in front of the moon as Kirn lay on his back in the Normandy grass. His left eye wouldn't open.

He thought of Alois and Brunner and Misch and Böse and Stecker and Muffe, and all the other names, forgotten, long left behind in Russia, never found in France. He thought he should say Hillie's name, but as he stared up at the moon with his one good eye, all he could think was how Muffe's helmet had always been so small for his head.

"Stay awake," someone said to him. Paul Stecker, he thought first, talking to him while he lay in the Russian mud after the big bang and the numbness in his right hand.

"I can't feel my legs," Kirn said.

"Help is on the way," the voice said.

"Doctor . . ." Kirn said. He wondered what made his cheeks wet. "The aircraft—"

"A pile of scrap beyond the trees," Brink said. The American was bent over him and his head blocked out the moon, now back from its hiding place. "We did it, you and me."

"You lie," whispered Kirn. There was no aircraft in pieces or flames. They'd failed. He'd let fucking Wollenstein kill his friends.

"No lies, remember?" Brink said.

"I want to look." Kirn tried to raise his head; he wanted to see how he'd saved his friends, like Brink said. But the American put a hand on his shoulder.

"No, you have to be still. You'll be fine if you stay still," Brink told him.

That was a lie. Kirn knew, the way he was cold inside, he would die in this *Wulewuh* field. It felt wrong to have only wet grass for comfort. Foolish, somehow, to die so far from home and without friends.

"If I'd known, I would have shot him in Bordeaux," Kirn said. His mind strayed a moment. Brink didn't answer, how could he, he knew nothing of Bordeaux and the ship and wooden box.

Or how cold it had been on that dock. Or in the East.

"We put newspaper in our clothes to stay warm," Kirn said, suddenly feeling the Moscow wind cut into his bones, "and then we ran out of newspaper." He heard the crackle of the hard snow, the sound like faraway shots, and realized he did have friends still.

"*Du bist mein Kamerad,*" he said, hearing his words slur. He grabbed tight to Brink's hand with his good one, afraid to let go.

The wet grass soaked through to his knees, but Brink didn't think he could stand, so instead he laid Kirn's hand on the man's chest, then felt inside his coat, found the bronze identity disc, pocketed it. He busied himself that way because he didn't want to think about what had just happened beyond this man calling him a friend.

The airplane had gotten off the ground, no matter that he and Kirn had put holes in it. Brink put a hand up to his nose, sniffed, and smelled gasoline.

It was flying for England or the ships that must be off the coast by now or just to loiter over the beaches until the boats brought men ashore. Wherever its destination, it would spray the *Pasteurella pestis* from the shiny metal tank under its fuselage. And once news reached Paul Childess and the Scotsman Gubbins, they'd talk a minute or two, nod their old heads, and decide on revenge. The linseed cakes would be boxed into Lancaster bombers and they'd drop them over Germany. If tens of thousands died from the pneumonic plague, millions more would perish from the anthrax.

The game was over.

Twenty-three

The shots, once long ropes of noise, broke into individual knots of sound. Then they died altogether, and the silence, such as it was, returned.

Oppel approached the tree behind which Kammler crouched. "It's safe," he said, and extended a hand.

Kammler took the time to pick leaves from his tunic, and let Oppel lead him back to where they'd stood and shot holes in the Messerschmitt, where the parachutists tried to finish them off. A few meters from his hiding place, the bodies began. The petrol-stoked fire was more than enough to light the scene, but the smoke from it stung his eyes and burned the back of his throat when he breathed.

The first body was one of Oppel's men, shot through the mouth. A few meters more were two others, one tucked under the shelter of the stone wall, the other on his back in the grass closer to the hedge. Their helmets were wrong and in the light he saw a flag—white stripes, dark stripes—

stitched to the shoulder of their uniforms. Both had been shot several times, the stomach of the second shredded so that viscera spilled onto the ground.

"Americans," Oppel said.

More, three all told, tumbled in the grass farther to the left, two of Oppel's and another American, his face surprised and blank, a black line of blood streaking his cheek and disappearing into his tunic. "One more we chased into the brush," Oppel said. "Mine went after him."

Escaped, like Wollenstein. That was him in the *Tante Ju*, Kammler had decided. The Doktor had sent the Me-110 to draw their fire—a good plan, a smart plan, Kammler thought, glancing back at the fuming, flaming Messerschmitt—then had fled in the second. Kammler glanced north where the Ju-52 had vanished into the cloud cover. The traitor had gotten away.

I am a dead man, Kammler thought.

Oppel coughed, spat, pulled at his nose, even pressed shut a nostril with a finger and huffed to clear the other.

"How many?" Kammler asked. He felt the wreckage of the Me-110 pulling at his eyes. Something. It tickled in his mind, this thing, like the smoke tickled his throat.

"Seven. Five dead, two not so bad. That leaves three, four counting me. Five with you."

Kammler looked at Oppel's black face; he wasn't sure if the man mocked him. He'd crouched behind that tree to keep it between him and the rushing Messerschmitt, and when the shooting started, he'd stayed there, one hand tight on the bark of the tree, the other damp around the grip of his PPK. A woman's gun, Himmler had called it.

"Nimmich, the boy with the bad eye, what happened to him?" Kammler asked.

"I don't know."

"Adler? The fat one."

Oppel's head shook back and forth. "Don't know. But there are others that way," Oppel said, pointing up the wall in the direction of the Messerschmitt's and Junker's hiding places. One huge tree towered over the others there.

"Americans?" Kammler asked.

"I got close enough to see two or three, not hear what they said or how they said it. Ground crew for the aircraft perhaps?"

Aircraft.

Wollenstein had a Storch, didn't he? Where was it? Kammler stopped. Wollenstein's Storch near Flers had had its potato sprayer tucked under its wing, a silvered tank under its thin fuselage.

Kammler turned to look at the Messerschmitt, still afire, its wings collapsed over the stone wall, one propeller missing, its tail the only major piece not burnt. He followed the swirls of smoke that rose into the air, saw for the first time its dirty yellow color. Wollenstein had finished building the potato sprayer, Nimmich had said. Wollenstein would spray the beaches. But Nimmich had said nothing about how many aircraft Wollenstein had, and he'd not thought to ask. He'd assumed the boy meant just the little Storch. But no.

The Messerschmitt and the Junkers had their own potato sprayers, their own tanks. And they were not just for Wollenstein's escape. Which meant that the *Tante Ju* winging to . . . England. And this one . . . Kammler stared at the smoke tinted like beer's piss, at the fire, all dark yellows, too, at the smoke again. He was an idiot for not seeing this sooner.

The *Grabbringer*. Kammler blinked. "Give me water!" he said. Oppel stood there. "*Water, get me some water and get this off my face!*" he yelled. He grabbed the canteen from Oppel, tilted it over his face and let the water flush his skin, took a mouthful, swirled and spat, again, then threw down the canteen and scrubbed with his free hand at his lips and his nostrils, anywhere the fucking illness of Wollenstein might have found an entrance.

But if Wollenstein had told him true, and he supposed he had, there was no use washing. If it had found the lungs, tiny things had already crept inside. And he'd been breathing it all this time, ten minutes or more.

"We have to get away," he said, hearing his voice tremble. "Now, right now."

"Where should we go?"

Anywhere but here, Kammler wanted to say, but he didn't take the time to say it. Instead, he gripped the PPK tighter and walked toward the largest tree far to the left. Perhaps Wollenstein had not been in the Junkers after all. If its purpose was to spray England, he couldn't imagine Herr

Doktor brave enough to go along for that ride. Perhaps he was by the Storch, perhaps he had the *Tiefatmung* like he said.

If he's there, I'll have the *Tiefatmung* first, then Wollenstein. I won't give him to the boys of Prinz-Albrechtstrasse. I'll lean him against a wall and put a bullet in his neck.

As long as Wollenstein hasn't yet run to England, as long as I have a body to show, Himmler won't care what I do, Kammler thought.

Dear God," Alix said to Juniper as the moon came out again. "What did they do to you?" She reached out a hand, but he jerked away.

It was broken, his once beautiful face. One hand was black and huge as a crab's claw, and hung useless at his side. The other held tight to a big thick revolver.

"Shot, too?" she whispered, seeing the round, ragged wound through the back of that claw.

"Friends let that happen sometimes," he said.

"I begged him to stop the truck."

"Did you now?"

Alix stepped closer and this time Juniper stayed in place. "Let me help you," she said. "I'll find a doctor to look at—"

"I suppose there's one around here somewhere," he said, his voice evil.

"I'm sick with the pestilence, Juniper," she said, putting a hand against her chest to feel it rising and falling too fast. "Like Papa."

"I can't help you. Ask your friend."

A noise behind Juniper made Alix turn. Nearly hidden in the shadows cast by a gigantic oak, the little aeroplane looked like a delicate, fragile toy compared to the monsters that had thundered down the grass before. Something shifted behind the dark glass of its windscreen, something clicked inside its engine.

"Juniper . . ." she began, paused to cough into her hand. The fever tried to return and she put a hand against her damp forehead. "What is . . . what are you . . ." She coughed again and tried to get her wits.

A figure stepped from under the high wing of the small aeroplane, a satchel in his hand. Tall, taller than Juniper, almost as tall as Frank. He wore a peaked cap, and even in the dark, Alix knew the man was *boche*.

The tall one said something. Juniper listened, said something back in *boche*, all without turning. "He says it's time to go," Juniper said in her tongue.

"Go? Go where?"

"Home," he said flatly, but with a faint whistle again.

"I don't understand," Alix said. The fever crept up and surprised her. Why couldn't she understand? Juniper was *boche*? How could that be? The moon disapppeared a moment, then cleared from the clouds again, and the *boche* was in plain view. Above the brim of his cap was the crossed bones and skull.

Fuzzy, she felt fuzzy. Like a hot summer day, it seemed as if time stretched to the sea's end. She looked again at the *boche*. A satchel, like a doctor's. SS.

There was a moment when the edges of things suddenly became sharp, and she stepped toward the one who had murdered the Jews, Papa, her. She reached for the revolver Juniper held.

Juniper pulled his hand away. "Can't let you have it, love. I'm taking him home, Alix. He's an important man. Very very important."

If she'd had a gun, she would have pulled the trigger. Kill Juniper if he got in the way, then kill the devil with the bones on his cap. But all she had was the cloth-wrapped knife in her coat pocket, the long blade pulled from the dead *boche* overlooking the ocean. And that wouldn't do against Juniper's revolver.

"You came for him," she said, not believing and understanding at the same time.

He nodded.

"You're protecting him?"

"I'm taking him home, dear," Juniper said. That whistle in his voice made her want to strangle him.

He was soulless, he had to be. "The first time, before, you were looking for him then, too?"

He nodded.

Her anger boiled up. "My papa, my Jules, my Alain, they died for this *boche*? Your precious Sam, he died for this *boche*, too?" she asked. "You killed your Sam, for what, this miserable man?"

"No, Sam's dead because you wouldn't listen to me."

"You bastard," she said softly.

"Don't you want to ask me, Alix? To take you with me? Go ahead, ask me. Ask me after fucking that arsewipe. *Ask me, goddamm you!*" He waved the revolver.

"Take me with you," she said very quietly as she put her hand in her coat pocket to touch the cloth, and feel, under it, the knife. He had been hurt by the *boche*, not just his face, but in his mind. He'd gone mad.

He shook his head. "It's built for two, takes three with careful crowding, but there's not room for a fourth. I'm sorry, I really am." In the moonlight she saw him smile, saw missing teeth in the smile, not just that one chipped tooth.

Juniper moved then and she got her first good look at the devil, Wollenstein.

Under his cap was a face with a narrow, pointed chin. Young, that face, and clean-shaven. He was rubbing his hand along the side of his trousers in an odd manner. He looked nothing like she'd imagined.

"All this for him?" she asked, wrapping fingers around the haft of the knife in her pocket.

Juniper translated her words into *boche*. The devil spoke, and Juniper translated again. "It's not what he expected either, that's what he says." Juniper's fury was gone, washed away by her asking to be taken to England.

"He has medicine, Juniper," she said. "He gave it to Mama." She pointed to the devil. "At least make him give me the medicine." She had her hand around the knife now, and was thinking of what moment in the next few when she would pull it out of her pocket and stick it in the devil's eye.

"Yes, the medicine," an older voice thick from cigarette smoke said behind her. But before she could turn, someone jammed something hard in her ribs. "Tell me all about the medicine."

W here is it?" Kammler asked, changing from the French. He blinked several times to clear the sting in his eyes. Standing near the front of the Storch, Wollenstein only stared and shifted the satchel to his other hand. Thank God he was still here. Kammler raised the PPK. "Is the *Tiefatmung* in there, Doktor?"

Oppel shoved aside the woman and waved his MP-38 at the English, who threw down a revolver. Oppel shouted to the one sitting in the cockpit of the Storch, and he dropped out and came from under the wing.

"Do you have it?" Kammler asked, pushing aside the thought that Wollenstein's *Gräber* was on its way to England, and surprise now lost. He had other worries, personal worries, secret out or not. Wollenstein refused to answer, only glared with those snake's eyes of his.

"Give me the fucking medicine!" Kammler shouted. It was all that mattered.

"So you can give me to the Gestapo? No," said Wollenstein finally as he held the satchel in both hands, the case solid against his chest like a shield. He shook the satchel and the sound of glass on glass chimed dully from inside it. He shook the case again, more vigorously.

"Stop," Kammler ordered. But Wollenstein rattled the satchel a third time. Kammler heard glass break. *"Stop it!"*

Wollenstein stopped, but awkwardly changed his grip on the case so that only one arm was wrapped around it, the satchel still held close but now lower, across his stomach. Kammler glanced at the English.

"You can't have him," Kammler said. "Oppel, shoot him."

"Shoot who? Which one?"

"The English, you imbecile!" With eyes still on Wollenstein, Kammler waited for the shots. Nothing. "Oppel?" he asked, daring another glance that way.

But Oppel had let slip his machine pistol, and as Kammler watched, the man dropped to his knees, then flopped to his face. Something bounced through the grass. There was a small whir close by his ear and a following ping against the Storch. Bullet? But he'd heard no shot. Kammler twisted to the right, his woman's pistol in his hand, only to feel a sudden flashing pain and the cool night air on his head as his cap went flying. He tried to stay awake, but the grass called and everything went first white, then gray, finally black.

Brink tossed the unnecessary rock into the empty dark of the field and walked to the airplane. Two out of three, he saw as he got close. He'd been lucky, what with the light so crappy, but then he'd always been lucky when it came to throwing.

"Very impressive," Wickens was saying, and Brink glanced away from the two Germans stretched out. The Englishman drifted to the second and pointed the Webley at the man's head.

"Don't. They'll hear," Brink said. "They're near the wreck, two or three of them. They'll be here soon enough. Shoot and they'll be here now."

Wickens had been roughly handled. Brink took in the crooked wrist so large it looked like it wore a dozen gloves. Wickens's face was puffed up, and there was dark that could only be blood daubed on his cheek and around his mouth. "You're taking him?" Brink asked, nodding to Wollenstein, who held a black case.

"I should never have told you," said Wickens. "That was a mistake."

Brink looked at Alix, whose face was whiter than the moon now heading for the west. *Erreure monumentale!* She listened to them, not understanding because he and Wickens spoke in English. She had her hand in a pocket.

"Don't let him take the devil," Alix said. She sidled closer. "He wants to save him to make his pestilence for the English."

Wickens shook his head, laughed a strange half-choking laugh, changed to French. "Didn't you know? He never told you, did he, your new sweetheart? How he's a brother in medicine to our dear Herr Doktor Wollenstein? How he made pestilence for the English?" *La peste*, the words came out. "How he came here for the same reason as me."

"Frank, is that true?" she breathed.

He let the moment slide by, unable to answer.

"You are like him. The same?" she asked.

"No," he said. He let another second slip through his fingers. "Yes, like him. Once. Yes."

"And now you want him," she said. "To help you. To make this pestilence for you."

"No."

"Then kill him!" she shouted. *"Shoot him!"*

He pointed Kirn's gun at Wickens, swung the muzzle to Wollenstein, touched the trigger. One moment passed, two.

"Don't," Wickens said.

From the corner of an eye, Brink saw Wickens turn the revolver on him. "Put the weapon in the grass, Doctor," said Wickens.

Brink shook his head. "No." He moved closer to Wollenstein and Wickens's revolver followed him. Brink stayed with English, but now talked to Wollenstein. "Where did that airplane go?" he asked.

"England," Wollenstein answered straightaway. There was some pride in the voice. "With the *pestis*."

"Oh, Christ," Wickens murmured.

Brink took it in. "Kirn said it was the beaches."

"Too early for that, isn't it?" Wollenstein said.

"And it will work."

"Yes, it will work." Definitely pride.

"Tuez-le!" Alix hissed in his left ear, her breath hot and, to his mind, stinking of the bacilli.

Brink pointed the gun at Wollenstein again. He'd do what Alix said, shoot him here and now. If the world had to do without an antibiotic, tough.

"Doctor . . ." Wickens said. The game between them continued, Wickens leveling the revolver each time Brink moved the submachine gun.

"Think what happens if they don't have this," Wollenstein said. He saw the gun, too, and rattled the case still held against his chest. "Thousands on your head if you shoot me," Wollenstein added.

"On yours, not mine," he said. He gestured at the case. Far away, guns spat. Closer, there were voices, loud, in the thick trees and brush along the wall, toward the fire.

"I want to know about Mama," Alix said from his shoulder. "Make him tell if his medicine cures her." Her voice was cold and sharp for the first time in hours.

"Was ist mit denen passiert, denen du die Medikamente in der Kirche gegeben hast?" Brink asked Wollenstein.

"All of them who were in the gendarme station are dead. It was leveled by English bombs," Wollenstein said in German. He shook his head, shrugged. "All dead." *Alle tot.*

Alix disappeared from his shoulder.

Shoot him, Brink told himself again. A second chance, that's what Childess had called it. This wasn't what he'd meant, but what did that matter now? Shoot because the airplane got away and because Kirn mumbled about how cold it had been at Moscow and because Alix would die from the *pestis*, him, too, probably.

"You're just a thief," Wollenstein said, and shook the case again, "here to steal something *I* made. You have no right to this."

The *Pasteurella pestis* will infect thousands in England, tens of thousands maybe, and without Wollenstein's antibiotic, kill them. Childess would counter with the *Bacillus anthracis*, and more would die. Even if Childess didn't, how many would perish of tuberculosis or plague or a score of other bacterial infections before Frank Brink put the pieces together with his own version of what Wollenstein already had in that case?

What if he *never* put those pieces together? What if no one *ever* did? Should he count those dead, too?

"Give me that," Brink said again, raising the weapon again.

"Doctor, put down the *damn weapon*," Wickens shouted.

He wanted to pull the trigger. Send this piece of shit to Hell for what he'd done.

"I am the only one who can save them," Wollenstein said clearly.

Brink caressed the trigger. "As evil as them," Childess had said. No, he wasn't. He wanted to be, but he couldn't.

"Doctor, put down the gun!"

The dead faces in the Bedford and the live ones in the church decided it for him. The only way there wouldn't be more of them was if Wollenstein lived to make his antibiotic. Fuck.

"Take him back," Brink said in English to Wickens, and dipped Kirn's gun for the grass.

But as he did, Alix reappeared at his side. "I know *tot*," Alix said. "Dead it means." The snout of another gun pushed into view. Wickens shouted *"Alix, no!"* and its barrel smoked and spit, the noise like a landslide over sheet metal. Bullets struck Wollenstein's leather case first, then Wollenstein, punching him to the grass like a boxer's fists.

"You can't talk to the devil," Alix said in the quiet. "Talking never does any good."

Brink kneeled next to Wollenstein, but didn't bother pulling aside his coat to get at the wounds. Instead he grappled with the metal clasps of the punctured case until he had its mouth open and his hands inside. Glass nicked his fingertips and he probed more carefully, pushed aside the wet papers in folders and the thick, damp, bound notebook and sifted through the shards hoping to touch something whole. He should be tending to the man, not going through his things. Every second his hands were in the case was one less he had to save Wollenstein, but he didn't stop. Alix needed what was in here.

He pulled out a syringe and then a pencil because it felt like a syringe, and put them in the grass near his knee. The hand went back into the hole that was the case, like groping in the haversack there outside Dakar's quarantine, and he felt and felt and felt but found only glass shards. Brink's stomach began to cramp with nerves, knowing that if there was nothing intact, Alix would die of the pneumonic plague and he would probably follow. Then he touched the small bottle. He held it up to the moon and shook it be sure there was something inside.

"He's still alive," Wickens said from his spot at Wollenstein's head. Brink heard the gasping, sucking sounds from the German's chest. "Fix him up! Do a damn better job than with Sam, or so help me . . ." Wickens said.

Brink touched every inch inside the case but found nothing more. He snapped it shut. "This is more important." The single vial and the syringe and the pencil he dropped in his coat pocket.

"Fuck the case, do something," Wickens said.

Brink eased Wollenstein's overcoat open. Alix's short burst had put three bullets in the German, one low on the right abdomen, the second higher, piercing the right lung, the third. . . . The third was the worst. Brink yanked open the tunic and tore the buttons on the shirt underneath and ripped at the thin cotton undershirt beneath that.

Just left of the sternum and above the nipple the blood was flowing thickest. The bullet had nicked something, maybe the left anterior descending, for the blood looked unstoppable. And glass from the things inside the leather case, swatches of the case, even fragments of paper, had been shoved by the bullets through the man's coat to pepper the skin.

"He's going to make it," Wickens said, like a question.

No, no he wasn't—it didn't take a doctor to see that. Wollenstein had only a few minutes at the most. Brink leaned close enough to put his breath in Wollenstein's face.

"Look at me," Brink said to Wollenstein. The man's eyes didn't focus, but they were open. "Is this all?" Brink held the small vial in front of the German's nose with one hand, took hold of his chin and pointed the face with the other. "Look at me. Is this all there is?"

Close gunfire made him flinch. A quick stammer of shots, a pause, then another.

Brink leaned so his ear was close to the German's mouth, and all he heard at first was one slow breath, but after licking his dry lips, Wollenstein wheezed out, "You will have to share."

"Get it started," Wickens was shouting in German to someone.

Brink swore the German beneath him was trying to smile.

"Do something!" Wickens yelled. The gun hammered behind them again. Alix, it had to be Alix doing the shooting.

Wollenstein reached out a hand, dark and wet, clawed at Brink's, the one holding the vial, grabbed hold and squeezed. Brink pried the doctor's fingers from his and pushed the hand away.

"You could have been famous," he whispered to Wollenstein. "Like Pasteur." One of the man's eyes was darker than the other in the moonlight; both were large.

"Help him!" Wickens screamed. *"Help him, you're a fuckin' doctor!"*

"Yes, I am," said Brink, but there wasn't a thing he could do to save this bastard.

Brink convinced Wickens that Wollenstein would live long enough to get him back to England, and to aid in the convincing he sponged up the blood on the German's chest and stomach with the remains of the dying man's shirt. While he did, he disguised the wounds by wrapping the dirty overcoat tight around Wollenstein's torso.

He has to get to a proper hospital, he told Wickens again and again. He'll live, don't worry, he'll make it. Lies. But good lies, like the ones he'd told Kirn, or even better.

Brink dragged Wollenstein to the little airplane and with what help Wickens gave, they swung him up and shoved and pushed and jammed the limp, silent doctor into the cramped space behind the second seat.

The pilot, already in the cockpit, flipped some switches, pulled out a knob, and pressed the starter.

The starter screeched and the propeller jumped a half revolution, another, and the engine caught and the propeller whirled into a hazy circle. The wind pushed at Brink. Alix fired her gun again and someone shot back. June bugs buzzed by the plane, one hit a wing and glanced off, drawing a long white spark.

He had to lift Wickens into the airplane, and even then Wickens cursed and once screamed when his wrist caught at the high door.

Wickens settled into the seat and Brink handed him the revolver. The Englishman brushed his hair from his forehead, the hair tousled by the propeller's wash. That girl's gesture. But Wickens didn't turn the revolver on Brink, as he'd been ordered to do.

"I won't forget this," Wickens shouted over the engine.

Not forget what? Saving his life? Or Eggers's death?

Brink felt the wind tug at his coat. Wickens's retribution, if that's what he meant, would come only after Brink had settled the score with Childess. In his heart, Brink knew that.

Brink pulled the black-edged piece of paper from his coat, the sheet that had blown out of the burning lab. He'd not looked at it, didn't know what was on it—not that it mattered. Then he took out the pencil, smoothed the paper on the skin of the airplane, and in the light from the moon, printed a message. The paper tried to blow away, but he held it tight. He folded the paper, gave it to Wickens, leaned close to shout in Wickens's good ear. *"Give this to Childess!"* Brink tapped the paper.

Wickens shrugged first, then nodded, and Brink pulled down the airplane's hinged door and slammed it shut, twisted the latch, and banged on its glass. Wickens put the tip of the Webley against the back of the pilot's head, and as Brink stepped back, the engine revved and the machine, after a jerk from its place, inched forward.

The airplane rolled away, slowly down the field, faster next, until its engine whined. It bounced off the grass, jumped into the air, wagged its tail, and slipped sideways before banking hard left toward the north, kept turning for the west, then vanished from sight.

Bearing his penciled message to Childess.

PAUL

HOSEA, I THINK

FOR THEY HAVE SOWN THE WIND, AND THEY SHALL REAP THE WHIRLWIND

Brink went to the spot in the grass where he'd left Wollenstein's shattered case, and called to Alix.

Twenty-four

She had shot the devil and still she felt unforgiven. So she fired a long burst into the dark boscage where the *boche* snakes hid, pulled the empty magazine from the machine pistol, and tossed it away.

Juniper was gone for good and Frank, where was Frank? But the pestilence, she still had that to keep her company, didn't she, and she wanted to laugh at the madness.

Alix felt the fever on her. She couldn't stand, and went to her knees, the grass wetting them as her dress hiked up. She sat still but her head spun and the scene blurred. Alix looked at the machine pistol, but she couldn't feel it.

Frank was at her side and she felt a prick on her arm, a solid sting like a bee makes but much longer, and she looked at the needle he'd stuck in her, too late for her to stop him. "The medicine," he said.

Alix waited for the fever to fade, the thickness in her chest to thin, but she didn't feel any different. Frank helped her stand. A moment she swayed there, but she gathered what she had left to make the spinning stop, breathed as deep as the pestilence let her, and although her head stayed light, she thought she could walk. "Where now?" she asked.

"That way," Frank said, pointing north.

"I'm well?" She touched where he'd stuck the needle.

Frank shrugged. "You may need several injections."

"How do you know the number?"

He shrugged again. "I don't," he said flatly.

"This killed Mama, the *boche* said so."

Frank told her that it was the bombs from Juniper's aeroplanes that had killed Mama. Not the medicine. She nodded slowly.

He leaned down to pick up her machine pistol, made her take it, and together they shuffled from the field and into a lane that bent north. Her legs ached and they moved slowly, but although she heard *boche* voices behind them, those voices paused where the little aeroplane had sat, perhaps to help the men Frank had knocked down with his rocks.

After a hundred meters slipping on the wet lane they came to a hole in the boscage, and Frank stopped, sniffed the air as if he thought a trap was ahead. She heard it, too: a voice from the field. A weak voice. A woman's voice. In her fever, she really couldn't tell what it cried.

What was he thinking? "The *boche*, they're following," she whispered. Behind them sounded one of their damn whistles.

They moved on fifty meters, sixty, until they came to a dead man hung in the middle of the lane, his body twisting like a luffing sail. Taunt white lines climbed from his shoulders into a dark tree that arched over the lane, and in the leaves of that tree was a billowing ghost. Frank flicked Kirn's cigarette lighter and held it near the man's shoulder. A flag stitched there, red and white with blue. American, Alix knew that much. A parachutist, and the ghost in the tree was his parachute. The man's boots were less than a meter off the ground.

Frank reached up for the man's neck—the parachutist was dead, what was he doing?—and slipped a hand inside the tunic and with a snap the hand reappeared, now holding a lace with a pair of clinking squares strung on it. He put them beside the *boche* lighter's flame. He said nothing, but they turned and went back the way they'd come to the gap in the boscage.

"Wait here," he said, and led her to a shallow ditch next to the hedgerow. Did he mean to leave her?

He and Juniper had used her to find Wollenstein, and even though she'd shot the devil, Frank had packed him into the tiny aeroplane and sent him, dying, toward England. Alix gripped his hand and squeezed hard, angry at the betrayal. Or was it something else she felt?

The words *I am* . . . came out of her mouth, but the remainder, . . . *not afraid*, she kept to herself as she realized this was denial. Frank kneeled, his face close enough to smell him, wet leaves over sweat over blood's metal scent.

"You're what?"

She couldn't answer. There was a long quiet there in the ditch, although the woman's voice kept calling. "What?" Frank asked again. "I'm coming back." Another silence stretched out, the woman and the distant patter of gunfire the only interruptions. She heard the woman's words then. *"Nous sommes juifs."* Jews. We are Jews. Again, Jews. Alix shook her head to clear it. Jews had started this, destroyed her entire family, and now it seemed they would end it.

"Alix?"

The Jews made her remember how this had begun, and she found the same words she'd said to herself there in that lane off the N13 so many worlds ago. "I don't want to be alone," she said, not a whine or a plea, but as a fact that wouldn't change.

"I won't be long." Another long silence sat between them. "There's something I have to do," Frank said finally. He put the devil's black satchel at her side. "Stay here." And he slipped into the field.

She covered her ears with her hands but was still able to hear the damned sick Jews who wouldn't shut up.

It wasn't the woman's call that drew Brink back, nor the dead paratrooper twisting under the tree. The man hadn't been anyone he knew, had an eagle on the shoulder patch so he was from the 101st Airborne, in fact, not the 82nd, lost and far from friends. And the woman's voice, although he heard it clearly and knew instantly whom it belonged to, hadn't been enough to make him stop or later reverse course. It had been the dead man's dog tags and the "T" punched into the metal, the letter and the two numerals after it marking the year for his tetanus inoculation.

He needed to know how far he could stretch the lone vial in his pocket. And there were people who could tell him how many times the needle had pricked their skins. All he had to do was ask them.

He cut a shallow arc across the field, sticking close to the hedgerow because the moon was out again, and drew near the front corner of an unlit shed. He sniffed, almost gagged, and tried to breathe through his mouth.

"We are Jews. Let us out," a voice said faintly. Brink slipped along the wood wall of the shed. "Let us out." Like a record played on that windup Victrola Grootvader had, it was softer this time around than the time before.

He crept closer and when the voice said the same again, it had a hollowness as if spoken through cupped hands. The moon's light showed a pale face pressed against a jagged hole cracked in a very small pane of glass, a thin dark line where the face touched the bird claws' shards. "Let us out."

He struck the flint of Kirn's lighter, a mistake because it ruined his night vision, and all he saw was the shock in the woman's dark eyes.

"Someone is here," the woman said. He punched in more of the glass with the butt of Kirn's gun and stuck the hand with the lighter through the hole. The smell that wafted out to the clean air was sweat and feces and urine. But not death. That browner stink was strong, but it came from the other end of the shed.

The flame guttered out and he struck the flint again. In the sudden light, he saw the yellow star stitched to her dress. She was thin, face drawn over hard bones, her nose a sliver, her cheekbones almost swallowing her eyes. But she wasn't sick with the *Pasteurella pestis*. Her face was pale, parchment pale, but without a tinge of blue.

"Show me your arms," he said, and she wouldn't understand. *"Show me your arms!"* he bayed like he thought Germans might. She stuck an arm through the opening. He waved the lighter over it, looking looking looking, and put the flame so close she cringed, thinking he was going to burn her. Nothing. "Show me the other! *The other!*" There. Needle marks.

"Are you sick?" he shouted. *"Are. You. Sick!"* *La peste*, he said over and over. A clatter of voices murmured *non* and *non* and jabbered *nous ne sommes pas malades*, the broken window framing half a dozen faces now crowded behind the first. "How many shots?" he stormed. "How many times?" and "When was the first time?" he boomed out and they answered in a ragged chorus of *"quatre"* and *"cinq"* and one over the others *"un jour après qu'ils nous declarent malade."* They pressed against the window so that he was afraid one would end up sliced from chin to crown by the broken glass, and he ordered them back, back, back. When they wouldn't listen, he shouted *Haut ab!* once in German and they retreated like automatons.

He groped along the wood wall until he found a narrow door held fast with a metal clasp and a padlock half as big as his fist. The Jews beat their hands against the other side, and no matter what he called through, they wouldn't stop and so he couldn't shoot at the lock, but had to smash it with the metal stock of the German gun. The padlock held. He jammed the barrel under the clasp and gave it a good wrench and the nails screeched out. A hard minute more and the clasp swung off the door and the Jews shoved and rushed him to sob and cry and clutch at his coat. Five women, two children, and one old man whom he figured for blind because he kept running thin fingers over Brink's face. The instant closeness and grabbing hands forced him back, and as he retreated he caught his heel in the grass and fell. As he looked up at the night sky, a circle of faces haloed his vision.

"Frank!" Alix screamed from across the field. He didn't know his name could last that long.

Alix heard sounds coming from the field—there were Jews out there, she heard, Jews, why was Frank bothering with Jews?—and the fever came in waves so loud she couldn't hear anything but their white crashing. Had she left Frank? What had she said? Where was Juniper? Mama, was she truly dead? The fever wouldn't let her remember exactly.

That was how the *boche* crept up on her, she decided after a hand picked her up by her dress collar and shook her like a toy. That hand pushed her into the lane, picked her up again, shook her again, shoved her toward the field. She had dropped the machine pistol in the haze of the shaking. But she managed to wriggle out of that hand's grip to walk without help.

If she was free of this fever, she wouldn't have let them surprise her. She would have heard them and killed them all. But then she remembered the machine pistol had lacked a magazine, so she could not have killed anyone.

There were four *boche*—no, only three; the third was so fat he seemed like two. The fat one held a pistol, the thinner man in front of him without a weapon. The one who had picked her up from the ground, short as he was, had no hat but wore a white swath of cloth around his head. She recognized him as the *boche* who had barked to the devil before the little aeroplane jumped for England. Frank had hit this one's head with the rock, but like the devil, he was hard to kill.

They stopped a few meters from another small crowd, one led by Frank. She first smelled that crowd, saw it second. They were rank, unwashed, but the stink from the shed behind them was worse, a stink the same as what had billowed out of the hold of Papa's boat.

She sank to the grass, not caring what anyone did to her. The medicine Frank had stuck in her arm did nothing to keep her head clear, and she had to sit to quiet the pounding in her chest and defend from the lightness that made her feel faint. Alix tucked her cold legs under her, and her dress lay across them. She sat there, fought off the black that tried to choke off her vision, and paid no mind to the conversation, which was all in *boche*. She focused on just one thing: the long knife in her coat pocket.

Put down the gun," the German said from ten feet away. He had a dressing wrapped around his head. Brink tossed aside the weapon. They had Alix, who was a bundle on the grass, her legs folded underneath her, her gaze vacant.

"Does your head hurt?" he asked the German. The man touched the bandage, showing the little pistol in that hand. In his other he held the handle of Wollenstein's case. He had small ears close beside his head, smaller eyes above a nose too long for the face, and a thin smile, a wickedness in the smile that reminded Brink of Wickens.

"*Du?*" asked the German. "You let Wollenstein go, why?"

"Let's be done with this," the big man in the foreground said. He had an unlit cigar in his mouth and a hand pinched on the narrow shoulder of the other man.

"You let Wollenstein go," said the bandaged German. He was short, about Wickens's size, and he held himself ramrod straight, looked a line into Brink's eyes. This one was like Gubbins, used to ordering, not asking. "I am Kammler. Obergruppenführer Kammler is my rank and my name, and so that is who I am. Wollenstein, you let him get away in that little air-craft of his."

"He's dead," Brink said.

"Don't think I—"

"He's dead, I tell you. My . . . friend . . . took him home to prove to my people that he's dead," lied Brink.

"He's spraying the *Grabbringer* on England by now." The German glanced at his wrist, as if he was going to look at a watch, but it was too dark for that.

"I know," Brink said.

"You know . . ." Kammler went quiet for a moment. "You swear? He's dead? Well and truly?" That last came out *klip und klar;* Grossmama's words every supper just after slapping shut her big Bible. *Klip und klar.* Yes, indeed.

"Ask her," Brink said. "She's the one shot him." He nodded to Alix.

"*Scheisse,*" Kammler whispered. "*Womit hab'ich das verdient?*" Kammler scratched at the bandage as he whined about what he'd done to deserve his fate. "What about the medicine, the *Tiefatmung?*" Kammler asked.

Tiefatmung? Only after a long thought did it come to Brink. Deep breath-ing. A deep breath, that's what the word meant. It's what they called Wol-lenstein's antibiotic.

"*Tiefatmung.* You know it?" Kammler asked, now louder. "For the *Grab-bringer.*"

"Yes," Brink said. *Grabbringer.* Grave bringers, like Childess had said so long ago on the curb outside 10 Downing.

"Why are we wasting time? Kill him," the big man said. "Kill all of them. We must get out of here. We must pack up the machinery and get—"

"Shut up, Adler," Kammler said. His next words were to Brink. "Nimmich here said there was a supply of *Tiefatmung* with the Jews. But I think he's lying."

The thin one in front shook his head, but the fat one hit him at the base of the skull with his ham-sized hand, and sent him to his knees.

"Nimmich?" Kammler asked.

The thin one choked out a "No," caught his breath and his nerve at the same time, and shouted, "It was me, not Wollenstein, don't kill me, I can—" but before he could finish, Kammler pushed aside the big man and jammed the muzzle of his pistol against Nimmich's neck. The thin one shut up instantly.

"This one, he can make the *Gräber*. Can't you? Nimmich, you can make it as well as Wollenstein?" Kammler asked quietly. But the muzzle didn't leave the man's neck, so Kammler'd get just one answer, wouldn't he?

"Yes, yes, yes, I can make the *pestis*. It's nothing more than biology, I know exactly—"

"Enough, Nimmich, we believe you," Kammler said. Then he turned to Brink. "You see how serious I am, yes, about the *Tiefatmung*? What I'll give up if you only hand me the *Tiefatmung*?" Kammler asked, and pulled the trigger. Blood jetted out Nimmich's mouth and he tipped onto his face.

Jesus Christ.

"I was very close to the crash," Kammler said quietly. Brink heard the words, but he kept looking at the man in the grass. Nimmich's arm spasmed, his hand drew into a claw, and Brink heard grass tearing from roots. Jesus. Christ.

"Why did you kill him?" the fat man bellowed. "He said he could make the sickness!" Spit flew from his mouth.

"Anyone can make the sickness, you fool," Kammler said, so calmly. "All that's needed are the things here." He raised his other arm and the case in it, then let the satchel thud into the grass. "Doctor?" asked Kammler. "Did you hear me? I was very close to the Messerschmitt."

"*Obergruppenführer!*" shouted the big man.

Kammler swung to the fat one, idly pointed his pistol in his direction. "Please, Adler, be good and shut up." Back to Brink now. "I want the medicine," said Kammler.

Brink looked away from the dead man on the grass. There were two things here. The airplane crash, its yellow-black smoke, was one. *Pasteurella pestis.* This Kammler had breathed that smoke and likely had the bacilli deep in his lungs. Unlucky, really, because once the sun came up, a few hours of daylight would ruin any *pestis* not inside a warm body and the clearing would be just a meadow again, albeit littered with corpses and blackened metal. The second was that this Kammler was the one really responsible here. This one was Childess.

"You need the medicine," Brink said, keeping his eyes on Kammler. "Or you'll cough out your insides in a week and you'll be . . ."

"Give me the medicine!" Kammler shouted.

"Dead," Brink finished. In the German, *tot*, it sounded so much more final.

"We don't need to listen to this," said the big man.

Brink put his hand in his coat pocket—Kammler's pistol stared at him— and he tugged out the single vial of Wollenstein's antibiotic. He lifted the stopper that plugged the vial. "This is all there is. This little bit." He tilted the vial a fraction and Kammler flinched. "If you shoot me, I'll drop it. You'll have nothing." Brink swirled the vial in small, tight circles.

"Don't," pleaded Kammler. His pistol's mouth wavered.

"Shoot them all," the fat man said. "Make him give it up. Shoot her." He stepped to Alix, loomed over her, put a meaty hand in her short hair and tugged a forelock to bring her head up.

"The pestilence, it turns you blue. You start pink and come out blue," Brink said. The big man tugged harder on Alix's hair to make her neck strain and force her to look up. "She's sick with it," Brink said. "She's breathing on you, that's how you get it." The corpulent German stepped backward to escape Alix, and Kammler snorted.

"Shoot her!" shouted the big man from a safe distance, his arm pointed at Alix, his hand with the pistol shaking. He tossed the unlit cigar he'd had locked in his teeth at her, and it struck her at the neck.

"You're not the one gambling, are you, so shut your mouth," Kammler said. He turned to Brink. "Give it to me and I'll let you go," Kammler said.

Brink looked at Alix. As soon as he'd heard her cry out his name, he'd known it would come to this. It was all he had to bargain with. She coughed a dark clot into the grass. But the second he handed it over, he'd be . . . Brink glanced at the thin boy flattening the wet grass.

"You can't let them go!" the fat man yelled. "What they've done, you can't. Obergruppenführer, this is wrong. *This is treason!"*

The word clicked in Brink's head, reminding him of the secret he'd spilled to Kirn, who had told it to Wollenstein, who might have told others. But it didn't seem to have mattered. Secrets. What secret would Kammler most want to keep? He looked at Kammler and thought he understood. "Wollenstein sent the aircraft to England," Brink said. "With the *Grabbringer*." He tried out the words. "*Mit den Grabbringer.*"

Kammler turned toward him, the white dressing wrapped around his head catching the moonlight. "Potatoes," he said, speaking nonsense. "He told you himself it was on the aircraft?"

"Yes."

Brink gathered his thoughts. "We've known all about the . . . the *Grabbringer* . . . for months," he said. "We have a . . . medicine . . . like the *Tiefatmung*, that cures the sickness," he lied. "Send a thousand airplanes, it won't matter."

Kammler said nothing, but turned to look at the Jews behind Brink.

"I was Wollenstein for the English," Brink said. "That's how I know."

Kammler's attention wandered from the Jews, and the German rubbed his temple under his peaked cap. "A pity," Kammler finally said. "Are you insane, like Wollenstein?" He licked his lips again, shifted the small pistol to his left hand, wiped at his mouth with the back of his right, then returned the pistol to its original place.

When Brink moved the hand holding the vial, Kammler's eyes moved, too.

"Just shoot them and be on our way!" The big man sidled toward them.

"Wollenstein wanted to kill us all, the fool," Kammler said, staring into the dark. "I had the idea, put Wollenstein's *Gräber* on my rockets, a hundred rockets in one day, and Himmler agreed. I could turn your insignificant island black as Africa. Turn it into the biggest corpse heap ever, a thousand times bigger than anything in Russia." He looked down at his pistol, pulled back the slide to eject a cartridge and rack a new one in the chamber. Making sure it was ready. "Now, however, it seems I am the one who deserves pity." Kammler nodded to the vial.

That moment, Brink's fury came uncorked at the nerve of this man. All the things bottled up since the little colored girl had arched in the Dakar dirt came loose, from the Bedford full of dead Jews, to the flies around the Tardif's chamber pot, to the faces in the church wanting him to tell them what to do, through the killing in the lane and Kirn clutching his hand and the ruined face of Juniper Wickens. He stepped toward Kammler, forgetting the little pistol the short man held.

"I know someone just like you," Brink said slowly. He stepped forward, but the gun came up to stop him.

"Wollenstein was the one who made it, not me. I'm only—"

"You're responsible," Brink shouted, the anger in him at the surface, wishing he could have yelled the same to Childess before.

"I don't have time for a lecture. Give me the *Tiefatmung*," Kammler said. "I swear I will let you and the others go." He pointed the pistol at the Jews, who had shrunk back against the shed.

"No," wheezed the fat man behind him. "No."

Brink finally put his conscience in the cupboard. He knew what he needed to do. He would get the big man to do his dirty work and then he would eliminate him.

"You're right," Brink said, turning to the fat man now. "How do you think I found this place? *He* gave Wollenstein's secrets to us. *That's how I got here! Him!*" As his voice boomed across the field, he pointed the hand holding the vial at Kammler.

Kammler stared at him.

"He led me here," Brink said quietly. "A fat one might be in the way, he said, but he'd handle him. So *he* said." Brink stepped back and almost trod on Alix. The big man leveled an enormous arm at Kammler, a pistol at its end. "And you heard the boy," Brink went on. "The boy said he could make the *Gräber* like Wollenstein, and still he shot him."

"You're believing his lies? Put down the gun and I'll forget this," Kammler said.

"I heard you," said the fat man to Kammler. "You said you'd let him go. You killed Nimmich, and we need him now."

"You think I'll let these English live?" Kammler shouted out.

Brink held his breath for the shot.

Instead Alix killed the wrong man.

Alix watched the pistol in the fat man's hand. At least the worst of the spell had passed. The longer she sat in the grass with her dress hiked above her knees, the air on her legs cooling the furnace of her fever, the better she felt.

The fat one's voice became more familiar as he sputtered and shouted. She'd pierced the cloud in her head and realized he was the one from Mama's kitchen, the voice she'd heard with her ear at the floor.

The *boche* had them on the hook and had only to pull on the line to drag them aboard; they would all be dead soon. But she could kill this one who had murdered Alain. It was all she had left, revenge, her head so fuzzy that it was enough just to think of that one thing, over and over, to remember Alain's face as it had looked when he lay dead on the kitchen table.

The fat demon stepped nearer, shouting again. The bandaged one spoke, Frank spoke back, and Alix concentrated on her hand tucked into the coat pocket as her fingers unsnarled the knife from its cloth sheath.

She unfolded her legs in one graceful motion to kneel first, stand second. Because the fat *boche* paid attention to the one wearing the bandage, she was able to reach him before he saw her. He was too big to stick with the knife—his heart was protected by layer on layer of flesh and fat. Instead, Alix snagged a fistful of the fat one's collar and pushed, with not nearly enough strength to shove him down but enough to make his head move forward so the blood vessels in his throat would not be protected by the muscles there. She wiped the knife in her right hand across his throat, cutting so deep her wrist was instantly drenched. The sharp *boche* steel cut through his windpipe before he'd said a word.

For Alain, she thought. The fat man shrugged off her hands and put his to his throat. He stepped forward, leaned back, half stepped again. Finally, before she could get out of the way, he toppled backward, to crush her into the soft earth that smelled of dead leaves from last autumn.

Kammler flicked his pistol's muzzle, but Brink edged toward Alix anyway. She was trapped under the big man.

All that showed was her hand. Its fingers raked the fat man's arm, each time softer than the time before. She was being crushed. Brink edged closer still.

"Not another step," Kammler said, the voice at the end of that pistol. Brink dared look away a moment, and stared at Kammler. "Give me the *Tiefatmung*. Then you can help her," the German said.

Brink looked back at the big man. His hands were only faintly pressing against his cut now; he was fading quickly into unconsciousness. The blood was a river across his shoulders. Alix's knife had severed the left carotid, the exterior jugular, too, sliced through the trachea, maybe even nicked the right carotid. The man was bleeding out.

"The *Tiefatmung*!" shouted Kammler.

Alix's hand still protruded from under the mountain, but it was motionless. He wasn't going to leave her like he'd left Kate.

Brink found the stopper in his pocket, walked the three steps to Kammler, plugged the vial, and held it out. In the creamy moon's light, the vial only looked empty, but he knew 4cc still sloshed in it. Kammler's hand folded around the narrow glass bottle. For a second, their fingers touched.

As soon as he gave up the vial, Brink kneeled at the big man's side to pull him off Alix, but all he did was stretch the overcoat's sleeve. He couldn't get any leverage pulling, and so pushed instead. He got one arm flung across the chest but still couldn't roll him over. A pair of hands appeared beside his then, a woman's hands. Brink looked up, saw the raw-boned face of the Jew with the blood lines etched along her face. More hands, these belonging to the old man, clearly not blind like he thought, joined them. Without a glance of acknowledgment, they pushed at the fat man's shoulder. Together the three of them rolled his weight off Alix.

Her face was smeared with the big man's blood. He felt for a pulse at her neck. He moved the finger to her wrist. He bent over her and gave an ear to her mouth. Not a whisper. The moon's light wasn't enough, so Brink lit Kirn's lighter to put it at her lips. The flame wavered from the breeze, went straight as the air stilled. He clicked shut the lighter.

"Alix," he said, touching her cheek.

Brink put his hands on her ribs, six inches under her breasts, and pushed in and up. Again, then leaned to listen for a breath or feel it in his ear. Again and again, listening, then repeating.

Brink put his face close to Alix's. She was a balloon filled with *Pasteurella pestis*. But he didn't care. He put his mouth over hers and breathed into her.

Her nose whistled. Her chest rose. When he pulled away, he heard her sigh, a long, slow shudder of *huh-huh, huh-huh*. But it was just the air he'd pushed in coming out again.

He licked his lips, swallowed. The *pestis* tasted like apples.

They'd make it to the coast, then England, and once there to Childess. He'd carry the satchel with Wollenstein's secrets in exchange for the actinomycin-17 that was by rights his. They'd take the actinomycin and pray that it worked.

He pinched her nose closed with two fingers and leaned down and blew into her again, and he pulled away to watch her chest rise.

Brink didn't quit, wouldn't stop even when Kammler stood over him and he thought the German would put a bullet in the back of his neck. From the corner of his eye Brink saw a boot kick the big man's leg, maybe to see if the fat man was still alive.

He kept at the artificial ventilation for two minutes, three. As he blew the last breath he had in him, she coughed gently and he felt her cough against the back of his own throat. He took away his mouth and let go her nose and rubbed her hands and talked to her.

Alix coughed and breathed, breathed and coughed.

Alive. Her eyelids fluttered open.

In the distance, sounds began to thunder in a regular rhythm. When he looked at the sky over the trees that way, he swore it was lighter. They'll be ashore soon.

Alix touched her hand to his face and he wondered if her eyes were green.

"Merci," she said, the word staying in the French in his head because it sounded English. They would all need mercy.

Alix reached out to hand him the pistol suddenly there.

"The fat man's," she whispered.

Brink took it from her, their fingers brushing, and he gripped the butt, the Bakelite wet and sticky. Fallen into the grass after Alix had slashed the big man.

"How much of this do I take?" Kammler asked behind him.

Kammler stood between them and home.

"Doktor?"

If Brink answered, Kammler would kill them. Brink looked at the pistol in his hand. His father's Calvinism had taught him that God chooses the saved, but the damned choose their own damnation. He had to become as evil. There was no one else to do the work—no Kirn, no Wickens, no Addison—and no Alix, who had killed her two demons. His turn.

Gubbins had asked only for five minutes. All he had to do was be brave for another five minutes. Brink thought he could do that.

Brink stood, turned to face Kammler, and pointed the pistol. It had been years, nine or ten at least, since Brink had fired a gun, and that had been a bolt-action Springfield his father had brought home from the Great War. But he didn't hesitate—he pulled the trigger. The sound, so small in the large field, took him by surprise no less than Kammler.

Kammler went slowly to his knees, the pistol slipping from his hand. "I . . . I don't," he said hoarsely. "We had . . . we had . . ."

This was Wickens's way of stopping the *pestis*. Childess's way. Gubbins's way. Wollenstein's way.

My way now.

Brink pulled the trigger again, Kammler flinched and his hand convulsed. The slim bottle skipped out of his hand and rose in the air, tumbling as it caught the moon's light.

He watched the bottle climb the foot or two, reach the momentary pause of its summit, and arc down. Without thinking, Brink reached out a hand and caught it.

Addison came to them across the field. He'd lost his Thompson somewhere. Now he held a Garand, the barrel pointing down, the stock up under his arm.

"Where're the others?" Brink asked. He put Wollenstein's precious antibiotic into his jacket pocket.

"Gone," Addison said. His voice was flat, his accent almost gone. "He's still breathing, you know." The Garand's end aimed at Kammler.

Klip und klar. Yes, he was. Brink bent over the German.

"Help," Kammler said softly.

Brink flicked aside the overcoat. The first bullet had entered in the abdomen's upper-left quadrant, perhaps perforating the lower stomach or the small intestine. The second went in the upper right, and in its downward track—Kammler had been kneeling then, he remembered—it would have plowed through the liver certainly. He wouldn't live much beyond noon, if that, even if he got to a good doctor.

"Help me," Kammler said.

"Es hat keinen Sinn, mit dem Teufel zu sprechen," Brink said back, repeating the words Alix had said to Wollenstein. It doesn't do any good to talk to the devil.

"What now?" Addison asked. He paid the wounded German no mind.

Brink helped Alix stand. She'd make it. She was tough. With Addison's help they'd find a place to hide, a barn or Frenchman's house, for a day or two until the fighting on the beaches was over. He'd give her three more injections of Wollenstein's antibiotic. By the time he started coughing himself, he'd have gotten them back to England and Kate's actinomycin. And he'd have to hope Morton had been very wrong about the colored girl.

Then he'd have to take Wollenstein's wet, holed notes from the black case, follow in the genius's footsteps as best he could. He'd make more of the antibiotic, the *Tiefatmung*, to save some of those who breathed what Wollenstein's single airplane might have sprayed. But he'd also make it so it would cure those coloreds in Dakar of *la peste* and the wogs in Bangalore of *mariyamma* and maybe even Dutch and German and Norwegian farmers in South Dakota of tuberculosis. Not so he'd be a hero, his five minutes of being brave were over, but so he could count up those he'd saved to balance the one he'd killed here, and the one he planned to kill someday in England.

Primum non nocere. First, do no harm. Well, that wouldn't work anymore, would it?

Brink looked at the Jews, the eight of them, standing close now to the shack that stank like the back of that Bedford. They would come, too. He touched Alix's hand, felt it warm again, dry. She smiled weakly, but it was that smile of hers that made her so pretty.

Epilogue

Pilot Officer Oliver Breeden glanced past the Mosquito's wing, and in the full moon's light saw the armada stretched across the Channel. Its head was tucked into the darkness ahead that must be Normandy, its tails were just clear of Southampton and Portsmouth and Plymouth far behind them.

"Bloody hell, that's a lot of ships, ain't it, Ollie?" the voice came over his headphones.

"Pay attention to your screen, Tick," Breeden said. "Only one of us plays tourist."

Tick didn't answer, just sighed into his microphone and the sigh amplified in Breeden's ears. He looked out, searching for moving specks among the scattered cloud cover and the bright moonlight. Nothing.

His headphones clicked, went dead, clicked again. Breeden wondered which ground controller they'd have tonight. "Bogey one-three miles," a soft, calm voice said in his ear. "Steer to three-two-five. Angels two."

Shits. Behind them, back toward home. "Turning, don't get your stomach up now," Breeden said to Tick. He put the aircraft in a gentle curve to left, delicate on the rudder so as to make sure his radar operator didn't get nauseous while he watched the tube between his knees. Breeden pressed the microphone at his throat. "Understood, ground. Range one-three, heading three-two-five, angels two." He watched the compass circle in reverse from 120 to 90 to 0 to 340. He let up on the rudder and centered the stick, and the compass jiggled to a stop right on the dot: 325. As soon as he had his heading, he throttled up the Merlins to full and the Mosquito thrummed for England.

"Is that you, Barry?" he asked the controller. It was the Queen, that soft voice. Not that anyone called Barry that to his face, not those who wanted to keep their faces in fettle. "What's the word, Barry?"

"He only popped up," the Queen said. "Heading still three-two-five, range one-two, angels two."

The invisible aircraft they now followed couldn't be Jerry. Its IFF must be shot, that's all. Jerry would have seen the ships and bounced back to France with the word faster than you could say Bob's your uncle. That's why he and Tick were up here, along with the rest of the squadron and who knows how many other night-fighters, to make sure no Jerry recce got a peek at the big secret.

Ground radar sometimes couldn't tell altitude worth spit, but Breeden put the nose down and watched the altimeter start its backwards spin from ten. He pressed the throat microphone again. "On his tail, Tick, range one-two, I'm taking us down to angels five."

"Speed estimated one-two-zero," the Queen whispered in his ear.

"Slow bugger," Tick said from the seat behind him, that voice in his earphones, too. "Maybes one of the Dakotas lost its way, maybes lost an engine."

Breeden figured that was it. Slow like that, a fat transport was a good guess, one with its IFF shot out so it didn't show on the Queen's screen as a friend. That's why the rules required visual sighting before firing, tonight of all nights, what with the air filled with bombers and Dakotas and gliders.

"Heading now three-four-zero, range zero-eight, angels two," the Queen said into the silence after a bit.

Breeden slipped the Mosquito right, kept looking out the windscreen. He swept the sky from sea to their own altitude, searching for anything that moved.

"Heading three-four-zero, range zero-five, angels two," the Queen said. "Bogey about to cross the line." Breeden knew where he was: east of Portsmouth, with the black mass of the Isle of Wight to his left back. If the Dakota was crippled, it would soon lose altitude looking for a place to land, and vanish from the Queen's phosphorous screen.

"I've lost him," said the Queen in that peaceful voice of his. "He's gone to ground, I believe."

Bloody hell, Breeden thought. "Tick, have you got him? Where's he at?" There was a good chance Tick's Mark VIII tube would show the aircraft even though the Queen's radar had lost it—they had the altitude.

But Breeden heard Tick clear his throat. They'd been together long enough for the sound to mean something. "No, Ollie, don't see him. Sorry."

Breeden immediately throttled down the Merlins—the last thing he wanted was to overshoot—and looked hard into the dark. The moon was bright, wasn't it? They might spot the aircraft visually. He looked. And looked.

It was the flame that gave it away, a guttering blue dot far off and below. Has to be one of ours, Breeden thought. Jerry's flame dampeners were first-rate; he'd rarely seen one off sorts and showing engine exhaust.

"I've got him," he told Tick. Tick sighed.

Breeden put the Mosquito into a dive, for the Dakota was at fifteen hundred or two thousand, and under the illumination of the full moon, the dot became a small square and then became a cross, the flame always his guide. They closed too fast, for he'd been high and the aircraft ahead crawled over the demarcation between Channel and coast slowly. Then he realized it was no Dakota. Where were the rounded wings and the bulb nose? Instead, he saw a Junkers, the slab-sided triengined box the Luftwaffe flew to ferry supplies and drop paras. Paras. Little late for invading England. Were they jumping on West Wittering? That was the little town under the Junkers, he was pretty sure.

The Iron Annie was on just two engines, the starboard feathered and motionless. Even so, it was the one afire and the flame's origin, for the blue changed to orange, back to blue, and licked over the cowling, suddenly withdrew into the engine, then burst out again in yellow. Someone had beat them to it, shot up that engine, and since the Junkers had no built-in extinguishers, Jerry was out of luck.

Breeden flipped up the guard on the stick and put the black cross into the gun sight. He was coming in high and hot, not from up the tail matching speeds like he should. Then the Ju-52 lurched left, so when he pressed the trigger's button and the Hispanos hammered, the tracer shells arched right and under the Ju-52. Hell. Someone lived down there, and those 20mm shells could smash roofs and pit streets. They screamed past.

Breeden twisted the Mosquito into a great banking turn to right, tight and tighter to bleed off airspeed and get behind the Junkers for another pass. Tick had a better view from his seat. "He's over water now, Ollie," Tick said. "Chichester Harbour, ain't it? He's after Portsmouth sure." Breeden pulled the Mosquito out of its turn. The Junkers streamed a twist of smoke from the starboard engine. Breeden put his finger on the trigger button, the Hispanos banged out shells and tracers again, but he was still too hot and the Junkers seemed to be in his head, because it took that second to drop. A shell or two clipped the top of its corrugated fuselage, but there was nothing important there, and then they were by, Jerry under them as Breeden pulled on the stick.

"Christ," Breeden swore, and yanked the stick to take the Mosquito in a left turn, watching the altimeter and airspeed, throttling up to make sure he had enough air beneath him, close as they were to the water of Chichester Harbour.

"Can't see 'im Ollie," Tick yelled over the earphones. *"There he is! Over Hayling!"*

The Mosquito leveled and Breeden saw the Junkers. It was throttled wide, not more than two hundred feet above the dark, narrow island, heading west with its burning engine lighting the way toward Portsmouth. Three, four miles, a minute or two flying time. What did the Annie want with Portsmouth? After the jack tars there?

Breeden pushed the Mosquito's throttle full to catch up, still swinging on the bowline toward the Ju-52. The flame from the Junkers's starboard engine now stretched clear across the metal wing and licked the emptiness behind its ailerons. They caught up just as Jerry rumbled over the beaches of west Hayling and dipped even lower, as it aimed for the city ahead.

A faint plume escaped from beneath the Junkers's port wing. Another engine afire? But it was different, this new smoke, or something like smoke, its color light against the dark water of Langstone Harbour. As the smoke got into the cabin, it tasted off as he sucked it into his lungs.

Gas. What if the smoke was gas? Like mustard or phosgene. The fuckin' Huns were going to gas Portsmouth.

The east edge of the city was just a mile or two away. The same light smoke plumed from under the starboard wing now and mixed with the oily smoke of the engine burning merrily. Breeden pressed the trigger again and the 20mm Hispanos banged away. This time they found a home, and the shells must have touched the Junkers's petrol, because the plane went to pieces. Flaming spears arced for the water. As he pulled up, Jerry was gone.

Breeden clawed for altitude, forced out a grunt and heard Tick do the same when he put the Mosquito into a weight-making climbing right turn, dipped a wing, rolled over, down-up and up-down, and then returned the way they'd come to finish the split S.

Below them flashed the bit of burning petrol on the water that marked the wreckage of the Junkers. As the Mosquito skimmed the waves, the odd smell rushed into the cockpit again.

"*Got 'im!*" shouted Tick. "On home ground, too, that's a first, eh, Ollie?"

Breeden realized his heart had been pounding, but that was always how it was. He only really had time to get scared after it was all over. He tried to swallow, but it was so dry there was nothing to swallow. God, he could use a drink.

Tick piped in from the rear. "Call it in, Ollie, you got to call it in," Tick said. This was only their third kill in three years, and fat, slow Junkers or not, Tick wanted the credit. Breeden did, too.

Breeden pressed the throat microphone. "Ground, Junkers-five-two down in Langstone Harbour, one mile east Portsmouth." Breeden wondered if he should say anything about the smoke. But he and Tick were fine, weren't they, not gasping for breath or anything, and the Annie had been over the water the whole time it had spewed anyway.

"Understood," said the Queen.

"Outstanding, Ollie," Tick said from the rear. "Bloody great shot."

ACKNOWLEDGMENTS

They say the second book is tougher than the first. Whoever "they" are, they're right.

Because some characters in *Midnight Plague* fought tooth and nail any attempt to make them do what they were told, I depended on the kindness and help of even more people than the first time around.

Jennifer Hershey, my editor at G. P. Putnam's Sons, may have moved on to the publishing world's equivalent of "another network," but she's not forgotten. Jennifer's pencil was even sharper this time than last, to my, and the story's, great benefit. She'll be missed.

I'd also like to thank Brendan Duffy, who gamely stepped in at Putnam's to shepherd the book through to publication, even though he didn't know me from Adam.

Don Maass, my agent, did his usual best to remind me of what was important and prod me to put that on each page.

Acknowledgments

Yves C. Chabu and Matthias Vogel, both of the University of Oregon, translated dialog into French and German, respectively, crucial since my French is on the level of *Parlez-vous l'anglais*, and my German not much better.

Lori, my wife, and Emily, my daughter, also deserve more thanks than they received last time, and more than I can give. They have become, through necessity, readers of historical thrillers, and provide greatly appreciated support and encouragement.

Finally, I would like to thank the discoverer of streptomycin, the real discoverer, not the fictional one in this novel. In 1943, while a graduate student at Rutgers Univesity, Albert Schatz isolated, cultured, and tested *actinomycetes* for their ability to retard the growth of the tuberculosis bacillus, *Mycobacterium tuberculosis*. Dr. Schatz, who was eighty-four, died January 17, 2005.

Streptomycin remains one of the antibiotics of choice in cases of pneumonic plague.

I never met Dr. Schatz, nor spoke with him, but we all owe him, and others like him, a debt for defending us from the disloyalty of nature and the potential treachery of man.

As always, naming others removes no blame from me for any errors. Consider them all mine.